**Also available from Rhenna Morgan
and Carina Press**

Rough & Tumble
Wild & Sweet
Claim & Protect
Tempted & Taken
Guardian's Bond

Coming Soon

Down & Dirty

Also available from Rhenna Morgan

Unexpected Eden
Healing Eden
Waking Eden
Eden's Deliverance

For those of you facing your past, your fears or both.
One foot in front of the other is all it takes.
You've got this.

HEALER'S NEED

—

Rhenna Morgan

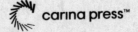 carina press™

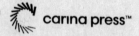

carina press™

Recycling programs
for this product may
not exist in your area.

ISBN-13: 978-1-335-46005-9

Healer's Need

Copyright © 2018 by Rhenna Morgan

www.CarinaPress.com

Printed in U.S.A.

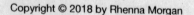

HEALER'S NEED

Chapter One

No signs of movement. No shadows moving as the early evening sun sunk behind the isolated cottage just thirty feet away from where Tate watched. No wavering of the curtains that shielded his mate's window.

But Elise was in there.

In coyote form he'd scented her. A faint mix of some exotic flower a man like him didn't stand a chance in hell of identifying, and a sweet treat warm from the oven. He had prowled the heavily wooded perimeter of the outdated home Elise shared with her mother, Jenny, and choked back a frustrated howl as the soft patter of water filled the old claw-foot tub and painted vivid images of her lingering in the warm water.

He backed farther into the trees and scanned the footpath that had begun to form between Elise's home and the one Tate shared with Priest, Kateri and Jade. The jaunt wasn't a difficult one. A brisk five-minute walk at most that wound through the unspoiled woods near Eureka Springs's Beaver Lake.

And Jade was supposed to have made that trek twenty minutes ago.

His hackles bristled, and a low growl rolled up his throat, his beast chiming in with its own displeasure.

In the two weeks since he'd met Elise, his companion had grudgingly played along with the self-imposed distance Tate had kept between them. A distance his instincts insisted was crucial to learn and prepare for the hunt ahead. Hell, the way Elise's heart had hammered in those first few seconds, distance had been downright necessary. The only reliable action that kept him from pinning her to the floor and taking her right then and there.

But his coyote was done with waiting. Had exhausted its patience and was ready to get on with the business of winning their mate.

Almost time. Just a few more hours.

It was more thought and emotion than actual words, the connection between man and animal as natural as his heart and lungs working in synchronization.

A twig snapped.

Tate spun toward the sound, ears tweaking in the direction of soft but steady footfalls against soil softened by April's steady rains. Logic told him it was Jade finally showing up to do what he'd asked of her, but with Draven still on the loose and hunting clan primos, the warrior in him wasn't willing to run on logic alone.

A second later, Jade strode into view, her long dark hair loose and swinging with each confident step, and the silver charms she'd woven into braids on one side of her head sparking in the waning sunlight. While she wasn't his sister in the truest sense, they may as well have shared blood. He sure as hell wanted to strangle her right about now the way a blood-bound brother would.

He waited until she was within ten feet to welcome his shift, the snap and burn beneath his skin as he relinquished his animal form to the Otherworld nothing compared to the impatience twisting his insides. "You're late."

Apparently, he and his coyote weren't the only ones in a nasty mood, because Jade snarled back at him as only a woman could, a little of her lynx mingling with the sound. "Elise is my friend, not an assignment. If you don't want to work with my timetable, then get off your ass and engage with your mate the way you're supposed to."

"She's new."

"So? Katy was new, too, and Priest barely let her out of his sight."

Oh, Elise hadn't been far from him. Maybe not always visible, but aside from time spent at work with a tattoo iron in his hand or running down leads on Draven and their missing seer primo when Priest demanded it, Tate had stayed close to her. It'd meant a lot of time in coyote form to maintain control and sleeping hidden outside her home, but he'd kept as tight of a connection as he dared. "She's different."

Jade opened her mouth as though she meant to argue, then frowned and snapped it shut. She'd been around Elise enough to sense it. The careful distance his mate kept between her and everyone. The watchful, sometimes skittish gaze so common to easy prey. The hesitancy craftily hidden behind a determined mask when she interacted with new clan members she met. The woman Elise presented to the outside world wasn't the real deal. It was armor. A protective shield his gut said had been honed from something painful, and he'd be damned if his predatory actions did anything to fortify that armor.

He wanted it off her. Wanted the woman he'd glimpsed in the unguarded moments when she hadn't known he'd been watching. To help her live and experience what it meant to be Volán without fear. To free the soft and sensual creature he sensed caged underneath.

"She might be different," Jade said, "but pretending to be someone you're not is no way to build a relationship."

The soft but pointed sentiment struck hard and deep, rattling a truth he'd worked hard to ignore. "I'm not pretending. I'm being careful."

"You're a predator. A man who thrives on the hunt. I've never seen a male in our clan more primal with a woman than you, but you've barely allowed yourself in the same room with her. That's more than careful. That's avoidance. Don't tell me there's not more to this than being cautious with Elise."

More? That was the understatement of the century. More like a gaping black hole of uncertainty he had no fucking clue how to cross. He'd thought he'd find his mate later in life like Priest had. That he'd be more grounded in his place as a clan warrior. Not twenty-seven and primed with more animalistic drive than he knew what to do with half of the time. A double whammy considering Elise was an intoxicating mix of sensual faery and untouched innocence. Winning her trust without losing control was going to be the miracle to trump all miracles.

"Tonight." The simple admission ripped up the back of his throat with all the comfort of a double-edged blade. Sharing meant a commitment. Someone to hold him accountable if he altered his plans, and Jade would call him on his shit in a heartbeat. "I want to talk to her mother first. Let her know…"

Out of nowhere, one of the many erotic images his mind had painted in the last few weeks derailed his thoughts. Elise on her belly. Moonlight covering her bare skin. Her knees cocked and her ass lifted for him. His hand pinning her to the ground at the back of her neck while the other gripped her hip and held her steady for his cock.

He shook his head to clear the image and swallowed back a low growl.

A sly grin crept across Jade's face. "Yeah, whatever explanation went with the look that just crossed your face probably isn't the one to use with her mom."

No shit. But he couldn't keep her mother in the dark either. She might have had the benefit of knowing about their clan growing up, but she'd had zero direct exposure to it and hadn't accepted her gifts when given the chance. "She needs to know Elise is my mate. Needs to understand what's going on."

"You don't think Naomi's told her already? Surely, she's at least laid the groundwork."

Maybe. Katy's grandmother wasn't just an elder seer in their clan, but the queen mother of all meddlers. She'd been there the day fate had hit him with a thunderbolt. Had done her part to cover the awkward silence while he wrestled to comprehend he'd just come face-to-face with his mate. No Volán man could miss that reality. The white aura around her had been as unmistakable as the awareness that had roared to life in her presence. The pull and insistent lash to take and claim what was his.

"Just get Elise to Beltane," Tate ground out. "I can't…"

He cleared his throat and forced another huge breath. "I can't think straight when Elise is close, and I need to get this right with her mom."

Jade studied him a moment, the early evening sunlight slanting from between the treetops brightening her shrewd green eyes. "The Keeper gave her to you for a reason, Tate. You won't get this wrong. No matter what you do."

Easy for her to say. She hadn't been semi to fully hard for over fourteen days with a hunter's urge to overtake a sweet woman who hadn't known their clan, shifters or magic even existed a month ago. He jerked his head toward Elise's house. "Go. I'll follow you to the party then circle back and talk to Jenny."

Snapping back to her usual sibling-combative self, Jade scoffed, pushed him out of her way with a none-too-gentle shove of her shoulder and strode toward the cottage. "Whatever. We're on protected land. Draven couldn't have gotten past Priest's wards a month ago. Now that Katy's practicing her magic and adding to them, he doesn't have a prayer of touching Elise while she's here." She paused just before she stepped past the tree line that opened out into the main yard and glared back at Tate. "Tonight, Tate. I love spending time with Elise and would do anything to help you, but she's your gift, not mine. Take it, or I swear to God, me and Katy are going to make Naomi look like a sweet little old woman who knows how to mind her own business."

As effective threats went, it was a doozy, the host of possible complications Katy and Jade could conjure for him effectively scrambling his focus.

Until the heavy door chunked open and left Elise framed in sunlight through the open doorway.

He'd seen her in jeans. Seen her in leggings and those sinful as hell yoga pants that showed off every curve he'd eventually explore. But he'd never seen her in shorts. Insanely *short* shorts. Denim ones that were faded and well frayed around the edges, effectively drawing his focus to the tender juncture where the back of her thigh shifted to the lower swell of her ass. According to the chats he'd had with her mom, and based on the trophies and medals he'd spied in Elise's room, she'd been an athlete once. Gymnastics, track and dance. He still hadn't learned why she'd given them up, but the fact that she was still an avid runner was evidenced in her toned muscles.

As if the bottom half of her outfit wasn't enough to keep him strung out, there was even more sun-kissed skin up top. Nothing fancy. Just a simple loose tank the color of a blazing summer sunset, but a pale teal bra strap peeked from behind the neckline, practically begging a man to explore underneath. Which all but guaranteed he'd be having his conversation with Jenny in record time and getting back to the party. No man was getting within five feet of his mate. Not without him by her side.

Elise laughed at something Jade muttered too low for him to catch, ducked her head so her golden-blond hair fell forward to cover her heart-shaped face and smoothed her palms along her hips—a self-conscious action that said she was as uncomfortable with her wardrobe as he was with her wearing it. When she lifted her head again, her cheeks were flushed, and her big green eyes were loaded with doubt and uncertainty. "I can't believe you talked me into wearing these."

"Oh, they're perfect," Jade answered, twisting her

torso just enough to make sure her answer reached Tate
as well. She might not have looked him straight in the
eye, but with the amount of smugness in her voice, she
didn't need to. "They don't look nearly as good on me.
Someone needed to put them to better use and you've
got the hips for them."

So much for Jade waiting to interfere. In that second,
Tate couldn't decide if he wanted to hug her, or hide
a handful of tacks in her bed like he had when she'd
ratted him and his *Playboy* stash out to Priest when he
was sixteen.

It took another few minutes' worth of hesitation and
a whole lot of encouragement from Jade to get them out
of the doorway and headed into the woods. Every second of it Tate spent with a death grip on the tree that
shielded him from Elise's sight. By the time only their
retreating footfalls and Jade's bold laughter remained,
the bark had bitten so deep into his skin it stung when
he released his grip, and his muscles were strung painfully tight.

He forced one foot in front of the other, the impor-
tance of what he was about to share with a woman
who could either help or hinder his progress with Elise
like a sharp dagger poised to pierce between his ribs.
Jenny was smart. Reasonable. Patient and giving with
her warm, welcoming smiles. Or at least she had been
in the time he'd spent doing odd jobs around her house,
helping restore the most immediate things they'd needed
to make their new home more comfortable.

But what if that changed when she learned what Elise
was to him? He was a tattoo artist, for fuck's sake.
Granted, he made decent money doing it. And while his
work wasn't as sought after as Priest's was, he wasn't

hurting for clients either. But Elise was on track for a solid career in sports rehabilitation. A kinesiology degree that would let her work with athletes and doctors pretty much anywhere she wanted to go.

And then there was the whole Draven thing. Elise and her mom had already had their whole world turned upside down and been forced to leave their home to keep Elise safe on warded ground. What if Jenny's lack of clan knowledge and fears for her daughter's safety worked against him? What if she didn't think he could protect her?

An inner snip and growl from his coyote knocked him out of his spiraling thoughts just as he stepped onto the raised wooden porch. That was the blessing of having a companion. The most genuine of connections to nature. Animals didn't overanalyze. They lived by instinct. Honored and utilized the gifts given by the Creator and simply *were*. And thank God for that, because in the last few weeks he'd relied on that balance more than he had the whole time since he'd accepted his soul quest and received his gifts.

He squared his shoulders, let out a hard breath and knocked, the reverberations of the thick wood door rattling down his forearms.

Elise's scent still lingered around him, mingled with damp forest soil and the lake's crisp bite. For the first day of May, it was warmer than normal. By nightfall, the temps would be perfect. Not cold enough Elise would be uncomfortable, but chilly enough she'd crave his heat.

Quick footsteps sounded on the hardwood floors beyond and the door swept open.

"Did you forget…" The fond humor on Jenny's face

shifted to open surprise. "Tate! I thought Elise had forgotten something and locked herself out." She scanned
the front yard, then eyed him from top to toe. While
he hadn't strayed from the tee and jeans he normally
showed up at their house in, tonight his hair was loose
and the quality of what he'd picked wasn't something
he'd do fix-it work in. "Why aren't you at the party?
Did Naomi send you? I told her I could cart the food
I'm making there on my own."

"No. Naomi didn't send me." Though, now that he
thought about it, he'd known Jenny was planning on
bringing a load of food to the celebration and should've
planned on helping her get it there himself. "But you
don't need to carry food alone. I can help."

Like her daughter, Jenny was petite and had startling
green eyes, big and wide set so they gave her an ageless
and guileless appearance. But where Elise's hair was
long and a rich gold, Jenny kept hers cut simply at chin
length and had probably been a deep chocolate color
before the soft gray had started taking over. She cocked
her head to one side, wisdom borne of hard choices and
a life alone narrowing her sharp gaze. "But that's not
why you're here."

"No." For a second, the urge to dodge the truth and
come up with some lame excuse for checking on one
of the many repairs he'd done nearly knocked him off
course.

Then he thought of Elise. Of those unguarded moments where he'd spied the woman beneath the neutral
mask. Of that concentrated look she got on her face
when she stared out at the lake from her window and
how it always made him want to know what she was
thinking. Of how she'd looked walking away from her

house tonight, dressed to innocently tempt him and who knew how many other men.

But she was his. *His* gift. And it was high time he started acting like it.

He met Jenny's stare head-on and let the same certainty he'd felt in those first moments near Elise billow up and bolster his words. "I'm here to talk about Elise."

Chapter Two

So many people. At least a hundred, if Elise had to guess, all of them milling from one group to another in the wide gorge behind Priest's big lake-view home. From her place between Jade and Priest's mate, Katy— or Kateri, as Priest insisted on calling her—Elise kept quiet and soaked in every detail. The torches that Katy had lit with nothing more than a flick of her hand. The treetops full of rich green leaves softly rustling over- head. The comforting rumble of easy conversation peppered with genuine laughter, and the strains of a laid-back alternative playlist piped through speakers she couldn't pinpoint.

A chance for a clean slate.

Finally.

From the year Elise had turned fourteen and been brutally indoctrinated into just how cruel teenage girls could be, she'd wanted to rewrite her life. A do-over to see if she could handle things differently the next time around and come out whole on the other side.

Now her chance was here. A new town more than four times the size of the one where she'd grown up, new people who had no knowledge of her past, and a clan of shifters gifted with varied types of magic. Granted, fate's gift had come with a nasty flip side. Namely, her being a prime target for a rogue Volán shifter who everyone said either wanted to possess her or steal the magic she hadn't even earned yet.

A strong hand clamped on her shoulder just as a man squeezed between Elise and Jade on her left. "Ladies, I come bearing female reinforcements and ice-cold beverages for your pleasure."

The second the rich voice clicked and her eyes settled on the big rugged blond man next to her, Elise's muscles uncoiled and she let out a relieved exhale. Not many men put off a vibe that made her feel instantly safe in their presence, but Katy's brother, Alek, was one them. Him and Priest. She still hadn't figured out why. Maybe it was merely the fact that Priest was the clan's high priest and Alek the clan's warrior primo, but she'd not once struggled with the need to shield herself from them.

And then there was Tate.

The same light and giddy buzz that always followed behind thoughts of the man who'd all but consumed her waking hours blossomed beneath her sternum and sent her pulse thrumming. She felt safe with Tate, too.

Sort of.

Not in the brotherly, tousle-your-hair and bear-hug way she got with Alek and Priest, but more like a protector. As if some part of her sensed that, if she needed him, he'd be there in a second. Which was insane because he rarely got close to her. Certainly not within touching distance. And if she'd learned nothing else about Volán culture in the last few weeks, it was that they were a physically affectionate lot.

But he'd watched her. Not once had she caught him

in the act, but she'd swear she felt it. Knew every single time he'd walked into her house to help her mom with odd jobs and shivered at the sound of his voice.

Alek dipped his head to a late-twenties dark-headed girl who'd moved in next to Katy, handed one Dos Equis to Jade and another to Elise. "Elise, this is Sara. Sara, meet Elise."

Rather than offer her hand, Sara aimed a sheepish smile Elise's direction and semi-bounced on her toes like she was trying to keep her excitement in check. "Hey. It's really nice to meet you. I'm part of healer house, too."

Ah. That explained the excitement. Priest and everyone else seemed certain she was destined to lead the clan's healers someday. "Well, I don't know what my magic is yet. I haven't had my soul quest."

"You don't know for sure, no, but you're the best bet for our healer prima," Sara said. "Primos almost always stay within a family line, and no one remembers anyone outside your family ever leading healer house. If you had a brother or sister maybe things would be up in the air, but as an only child?" She blushed, jammed her hands in her jeans pockets, and shrugged. "Well, everyone's just super excited you're here."

They were?

Directly behind Sara, three couples stood chatting, two of the women quickly shifting their gaze from Alek and Elise back to the others around them. An older bunch of women sat around a fire pit in comfortable patio chairs, some of them balancing plates of food and chatting, while others openly stared her direction with happy glints in their eyes—one of them being Katy's grandmother, Naomi.

But it was the handful of women standing in a cluster just behind them that struck the hardest. Five to be exact. All of them roughly Elise's or Jade's age and dressed to impress despite their casual attire. And every one of them aimed suspicious, almost calculating, glances her way.

She knew that look. Had suffered the backlash that inevitably followed.

Elise tried to shift slightly behind Alek's broad body and out of everyone's line of sight, but he caught her with a strong arm around her shoulders and guided her back to his side. "Whoa. What's that about?"

A quick glance at the rest of the women gathered around them showed the same concerned expression etched on their faces.

Dammit.

Clean slate.

Clean slate.

Clean slate.

She didn't have to be something she wasn't. Didn't have to hide what she thought, or what she looked like to fit in. Not here. Not this time. She forced her shoulders back an inch or two, even if it did make her breasts stand out even more than they already did. "I get self-conscious when people stare at me."

Katy scoffed, but the sound had a boatload of empathy behind it. "Boy, do I understand that feeling. The day I walked out in front of the clan knowing I was the first sorcerer since Draven worked his bad juju and nearly killed everyone was one of the hardest of my life." She frowned, zigzagged her attention between the beer in Elise's hand and the one in Jade's. "And where the hell is my beer?"

Just that fast, the awkward moment was over. Swept under the rug like it was no big deal.

Alek chuckled and tucked Elise tighter to his side. "I only deliver beer to pretty girls. I mean, you're pretty and all, but you're my sister, so that knocks you off the auto delivery list."

An indescribable awareness danced beneath her skin a second before Tate's low and eerily menacing voice registered close behind her. "Take Elise off your list, too."

Before she could spin to face Tate, Alek's arm clamped down tighter, holding her firmly in place, and she'd swear Alek grinned before he masked the humor with a blasé expression and peeked over his shoulder. "Oh, hey, Tate. 'Bout time you got here. I was just about to introduce Elise around to the rest of the clan."

Katy covered her mouth and ducked her head.

Sara's eyes got big as dinner plates.

Jade just snickered and grinned like she'd just pulled off a huge coup.

A warning growl that was unmistakably animal rumbled behind her and rippled up her spine. Jade had told her Tate's companion was a mountain coyote. A big one with above-average hunting skills, but she'd never seen it. And while logic told her Tate was fully human behind her, there was no mistaking his beast was close to the surface. "Let go of her. Now."

Alek squeezed her shoulder as if to reassure her then lowered his arm and casually turned, placing himself slightly in front of her. "You sure?"

Elise twisted just in time to catch a muscle at the back of Tate's jaw twitch. The impact whenever she saw him was always a punch. Sandy-blond hair to his shoulders with a wave to it that made him look like he'd just ambled in from a day at the beach, a full, but well-trimmed beard slightly darker than the rest of his hair that made her wonder what his kiss would feel like and a lean, but muscled body that always crackled with a lethal energy. Dressed in a black T-shirt and faded jeans, he looked like the predator he was, and the way he was holding his body made it appear he was a nanosecond from tackling his primo.

Which was insane. He'd barely spoken to her. Barely looked her in the eye since the first day they'd met. But here he was, trading some silent but deadly man-to-man communication she couldn't translate. Given the amused expressions from Katy, Jade and Sara, she was the *only* one in need of subtitles.

Tate's nostrils flared, and he edged closer to Alek, shifting as he did to put himself between Alek and Elise. When he spoke, his words came out grated and pulsing with power. "Don't push me. Primo or not, I've got incentive in the fight you're pushing."

"Enough." When Priest had moved in behind Katy, Elise couldn't say, but the single word vibrated with such command the whole clearing quieted.

For a second, neither Alek or Tate moved.

Then one corner of Alek's mouth twitched. "Something tells me I just earned payback when the time comes, but I figure it was worth it."

"You think that now," Priest said, his tone shifting to something closer to wry amusement. "Wait 'til it's your ass in the wringer."

Alek's smirk shifted to a full smile, but he dipped his head in a silent truce toward Tate. "If she's half as amazing as the one Tate lucked out with, I don't care what he dishes out."

"Who's amazing?" The question was out of Elise's mouth before she'd even realized she wanted the answer, the frustration of not knowing what was going on while everyone else watched with avid curiosity fueling her impatience.

An ugly snarl ripped up Tate's throat.

"Alek," Priest warned.

Alek barked an unrepentant laugh and threw up his hands in surrender. "Yeah, yeah. I'm going. I'm going." He snatched the beer Elise had all but forgotten from her fingers and saluted with a naughty glint in his eye. "Don't think you'll be needing this." Then he eyeballed Jade. "Come on. You started this mess. The least you can do is keep me company while your brother plots my murder."

For the first time since the standoff started, Tate's focus broke from Alek and whipped to Jade. While he didn't look like he was a hairbreadth away from shredding anyone anymore, Elise wasn't sure he'd found the same mental grounding Alek had.

Jade didn't seem to care. Just giggled and waggled her eyebrows at Tate. "Ya gotta admit. It was effective." Not waiting for a response, she sidled up to Elise, wrapped her in a friendly hug and whispered, "Don't worry. Tate'll take care of you. I promise."

"Take care of what?" she whispered back.

She pulled away, squeezed Elise's shoulders and winked. "Everything."

Chapter Three

The frantic beat of her heart. That mysterious yet sweet and innocent scent he'd come to crave. Her body well within touching distance and a wealth of unmarked skin on display. The weight of at least half the clan's attention, if not all of it, was firmly locked on Tate and his mate, but those were the only things he could process. That and staking his claim in a way no other man would dare to put his hands on Elise.

Although, given the maneuver Jade and Alek had engineered to trigger his protective instincts in front of everyone, no one gathered here tonight would question what she was to him going forward.

Well, no one except Elise.

Beside her, Priest, Katy and Sara waited and watched. While he knew Priest only lingered to make sure Tate kept his shit in check and Tate appreciated the mix of sympathy and humor in Katy's expression, he could have done without Sara having such a front-row seat. She was a sweet girl. As honest, open and sincere as a woman could be, but talkative, too. Whatever happened in the next few minutes would be grapevine fodder for the whole clan by morning.

Elise twisted, peeling her gaze away from Jade and

Alek as they sauntered away and peeking over her shoulder first before she fully faced him. "What was all that about?"

A question that should be simple to answer. One that would've been painfully obvious to her if she'd been raised with knowledge of their clan. Not that her mother hadn't tried to share what it meant to be Volán and the things they could do. Elise just hadn't believed her. And, since Jenny had rejected her gifts, she couldn't prove a word of it. "Alek touched you."

"So?"

This was it. Once he gave in and made physical contact, she'd grow to crave his touch every bit as much as he needed hers. Would feel the pull that started as a subtle tug and grew toward something neither one of them could fight. An inextricable bond that would tie them to one another.

He'd tried to give her time to adjust. To grow accustomed to their clan and the gifts of their race. But he couldn't have stopped himself any longer even if the hounds of hell descended in mass, determined to kill them all. He dragged in a long, slow breath and inched forward, careful not to startle her. "No man touches you." The denim at her hips whispered against his palms a second before he settled his hands more firmly against the luscious curves. "No man but me."

Her breath hitched on a tender gasp and her body jolted at the careful, yet intimate contact. Whether it was the surprise of his words, his touch, or a combination of the two, he couldn't say, but the impact was heady. Her full, parted lips. Each ragged inhalation and exhale. Those gorgeous and expressive green eyes of hers, wide with surprise and untapped sensual awareness.

Her gaze dipped to his mouth and she pressed her hands to his pecs. She jerked them away almost as quickly and nearly knocked herself off balance in the process.

Tate moved in tighter, bringing her body flush to his and anchoring one hand low on the small of her back and one at the back of her neck. "Easy."

The need to pair the soothing word with the brush of his lips against her neck—across her forehead or cheeks—nearly crippled him. But he held it in check. Barely. Her mother had all but confirmed Elise's past was a difficult one. And while she'd insisted the details were of a personal nature and up to Elise to share, she'd made it painfully clear the scars ran deep. No way was he opening those old wounds when they weren't in a place he could give her the attention she needed to heal them properly.

Instead, he stroked the length of her spine and centered himself in her scent. In the feel of her soft body trembling against his. "Just breathe. I've got you."

Her fingertips skimmed the length of his triceps and up to his shoulders, the touch tentative and uncertain. She shifted just enough to meet his eyes and opened her mouth, more questions than he had a prayer of answering without scaring the hell out of her burning behind her eyes.

"Tate?" Priest's low inquiry saved him before Elise's questions could meet air. "You good?"

In the last two weeks, runs in animal form with Priest in the darkest hours of the night had been one of the few things that had kept him sane. That and the patience Priest had shown in listening to him ramble about every fear that bubbled up. Tate twisted his head just enough to meet Priest's gaze and gently squeezed the back of Elise's neck before grudgingly releasing her and letting her get her bearings. "We will be."

Priest's tips twitched in that smug way mates who'd already run the gauntlet seemed prone to do and tucked Kateri closer to his side. "Right. You will be."

On the other side of Priest, Sara beamed like she'd just confirmed she was the owner of a grand-prize-winning lottery ticket, and her cheeks were flushed enough to rival Elise's. "Wow. That was *sooo* rom—"

"Intense," Katy cut in before Sara could dig Tate an even deeper hole to climb out of. "When I first got here, all the male posturing weirded me out a little bit," she said to Elise with all the exaggeration of a woman well-versed in clan life. Which was funny as hell considering she'd only shown up at Priest's shop for the first time a month and a half ago and had been in an almost identical situation to Elise, barely having any knowledge of what it was to be Volán.

Still, she was throwing him a bone and giving Sara what he hoped was a solid clue to shut the hell up, so he rolled with it and moved in close to Elise's side, settling his hand low on her spine. "Sorry if the thing with Alek startled you."

Elise twisted as if to confirm his hand really rested where she thought it was, then studied him like she couldn't decide if she'd actually experienced the last ten minutes or conked her head on a hard surface and dreamed it all.

Yet again, Katy moved into damage control. "Hey, Elise. Why don't we plan some time away from the house tomorrow? Maybe see if Tate and Priest could take us along the strip and let you explore some of the shops. They're super touristy, but a fun way to turn your mind off for a while."

"She's got finals on Wednesday," Tate said, startling even himself with the answer.

Elise craned her head to stare up at him. "How do you know that?"

Because he'd stalked her from the day he first saw her. Because he'd been fascinated with the degree she'd chosen and had spent an inordinate amount of time wondering how she'd ended up choosing it. Because he'd just spent an hour and a half prying every detail he could out of her mother so he could arm himself to win her and not hurt her in the process. "Your mother mentioned it when I was painting her bathroom," he said instead.

"Then we'll go after your finals are over that night," Katy said. "Make it a celebration."

Tate scowled.

Katy took one look at his face, apparently realized maybe taking the first open slot on Elise's agenda wasn't the best idea and adjusted plans. "Or Thursday. Maybe Friday." She waved her hand in one of those *no big deal* maneuvers and smiled up at Priest. "You're flexible, right?"

Clearly, Priest thought the whole debacle was hysterical, but he was doing his damndest to rein his laughter in. "We'll work it out, *mihara*." He squeezed her shoulder and lifted his chin toward Tate. "I think we'll let you focus on introducing Elise to everyone." Thankfully, he shifted his attention to Sara and handled the last remaining complication while he was at it. "How about you help my mate make the rounds and make sure everyone's got what they need?"

While she'd apparently gotten the message to keep her revelations to herself, Sara's eyes sparked at the opportunity to cast her front-row experience far and wide. "Absolutely." She grinned at Elise and waved her hand. "It was really good to meet you. My healer magic's not that impressive. Nowhere near what Vanessa has today, or what you'll have after your soul quest, but if you ever need anything…anything at all… I'll help."

With a shake of his head and one last commiserating smile aimed at Tate, Priest steered her away, keeping Katy tight to his side.

"You're a rock star and you didn't even know it," Tate said, hoping to keep conversation on neutral ground.

It worked because Elise frowned and tracked Sara's progress moving from one group to another. "She thinks I'm going to be the healer primo."

"Everyone thinks you're going to be the healer *prima*. Me included."

The frown shifted to something closer to a scowl and her focus seemed to drift, as though her thoughts had turned inward and the activity around her was just extra input. She definitely hadn't picked up on the subtle language distinction between *primo* and *prima*. "I'm not sure how I feel about that." She glanced up and over her shoulder at him and tucked her fingertips into the front pockets of her shorts. "I know almost nothing about our clan. And maybe that Keeper person won't want to have our family keep the whole primo deal after Mom rejected her gifts."

"Prima."

The clarification wiped the frustration from her face long enough to generate some curiosity. "What?"

"It's *prima* for females." He let his gaze travel the

length of her, leisurely enjoying every curve and valley along the way. The bra she had on lifted her amazing tits up for an insane amount of cleavage and made him want to kill Alek all over again for being close enough to see the same view. "And you're one hundred percent female."

For a split second, she responded, her shoulders just barely inching back in a subtle offering he doubted she was even aware of. Just as fast, she spun away and started to leave.

Tate caught her wrist before she could gain any distance. "Please don't."

Beneath his fingers, her pulse raced. While her scent had taken on a hint of the sharpness that came with fear, there was another thread to it now, too. The rich, intoxicating bite of arousal. Faint, but there.

She wanted him.

Had responded to the feel of his lingering perusal. Hadn't broken the loose, yet firm contact at her wrist. She just didn't have a clue how to process what to do with the aftershocks. And fuck if that didn't make him want to howl his triumph for everyone to hear and cart her off no matter who was watching.

He tightened his fingers only enough to gauge her response. To pair the truth of his words with tangible touch. "I want you with me."

She shivered and focused on the single point of contact for too many excruciating heartbeats, then lifted her wide eyes to him. "Why now? You've barely said a word to me since I moved in."

A smile split his face, the fact that she'd inadvertently admitted she'd wanted his presence bringing the response too quickly for him to mask it. He stroked his thumb along her pulse point and moved in close. "Wanting something and being ready for it are two different things."

"And you're ready now?" It came out a little sassy. A delicate dare tangled up with genuine curiosity.

And his beast loved it. "I was ready the day I saw you." Giving in to temptation, he traced her jawline and cupped the back of her neck. Her hair was thick. A silky weight along the back of his hand that made him want to shift his grip, fist it tight and angle her mouth for his kiss. "The wait was for you. To give you time to settle."

God, those eyes. So big and expressive. Loaded with pleasant surprise and a fragility that made him want to wrap her up and keep the whole fucking world at bay. He couldn't wait to see them heavy and dazed with lust. To see what moved behind them the first time he slid inside her.

"What if I'm still not ready?" she nearly whispered.

Inside him, his coyote stilled and let out a short huff. A warning and a keen nudge to keep his derailing thoughts on track. Elise wasn't the coy type. If she'd dared to utter such a statement, it wouldn't be based on flirtation or dressed up as an innocent challenge the way some of the other more aggressive clanswomen would. She'd mean every word of it. And damned if that didn't suck for him because he was absolutely on board with getting her ready in the most tactile way possible.

He filled his lungs with her scent and forced his fingers to uncurl from the back of her neck. "It's always your choice, *mihara*." The second he lost contact and stepped out of her personal space, an empty coldness he'd never felt before settled behind his sternum.

His beast whimpered and paced, fighting the same compulsion to take and claim that burned inside him.

But this was a long hunt. The longest and most important one of his life. To push and try to steal her surrender might be faster and gratifying as hell in the short-term, but it wouldn't build the foundation he wanted. The foundation she'd need to hold her own between them. He held out his hand. "Do you want my company?"

Of all the fights he'd been in—of every hare-brained, thrill-seeking stunt he'd pulled in his life—none generated the raw exposure of that moment. The gut-clenching fear as she stared at his hand with open indecision. His lungs burned with the need for more air and his muscles ached to move, the itch and strain no different than if he'd purposefully splayed his hand on a flaming stove. But he kept his hand steady. His breaths slow and even.

Gaze rooted on his palm, she swallowed hard and rubbed her own against her hip.

"Trust me, Elise. It's just a party. Let me introduce you to everyone and get to know you in the process."

She met his stare, such stark uncertainty reflected on her faery face that his whole body seemed to shut down, and he braced for her to walk away. Instead, she slowly placed her hand in his, her fingertips trembling as they skittered across his palm. "I'm not great at social things."

His heart lurched back into motion, the ricochet of its furious rhythm as it tried to catch up a deafening crash in his ears. For the first time in days, he felt balanced. Borderline normal. As if her acceptance had not only latched on and yanked him from the eye of a tornado, but opened up a whole new terrain to explore.

"You don't have to be great at it." He laced his fingers with hers, relief and determination jetting a fresh wave of adrenaline through his bloodstream as he tugged her closer and steered them into the celebration's fray. "I'm a master. Just sit back and enjoy the ride."

He started with a cluster of mated couples who'd been together awhile, most of them Priest's age or older. Where the grip she kept on his hand had been painfully tight when they'd joined the group and her input to the lighthearted conversation limited at first, by the time they'd meandered away, she'd unwound enough to comfortably stroll by his side and a small smile lingered on her lips. The next group was even easier, Katy's grandmother, Naomi, and one of the clan's elder warriors, Garrett, each pulling her into warm hugs like a favorite granddaughter and taking over with introducing her to the others around them.

Fortunately for Tate, all the hugs and handshakes had forced Elise to release her hold on him. A fact he took prompt advantage of the second all the hi-how-are-yas were over by moving in tight beside her and sliding his arm around her waist.

She sucked in a quick, indrawn breath. A barely there gasp that would have gone undetected to anyone who'd not yet received their heightened shifter senses, but considering the people around them had all answered their quest years ago and been alive for well over a hundred years each, they all caught it. They may not have turned their heads and openly made note of it, but the quick smiles and chuckles in the wake of her innocent response had obviously triggered fond memories.

Even if they'd turned and pointed, Elise would have likely missed it. She was obviously too flustered, first folding her arms across her chest, then tucking her fingertips inside the front pocket of her shorts.

With a smile he hoped she didn't catch, he leaned to the side and murmured, "It's okay to touch me, *mihara*."

She peeked up at him through her lashes then scanned the people gathered around the gorge as though looking for examples to work from.

Tate smoothed his hand along the ample curve at her hip. A gentle, petting stroke when what he really wanted was to squeeze, pull her in front of him and make it so she could simply lean against him. "Put your arm around my waist. See how that feels."

The hesitation that followed was nowhere near as long or painful as the wait for her to take his hand had been. But the feel of her fingertips tentatively sliding low on his back from one hip to the other? That was a whole different level of torture. Especially, when she dared to snuggle in closer and pressed her free hand lightly on his sternum. "Like this?"

Yes.

No.

Both answers hit him at the same time, part of him insisting the wiser course of action was to let her take her time and explore however she wanted, while the other part fought the temptation to pull her flush, front-to-front, and devour her mouth.

Patience.

His companion might have uttered the message, but even his coyote's confidence was wavering. Patience strained to the point of pain and frustration.

"Perfect," he said, instead. And it wasn't a lie. It

might not be as much as he craved, but without the tension of when he'd steadied her against him and calmed her before, now he could savor the contact. Could let the conversation bouncing around them idle as nothing more than background noise and focus on the way her soft body gave way to his and fit so perfectly. The press of her full breasts against his side. The whisper of her hair against his chin, and the heat of her skin even through her tank and jeans.

He was so lost in soaking it all in, he barely registered the overly perky and feminine voice at his opposite side. "Hey, Tate. Aren't you going to introduce us to your friend?"

Elise went tense within his arms, her fingertips pressing more firmly against his chest and her hard, impassive gaze lasered in the direction the words had come from.

In less than a heartbeat, both man and beast went on full alert, his brain finally tying the voice with who it actually belonged to. Tate tightened his arm around Elise's waist and gave her hip a reassuring squeeze before he shifted them both to fully take in the new arrival. "Hey, Nessa." Though, as he offered the greeting, he realized it wasn't just one person who'd strolled up to the group. It was bad enough he was going to have to introduce Elise to someone he'd been intimate with before he had a chance to cover that ground with her, but apparently, he was going to have to handle it with Nessa's gossiping posse in tow. Four of them, to be exact, and all of them eyeballing Elise tucked tight to his side with calculating expressions.

He dipped his head to the lot of them. "Ladies."

Each offered anything from laughter to sly smiles in

answer, but it was Nessa who kept things going. "So? Who's your friend?"

Funny. Once upon a time, he'd found Nessa ridiculously attractive. With her cool blond hair, pretty blue eyes and willowy body, she was definitely easy on the eyes, but after a few outings with her, he'd realized the depth behind her beauty was almost nonexistent.

He stared down at Elise's still guarded face, the same pride that had nearly choked him every time he'd introduced her tonight pushing up from his chest. "This is Elise Ralston. She just moved here from Louisiana." He lowered his voice, hoping the tone of it would help calm whatever had Elise drawn so tight. "Elise, these are some of our clan's healers and seers. Bren, Taya, Daycie, Renda and Nessa."

"It's Vanessa, actually. Only my friends call me Nessa."

The bite behind her saccharine sweet words slapped like a subzero wind chill to the cheeks. If Elise noted the barely veiled slight, she didn't show it. Just dropped her hand from Tate's torso and straightened to the max of her five feet two inches and lifted her jaw. "It's nice to meet you."

Bren, a seer and the friendliest of the group, cocked her head and offered a neutral smile. "Where did you live in Louisiana?"

Elise studied her for a second, the shrewd focus of a crafty animal accustomed to assessing and dodging dangerous aggressors. "Butte La Rose."

"Where's that?" Renda asked.

"Just outside Lafayette," Elise answered, though the clipped delivery didn't encourage diving deeper into details about her hometown.

Toying with the straw that peeked out of her red Solo

cup, Daycie weighed in anyway. "Sara said you're from the healer primo family line, but I thought their name was Rallion."

"Rallion is the name her family used to go by," Tate said before she could answer. Whatever it was that had Elise poised for flight, neither he or his companion liked it and were ready to shut the awkward situation down by any means possible. "They go by Ralston now."

"Well, just because she's from the former line doesn't mean she'll be prima," Nessa said. "I mean, her mom didn't take her gifts, so the Keeper might shift things to a new line. Why keep the honor in a family who doesn't appreciate it for what it is? And isn't your dad a singura? You may not even have a soul quest, right?"

And there it was. The catty attack his mate had obviously sensed coming that he'd apparently done a piss poor job of blocking. Yeah, he'd listened to Jade cry and rant when women had tried to pull that backhanded bullshit with her growing up. Had even heard Nessa and her crew bad-mouthing women they obviously viewed as competitors in high school, but now? For fuck's sake, they were all mid- to late-twenties, not fourteen and maxed out on hormones.

Beside him, Elise went eerily still, her heart's once agitated rhythm settling into that of a warrior pre-fight. Even the energy around her seemed to settle into an impenetrable shield. "Whether or not I'm given magic, or what titles I hold doesn't define me. Character does."

Silence.

One by one, the women around Nessa lost their smiles and looked to their fearless leader as though they'd entirely lost their rudder.

Nessa glanced at the elders beside them who'd ceased

their conversation in favor of the drama unfolding and let out one of those awkward laughs reserved for people up a social shit creek. "I think what I said came out the wrong way. I just thought you might be feeling some pressure and wanted to point out some other possibilities. I mean, being the healer prima is a big thing and you don't even know anything about us."

"Neither did Katy and she's Priest's mate," Tate said. "Not to mention our first sorcerer in years. You wanna throw around possibilities, maybe the Keeper's decided to give our clan primos who don't have sticks up their asses and can actually function with a little humanity."

"Oh, come on, Tate," Vanessa said. "You know I didn't mean anything bad by it." She slipped in closer and actually had the audacity to drag a familiar stroke along his arm. "You *know* me."

Elise jolted against him, a faint movement she did an astounding job of hiding from everyone else, but pressed against him, he felt every pain-laced bit of it. She tried to move from within the shelter of his arm.

Tate clamped down harder. "I have a woman next to me and you dared to touch me in front of her. She's new to our clan and from an honored family, but you gave her the coldest welcome of anyone here tonight. Worse, you'd rather try to brush the slights you've handed out as misunderstandings to save face rather than own up to them. Apparently, I don't know you. And just to be clear, any right you once had to touch me is gone."

His gaze slid to Jade who'd meandered to the edge of the crowd, her feet planted hip width, arms crossed and a proud grin on her face. She might be a seer for the clan, but in that moment, she looked more like a warrior weighing whether or not she needed to wade in and kick a load of female ass. As pissed as he was, a part of him wanted to hang around and see if she actually pulled the trigger.

But Elise needed him more. Preferably without the bulk of the clan looking on. "I think we're done here." He steered Elise away from the group, but tossed a final dig over his shoulder as he left. "Nice talking to you... *Vanessa*."

Chapter Four

Women were bitches. Backstabbing, underhanded, devious bitches.

Perched atop a big boulder at the lake's edge with Tate beside her and a crescent moon high in the near-midnight sky, the thought seemed incongruous. A hairy wart in the middle of an otherwise picture-perfect scenario.

Deep down Elise knew the sentiment wasn't true. Had actually met many decent women in the years since she'd escaped high school—Jade and Katy being among them—but with the dregs of her encounter with Vanessa still lingering like a stubborn hangover, it was hard not to generalize.

It was also hard not to run and hide. Actually, she *would* have run if she'd been able to swing it. At least five times she'd tried to make excuses to Tate and escape down the path back to her house, but he'd stubbornly either kept her fingers laced with his, or wrapped a possessive arm around her waist whenever they stopped to mingle with other people from the clan.

And then he'd brought her here. Led her unerringly through the dark, still woods without a single light to help navigate the terrain and peppered her with questions about her life. About her mother, her father, and what life had been like living in a small town like Butte La Rose.

Moonlight rippled on the lake's wavering surface, the wind just strong enough to leave a chill on her skin. Not that she minded. With Tate this close, subtly leaning in every now and then and brushing his shoulder against hers, it could have been fifteen below zero and she'd have been content.

"So, why major in kinesiology?"

She ducked her head and smiled at his new topic. "Normally, the first question I get isn't how I ended up majoring in it, but what the heck is it?"

"It's about body movement, right? Using it to make people healthier, or rehab them after injuries?"

And here she'd thought he hadn't noticed her. Clearly, he'd not only been watching how she spent her time, but he'd done his homework, too. "I'm impressed."

The smile he answered her with reminded her of a little boy she'd worked with during a physical therapy internship rotation in Lafayette. His leg had been significantly damaged in a horrible car wreck, but he'd been fearless in his recovery. The day he'd taken three steps in a row, he'd beamed at her with such pure delight it made her heart sing.

"Don't give me too much credit," he said, twisting on the wide rock so he faced her rather than the lake. "My time with Google only went so far. When they started throwing out things like biomechanics and neuroscience, my eyes kinda glazed over." He studied her for a beat then shifted one leg, anchored it behind her back and scooted closer. "So? Tell me how a girl from a tiny town in Louisiana ended up with an unconventional major like yours."

Unconventional was a choice word. Some people in the medical world even went so far as to scoff when kinesiology was mentioned, but she'd gotten to the point where she didn't care anymore. "I was really active with sports growing up—dance, track, gymnastics. Up until I was sixteen, my poor mom spent more time in a car driving me from one thing to another and finding me whatever gear I needed than she did doing anything else."

"Well, you were good at it if the number of trophies and ribbons in your room are any indication."

Ugh. Those trophies. They'd been a joy and a weight all at the same time. "If it was up to me, we would have left them back in Louisiana. Or better yet, they'd be gone altogether."

"Why? You worked for them."

And paid for them through more than competition. She dared a look at Tate beside her. "I got hurt about halfway through my junior year in high school. A knee injury. Mom keeps the stuff around me as a way to try and get me to reconsider dropping out of sports."

"You never went back?"

"Nope."

The night swallowed her answer and the soft spring air danced along her skin. As if it dared her to share more.

Tate waited.

Odd. For the first time since the day she'd limped and crawled her way back to her house, the devastation and pain that normally swarmed her remembering what had led to her injury stayed blissfully at bay.

As if his presence alone held the humiliation and hurt well out of reach.

"Anyway..." She anchored her heels on the boulder and wrapped her arms around her knees, hugging them tight. "The whole injury process—the doctors, the nurses, the rehabilitation—it all fascinated me. When I started college, I planned on going the doctor route, but the more classes I attended, the angrier I got. It felt too rigid. Too textbook."

"So, you switched to the therapy side of it?"

"Not right away. There was a semester where I explored the nursing angle first, but then an advisor at school suggested I look at kinesiology." She shrugged and twisted to meet his gaze. "It fit."

Never in her life had a man looked at her the way Tate was right now. Totally focused. As if there was absolutely nothing else in the world except her and what came out of her mouth. More than that, he seemed intent on committing every response to memory. The way she moved. Her smiles. Her mood. "You don't like to talk about how you were hurt."

It was a gentle nudge. A careful approach delivered on the rich baritone of his voice. Part of her wanted to answer it. To open up and let it all spill out. The embarrassment. The shame and the loss.

But the rest of her was too greedy. Too hesitant to risk a moment like this slipping away. "No."

He held her gaze, an emotion moving behind his amber eyes she couldn't quite identify.

But she'd never felt safer. More accepted than in that moment.

The wind teased her hair from behind her ear and across her face.

Tate swept the errant strands back, softly tracing his thumb along her cheek. "I want to know you, Elise. Even the parts you're afraid to share." He cupped her nape, the careful yet deeply possessive contact lighting a heightened awareness. As if the air around them had grown thick and rich with a pleasant electricity. "I won't rush you. Won't ever take more than you're willing to give." His thumb skimmed along the pulse at her neck. "But I want it all."

Her heart kicked and her belly spun to rival some of the flips she'd once mastered in her floor routines.

All as in her secrets?

Or all as in *everything*?

Who cares?

Looking at him in that second, bound to him by the magnetic moment and barely capable of reasonable thought—let alone fear—neither prospect seemed daunting. "What about you?"

"What about me?"

"I don't know anything about you."

His full lips twitched. "You know I'm a warrior. You know I'm a tattoo artist and that I work and live with Priest. You know Jade's a pain in my ass."

"But I don't know why you live with Priest." As soon as she said it, she wanted to snatch the question back. Especially when his smile slipped and a wistfulness settled in his eyes.

He lowered his hand and leaned back. "You know what happened to our clan, right?"

Oh, she knew. Had heard about the presect rites performed at each change of season to keep the Earth's magic in balance. Had nearly cried at hearing the excruciating details of how Priest's brother, Draven, had stolen every primo's magic at the last rite over fifty years ago trying to overtake the clan. Draven had killed the primos in the process—Elise's grandmother, included— and nearly killed Priest as well. But Priest had won in the end, stripping the gifts Draven had stolen and taking them into himself. He'd thought he'd killed Draven, too, but they'd learned otherwise when he slaughtered Kateri and Alek's parents.

Elise nodded. "Jade said Priest still has the dark magic Draven used that night trapped inside him."

"He does. For a long time after the attack happened it was mine and Jade's mothers who kept him alive and protected. It took Priest years to get the darkness under control. Our moms are the ones who inked the marks you see on him today. Or most of them, anyway. The symbols helped contain it."

"Where was your dad?"

"You know our life spans are different, right?"

She nodded. "Naomi said she's 125."

"And Garrett's 163. Some of our elders have even made it to almost two centuries. The only one who lives longer is our high priest. The one Priest replaced was nearly 300 when he died."

Katy had shared as much early on, but it still was a shock to try and comprehend. "And?"

"So, my dad was a lot older than my mom. Died when I was ten. When my mom died, Priest took me in. I was sixteen then, but he'd always been a fixture in my life. Jade moved in with us a year later when her mom died."

"Your mom was a healer?"

He nodded, a slight smile playing on his lips. "A

strong one. Nowhere near what you'll be someday, but powerful nonetheless."

"You don't know I'll be prima." Sure, it would be an amazing gift. An honor she'd put everything into if it came to pass, but right now she'd be happy just to lean a little closer to Tate and run her fingers along his strong jawline. To feel his beard against her skin.

She hadn't even realized she was rubbing one thumb along the pads of her fingertips until Tate covered her hand with his, turned it so her palm faced up and traced a path along the center. "What are you thinking about, *mihara*?"

Mihara.

He'd called her that a few times tonight. She'd known it was an endearment of some sort from the times she'd heard Priest use it with Katy, but the exact meaning was still a mystery. "What's that word mean?"

His smile shifted, the devilish grin that replaced it whipping her heart into a jog. "That's *my* secret. But anything else you want to know about me is yours to have."

"Anything?"

Pure delight glinted in his eyes. "Anything."

A kiss was too much. Definitely more than her already exhausted courage could rally for. But there was something else. Something she'd imagined countless times, mostly at night with the windows open with the night's sweet sounds drifting in to lull her sleep. She swallowed hard, praying her request wouldn't make him laugh in her face. "Will you shift for me?"

His smile died, but the look that moved in behind it stirred something wild inside her. Heat. Desire. Raw and uninhibited lust. "Do you know what my companion is?"

Thinking was a challenge. Talking even more so. Especially, when the only action her body seemed interested in processing was how to initiate contact. Full, chest-to-toes, delicious contact. "Jade said it's a coyote."

"A mountain coyote." He cocked his head and studied her. "And you're not afraid?"

"Should I be?"

For a second, she swore a growl rumbled past his lips. "Not in the way you're thinking." He gripped her hand in his and gave it a meaningful squeeze. "But you're safe with him."

"Then I'd like to see."

He dipped his head, though she would have sworn it wasn't her he was agreeing with. More like an answer to a conversation she wasn't privy to hearing. "All right." With one last stroke from his fingers along the back of her hand, he slid from the boulder and paced a few steps away. Though, with Tate, even the simple action was a wonderful thing to watch. With his tight, compacted muscles and animalistic grace, he was pure alpha in motion. "Stand up."

"Why?"

He faced her, his fists loosely clenching and releasing at his sides. "Because it's past midnight and I don't want your mother worried. If my other half gets to come out and play, he at least needs to walk you home."

A weird mix of elation and disappointment dragged her to her feet. For the first time in her life, she didn't want to go home. Didn't want the night to end. But at the same time, she couldn't wait to meet his companion.

"Can I talk to him?" *Well, duh. Of course, you can talk to him.* "I mean, will he understand me?"

Tate's smile was lightning quick. "He's been here all night and heard every word. So, yeah. He'll understand you. We're two parts of one whole. If you need me, or you get scared, we'll both know, and I'll shift back."

So. Freaking. Cool. She barely stopped herself from bouncing like a five-year-old waiting for her princess birthday party to start. She'd seen Alek shift into his wolf the day she'd learned about the clan and had glimpsed Katy and Priest with their panther and lioness padding side by side through the isolated woods a few times, but somehow this was different. More important. Like a long awaited meeting she hadn't even been aware she was waiting for.

"Ready?"

She nodded, her answer as it slipped out breathy with anticipation. "Yes."

He hesitated for all of two heartbeats, his gaze locked with hers and the ten feet between them pulsing with a supercharged connection.

A soft light tinged with red blossomed against the lake and the sky's dark background.

It dimmed almost as quickly, but Tate was gone. In his place was a gorgeous creature that stood as tall as her thighs, his thick gold pelt accented with white, gray and black. Where she'd expected his build to be lean, or even wiry like some of the wild images she'd seen online, Tate's companion was pure muscle.

He waited, the same amber eyes as Tate's staring back at her, only now their shape was different. Slightly angled in a way that made his gaze seem sharper.

"Hi." It was probably a stupid thing to say. Tate had

basically just told her the animal standing in front of her was part of him, so it wasn't like an introduction was necessary, but the greeting felt right.

Strangely enough, the coyote lifted its chin, let out a soft yip and cautiously padded forward.

Instinct pushed her to back away. Or better yet, run. But another far more pressing need dragged her to her knees. The chilled damp ground cushioned her landing and sent goose bumps along her bared skin, but the closer he got, the less she cared about the discomfort.

He slowed and paused just out of reach.

She lifted her hand, palm up. "I'm okay."

His pert ears twitched and his avid gaze shifted to her trembling fingers.

Okay, maybe she wasn't rock steady, but she wasn't terrified either. "I'm excited, not afraid." When he still didn't budge, she opted for something with more weight. "I'm also a little cold. You're not blocking the wind anymore."

On a human, the huff her statement earned would have fallen somewhere between humor and mild annoyance. What it meant for a coyote was harder to gauge, but it did get him in motion, sidling slowly within reaching distance. He butted her hand with the top of his head and nestled closer, stopping when his fur tickled the inside of her arms and tops of her thighs.

And holy cow, was he soft. Soft with such a thick coat that when she combed her fingers just behind his ears the fine tips teased her wrists. She sighed and got her other hand in on the action, stroking the back of his neck and burrowing into his heat like he was a friendly husky instead of a deadly hunter. "That's much better."

A soft hum rumbled from his chest. He leaned into

her, nudged her neck with his cold, wet nose, then rubbed his cheek along the same spot. With the weight of him, his open affection and the playful swish of his tail, she toppled sideways, her laugher lifting out into the cloudless starry skies. "Oh my God, you're heavy. What do you weigh, anyway?"

He barked and crept close, snuggling alongside her like it was the most natural thing in the world. His warm breath buffeted against her neck and she would have sworn his parted mouth was a coyote's version of a smile. "Are you apologizing, or just angling for a better back rub?"

At that, he huffed and licked her cheek, drawing an unexpected squeak out of her they probably heard all the way back to Priest's house. "Okay, okay. Back rub it is. Though, if you lick me again all bets are off."

He let out a soft whine, stretched out on his belly and rested his chin on his paws, the picture of contentment. And that was it. Just the peace of two beings snuggled close to each other. Him sharing his heat and her sharing her touch. And the funniest part? She was comfortable. Totally void of the nervous sexual jitters she felt around Tate. As if, by shedding his human skin, she was able to peel away all her past hurts and fears and just *be* without worrying.

She didn't have a clue how long they lay there, but it was far too soon when Tate's companion lifted his head, met her gaze and slowly stood, rubbing the side of his massive torso against her as he did. "Time to go, huh?"

In animal form, there were no facial expressions to clue her in to his thoughts, but his eyes said he wasn't any happier about reality forcing its way into the moment than she was.

"Okay, fine. But don't go too fast. I can't see as good as you."

The trek through the woods was peacefully perfect, the whisper of her sandaled feet against winter's decomposing leaves, the soft rustle of leaves overhead and the forest's rich, earthy scents wrapping her in a reflective tapestry. The last few weeks had been a whirlwind. Uprooting from the small town she'd lived in her whole life. Meeting new people. Wrapping her head around the fantastical reality of magic and shapeshifting. Finding herself dumbstruck by a man she'd thought hadn't noticed her at all.

And then tonight had happened.

In the time she'd spent with Tate's companion, the heady buzz that had kept her spellbound and tongue-tied all night had finally eased, but the awareness was still right there at the surface. The near tangible promise that while the very human alpha who'd not only demonstrated quite publicly his interest, but stood up for her with someone he'd likely known most of his life, was only a shift away, just waiting to pick back up where he'd left off.

At least she hoped that's what happened. With her experience, or the lack thereof, it wasn't outside the realm of possibility she was reading everything the wrong way. But then why would he be so open with physical touch? Why spend his time with her? Or more importantly, want her secrets? The questions looped over and over, new ones popping up and jumping into the never-ending cycle while the forest slipped by.

Through it all, Tate stayed close. Only when a fallen log or outstretched branch might have tripped her up or injured her did he leave his place just ahead and to one side of her and draw her attention to the danger.

The light from her back porch glimmered through the tree line ahead.

Home.

It should have made her happy. Had always served as a safe space where the curious looks from boys and ugly taunts from girls couldn't reach her.

Tonight it meant the end.

For a moment, she thought about circling back toward the lake. To steal a little of the night back before the real world could toss her back into her ordinary, isolated routine. But that was only a delay. The one thing in life she knew with absolute clarity was that you couldn't prevent life or people from being what they were meant to be. God knew, she'd tried and failed miserably. No one knew what tomorrow would bring and to mourn tonight before it was fully over was a waste.

Tate moved into her path and stopped barely more than an arm's reach away, forcing her to do the same. Unlike the cautious or playful energy she'd sensed in him before, this time he was laser focused. A keen predator astutely aware of every sound and sight around him.

The beautiful red glow that had marked his shift before fired bold before her, the power of it so intense it surrounded her as well.

And then Tate was there. Shoulders back. Arms loose at his sides and feet braced hip-width apart. Nothing about his stance communicated danger. No threat of any kind.

But his expression was another matter. Harsh. Focused. Eyes blazing and scanning her face and body as though looking for something. "What's wrong?"

"What do you mean?"

"You were fine and then something changed."

Her heart lurched and took off at a jog, the rhythm uncomfortably unsteady. He couldn't have known what she was thinking. Voláns had all kinds of magic—healing, vision, physical strength and textbook sorcery—but she was pretty sure mind reading wasn't in the lineup. "What do you mean something changed?"

"Your scent. Most emotions have one." He cocked his head and narrowed his gaze. "Yours is sad. Why?"

Shoot.

Talk about your bad times to stumble onto clan knowledge. She shrugged and clamored for an answer that might somehow make her not come off like a pathetic loon. When one wouldn't come, she fell back on the truth. "Tonight was a good night."

He crept forward. "But that's good."

She nodded, her pulse ramping higher the closer he got. The next time she spoke, it was barely more than a whisper. "It's good until it has to end."

Comprehension settled on his face and a tiny grin lifted his lips. He stopped with only inches between them and cradled her face in both hands. His deep voice sent fire licking along her chilled skin and his warm breath teased her lips. "This isn't the end, Elise."

She braced both hands on his chest, torn between pushing him away long enough to get her emotions and mind under control, and simply allowing herself the joy of sampling the hard muscle beneath the soft cotton. Logic told her to follow up with another question.

To dig deeper and unearth what sounded like a whole lot of missing but pertinent information.

But the instinctive and purely physical side of her didn't give a fig about logic. Or questions. The only thing it cared about was the primal male in front of her. In the heat of his hands. In the tantalizing proximity of his full lips and the ravenous gaze locked squarely on her.

"What are you doing?" Her lungs barely managed to support the question, and given how light-headed she was, they weren't doing much to support the rest of her either. But man, if she was gonna go, dying from an overdose of Tate was a stellar way to do it.

"Unless you stop me, I'm going to kiss you." He shifted one hand and gently dragged his thumb along her lower lip. "Do you want that, *mihara?*"

Want? Was he joking? *Want* was staring at your favorite dessert when your belly was already full of Grade A fillet, tossing aside guilt and not caring how uncomfortable your waistband felt on the way home. Feeling his mouth on hers was *necessary.* A primal connection she had zero experience knowing how to claim for her own, but knew on the most intrinsic level would re-chart every truth in her life.

"Elise?"

"Yes."

She was pretty sure the word made it past her lips. Tried to at least pair it with a dip of her chin. Whether either worked was hard to tell. Not with the prickling anticipation skittering across her skin and his hot gaze holding her rooted in place.

He slowly lowered his head.

Her heart kicked and thrashed like a frantic animal desperate to escape a trap.

But her lips parted.

Willing.

Desperate.

Ready.

His warm breath fluttered against her skin a second before contact, her lungs reflexively drawing the unexpected gift into her lungs along with his earthy scent.

And then was *there*. The full press of his mouth fitted perfectly with hers. The soft whisper of his beard. The teasing glide of his tongue along her lower lip, coaxing her to open. His soft groan as she gave him what he wanted, and the wet heat of their kiss.

She was lost. Floating through a riot of sensations she'd never dreamed existed. Drowning in all that was Tate. Absolutely nothing else mattered except the taste of him. In following where he led with each slick glide of his lips against hers. In savoring the decadent feel of his tongue sliding against hers.

He angled his head and deepened the kiss, sliding one hand to the back of her head and holding her firm as his other hand slipped around her waist and anchored just above her ass, pulling her flush against him.

So much muscle and heat. His arms banded around her. His muscled torso against her breasts and questing palms. His powerful quads pressed against her hips and—

She gasped and jerked away, the startling realization of what she'd felt hard against her belly knocking her headfirst back to reality. She staggered back a step. Then another. Willing her lungs to function despite the air thick with need around her.

A low growl surrounded her before she could take a third. "Don't run." Chest heaving and chin lowered as though he were seconds from charging forward, Tate pumped both his hands in fists. "I won't hurt you. Not ever. But you can't run."

Something in his tone suspended her fear. A desperation that put the brakes on all thoughts of distance and made every protective instinct fire bright. "What's wrong?"

"Just promise me, Elise. Whatever you do...*don't run.*"

Common sense and every deeply entrenched self-preservation coping mechanism she'd built in her teenage years told her to just agree, give Tate time to gather whatever control he needed and not ask any questions. But apparently, common sense and self-preservation didn't hold much weight when Tate was part of the mix. "Why?"

The growl rumbled free again, this time lower and vibrating with so much energy the air between them pulsed with a living current. He prowled toward her. "Because I want to chase you."

Pleasure speared through her belly and her sex clenched, the image of him above her and pressing her into the soft ground all too easy to conjure.

He moved in close and cupped the back of her neck, trailing his thumb along her pulse point. "Why did you pull away?"

Diversion would be best. Some innocent half-truth along the lines of not wanting to go too far too fast so she wouldn't look like a naive idiot. But with Tate, anything less than complete honesty felt wrong. A slight dealt through lack of courage. "Because I don't..." She swallowed and tried to steady her voice, but it came out raspy and uncertain. "This is new to me."

His nostrils flared and his eyes widened with shock and comprehension.

She pushed against his chest and tried to slip from his hold, but his grip tightened and he pulled her closer, anchoring his other hand on her hip. "How much is new?"

Never in her life had she been so grateful for night's forgiving shadows. Though, with the way he'd been able to navigate the woods, he probably still saw the flush burning her cheeks.

Give him the truth. All of it.

The thought rang crystal clear in her head. One of those peacefully quiet messages that rang with divine certainty. A gift from the unseen to navigate an unclear path. She forced her mouth to move. "Everything."

Pure, masculine pleasure washed across his face. A predator who'd triumphed in the most primal of feats and earned the ultimate prize. And yet, despite the surge of power emanating from him, his grip gentled and shifted to cup the back of her head. "Was that your first kiss?"

She ducked her head—or tried to—but he stopped her with fingers at her chin before she could so much as steady her thoughts. "Elise?"

She was twenty-three. Far too old to be in this position. But it was who she was. "Yes."

Of all the responses she might have expected, the groan and all-encompassing hug he enfolded her in wasn't one of them. He rubbed his temple against hers, the rumble emanating from his chest oddly soothing despite the ferocity behind it. Only when her heart had settled and the rise and fall of her breath had evened did he speak. Even then, he kept her close, his voice low and deep at her ear. "Have you been on a date?"

"No."

He stroked the length of her spine and inhaled deep. "Then we'll start there. Wednesday night after your finals are over."

She snapped her head up and dug the heels of her palms against his chest, surprise and panic fueling the move enough to garner eye contact. "What?"

"A date." As if he sensed her growing panic and the need for time to process, he pulled away, but captured her hand with the same casual determination he'd used throughout the party and led her toward the forest's edge. "We'll grab dinner and I'll show you around town."

"But Priest said I couldn't leave the property."

"I'll talk to Priest. You'll be safe."

Safe.

Such a simple word with comfortable and confident implications. While she had no doubt Tate would do everything in his power to keep her out of Draven's hands and any physical harm, she wasn't entirely certain her heart was as well protected. She'd certainly not done her part in those early years to teach herself how to guard it on her own, and by the time she'd reached out for help after high school there'd been no real threats left to guard her heart against.

Skirting the back patio with its modest view of the lake, Tate released her hand and guided her to the front of the house with his hand at the small of her back. The raised wood porch that wrapped around the simple cottage had the same homey feel as the one they'd left behind in Butte La Rose, only the coloring was vastly different—a rich hunter green with terra cotta trim that would blend with the woods around them no matter the season. And it was far more isolated. More intimate with a single old porch light behind a heavily frosted globe painting a tiny perimeter close to the front door.

Tate stopped her at the top of the steps, halfway in and out of the shadows, and turned her to face him. He slid his hands around her waist and pulled her close with a familiarity her body still processed as if it were the first time, the jolt forcing her hands to his shoulders to keep her balance. "What are we doing?"

With the porch light at her back, the sharp angles of his face were more pronounced and his gold eyes as breathtaking as a cloudless sunset. His lips lifted in a lopsided grin. "Well, unless you stop me, I'm going to give you another kiss."

A shudder wriggled down her spine and her breath caught, her mind and body both chiming in with whole-hearted approval. But that wasn't the answer she was after, and there was no way she was walking through her front door without making sure her brain wasn't twisting the night into something it wasn't. She'd done that once before with painful results. Granted, it had been more along the lines of catastrophizing instead of fantasizing, but both were a dangerous game for her psyche.

"I meant what's going on with us," she said. "You said, 'We'll start with a date.' What's that mean?"

His gaze softened and he skimmed one hand up her spine to the back of her head. "Let me kiss you and I'll show you."

A request. Not a demand. Not a violation of her privacy, or an uncomfortable advance. Aside from the altercation between him and Alek tonight, he'd always given her a choice. Shown a forthright interest that lifted her up and empowered her despite her lack of experience. If she hadn't been so overloaded with surprise, wonder and sheer delight all night she might have recognized the gift for what it was sooner. "Okay."

The word had no sooner slipped free than his mouth was on hers. Tasting. Tempting. Nudging her deeper and deeper into an intoxicating place outside the real world. Here there was no need to think, rationalize or dissect. Only to feel. To let go and explore the sensations as they were given. The steady beat of his heart. The soft rasp of his T-shirt against her palms and the hot muscle underneath. The unscripted, but oh so perfect press and glide of his lips against hers.

She rolled up on her toes and circled her arms around his neck, the crush of her breasts against his chest pushing everything higher. Hotter. And yet it still wasn't enough. Something was missing. A hunger hiding in shadows with no ready path to feed it. An ache she couldn't ease. She rolled her hips and moaned at the unmistakable press of his cock against her belly.

Not a threat.

A promise.

He fisted his hand in her hair and tore his mouth away, resting his forehead against hers. Like hers, his breath sawed in and out in a ragged rhythm, but where she was soft and pliant, his body vibrated against hers with barely restrained control. When he spoke, his lips whispered against hers and his voice vibrated with hunger. "That's what we're starting, *mihara.*"

A start.

Good God, if that was the start, she wasn't sure she'd

be able to handle what came farther down the road. Or worse, the ending. And the start of what? A fling? Something purely physical? "I'm not sure I know what that means either."

Tate loosened his grip and lifted his head, his eyes smiling when they finally met hers. He cupped the side of her face and fanned his thumb along her cheekbone. "It means you'll never go without what you just felt again. You don't have to worry. Don't have to process what it means, or what comes next. With me, all you have to do is be who you are."

Never go without.

No worries.

Just be.

Three promises that whispered to her soul and cast a soft glow on every hope and dream she'd harbored close. Logically, she knew they were ideals at best. Definitely not absolutes. People were human. Fallible. But, the hope was there, striking a spark.

He sucked in a slow breath and tucked her hair behind one ear. "Go inside. You've got to study tomorrow."

Right. Like she'd be able to process anything except the things that had happened tonight. Still, standing there and clinging to him for fear that the memories might evaporate the second she let him go wasn't an option either. She slid her hands over his shoulders, then lower to his biceps, pausing for just a moment to savor the unhindered skin-to-skin contact the tee provided. "Thank you." Meeting his eyes, she stepped from his arms. "For everything."

He smiled as though she'd said something funny. "You're thanking me for something that was all pleasure on my end." He dipped his head toward the door. "Now, go inside before I can take even more."

It was the longest three steps of her life, the weight of his stare on her back and the sheer loss that came from simply walking away from him leaving her cold and empty. She twisted the knob and put a shoulder to the door.

"Elise?"

She paused with one foot across the threshold and twisted enough to meet his steady stare over one shoulder.

God, he was something to look at. All male. Rugged and dangerously alpha. "I need you to remember what I said. If you run, I'll chase you. Trust me and don't run." The sincerity in his gaze shifted to something heated and she'd swear both man and beast spoke to her at once. "At least not yet."

Chapter Five

"I'm tellin' you, we're dead in the water and the only way we're gonna change that is if we pull in someone from the outside."

Alek's comment should have bothered Tate more than it did. Hell, a few weeks ago it would have been one of the few things worthy of dragging his attention from work or honing his warrior skills, but with his date with Elise just over twenty-four hours away it was background noise at best.

With his hip propped on the waist-high windowsill, Tate crossed his arms and scanned the tourists and locals on Main Street from Priest's second-story office above the tattoo shop while one of the newer warriors who'd just relocated to Eureka Springs second-guessed the wisdom of outsiders. His first hurdle was getting Priest to agree with taking Elise off protected land. Then there was the delicate decision on where to take her for dinner. She'd probably be more comfortable with something casual, but the idea of taking her anywhere less than stellar and special rubbed him wrong. She needed spoiling. Attention and a whole lot of time and touch.

Of course, she also needed patience. And while he'd

done a halfway decent job of keeping himself in check last night, he wasn't sure how long his control was going to last. Christ, but the woman could kiss, and she tasted like heaven. How he'd kept from carting her off when she'd all but rubbed herself against him, he still didn't know. She might have been shocked and afraid the first time she'd felt how hard she made him, but that second time, she'd reveled in it.

"Tate?"

Tate jerked his gaze away from the old three-story brick building across the street and zeroed in on Priest seated on top of his old desk with Kateri standing between his legs, his arms loosely banded around her waist. "Sorry. I zoned out a minute. What's the question?"

One thing about Priest—when he studied a person the way he was studying Tate now, they felt it clear to their bones. Like their whole damned life and every secret harbored was being consumed in the span of a heartbeat. "Where's your head with using an outsider?"

"We already are. Or have been." Tate looked to Alek where he stood leaning against the far wall. "Your buddy David's been decent about getting us what we need so far."

Katy shook her head and intervened before Alek could answer. "We can't use him anymore. David's a nice guy and would probably do anything for me or Alek, but he's asking too many questions. We need someone who doesn't know about our past. Someone impersonal who'll do what we ask and not insist on knowing all the whys."

"We've got nothing," Alek said. "No sightings of

Jerrik. No seer leads. Nothing. We need someone with real connections to turn things around."

One of the clan's oldest warriors kicked back on the legs of an old wood chair that had occupied their building when they'd moved in almost ten years ago. Garrett's hair might have been full silver, but paired with its length hitting his shoulders and his physique, he looked like a retired rock star. No way any singura who met him would realize he was 163. "I'm all for supplementing where we can't handle things ourselves so long as we get someone worth their salt, but how are we going to explain to a PI why we're looking for these people?"

"Explaining the seer is easy," Alek said. "We find someone specifically for that search only, keep interactions with whoever we hire to just one of us and say we're looking for a high school friend or something."

"It's the other search that's gonna be rough," Priest said. "Looking for someone who's already wanted by the cops in Blacksburg is gonna raise a lot of questions, no matter how much money we throw at them."

Another of the newer warriors Tate barely knew piped up from behind Garrett. "Why not just hire someone farther away who's not as tied into what's going on in West Virginia?"

"Because the farther away they live, the less familiarity they'll have with the case and they'll need that kind of connection," Alek said. "At least to start. We'd do better to find someone closer to where Jerrik's parents were killed."

"And capable of keeping their mouth shut," Tate added.

Katy covered Priest's clasped hands low on her belly and idly stroked a path back and forth. A soothing stroke he couldn't help wishing Elise was here to give him. She looked to Alek. "Any chance some of the people you went to school with might have some suggestions?"

"Maybe. We can check it out if everyone's on board."

Behind Kateri, Priest nodded. "Do it. The more time we waste, the more time my brother has to hurt someone else. Until we find a PI, we'll keep working with the seers for clues. We'll give the clan an update this weekend before we train, but if you get any good names before then, we'll huddle up and reassess."

Alek nodded and straightened from the wall as if to leave, the young trio of warriors who'd followed him into their meeting today taking the cue and standing as well.

"Hold up, Alek." Tate eyeballed the new men and motioned toward the stairwell that led down to the shop. "You all mind if I talk to Alek and Priest for minute?"

From the clueless looks on their faces, none of the three seemed to realize he wasn't keen to have his conversation with them on board.

Garrett, on the other hand, proved to be a godsend. He stood and motioned to the door. "Come on, guys. Drake needs to get to know the town and the people in it, and I could use a burger and a beer. Might as well get him introduced to the Cat House."

Alek frowned for a second and watched them leave like he was a little envious to be missing out on food, but shook the perturbed look off his face as soon as they disappeared down the stairwell and refocused on Tate. "What's up?"

When Tate hesitated, Katy patted Priest's hands at

her waist and tried to move out of his hold. "I'll wait for you guys downstairs."

"No."

The sharp answer came from both Tate and Priest almost simultaneously, but Priest paired his with a tighter grip that she didn't stand a prayer in hell of escaping. "He'll need your help as much, if not more, than he'll need mine."

It took a beat for Priest's statement to fully register, but as soon as it did Tate's jaw undoubtedly slackened to match the perplexed expressions on Katy's and Alek's faces. "How do you know what I need?"

Priest dipped his head toward the window. "You've been staring out that window for the last hour like the answers to the universe might sidle up and dance a jig any second and only heard about half of the things we talked about. When I saw you disappear last night, you had Elise tucked up close to your side and a single-minded determination on your face. Not exactly a stretch to figure out what the primary topic on your mind is."

Katy ducked her chin, but not before Tate caught her rolling her lips inward to fight a smile.

Alek didn't give a shit about hiding his humor, because his smile was big enough to show teeth. "You struck out."

Fuck, but sometimes he wanted to punch his primo. "No, dickhead. I didn't strike out." He shifted his focus to Priest. "I've just got a logistical problem."

"A logistical problem." To his credit, Priest did a pretty good job of not cracking a smile, but his eyes held more laughter than Tate had seen in a long time. "Are we talking about the fact that your mate's mother is shacked up in the same residence as her and you're not comfortable bringing her to yours with a ready audience in attendance?"

"No." He'd already figured out a plan on that score and told Jade first thing this morning that the tiny lakeside cabin Priest had built to give them a private space was off-limits for the foreseeable future. "I want to take her off property."

The comment sobered all three of them in a blink.

"Why?" Alek said.

Priest stared at him, a whole host of thoughts obviously moving behind his eyes, the foremost, no doubt, motive and possible ramifications.

Katy, though, got to the heart of things the fastest, her mouth softening to an understanding smile and her voice moving through the room like a mother's caress. "Because that's what she needs."

That.

That *right there* was why Kateri Falson was exactly what Priest and their clan needed. An alpha female with an insightful heart.

Priest must have echoed the same thought in his own head, because he dipped his head and kissed the top of her head, the reverence on his face one Tate wouldn't have fully understood until last night.

"What she needs is to stay alive," Alek said. "Taking her off property makes her vulnerable to Draven."

"She doesn't have her magic yet," Priest countered. "Without it, Draven can't track her. That means he's stuck to physical means of finding her, and we're more than capable of guarding her."

"Where do you want to take her?" Katy asked, pure feminine curiosity sparking in her blue-gray eyes.

And just like that, he was back to square one. Worse, he felt as uncertain and awkward as he had when he was fourteen and faced with asking his first crush to go to a football game. "I don't know. This is new to her. I don't want to freak her out with too much, but I don't want to downplay it either."

"What do you mean it's new to her?" Alek said. "She's twenty-three years old, not sixteen."

Fuck.

He should have been more careful. While he didn't doubt Alek's honor or ability to keep details to himself, the more people who knew about Elise's knowledge, or lack thereof, the more risk for speculation or ridicule. While her mother might not have spilled all the details on what happened to her in high school, the way Elise had responded to Vanessa last night told him she'd already had her share of unfriendly jibes. "That's between me and Elise. No one else."

Something shifted in Alek's expression. Not the inquisitiveness of a man who'd just picked up a scent worth chasing, but something far more protective. A comprehension that clicked on the most primitive level and a vow to have Tate's back all rolled up into one. And damned if that didn't make Tate appreciate his primo more than ever. "Take her someplace nice."

"Ooooh. How about Le Stick Nouveau?" Katy said, jumping right on board. "I heard one of the seers telling Jade about it the other day. She said the food was amazing and done up like one of those crazy expensive fancy places in big cities and the atmosphere is amazing."

"We could make that work," Priest said. "And Katy's right. The location's pretty amazing. It's under the New

Orleans Hotel and is impressive without being uptight. When did you want to go?"

"Tomorrow night."

Priest cupped Katy's shoulders and squeezed. "We can do that. Kateri needs more practice with her wards, so we'll spend some time tonight getting them in place."

She twisted enough to meet his gaze and grinned. "Does this mean you're going to feed me while we're there? I mean, in the name of research and all. Just to make sure we know the layout ahead of time."

"I imagine we could make that work." His lips twitched and despite his playful tone, pure devotion blanketed his face. "Though, you're lucky they have steak. Those other bite-size entrées wouldn't last me long."

Alek scoffed and crossed his arms. "Steak I can do, but I'd rather pass on the fancy." He eyeballed Priest then Tate. "We good?"

Tate and Priest both nodded, but it was Priest who answered, his focus on Kateri. "Just give me a minute with Tate and I'll be down."

His gut clenched and, for a second, he gave serious consideration to making an excuse that would let him follow Alek and Katy out the door. Alone time with Priest was normally a good thing, his whole life sprinkled with memories with one-on-one experiences he wouldn't trade for anything. But something told Tate this particular round was going to fall in the more introspective and uncomfortable category.

Priest waited, his gaze aimed at the floor, feet crossed at the ankles and his hands curled around the edge of the desk. But as soon as the security door at the bottom of the stairwell slicked shut he lifted his head. "Now, tell me the rest of it."

"The rest of what?"

Huffing out an ironic laugh, Priest crossed his arms and cocked his head. "I've known you since the day you were born and watched you chase a whole lot of tail after you realized girls might not be all that bad, but for the last two weeks, you've been withdrawn. Quiet. That's not like you, Tate."

"I'm not withdrawn." Well, maybe he had been a little, but that was over now. Or at least him staying on the sidelines was over. "I'm being careful."

"Of what? You've never hesitated pursuing a woman who piqued your interest. Now you've got a mate and you act like she's a whole different species. I told you the day you met Elise—this is a good thing. Don't fight it so hard."

"I have to fight it."

"Why?"

"Because she's innocent."

"Yeah, I gathered that. So?"

"Godammit, I want to hunt her!" The confession all but exploded through the room, the sheer velocity of it leaving him shaking and short-winded. He paced away from the window and fisted his hair on top of his head. "She's never had anything. Not a kiss. Not a date. Nothing. And all I can think about is pinning her down and taking what's *mine*."

He stopped at the far end of the room and glared out the window at the street below, the weight of Priest's stare heavy on his shoulders.

Priest kept quiet. It was a tactic his guardian had

used on both him and Jade for years and was effective as hell when it came to making them talk.

Today was no exception. "I love the hunt. I hear the way her heart beats when I'm around her—smell the mix of fear and excitement—and it makes me insane. She's everything I never knew I wanted in a woman. Curves everywhere. Sexy as fuck, but in a way that's so innocent all I want to do is dirty her up." He sighed, all the fear and pent up frustration he'd stuffed for days rushing out behind it. "She's the polar opposite of everything I know."

"You only think she's the polar opposite of you."

The comment was so understated and matter-of-fact, it took Tate a seven second delay to rewind and reprocess. Still not certain he'd heard him right, Tate slowly faced Priest. "What's that supposed to mean?"

"Just because Elise hasn't ever been hunted doesn't mean she won't like it." He paused a beat, studying Tate as if to gauge just how deep the idea resonated. "You think the Keeper gave you a mate who's everything you're not, but the reality may be you're who Elise needs to guide her into our world. Your mother was a healer. One of our strongest. You're a warrior and she's likely our healer prima. Who better to teach her and protect her at the same time?"

"I don't want to protect her, I want to *take* her. I don't want her away from me. I don't want to share her with her mother, you or anyone else. I want her under me. In my bed, outside and any other place I can keep her pinned down and powerless."

The admission should have rattled Priest. Or at least drawn a scowl. It sure as shit made Tate feel like an ugly predator just saying it out loud.

Instead, Priest smirked. "Spoken like a Volán male who wants his mate."

"What?"

Priest chuckled, straightened from the desk and paced toward him. "What you want's not bad, Tate. It's primal. Primitive. And yeah, probably not something Elise is used to or prepared for yet, but it's natural. Your coyote knows it. It's your human side that's messing with your head." He clasped Tate on the shoulder and gave a reassuring squeeze. "But, I will tell you this. Going slow for your mate is one thing. Ignoring who you are is something else. You are who you are for a reason. Trust the process. Listen to your companion. Talk to your mate and show her who you are. What's she's inherited."

"I don't want to hurt her."

With a wry grin and one last affectionate squeeze, Priest dropped his hand and prowled for the door. "Maybe it's time you stop worrying about all the things that could go wrong and just accept the gift you've been given."

Chapter Six

Another semester done and only one more to go before Elise finally had her degree. Though, staring at the confirmation message on her screen, it was the first time since she'd started working her way through college that she didn't have a clue how she'd done on a final. If it hadn't been for the intensive studying she'd done before Beltane, odds were good she'd have failed entirely. God knew she hadn't been able to concentrate yesterday.

Well, that wasn't entirely true. She'd been able to replay every single detail from Monday night just fine. The question she still hadn't figured out between then and now was, what changed? And why?

With a frustrated huff, Elise clicked out of her browser session, pulled her earbuds out and shifted her laptop to the comforter beside her. Without PVRIS crooning in her ears, the silence was almost deafening. A stark reminder of the single fact that scared her most of all.

She had no idea what she was doing.

She pulled her knees in close, hugged them tight and rested her forehead on her knees. Maybe a run would be smart. Aside from the strength training needed to keep her body healthy, her daily runs were the only source of exercise she relied on anymore, but they usually served her mind as well as her body. A chance to let everything but the moment go and empty out all the chatter in her head.

On the nightstand beside her, her phone chimed, the soft understated sound triggering a far more abrupt and startling response in her body.

Tate.

She didn't have to look to know it was him. While she'd built a small, but solid cadre of friends since graduating from high school, most worked at Butte La Rose's only assisted living center with her, or were fellow students, but messages from them were rare. Tate, on the other hand, had started up with steady messages, starting with a simple Good morning text yesterday morning. They weren't elaborate or overzealous in number. Just simple one liners that let her know he was thinking of her and didn't require much from her in return.

Honestly, she'd thanked her lucky stars for every one of them. Aside from the giddy flutters and goofy smiles that always triggered in their wake, they were proof she hadn't imagined Monday night. That her penchant for vivid fantasies hadn't taken over and left her trapped in a dream world of her own making.

Finished with your finals?

Yep. Definitely real. And frankly, reality was turning out better than some of the scenarios she'd come up with on her own.

Just submitted the last one. Not sure how well I did, though.

In the time it took for the little bubbles to do their wavy thing, she read and reread every response she'd made over the last twenty-four hours. Were they too much? Not enough? Maybe she needed to come up with more clever replies.

I've watched you study and you love what you do. That means you probably rocked them and it's time to celebrate. I'll be there at 7. Dress nice.

The pleasant buzz that had permeated every one of their innocent back-and-forths since yesterday morning downshifted to panic.

How nice?

Nice enough I'm not wearing a T-shirt.

Shit.
Shit, shit, shit.
She stalked to the closet and pulled open the bifold doors, nothing but casual clothes and workout gear glaring back at her. She didn't do nice. Unless you counted the two token interview outfits she kept tucked behind everything else, and no way was she eating dinner with Tate looking like a buttoned up, old-fashioned librarian.
One by one, she worked her way through the garments. Like some kind of faery godmother was going to pop in and magically insert something hot yet un-

derstated between her favorite jeans and well-worn leggings.

Mom would have something.

The thought paused the full-scale alert blaring in her head and sent her hauling butt down the split-level staircase. Jenny Ralston might not be the height of fashion sense, but she was always prepared for any occasion. The downside? While they were close height-wise, her mom hadn't exactly been graced with the same generous proportions as Elise. Still, there had to be more options in her mom's closet than the big fat goose egg hanging in her own.

She cut through the cozy living room. "Mom?"

"Yeah, sweetheart. In here."

In here nearly always meaning *in the kitchen*. From a leisurely cup of coffee in the morning perusing her favorite websites, whipping up one of her experimental casseroles, or tucked up in the cushioned bay window reading a book at night, the kitchen was always her mother's favorite hangout.

"Hey." Elise paused long enough to catch her breath and take in the computer in front of her mom at the kitchen table. "I need a favor."

Her mom levered her head down enough to peek over the top of the readers. "I thought you were taking your finals."

"I am. I mean, I was. They're done."

She smiled huge, tossed her pen to the table and sat back in her chair. "Well, congratulations. That went faster than I thought it would."

Yeah, faster than she'd thought, too. So, either Tate was right and she'd aced them, or crashed and burned abysmally.

"So, what's the favor?" her mom said.

The question triggered a whole different layer of panic, the belated realization she'd yet to share anything about what had happened between her and Tate after the party skidding into play about twenty seconds too late. "Well, I…uh…"

Not a big deal.

It's just a date.

Granted it would be her first one, but her mom was cool.

Most of the time.

Elise cleared her throat and tried again. "I'm going out and need something to wear."

"Oh! Katy mentioned she was going to talk to Priest and see if you could get out of the house a little after finals were over." Her mom peeled her glasses off and tossed them to the table, standing as she did. "I don't think most of the places here need anything more than jeans, but I can help you put something together if you want."

"I'm not going out with Katy."

Her mom paused, more than a little confusion leaving a deep furrow between her brows.

"And I need something dressy."

This time her eyebrows lifted high enough they disappeared beneath her longish bangs. "Dressy?"

Elise nodded, the nonverbal response about all she could manage with the claustrophobic grip cinching around her neck.

While her mom's shocked expression didn't fade, something behind her eyes shifted. A subtle comprehension that usually meant a cat Elise seriously didn't want out of the bag was loose and running rampant through the house. Jenny's lip curved in a sly smile. "But you're not going out with Katy."

"No."

"Or Jade."

Elise shook her head.

Her mom paused long enough to fight a smile. "I don't suppose this dressy outing you're dancing around has anything to do with you disappearing from the party with Tate Allen, does it?"

"You saw that?"

The depth of Jenny's chuckle spoke of age-old secrets and long forgotten memories. "It was a little hard to miss with Naomi offering color commentary every five minutes." She cocked her head and waggled her eyebrows. "I also noted that while you left before me, you got home way after I did. Must have been quite the scenic route you took on the way home."

Heat blazed across her cheeks and, for a second, she gave serious thought to boarding herself up in her room until she was thirty. "We were just talking."

"Mmm hmm. I remember *talking*, too. Lots and lots of *talking*. If you ask me, that was the best part of growing up. But I'd like to point out, you're lucky your grandfather's not still alive. He usually waited up for me. Or worse, if he didn't like the guy I was with, he'd meet us at the front door before any *talking* could commence."

Ugh. Seriously? Could this moment get any more awkward? "Mom, I just—"

Jenny chuckled and shook her head. "It's okay, Elise. I'm only teasing you." She closed the top to her computer, moved out from between her chair and the table and cupped one side of Elise's face. "I like Tate. A lot."

"You do?"

"Mmm hmm." She paused and studied her a minute. "Do you?"

Like him? She liked her chili and lime Takis. She liked lingering over a cup of coffee in the morning and not having an immediate agenda. She even liked helping her mom cook when the newest recipe idea she'd pulled off Pinterest wasn't too weird or complicated to put together, but none of those things made her full-on stoooopid the way Tate did. "If by like do you mean my brain doesn't function right when he's around?"

"Yes, that's exactly what I mean."

Elise swallowed hard, the actual process of admitting how she felt out loud generating more roadblocks than her throat knew what to do with. "Then yeah. I like him."

Her mom's gaze softened and she smoothed Elise's hair away from her face. "I'm glad, sweetheart. He's a good man."

"I don't have a clue what I'm doing." It came out as a terrified whisper, but the weight that lifted off her with it made the admission worth it.

"There's nothing to do, Elise. Not with a man like Tate. Nothing but enjoy the moment and get to know one another. The rest will all take care of itself. But more than anything, just be honest. About who you are and what you feel."

"No offense, but that didn't work so well for you."

The sadness borne from years of living without the man she'd loved knifed across her mother's face. She'd tried to tell Elise's father about her race. About the magic and shifting abilities those in their clan were offered if they answered their soul quest.

But her father hadn't believed her. Heck, Elise hadn't either, but at least she hadn't derided her mother's claims, called her crazy and laughed in her face.

"Tate's not your father," Jenny said. "He's a trustworthy man. One I'm thrilled to see you with. The kind of man you can share your secrets with and know he'll not only listen, but protect them."

"How do you know that? I mean, I know you've talked to him a lot when he's been here, but you haven't spent *that* much time with him."

"Oh, Elise." For a second, her expression pinched like she wanted to share something more, but instead, pulled her into a comforting hug and sighed. Her words were whisper soft. A secret shared from mother to daughter. "I just know you're safe with him. And soon, you're going to realize that, too."

Emotion swelled behind her sternum, the peace and acceptance that came from her mother's simple embrace loosening the knot in her gut. "I still don't have anything to wear," she grumbled.

Jenny laughed and backed away. "I've got clothes."

"Yeah, but my boobs are way bigger than yours."

Her mom opened her mouth, the wry expression on her face promising one of the friendly but jealous jibes they'd shared about their disparate figures over the years, but the doorbell rang before she could speak.

Jenny frowned. "What time's your date?"

Elise checked the nonexistent pockets in her leggings looking for the phone she'd clearly left upstairs and followed her mother toward the tiny dining room. "Not until seven. It's only a little after three." And she had no makeup on. And a craptastic ponytail. *Awesome.* "You didn't invite him over, did you?"

"No, I didn't invite him over." Her mom peeked out the picture window overlooking the front yard, the same confounded look on her face as Elise…right up until she spied whoever was on the front porch. Then her expression shifted to pure delight.

"What? Who is it?"

Her mom waved, backed away from the window and hustled to the front door. "Well, from the looks of things, it's what my dad referred to as the date brigade."

Elise followed her. "The what?"

"The date brigade." With no more explanation, she opened the door to show Katy and Jade standing side by side, their goofy grins almost identical to the one her mom was sporting. "Hey, girls! That's quite a haul you've got. Need any help?"

"Nah, we've got it." Jade slung a garment bag thick with God only knew how many outfits inside it over one shoulder and stormed inside like she lived there. Under her free arm was a smaller box like you'd use to pack books for a big move.

"Um," Elise said. "What are you doing?"

Jade paused at the bottom of the stairs and gave Elise a perplexed look. "We're here to help you get ready for your date. What else?"

Still rooted outside the door and loaded down with a carry-on suitcase in one hand and an overnight bag in the other, Katy cocked her head. "Well, assuming you want our help. We didn't mean to ambush you or anything. We just thought it'd be fun."

"Ha!" Jade said. "Maybe you're here to play nice, but I'm *totally* here to ambush. I just saw my brother drag a suit out of his closet. *A suit.* Tate never drags out the big guns for a woman. Ever. If you think for a second I'd miss out on a chance to meddle and get a girlfriend dolled up enough to make him swallow his tongue, you're nuts." She shifted her load on her back and eyeballed Elise. "So, are we doing this or what?"

"He's wearing a suit?" Elise said, the picture in her head enough to make her light-headed.

"Mmm hmm. A nice one."

"And he's taking you to Le Stick Nouveau," Katy added. "Which is crazy nice, by the way. Priest and I went there last night and put wards up and everything."

"Priest knows?"

"Of course, he knows. You didn't think Tate would take you off property without making sure you were safe, did you?" Apparently tired of waiting for a formal okay, Katy strolled across the threshold and nudged the door shut with her hip. "So, what do you say? Is it all hands on deck, or would you rather fly solo?"

Elise glanced at her mom who was doing a terrible job of keeping her mirth in check. Then up at Jade who looked like she was stoked to do battle.

A comfortable warmth spread along her shoulders and the world steadied beneath her feet. She wasn't alone. For the first time in her life, she had a chance not just to go on a date, but to be girly and giddy with other women who genuinely seemed to want to help her. All she had to do was open up and go along for the ride. To trust and throw herself into the moment.

She dipped her head toward the garments weighting down Jade's back, the movement not nearly as casual as she'd have liked it to be. "I don't suppose you've got a dress in there that might work for a busty girl like me."

Jade's grin was flat-out wicked. "Oh, girl. I don't have just one. I have *several*."

Chapter Seven

It was weird what having *the* woman in your life did to a man. All of a sudden, things that used to mean nothing to Tate—things as simple as remembering she liked unsweetened tea more than sweet tea, to bigger shit like the car you drove and where you lived—got *crazy* important. And not because they were things, but because he didn't want her thinking for a second he didn't notice what she liked, or to have her riding or living in anything but the best.

He forced his attention to stay on the road instead of the passenger's seat and the insane amount of thigh Elise's dress showed.

Fucking bucket seats.

Yeah, he loved his Camaro. Or he would as soon as he knuckled down with the '69 classic and finished restoring the exterior, but the way the low-slung seats were angled, Elise might as well have been reclined back on a chaise like a bedroom pinup.

Nope. No way. No thoughts of bedrooms. Or pinups. Or the fact that the body hugging dress she'd worn made her a prime candidate to star in one.

He squeezed the steering wheel a little harder, but damned if his eyes didn't stray of their own free will to her legs and the strappy heels that matched her black dress. He didn't dare look at her chest again. Not the way the dress accented her amazing rack. Honest to God, he didn't know whether to hug Jade and Katy for their intervention, or take his sweet time strangling them both.

Elise slid her feet a little closer to the seat's edge, gripping the hem of her dress like she had a chance in hell of covering more skin. "Are you okay?"

Peachy. Burning alive on the inside and ready to claw his way out of his skin, but on top of the fucking world. "I've got you stretched out in my car in a dress that looks like sin and am on my way to what Priest says is an outstanding restaurant." He peeled his eyes away from the road long enough to meet her gaze. "*Okay* falls a little short."

One smile. One sweet, tremulous smile accented by those big, trusting eyes of hers, and he was back on track. Grounded and centered. "You sure? You seem tense."

Crummy timing and a fast approaching parking lot made him put his response on hold long enough to get his car in park, but the second he had the stick out of gear and the parking brake pulled, he twisted to face her, covered her hand with his and gave it a gentle squeeze. If he wanted her honesty, then the least he could do was set his own macho bullshit aside and go first. "I *am* a little tense. But it's not because of anything you've done or aren't doing. It's because this is a big deal for me."

The shock on her face echoed the sharp surprise in her voice. "It is?"

"Yeah. A huge deal."

"Why?"

Way to go, smooth. Talk your own ass right into a corner, why don't you?

Telling her what she was to him wasn't an option. Not yet. But there was a more fundamental truth he could absolutely share. One he didn't even have to think twice about. "Because it's for you."

No movement. No outwardly visible response of any kind. Just her eyes on his and the steady in-and-out of their breathing. But he felt it. One split second of an astounding connection that left him rattled.

She ducked her head as if she'd felt it, too, the gold-blond strands she'd curled into loose waves falling heavy around her face. She smoothed a nonexistent wrinkle near the bottom of her dress. "Thank you."

Damn, but he wanted to kiss her. Wanted them anywhere but in a car where he couldn't pull her close and just hold and pet her until whatever feelings she was wrestling with let her go and she could relax the way she had by the lake Monday night. But what he couldn't make up for with touch, he could handle with humor. At least for now. "Don't thank me yet. Priest said the food was good, but he also said it was fancy and that the portions were better suited for a mouse. We may have to hit McDonald's before I take you home."

The quip worked, drawing a quiet chuckle from her as she lifted her head. "McDonald's I might actually be able to navigate without being a nervous wreck. Dresses are pushing it for me, but adding heels to the equation is just begging for disaster."

Ease up there, buddy. Forget the heels, the dress, or any offensive maneuvers to get her out of either one.

"Trust me, Elise. There's not a man breathing who'd

look at you tonight and even think the word *disaster*."
His gaze slid down her legs despite the coaching from
his common sense and he slid his hand from hers just
enough to brush the top of one thigh. "Now stay right
there and let me get your door."

Inside the restaurant, things were blessedly low-key.
No doubt, thanks to the fact it was a Wednesday night
in a town predominantly driven by weekend tourists.
The hostess recognized him from his visit earlier in
the day and greeted them both with a warm smile, but
there was a wry quality to it as well. One that said she
was both shocked and a little humored at the change in
appearance from the ponytail, jeans and T-shirt he'd
been in earlier. "We've got your table ready for you,
Mr. Allen. If you'll just follow me?"

Elise started forward, but twisted just enough to quietly murmur over her shoulder, "Mr. Allen?"

"I know," he answered back in kind. "Makes me
think my dad's standing behind me." He splayed his
hand low on her back and walked with her to the alcove
he'd picked just for them. Normally the small room held
four four-tops, but with a little finagling this afternoon,
he'd talked the manager into removing all but one. Gold
curtains separated the private space and were drawn
back just enough to let them watch the comings and
goings of other guests, but still kept them isolated. The
only light came from an ornate fixture in the shape of
a peacock on the wall, its cobalt, teal and white lights
artfully mixing with the rest of the rich mahogany and
granite décor.

Elise stood beside her chair and studied it, her head
cocked to one side and eyes wide with open appreciation.

The hostess laid their menus beside each chair. "I'll

just leave these for you here. Your waitress will be here shortly."

Nudged from her perusal by the hostess's quiet comment, Elise peeled her attention free and noted him patiently waiting for her by her chair, his hand resting on the top of the seat back. "Oh, right. Manners." She slid into her seat and sat her purse to the side of her place setting. While everything she did held a natural grace, the awkward moment seemed to re-inject some of the tension she'd relinquished since they'd pulled into the parking lot. "Sorry, it was just so pretty I couldn't help but gawk."

He guided her chair closer to the table, the upper swells of her breasts on prime display with him towering above her. As isolated as they were, he could easily skim the back of his knuckle along the soft skin. Could trace the plunging neckline of her dress and soak in every detail of her response.

Instead, he braced one hand on the table, leaned in and mimicked the touch he craved up and over her bared shoulder, across the simple tank-style straps and on to the curve of her neck. "There's no wrong action you can take with me, Elise. No expectation you have to uphold or model you have to fit." He cupped the back of her neck, the silky tease of her hair against his fingertips thick and tempting. "So long as we're honest with each other, there's nothing we can't figure out."

"Honest."

"Honest," he echoed back with the same depth she'd given him. "Even if it means you need to tell me no, or to back off. Understand?"

Her gaze dropped to his lips and damned if her own didn't part on a slow and shaky inhalation.

"Elise?"

Her focus shifted back to his eyes and she nodded, but a sharp resolve etched her features. As if in the span of seconds, she'd measured the width of a dangerous chasm and vowed to leap across it anyway. "I don't want you to back off."

One breath.

Then another.

The third one finally came easier and the crushing compulsion to take her mouth right then and there took a shaky step back. Even his companion was shaken to the core, the sheer need to touch, overpower and claim lashing at deeply entrenched instincts. By some fucking miracle, he brushed a kiss against her forehead, the soft contact nowhere near the iron fist locked around his control. "I'm not going anywhere."

Dinner passed at an easy pace. A little awkward and tentative at first, then easing into a steady rhythm of lighter questions through dinner. Her curious as to how he'd come to work as a tattoo artist with Priest. Him peppering her with details on sports and what she liked about her studies. A seamless back-and-forth exchange that seemed to push the rest of the world farther and farther away and left her open at a level he'd only seen when she'd thought no one was watching.

But as soon as the dishes were cleared, her demeanor changed. Not a shutdown, exactly. More of a cautiousness that pricked at his awareness.

She cleared her throat and opened her mouth to speak, then promptly clamped her lips shut and stared at the table.

Long-honed social reflexes prodded him to fill the

silence. To nudge and open the door a little by asking what was wrong.

But his beast sat quiet. Waiting. Patient. Urging him to do the same.

He settled for stretching his arm across the intimately sized table and offering his hand palm up.

She stared at it for long moments, her back perfectly straight, her hands fisted in her lap and her gaze distant as though combing through a wealth of memories. Finally, she placed her hand in his and met his eyes. "Will you tell me something about you? Something unique to you. Something…important."

Important.

Not some random data share about why he was who he was, but something tangible. An offering. Or maybe just a request for someone else to go first.

The memory that raised its head was one rarely revisited. Not because of the remembered pain, but because the hurt that had come with it had long-since served its purpose and been released.

"Our clan's a lot different today than it used to be," he said. "Or at least that's what Mom used to say. Priest isn't like the high priest who served before him. While he's got access to all the magic the different houses hold, he honors them all. One house isn't more important than the other and no one person outranks another. Everyone holds value, no matter how much magic they're given or what their companion is."

"How was it before Priest?"

Just like it was yesterday, the old shame and fear of disappointment he'd harbored for years growing up resurfaced. "More segregated. Locked in old traditions and highly competitive."

Elise wrinkled her nose. "I don't think I'd like that very much."

"No. I didn't either."

She cocked her head, quickly homing in on the distinction in his response. "But you weren't alive then."

"I wasn't there when the old high priest was still alive, but my dad was deeply grounded in the old ways. And the most competitive house of all were the warriors."

"So, your dad was a warrior?"

He nodded. "A strong one. Strong enough he gave Priest a run for his money a time or two. And back then, when the darkness was still riding Priest's ass all the time, that was really saying something."

She held her silence, her body slightly leaned in and her eyes wide. Captivated.

"I wanted to be like my dad. Was just like every other eight-year-old boy and wanted to make him proud." He shrugged. "Only problem was, I was a runt of a kid."

"No way."

"Oh...way." For the first time in a long time, he was able to look back on the day that had marked him so deeply and actually see it without the judgment. Without all the hurt and agony of an innocent kid's heart, thanks to Priest's patience in the months and years that followed. "I was small and weak enough my dad never took me with him to train. And back then, even without a lot of us located in one place, they trained *every day*. It was a thing with them—they all brought their kids if they thought they'd end up in warrior house."

"But you wanted to go."

"Oh, I more than wanted to. I *went*. Followed him on a boar hunt one day."

She must have sensed the ending wasn't a good one, because her shoulders curved in just a little. As if she were bracing to bear the brunt on her own. "What happened?"

"The short version—I came about three inches from taking a tusk to my right lung, another kid was almost fatally wounded and my dad ended up bearing the brunt of my stupidness for months. A few of the men actually told my dad the clan would've been better off if he hadn't pulled me out of the boar's attack and kept the other kid safe."

"You're kidding me."

"Nope."

Pure anger fueled her gaze and the way she held her body, Tate was a little surprised she didn't get up and pace just to blow off some steam. "That's cruel."

"Maybe. But it was the way they lived then."

"That's no excuse. No child is worth sacrificing. Never."

"No, they're not." Tate squeezed her hand and lowered his voice. "I'm not going to lie. That day hurt and it put a huge hole between me and my dad. One we never got over before he died. But it also made me who I am today and was kind of a turning point for our clan."

"How so?"

"Well, for starters, Priest put his foot down. By that point, he already treated Jade and I like we were his own kids. Learning people in his clan would value one kid over another made him realize how segregated things were. So, he shifted how training worked. Made them like they are today and shifted the focus of warriors from beating their own chests to being all about protecting the other houses."

She studied his face, openly soaking in the details and piecing together the information as though painting a picture of her own in her head. "And you?"

He chuckled and hung his head, the stubborn determination he'd nursed back then somehow funny when he looked back at it. "I worked my ass off." He met her gaze and let the warm memories he'd earned in the days that came after wash over him. "Not one day went by I didn't train. For every one of them, Priest was with me. Jade, too, when she got older. Or, she was when she wasn't too busy running around with her friends."

"You grew up," she said softly.

"I grew into who I knew I was, but it took the pain to push me. To take the bad and make something of it."

Her gazed drifted to their hands. "You make it sound easy."

"It wasn't. Not even close. But I had people to help me."

He waited, a heated back-and-forth debate going on in his head on whether or not to say more looking like Wimbledon on fast-forward.

She kept her focus on their hands and, when she spoke, it was so quiet he'd have missed it had it not been for his heightened hearing. "Do you think it's weird a twenty-three-year-old woman's never been on a date? Never been kissed?"

This was it.

His first real chance to show her she was safe. To build a foundation that would hold her steady. And he'd never been so terrified of fucking up in his life. "I think it's rare."

She frowned and lifted her gaze to his. "What's the difference?"

"*Weird* implies it's something bad or awkward. Things that are rare are precious." He stroked his thumb along the hammering pulse at her wrist. "Considering I got to claim both of those firsts with you makes them pretty damned precious in my book."

The current that moved between them was potent. A palpable and startling energy drawn tight and untamed. She must have felt it, too, because her hand trembled in his and her lips parted. She snapped them shut just as fast and ducked her head. "I want to tell you something."

He was too far away. Too physically disconnected to give her the tangible support both his human and animal halves insisted she needed. But at the same time, he was too afraid to move. Too worried he'd startle her out of the moment and ruin it. "Okay."

She splayed her free hand on the table then ran a finger along the side of her silverware, the entirety of her concentration fixated on the motion. "When I talk about it now, it feels stupid." She peeked at him first before fully lifting her head. "Kind of like realizing you made a big deal over something you shouldn't have, but it didn't feel like a small thing at the time. It felt huge."

"Everything feels bigger when we're in the middle of it. It's instinct. How we're engineered to survive. Dealing with the fallout's usually a much bigger proposition."

She huffed out an ironic chuckle. "The therapist Mom took me to for about a year after high school said the same thing. Though, you're a lot nicer to look at when I talk and you got the point a lot quicker."

A quip to lighten the mood was tempting. Hell, at the moment his torso was locked tight enough it hurt to breathe, and he wasn't even the one poised on the edge of sharing something obviously uncomfortable. But dodging the issue further wouldn't help her get on with things so he kept his silence.

Her grip tightened in his for a second, then loosened enough to pull her hand free. With a sweep of her hands toward her torso, she shrugged and gave him a sardonic look. "So, clearly I'm more of a full-figured woman than one you'd find on a fashion runway."

Fuck, yeah, she was. And as soon as his gut gave him the all clear, he had big plans for showing her how much he appreciated every curvy inch. "That fact hasn't escaped me, no. Though, we're going to have an issue if you try to tell me that's a bad thing."

She pursed her mouth in a wry grin. "No. I don't think it's a bad thing." Her expression sobered. "Or at least I don't think it's a bad thing today. I used to hate it."

"Why?"

Her lips thinned as though forming the answer she needed sat bitter on her tongue. "Because it drew attention to me at a time when I didn't want it."

Breathe.

Don't react.

Don't assume.

Fine guidance from his far more patient companion, but hard words to act on when his brain threw all kinds of worst-case scenarios at him at once. Forearms braced on the table, he fanned his thumb along the tablecloth, forcing what he hoped was a casual response. His voice wasn't nearly as cooperative, the depth of it bordering on a growl. "Attention from who?"

"In a small school like the one I went to? Everyone." She shrugged. "I developed a lot earlier than the other girls and a lot faster. Which might have been okay and easier to cover up if I hadn't been so active in sports, but even the most high-impact sports bra can only do so much."

"And people rail against different."

She chuckled at that, the sarcasm in her tone thick with bad memories. "Boy, do they. Especially teenage girls."

Which explained her guardedness with Vanessa. "What did they do?"

Elise shrugged, but at least some of the tension in her shoulders eased. "What you'd expect. Teasing. Passive-aggressive comments. Spreading stories. I mean, I was used to the way they operated to some degree. A lot of us had competed for years and I was really good at dance and gymnastics, so I got a lot of jealous back-lash. But by the time I hit my sophomore year and I couldn't hide my figure anymore, the stories started changing. Boys I'd allegedly slept with at school. Things I did outside of school with men much older than me." She paused a beat and shook her head. "They weren't pretty. Definitely, not the kind of stories that died fast in a small school prone to gossip."

"What happened?" That there was still more to her story was a given. It practically hung in the air between them, a dark and weighty ghost that made his coyote pace.

"I think the girls meant for the talk to backfire and ostracize me, and it worked with other girls. But the boys?" She cleared her throat and hung her head. "It fired them up. Made them curious. Bold. Even the ones who'd been my friends."

"They hurt you?" This time covering the agitation

in his voice was impossible and his skin prickled with the need to shift.

"Not physically, no." She faced him with a sad smile. "But one of the guys took it pretty personal when I kept telling him no and kept him at a distance. He wanted a mark on his belt whether he'd earned it or not, so he changed tactics and somehow got access to the girls' locker room. Sports were all I had by that point, so I was there a lot. Turns out, he was pretty handy with a smartphone camera and graphic programs."

Tate fisted his hands on the table, but otherwise held perfectly still, modulating every breath the best he could. "He doctored them up and spread them around."

"And no one ever questioned the content. Not once. Not with all the other gossip that had gone on before they went out. The few friends I had dried up. One of them even told me that nice girls couldn't risk being seen with a slut like me. Said it right to my face."

God, no wonder she was so reserved. So hesitant to drop the mask she maintained around people she didn't know. And to think she'd spent what was supposed to be some of the best and most formative years of her life hiding mentally and physically made him want to hunt the lot of her tormenters and bathe in their blood. "What did you do?"

"In a nutshell? I lost it. Mom had an insane time getting me to go to school. My grades dropped, and my heart wasn't in sports anymore, so I did horrible there, too. One day I just lost it. I needed to run. To get away. So, I did. I took off after school and let it out. Unfortunately, running while you're sobbing isn't exactly the safest thing to do. I wasn't paying attention, planted my foot wrong mid-stride and ended up tearing my ACL.

After that, sports were officially over. Mom worked out a home school program for me and that's how I finished my junior and senior years."

"And that's when you figured out what you wanted to be."

The sad smile she paired with her answer nearly broke him. "Like you said—take the bad and make something of it."

Oh, he wanted to take the bad and make something of it. Preferably, broken bones and bruises for those who'd hurt her. Which was a lot better than the severed limbs and shredded flesh his coyote craved. "That's why you haven't been on dates? Hadn't kissed anyone?"

"Pretty much." She mirrored his pose and leaned her forearms on the table. "The thing about small towns is that not many people my age want to stay. Not unless they don't have other options. By the time I got some counseling and started looking at the things that had happened from a new perspective, most of the people I knew had moved on with their lives. Gone to college, or moved away for jobs. Plus, commuting to school in Lafayette and taking online classes gave me an excuse not to put myself out there."

"Well, you're out there now." Granted, hell would freeze over before he let anyone else get close enough to introduce her to the things she'd missed, but they'd cover that ground later. Hopefully well after he'd spoiled her and made it so she couldn't even imagine anyone else's touch. "You're on your first date. Had your first kiss. What do you think so far?"

For the first time since she'd started her story, her eyes sparked with lightness and a shy smile tipped her lips. "I think I'm starting to see what all the fuss is about."

Oh, she didn't have a clue. Had only brushed the surface. And it was going to be him who pulled her into the dark still waters and taught her how to swim. "Does that mean you're ready for another first?"

She froze the same as small prey caught unaware in the center of a clearing, but a heady jolt of excitement buzzed between them. An alertness that made him itch to hunt. "What kind of first?"

He reached across the table and captured one of her hands in his. She might not be ready for the kind of intimacy he wanted, but that didn't mean he couldn't get her next to him and show her how good it was to live and have fun on top of it. Plus, Rogue's Manor already had wards in place. "How do you feel about dancing?"

Chapter Eight

Dating and dancing were fun. Or at least they were with Tate leading the way. Granted, Elise's feet ached from the heels Katy and Jade had talked her into wearing, and both she and Tate were horribly overdressed for the casual bar he'd taken them to, but after the night he'd given her, she didn't care. For the first time in longer than she could remember, she felt normal. Alive. Feminine and desirable in a healthy way.

But most of all she felt free. Void of the weight of her past. As if in recounting her worst memories, she'd finally broken the anchors that kept them welded in her soul and let them drift away.

She shifted her cheek where it rested high on Tate's chest, closed her eyes and surrendered to the band's sultry blues rhythm and Tate's easy back-and-forth sway. He'd shucked his suit jacket shortly after they'd arrived and pulled her onto the dance floor the second the band kicked into a slow song.

Lordy, what a treat that proved to be. The hot, hard feel of him against the length of her. His hands on her back. Her neck. Her hips.

And his scent. It was everywhere. The earthy richness of it permeating her lungs. Buried in her skin. She loved it. Gloried in the fact that she carried such an intimate part of him on her physically. A mark no one else could see, but that resonated on the deepest level.

The bass from the song's final note played out far too soon, lingering in the room with the same sense of longing she'd wrestled all night. As if there was more that needed to be said, sung or felt, but the way to express it was still unclear.

Tate cupped the back of her neck and pulled away just enough to graze his lips against her forehead. "You liked that one."

Oh, she liked it all right. It and all the other slow ones that gave her an excuse to get close and cozy with Tate. She nodded and tried to fight the yawn that hit her out of left field.

Chuckling, Tate angled her face so he could murmur against her lips. "You're adorable when you're sleepy."

"It's the wine and the music." And the empty study time last night staring at her computer screen thinking of nothing but Tate. And how comfortable and safe she felt tucked close to him tonight. But that was probably too much information to share.

He pressed a soft, but lingering kiss to her lips, clearly not concerned about the change to an up-tempo song and the others dancing around them. "I should take you home so you can get some sleep."

He said it softly. Sweet and full of care. But it knifed so deep behind her sternum that drawing breath after the fact was almost impossible. She didn't want sleep. Didn't want the night to be over or to be without him. "Probably," she forced out instead.

Cupping the side of her face, he traced her lower lip, an understanding in his amber eyes that made her wonder if mind reading wasn't a part of his warrior magic after all. "It won't be the last time we dance, Elise. It won't be the last time for anything."

There it was again. That delightful dip and swirl in her belly paired with a lightness that defied gravity. From the time she'd opened the front door and he'd languidly taken in every inch of her appearance, to the possessive weight of his hands at her hips during their first dance, he'd stirred the disconcerting sensation over and over again. It was glorious. Downright addictive to a degree that made her want to demand a blood vow to go with his promise.

Shoving the thought away until she could dissect it later, she backed away and smoothed her hand along her belly like that might somehow calm the nervous flutters inside. "Okay. Just let me run to the restroom really quick."

He aimed that knowing look at her again and dipped his head toward the hallway she'd spied behind the band. "It's back there. I'll wait for you at the table."

She wove her way through the crowd, more cognizant of not just how much more dressed up she was than everyone else in shorts or jeans and casual tops, but how much more exposed she felt without Tate beside her. Not once tonight had she been aware of or worried about what others might think of her or what she had on, but now that she was alone, reality seemed sharper. Closer and more chaotic.

Fortunately, the restroom proved a respite of sorts, the lack of people and the muted thrum of the music giving her heart and head time to settle. No matter what happened after tonight—whether he was sincere in what he'd said about wanting more than just tonight—she had fantastic memories to hold close. A new start she could build on.

The click from the auto-mechanism that controlled the tap's flow sent cool water rushing over her hands just as the door swept open behind her. The music from outside swelled along with a cluster of feminine laughter then muted once more.

"Elise?" One word carried on a candy-coated, but incredibly snide voice.

Elise forced herself not to flinch, finished rinsing her hands and casually lifted her head to meet the cluster of women reflected in the mirror as she reached for the towel dispenser. "Hello, Vanessa." She let her gaze drift over the other women and tried for what she hoped was a confident smile. "Good to see you all again."

"Wow, look at you," one of the other girls said as Elise faced them. The way Tate had introduced them the night of Beltane, she didn't have a clue what the girl's name was, but she eyeballed Elise with a mix of shock and appreciation. "That dress is a killer."

"It sure is," Vanessa said, sauntering a little closer and doing her own head-to-toe perusal. "Not exactly the kind of thing most people wear here, but it sure explains why Tate's so into you."

The temptation to curl her shoulders inward and downplay the figure Tate had openly admired all night tapped between her shoulder blades. Even more pressing was the urge to simply duck her head, avoid the lot of them entirely and escape.

There's nothing wrong with you, Elise. Nothing to hide. Nothing to be ashamed of. How another person reacts to who you are is a reflection on them and their own insecurities. Nothing more.

Elise clung to the remembered words from her therapist, straightened as much as her five feet two inches plus heels would allow and forced her shoulders back. "I don't think you know me well enough to know what does or doesn't make Tate want to spend time with me, but I doubt he deserves being labeled as a man driven only by physical appearance."

The other women sobered from their lighthearted demeanors and volleyed their attention between Vanessa and Elise with wide eyes.

Vanessa glowered, pure venom burning behind the peaceful sky-blue color. She opened her mouth to speak.

Before she could, the bathroom door swept open leaving Tate braced in the entrance. His suit jacket was back on, obviously ready to leave. He held the door open with one hand splayed in the center and swept the scene with all the alertness of a SWAT team braced to infiltrate a hostage situation. His gaze rested for all of a second on Vanessa before it shifted to Elise. "Everything okay?"

Vanessa spun and faced him. "Tate, it's the women's restroom. You can't just barge in here."

"Funny. I just did."

"Everything's fine," Elise said answering his question. Granted, her insides were as shaky as her first steps in high heels and her palms were sweaty enough she wished she hadn't thrown her paper towels in the trash already, but she'd held her own and not backed down. She tipped her head politely to the lot of them and strolled toward him with as much grace as she could muster. "Vanessa and her friends were just saying hello and commenting on my dress."

Tate pulled Elise into the circle of his arm. "Which

part? The fact that you look amazing in it, or how you being here in it made a dive bar look classy?" Without waiting for an answer, he scanned the women behind them with a look that said he wasn't blind to the near showdown he'd interrupted. "Night, ladies."

Just a few subtle sentences and an understated fare-well, but the way he'd crafted and delivered them as he steered her through the doorway, he may as well have dropped a grenade in the room.

With the band playing their final set at full throttle, talking on the way to the exit wasn't an option. The thirty-minute drive back to her home seemed even less opportune for casual conversation, let alone addressing what Tate had walked in on or what had him so tense in the aftermath. In the end, she opted to let sleeping dogs lie, let the steady drone of the tires against pave-ment lull her into a peaceful place and surrendered to strains of Lissie's "Daughters."

The approach seemed to have worked, because by the time Tate pulled into the drive and circled around to help her out of her seat, he was back to his usual laid-back, yet controlled demeanor. He shut the car door behind her and guided her to the front door. "What are your plans for tomorrow?"

Given how quiet he'd been on the way home, the question startled her a little. "Um… I don't know. I hadn't really made it that far. Before we found out about Draven, I'd just planned to work at my assisted living job through the summer and save up some money for tuition and books."

"Good."

"Good?"

"Yeah, if you don't have plans then you can come with me."

"Come with you where?"

When she stopped at the bottom of the steps to her porch and faced him for an answer, he just urged her back into motion. "To work."

She put on the brakes again, this time turning more sharply. "I can't go with you to work."

"Why not? Katy goes with Priest every day."

"Well, yeah. But they're a couple."

"They're mates." A calculating look crossed his face. One of those sly expressions reserved for men fired up with a sudden bout of wicked inspiration. "Have you learned about mates yet? How that works with our clan?"

"What do you mean, *How it works*? Isn't it like how most couples work? They meet, things work out and they live happily ever after?"

His lips twitched and he inched closer. "Happily ever after?"

"Okay, maybe that's not how all couples work out. Priest and Katy are the type that make other miserable couples want to stab their eyes out with a spoon."

This time he couldn't fight the smile and the way he looked grinning down at her in the moonlight, she couldn't find the strength to bust his chops for laughing. What he shared next, though, knocked her completely off-center. "Voláns don't have miserable couples. Not unless they fight being with the mate they're given."

She rewound his statement in her head, then repeated it out loud for good measure. "The mate they're given? You mean like an arranged marriage?"

"Yes and no. Yes, it's a fated match, but it's not the

parents who arrange it. You understand what the Keeper is to us?"

"Jade said he's the one who does the soul quest. Like some right hand to the Big Guy who makes sure we're paired up with the right magic and companion animal."

"The Keeper's a *he* to Jade, but might be a *she* to you. He or she appears to every one of us in a form that will speak to us at the deepest level. The soul quest is a kind of test. A deep look into who and what we are."

Yeah, Jade had mentioned hers was intense and that no two experiences were ever the same. Given how hard it'd been just to sit through a year's worth of counseling, Elise wasn't too excited to dive into a mystical psyche session with a nonhuman. "What's that got to do with Volán couples?"

"The Keeper picks them for us."

"What? When?"

His brows lifted as if she'd caught him completely unaware. "I have no idea. Could be when we're born. Could be five minutes before it happens. I only know that it happens. And like our companions and our magic, the mate that's chosen is the one best suited for us. I don't think there's been one story in our history about any couple unhappy with their match. Only unhappy stories where they fought the connection."

Huh. Well, that was an interesting nugget to chew on. Definitely something to pester Katy about the next time they saw each other.

Tate cupped the side of her face, effectively dragging her thoughts from the topic at hand. "Come with me tomorrow, *mihara*. Let me show you what I do for a living and spend more time with you."

More time with Tate.

As tempting propositions went, it was the mack daddy of them all. Especially the prospect of seeing him work. Plus, she'd be able to pester Priest and Katy with more questions.

But as she'd learned tonight, time with Tate came with difficult complications. Complications she'd have to be prepared to face with or without Tate beside her. "I like being with you, Tate. I like talking with you and learning about who you are, but I know women like Vanessa. If I keep spending time with you, run-ins like tonight aren't going to stop. They only escalate and get worse."

His jaw hardened to the same stubborn line he'd worn most of the drive home.

She pushed a little more. "You were with her before me, weren't you?"

His lips thinned and a muscle ticked at the back of his jaw, but he held her stare. "A few years ago. It was casual and didn't work for either of us. I think the only reason she showed interest in me was because of my relationship to Priest."

The truth. Laid fearlessly in front of her for her to work with. Yet another reason she found him so appealing. "How did you know to come check on me in the restroom?"

"I saw Vanessa and her crew come in while we were dancing. When I went to pay the tab, I watched them head to the restroom."

And he'd moved in to protect her. The same way he'd stood beside her at the party. Why the action warmed her the way it did, she couldn't say, but it nudged some sleeping part of her to life. "You didn't have to save me. I'd have been okay."

"I know you can hold your own. I also know her bullshit has got to be digging up a lot of crap from your past. But you've also got to understand—there's a huge difference between what you went through in high school and where you are today."

"What's that?"

He lowered his head, his mouth close enough her lips tingled. "You have me." He brushed his lips against hers, a there and gone temptation that made her mouth part and her breath catch. "You won't go through this alone." Another kiss. "Not this, or anything else." The next time his mouth lingered, coaxing her lips apart with a teasing swipe of his tongue. "Say yes, *mihara*. Say you'll come with me tomorrow. One day at a time, say you'll take a chance and stay in this with me."

His breath mingled with hers, the ragged in and out of their escalating breaths and the feel of him pressed against her fogging what was left of her common sense. The past was over and gone. This was now. Her new story. Her new beginning. Whatever that looked like.

Beneath her palm, his heartbeat a steady, reassuring rhythm. Nothing like the galloping pace of her own. She pulled back just enough to fully meet his gaze and took the risk. "Okay. One day at a time, I'm in."

Chapter Nine

One nice thing about tattoo artists—their 10:00 AM start time sure beat Elise's 7:00 AM shift at work. A definite plus today considering it'd been nearly one in the morning by the time Tate had finished kissing her senseless on the front porch. It'd taken another hour and a half to stop floating through the memories of her first date and fall asleep. Even then, she'd tossed and turned, an odd flailing sensation leaving her out of sorts.

From her place in the passenger's seat, she nursed the coffee she'd brought from home and snuggled into her fleece jacket, letting her thoughts drift as the rich green trees along the winding roads and the isolated stores as they neared the town whipped by. "So, tell me how a day in the life of a famous tattoo artist typically plays out."

"Priest is the famous one. Not me. And I'm still not sure *famous* is the right word. More like *insanely talented* and able to charge ludicrous fees for his work."

"Right. Like I said. Famous." She flipped the top on her travel mug and shifted a little to better watch him while he drove. Like everything else Tate did, there was a grace about how he handled the curves. A casual confidence in the way his big hand gripped the stick and shifted from one gear to the next. His casual attire was back—this time sporting a white Glass Animals concert tee—and his hair was back in a low ponytail. Which really sucked because she'd had a fine time feeling it in her hands every time he'd kissed her last night. "Jade said there's more to his tattoos than just ink. That they're like talismans."

He glanced at her and grinned. "*Talisman* is a good word. They can also be a locator or a protection. Jade, Katy, Alek and I all have them. But he doesn't do them for just anyone. Mostly just the people in our clan. Every now and then, though, a singura will come in and he'll sense they need something. A boost to help them through something hard. It's one of the things he did to balance out the darkness before Katy came along."

"Something positive to offset a negative."

"Exactly like that."

"Do they know what they're getting?"

"People in the clan? Sure. But singura, no. Priest wants to get us more integrated with mainstream society—more modernized than what we were before the Keeper named him high priest—but singura aren't ready for us yet."

"More modernized?"

Tate nodded, downshifted for the traffic light ahead and turned on his signal. "I told you things were different for my dad's generation. It wasn't just attitudes. It was proximity and sophistication, too. We really lived like a clan. Mostly isolated to the forests that run through Colorado. That was fine before technology, but Priest knew if we didn't do something to integrate with the rest of the world, we'd die out, magic or not."

"Is that why Draven tried to get control?"

"Who knows. Maybe." He shrugged and turned onto Main Street. "Could just be he was a crazy fuck who couldn't stand his little brother had been picked to serve as priest instead of him."

For a Thursday approaching ten o'clock, the main drag where the bulk of tourists congregated was surprisingly busy. Most likely in part due to a quickly warming morning and a cloudless May sky. Unlike some touristy towns, the appeal for Eureka Springs was its quaintness. Like the people who lived there hadn't yet gotten the memo that malls and fast food were the way to go. The streets meandered up and down some pretty significant inclines and the buildings on either side were mostly two or three stories high, the architecture that of a classic 1850s American town house. But rather than an endless stream of buildings, there were trees, too. Lots of them. And where many tourist towns had a hotel every other block, Eureka Springs had mostly bed-and-breakfast options.

Tate pulled into an isolated parking lot behind a red-brick building with tall second-story windows and gorgeous ironwork. Well, calling it a parking lot was a bit of a push. More like an oversized alley someone had opted to completely pave forever ago so as not to take up precious shopper parking spaces out front. He parked between a Harley and a pretty teal convertible Mini Cooper, yanked the parking brake and killed the engine. "Ready for the high life of the tattoo business?"

Oh, she was ready. Honestly, he could have mowed lawns for a living and she'd have still happily followed him around all day. The fact that she was going to get to see how the whole process behind tattoos worked was just icing on the cake. She nodded and pushed her door open. "Please tell me the high life includes a functioning coffee machine. I don't think the cup I snagged on the way out is going to hold me."

"Already covered." Tate rounded the back of the car and grabbed her hand just in time to help pull her from the low-slung seats. "Katy got tired of making coffee runs and put one of those single brew coffee things in the break room about a week ago. I'm not sure who's happier—Priest because it means I'm not bringing in Whataburger breakfasts with my coffee hauls anymore, or me and Jade because we don't have to fight over whose turn it is to go."

"And none of you considered just putting in a coffee machine?"

Tate chuckled and wrapped an arm around her waist like they'd been together years instead of days, guiding her to the half flight of stairs that led to the building's raised back door. "Where's the fun in that? We're family. We gotta have something to bitch and hassle each other about."

Coming in through the back instead of the shop's storefront, it was a break room that greeted her first. A simple white Formica table that could have done duty at a coffee house sat in a corner with matching metal chairs around it. A refrigerator that was probably white ten years ago but was closer now to ivory sat tucked in a little alcove, and a long wall of dove gray counter space and cabinets with a sink in the middle ran opposite of it. It should have been depressing, and probably would have been combined with the industrial white tiles, but with the artwork adorning the walls, it was magical. Animals. Tribal designs. Flirty pinup cartoons and mystical beasts. If it existed in the real world or fiction, there had to be some rendition of it on the walls around her.

Vaguely, she clocked Tate setting aside his keys, billfold and phone, but most of her attention was rooted to the wall closest to her. "This is where you and Priest keep your designs?"

"This is more personal stuff. The ones you're looking at are mine. The other wall is all Priest's stuff. Nothing back here would end up on a random customer. It's more for clanspeople or people we're close to."

Near the center of the wall was a drawing so elaborate—the details and the coloring so rich—it looked more like a photo than anything handcrafted. And it wasn't just the skill of the drawing that caught her eye, but the content even more so.

A petite and fluffy fox snuggled trustingly next to a lounging black bear.

"Tate, this is beautiful." She lifted her hand to touch it, then thought better of risking any damage to his work and glanced over her shoulder. "What made you put the two of them together?"

His gaze drifted to the picture and a smile mixed with both sadness and pride curved his lips. He paced toward her, blanketing her back and cupping her shoulders. "They represent my mom and dad. He was a hard man and aloof to those who weren't close to him, but around her, he was an absolute teddy bear."

He'd captured that. Not just in the protective way the bear lay semi curled around the little fox, but in the peace radiating from his eyes. A powerful predator willingly tamed. "I don't know anything about art, but that one's exceptional."

"I'll need to start a new one after we see what your

animal is." He dipped his head enough to skim a soft kiss to her cheek. "Come on. I've got to set up and I want time to get you started on something before my first client gets here."

Even with her frequent trips to Lafayette and explorations in between classes, Elise had never once stepped foot in a tattoo shop, but she had a feeling this one wasn't like most. Where the break room's fixtures had been stark and void of color, the main area was a mix of urban art studio with exposed and weathered brick walls and a gothic heaven. Three rooms lined one side of the wide-open space, each with doors that allowed for privacy, where the primary section boasted every imaginable design on the walls and body jewelry in several glass cases. The room farthest from the door seemed bigger than the others and, while she couldn't get a visual from where she gawked at the center of the room, the low masculine voice told her Priest was already inside and working.

Jade popped up from behind one counter, her dark hair pulled up in one of those artfully messy buns Elise had never been able to pull off and her fitted T-shirt a surprisingly good match for the Mini Cooper outside. She smiled and carefully dumped an armload of small cardboard jewelry boxes on the countertop. "Hey, Elise." Her gaze shifted to Tate. "You're late."

"I thought you said my first one's at eleven?"

"I did. It's ten fifteen now, so you're pushing it if you want to get Elise set up."

Tate harrumphed and steered Elise toward the room in the middle with a hand at the small of her back. "Plenty of time. You get the stuff?"

"Yep."

Elise followed where he led in a distracted haze, the sheer volume of amazing designs on the walls making it hard to know what to take in first. Heck, just the bright and shiny jewelry and charms under the counter would keep her oohing and aching for a good long while. "Get me set up for what?"

She rounded the corner to the room Tate had steered her to and stopped dead in her tracks, the answer she'd wanted from Tate displaced by a more pressing interest. "Why are there like twenty plus honeydews and grapefruits stacked in a fruit pyramid on your table?" At least she assumed the configurable black table was Tate's. The artwork lining the room sure looked like his other stuff.

Tate strolled to the brushed chrome wall cabinet stocked with everything from cotton balls, alcohol wipes and black latex gloves, to razors, ink bottles and every color of Sharpie known to man. "The pyramid's Jade's way of yanking my chain. The grapefruits and honeydews are for you."

"Um…" She studied the artfully arranged fruit, then shifted her gaze to Tate who'd already dug right in to pulling things out of drawers and cabinets. "I'm not hungry?"

He grinned over his shoulder and split open a packet with something long, skinny and silver inside it. "They're not to eat."

Fascinated by his smooth, efficient movements, she padded closer to watch him work. "What are you doing?"

"Prepping you a tattoo machine."

"What? Why?"

Rather than answer right away, he tugged open a

drawer and pulled out a thin stack of art paper. He slid it onto the counter in front of her then thumbed through a holder full of Sharpies. "I had an idea last night on the way home, so I'm going with it." He waggled the pen in front of her. "Write your name on the paper."

"My name?"

"Yeah, your signature. It's pretty."

"How do you know what my signature looks like?"

"Because the day I fixed the sink in your kitchen, your mom got carried away showing me pictures of you at summer camp in junior high and there were letters from you folded up along with them." He nudged the paper closer and held the pen out. "It's just a signature."

No, it wasn't. She wasn't exactly sure what the real game was, but there was way too much clever calculation going on behind his eyes to be just a signature. Still, playful Tate was an awful lot of fun to be around and she'd promised herself to enjoy the day.

She took the marker and carefully wrote her name at the top.

Tate cocked his head and scanned it for a second. "Do a few more beneath it, but don't think about it. Just sign like you would if you were signing for a pizza."

"If I do it like that you won't be able to read it. I'm usually starving by the time I break down and order a pizza."

He grinned and shrugged. "Okay then. Somewhere in between slow and pizza scrawl."

Sighing, she did two more, the last of the three a decent mix of legible and artistic. "Now what?"

"Now I take these and finish getting set up while you hit the break room and get us both a cup of coffee."

"Seriously? You're not going to clue me in?"

"Absolutely." He paused in pulling something else out of the cabinets, leaned back and brushed a teasing kiss across her lips. "I'm just not stupid enough to do it until I know you're caffeinated."

Her grunt sounded like something more appropriate for his coyote, but he had a point. Everything was better with coffee. Dastardly plans from gorgeous bearded men included. "Fine." She turned and stomped a whole two steps away before she realized her grand exit was going to get derailed by a lack of information. "I don't know how you take yours."

"Black. But save the ones marked dark roast for Priest. I don't know where he bought 'em, but I think they could fuel a jet engine."

By the time she'd fumbled through the kitchen cabinets, brewed two coffees and meandered back, Tate had restacked the fruit at the foot of a small art table in the corner. All but one of them anyway. One honeydew sat in the center of the plain white tabletop and a machine just a little smaller than her hand sat mostly covered in plastic beside it. "Is that what I think it is?"

Tate turned from the cabinet with a smallish oblong shaped piece of paper and headed for the table. "I don't know. What do you think it is?"

"Something that looks like I should have brewed a double dose?" She padded close enough to slide the cup she'd made for Tate onto the countertop, then watched as he carefully pressed the paper to the honeydew's surface.

He peeled it away and spun the fruit around to show her name exactly as she'd written it transferred on the thick surface. "It's a day in the life, right? Might as well get you hooked up with a machine and let you see what it's like to do the actual work."

"You want me to tattoo my name on a fruit?"

"Well, I didn't think you'd be a fan of pig's feet."

She shuddered and stepped back.

Tate chuckled and guided her to the chair behind the table. "Come on. It's not as bad as you think."

In truth, it wasn't. A little noisy. A whole lot awkward, like a seriously weighted and bulky pen in her hand, and weird with the way the vibrations rattled up her forearm, but all in all, the process was pretty cool. Granted, her lines were a complete mess and the final product looked nothing like the name he'd transferred to begin with, but it'd been a fun experience. She spun the honeydew back and forth, admiring her atrocious work. "Okay, so giving up kinesiology for ink probably isn't a smart idea."

Priest's low voice from the doorway nearly jolted her from her seat. "Tate's first try looked worse, but look at him now."

One look at the fruit and tattoo machine in front of Elise and Katy hurried past Priest for a closer look. "Oh, wow." She ran her finger along the funky line that was supposed to be the lower curve of her *E* then locked stares with Priest over her shoulder. "How come you haven't taught me to do this?"

His wicked smile was enough to set an ice cube on fire. "Well, I was good with the marks you've been leaving with your nails and teeth, but if you want to add ink to the mix, I guess we could go there."

Jade poked her head between Priest's massive body and the door frame. "Hey, Tate. Your eleven o'clock's here." She scanned the room then locked on to Elise's morning project and grinned. "Not bad for a first time. You should have seen Tate's. Total disaster."

Leaning against the counter's edge, Tate crossed his arms and glared at Jade. "You gonna bust my balls in front of Elise or bring my client in?"

"That's a no-brainer. Busting your balls is way more fun and you can get your own damned client." Despite the sharp words, she paired the jab with a wink and shifted her attention to Elise. "Once you get the knack of ink, I'm totally teaching you how to do piercings. You wouldn't believe the guy I got to do a dydoe on last weekend."

Tate shoved from the counter and prowled toward Jade still leaning through the door. "She's not doing any dydoes."

"What's a dydoe?" Elise asked.

Kateri coughed and covered her mouth with her hand.

Priest tried to fight a smile, but did a terrible job of pulling it off.

Jade shifted just enough to keep Elise in her line of sight despite Tate moving in fast. "Oh, girl. We gotta talk. It's a piercing."

"You can talk all you want, but Elise isn't getting near anyone's dick but mine." With that, Tate herded her out of the doorway.

"Ha," she fired back as they both disappeared from sight. "You're assuming she even wants anything to do with your dick."

Elise shifted her gaze to Priest. "So, it's *that* kind of piercing?"

"One of many," he said with a chuckle. "But you'll have to stick to Google if you want to see what they look like. I don't think there's a chance in hell of Tate leaving you alone long enough to get any in-person viewings." He motioned Katy closer. "Come on, *mihara*. We gotta get back from our meet up with Garrett and Alek before two. I've got a client who's gonna eat up the whole afternoon."

Katy hesitated just enough to give Elise a hopeful look. "You'll still be here when I get back, right?"

Elise glanced down at the fruit stacked on the floor beside her. "If that pile is any indication, I might be here until the shop is closed."

"Oh, I doubt Tate's going to make it to close with you here, but I'm glad we'll have time to talk." She waved and slid into the crook of Priest's outstretched arm, but the glint in her eyes spoke of secrets and mischief. "Have fun playing with Tate."

Playing with Tate turned out to be a mix of fascinating hours spent watching him work and tedious repetition inking her name. Granted, the tedium wasn't all that bad when he didn't have a customer to work on. Those periods he spent straddled behind her in her chair coaching her on technique. Not that she remembered a darned word he said. If he'd wanted her to actually learn something he'd have had to take his hands off her hips and not talk with his lips right near her ear in that sinfully low voice, like he was right now.

He nuzzled her neck, tickling the skin exposed by her ponytail with his beard. "I think you've got the hang of it."

"Yeah, well, it's a miracle. Your mouth's a distraction."

"Mmmm." His lips skimmed downward as far as

the neckline of her tank would allow. "One more client and I'll see if I can't find other ways to distract you."

The bell above the shop's front door jingled, and Tate's warm breath whispered down her back.

She gave up trying to focus and killed the machine, the room's answering quiet almost as erotic as the press of his muscled torso against her back. "Is that your client?" It came out as ragged as her pulse.

Tate must've noticed because his fingers tightened on her hips. "If it is, then I'm that much closer to the best part of the day."

"What's the best part?"

"Alone time with you." He guided her face toward his with a gentle finger at her chin. "Do one more for me." With that, he kissed her soft but quick, stood and disappeared to the front of the shop.

She was still staring at her last attempt, trying to gauge her work and unsuccessfully getting her wits back together, when Tate led a woman almost as tall as him and built to dominate the fashion industry into the room. Given her toned muscles, the high-end yoga leggings and racerback tank weren't just for show, and her hair was an enviable dark chocolate that fell in beachy waves to her shoulders.

The stranger peeled off her tank with a casualness Elise would never be able to muster in public and stretched out on her stomach, casting Elise a polite smile over one shoulder. "Hey. I'm Emma."

One simple greeting, and Elise hated her. Absolutely, unequivocally *hated* her. Hated her freckle-free creamy skin. Hated the fact that, while Tate hadn't seen Emma disrobe and couldn't see her breasts now, one change in position would change all that. Hated the elegant and yet unfinished vine of exotic flowers twining down her back.

Tate had put those there.

Would finish it.

Would put his hands on her to do it.

"I'm Elise." How she managed to say even that much was a mystery. All she knew in that second with absolute clarity was that the tattoo machine lying innocently in front of her had a relatively narrow point to it and could do a decent amount of damage if she used it right.

Apparently, the lack of warmth in her tone was even worse than she'd thought, because Tate froze mid-prepping his machines and locked a concerned stare on Elise. "You okay?"

"Fine." More like seething hard enough to fuel the pits of hell, but no way would she admit otherwise. She fought the urge to throw the used honeydew at the gorgeous woman's head and placed it on the ground with the rest of the used ones instead.

"Elise?"

She ignored Tate and the soft tenor of his voice, snatched a fresh grapefruit and thunked it on the tabletop.

"Elise, look at me."

Hell no. Looking up meant looking at *Emma* stretched out and ready for Tate to touch her, and if she did that, she was pretty sure she'd end up in jail.

What is wrong with you?

The answer didn't come, but an overpowering urge to physically put herself between Tate and Emma left her muscles tight and burning and a cold sheen of sweat fanning out along her neck. "I think I'll take a break."

Even to her own ears, her voice sounded strained,

and the room around her registered as though it was a whole different reality. Like a camera projected the image from a remote location instead of from her own two eyes.

One second her gaze locked on to the safety of the break room door, and the next the world spun around her. Her back hit something solid, followed by the hot press of Tate's muscled body against her front.

And then she was drowning in his kiss. His devastating, all consuming kiss.

He fisted his hand in her hair and dragged her head back, deepening each wicked stroke from his tongue and growling into her mouth. The delicious sound rumbled through her, ricocheting out in all directions and soothing her tension in its wake. Emma didn't matter. Reality didn't matter. Only his taste. His touch. His scent.

Bit by bit, her muscles uncoiled and her breaths steadied to match Tate's.

Too soon, he gentled his grip in her hair and slowed his kiss, his words murmured against her lips. "That's only for you, Elise. Only you."

Only for her.

Why the simple statement meant so much she didn't understand, but she clung to it. Hoarded and protected the knowledge like a dragon with its jewels.

Around her, the room finally began to register. A foreign one she hadn't yet seen, but obviously belonging to Priest given its size and the artwork on the walls. She forced herself to uncrimp the death grip she had on his shoulders and sucked in a shaky breath. "I'm sorry." She smoothed her palms against the hard slab of his pecs, the trembling of her fingertips impossible to hide. "I don't know what happened. I just… I was fine and then I saw her. And then… I… Something tripped."

"I know what happened."

She froze and met his gaze. "You do?"

He nodded. "It's okay. Totally normal."

"No, it's not. Not for me. I don't act like that. Ever. But I seriously wanted to hurt her. I wanted to—"

"Elise." He paired her name with a gentle press of his thumb against her lips and kept it there until she'd drawn a steadying breath. "It's okay. What happened wasn't wrong. It's part of who you are and what you are to me."

"What I am to you?"

He held her stare, a mix of determination, hesitancy and fear reflected in his eyes. "What we are to each other. I'll explain it to you. All of it. But I need to get Emma done so we can have time to talk."

Emma.

The gorgeous woman stretched out on the table in the next room and waiting for Tate.

Right.

She could act normal.

Maybe.

She jerked a nod and tried to push away from the wall. "Okay. I'll just spend some time with Jade."

"No, you'll stay with me."

"Tate, I can't." She didn't have a clue why that was the case, but it was an instinct she knew better than to ignore.

"You can, *mihara.* You'll stay with me. Right beside me. So long as we're close, you'll be fine. I promise."

Her blood hummed and her muscles shook like a near miss in a car accident, and where her brain normally wouldn't shut up, now it just an empty flatline. "This is weird."

The last thing she'd expected from him was a smile. Certainly not one so big and full of pride like the one he gave her. "It's beautiful." He grazed his thumb along her cheekbone as though memorizing the line of it. "To you, it's a mystery, but for me it was a gift."

"I don't like mysteries."

"It won't be much longer. I'll explain it all, but you have to trust me." He pulled away enough to hold out his hand palm up. "One hour. That's all I need to finish her up and you'll get your answers. All of them."

"All of them?"

"Everything."

One hour. Probably the longest one of her life if the last five minutes were anything to go by, but if he could explain half of what she'd just experienced it might be worth it.

Maybe.

Assuming she could keep the inner animal she hadn't known existed under control.

She gripped his hand and nodded. "Fine. Just don't blame me if you end up with ink and blood on the floor."

Chapter Ten

The bond was growing. That single thought had rattled around in Tate's head so loud for the last hour and
a half he'd been a little surprised Jade hadn't stomped
in from the main room mid-tattoo and told him to keep
the racket down.

But it had to be true. No way would Elise's primal
instincts have kicked in like they had if the bond wasn't
growing.

And she'd run.

Holy hell…just thinking of the jolt that had gone
through him when she'd torn out of his room made it
hella uncomfortable not to fidget in the driver's seat as
he drove them back toward Priest's property. How he'd
kept his shit in check and not taken her against the wall
he still hadn't figured out.

In the passenger's seat, Elise straightened and
twisted, watching the long driveway to her house fly
past them. "Where are we going?"

"Someplace private."

She settled back into her chair, a tiny furrow etched
between her brows.

"Relax, Elise." He covered one loosely fisted hand
in her lap and squeezed. "You wanted answers to ques-

tions. I don't want to do that someplace where we run the risk of being interrupted every five minutes." Or worse, where Jade could poke and prod his coyote into doing something stupid. "Besides, there's something I want you to do for me and I want you to be able to concentrate."

The teaser worked, turning the concerned frown on her face to something closer to shy intrigue. "What's that?"

He grinned and downshifted enough to take the gravel drive coming up around the bend. "Hold that thought and I'll show you."

The long, winding path was a bear in his Camaro. Definitely not the type of surface he could take at the speed he wanted, but it did a decent job of distracting Elise from pushing for more before he was ready. When he rounded the last line of trees and the plain cedar cabin came into view her eyes widened and her smile guaranteed he'd just bought at least another five-minute delay. "Wow. Whose place is this?"

"Mine. Jade's. Priest's. Depends on who needs space the most." He parked right in front of the raised porch and killed the engine. "Every bit of it we built by hand. Priest swore it was because he wanted to save money, but that's complete bullshit. He's got more funds than he'll ever spend."

"He does?"

"Oh, yeah. Don't let the biker image fool you. He's seventy-seven years old and has a capacity for learning that would floor scientists. What he doesn't earn with his artwork, he more than makes up for in side businesses and investments." He popped his door and rounded for Elise.

Elise kicked in the second he opened her door. "So, why build it by hand?"

"You never know with Priest." Tate pulled her to her feet, gathered his bags from the trunk and guided her to the porch. "Could have been he saw it as a chance for the three of us to get over losing mine and Jade's moms. Could have been he just wanted us to stay out of trouble for the time it took to get the job done."

The inside was simple—one mostly open room with only a modest bathroom tucked into one corner for absolute privacy. The far end of the room faced the lake and had huge windows that provided the bulk of the light during daylight hours. A queen-size bed looked out at the view while a thick couch and coffee table sat facing the front of the cabin. Along the far corner opposite the entry was a kitchen and a small dinette.

Elise padded forward, her footsteps careful like she was afraid to make a sound. "Oh my God, I love it."

"Which part? The flower child style, or the bachelor furniture arrangement?"

"Both." She scanned the stunning scene of the lake below then trailed her fingers along the bed's teal silk comforter. "Let me guess…the flower child part is Jade."

"Yep. A lot of it came from stuff our moms had in storage, but me and Priest put our foot down when she tried to hang up the beaded wall dividers." Duffel in hand, Tate paused at the bathroom and motioned to the floor lamp in the corner of the pseudo bedroom. At nearly eight o'clock at night there wasn't much sunlight left. "Turn that on if you want. I just need a minute to get set up."

"Set up for what?"

"The thing you're gonna do for me." He ducked inside the bathroom before she could drill him any more and started prepping. What would have taken him five minutes at the shop took triple that tonight, adrenaline and the need to get things just right making his movements embarrassingly shaky. He'd already planned to do what he was about to spring on her, and after what happened at the shop, she deserved to know the truth. But that didn't mean his insides weren't churning like the day he'd woken up in the Otherworld and faced the Keeper for the first time.

Finally satisfied with his work, he pulled on his T-shirt and exited the bathroom to find Elise in the deepening darkness framed in the center of one window, her arms hugging her chest and her gaze locked on the lake and what was left of a fiery sunset. "Are you cold?"

She shook her head, but kept her focus trained on the lake. "Not really. Just thinking I guess." She peeked over one shoulder. "It's a good view for that."

"That's why we picked it." Tate dropped the duffel next to the big club chair near the window and got to work setting up. "I think Priest figured out early on that two teenagers and one high priest with a load of dark magic trapped inside him was a dangerous combination to have under one roof. So, he figured a place we could get away and be alone was a smart move. With the amount of property he bought when we moved here, we had a lot of options to choose from, but this one proved the best for view and accessibility. There's a path from here to Priest's house that's easy to walk."

Elise kept her silence, but she'd openly given up staring at the lake in favor of watching his every move.

Even noted the fact that he'd ditched his shoes and replaced his jeans with simple track pants with an open scan of his body. By the time he ambled back to the bedroom with a tray of everything she'd need, her face was pinched with a rapidly growing frown of concern. In about five more seconds, the questions were undoubtedly going to hit, so he set the tray on the side table next to the chair and diverted with his own conversation. "You know, I've been thinking about the thing with Vanessa last night."

That perked her up, shifting her concentration from the tattoo machine he busied himself putting together to his face. "What about it?"

"I think you're right. Her bullshit's only gonna escalate until she figures out no one will play her games, or someone stands off with her." With everything in place, he shifted the ottoman so it lined up just right with the club chair, flipped on the gooseneck light Priest used for reading and aimed it so she'd have optimal lighting while she worked. He pulled his shirt off and moved directly into her line of sight. "So, I say let's cut to the chase. Stand up to her and stake your claim."

Her gaze dropped to the outline of her name he'd transferred from the stencil to the space above his heart. "You're out of your mind." Her focus shot back to his face. "I can't tattoo you. I've worked on fruit, not people. And besides that, I don't have a claim to stake."

"Yes, you do."

"No. I don't. We've been on one date. You've barely known me more than a few weeks."

"Elise, you have a claim." He prowled forward and carefully grabbed her wrist and tugged her toward the chair. "You felt it this afternoon. There's a reason for

what you felt. All I'm asking for you to do is own it."
He sat on the edge of the ottoman and dipped his head
toward the supplies on the tray. "Take what's yours."

She dropped to the chair in front of him and leaned
in close, her hands clasped almost pleadingly between
her knees and a mix of panic and bewilderment coating
her voice. "Tate, what you're offering is sweet, but I'm
not putting a permanent mark on you just to get a bully
to leave me alone. You said yourself last night—Voláns
have fated mates. Don't you think yours is going to be a
little pissed off to have another woman's name on you?"

"My mate's not going to be pissed off. And dealing
with Vanessa isn't the main reason I'm asking you to
do this. There's a bigger one." He gripped both of her
hands in one of his. For all the times he'd imagined
this moment, none of them featured the tightness in
his chest. The ache and burn in his lungs and the slow-
motion surrealness of every detail around him. "You
asked me what *mihara* means." His voice caught, and
his heart kicked. "It's an endearment. One a man only
uses with his mate."

A shudder moved through her, a tiny current that
rippled from her joined hands into his.

"You're my mate, Elise. I knew it the second I saw
you. So, unless you've got an aversion to seeing your
name on my skin, I want your mark. I want everyone
to know with absolutely certainty, I'm yours. Vanessa
included."

"No." She shook her head and tried to jerk her hands
out of his.

He tightened his hold on her hands and cupped the
back of her neck with his free one. "Don't run." He
rested his forehead against hers, the animal half of him

ready to hunt and claim what it knew belonged to them, and his lungs churning double time. "Please, dear God, don't run right now. Talk to me. Scream at me or hit me, but don't run. *Please*."

Her body trembled and a soft sound far too close to that of a muted sob slipped from her lips.

He pulled her closer and kissed her forehead. Smoothed his hand up and down her back. He'd expected shock. Denial and even an argument, but not fear. Not the acrid scent of it or her salty tears. Inside him, his coyote whined and paced, the pain from her rejection a dull blade cutting from the inside out.

"You're wrong about this," she whispered. "You have to be."

Another slice, this one deeper and jagged.

"I'm not wrong, Elise. A male who's accepted his magic always knows when he finds his mate. The aura's unmistakable and we feel it. We know it the same way you know basic right from wrong."

She lifted her head, her eyes bright and eyelashes spiked with wetness. "But I don't know what to do. My God, I've been on one date in my whole life. Have never been with a man. How am I supposed to be a mate if I don't even know how to be a girlfriend?"

Not afraid of him.

Not a rejection.

A fear of herself. Of what she brought to the equation.

Confident she'd passed the state where she might bolt, he took a chance and cupped her face. "There's nothing for you to do. Nothing for you to know. All you have to do is be you. Give us time together and get to know what works for us. The bond between us won't seal until you're ready to accept it. You control everything."

Her breath caught on a hiccup and she swiped a tear from her cheek. "What bond?"

God, she was sweet. And gorgeous. Even with eyes red from crying and a tear-streaked face. "The connection between mates. Some couples say it's an intangible knowing between them. Like what twins claim to have, but at a more intimate level. Some describe it as an emotional tether. A link that lets them feel the things their mate feels and keeps them in sync. Priest says he and Katy can actually communicate between it. Not with words, but with thoughts the way they do with their companions." He wiped a fresh tear free with his thumb. "What you felt today…that was the bond, Elise. An instinct to get between your mate and someone you viewed as a threat."

"But that was awful."

"To you, maybe. To me… I was floored. Honored. And the only thing I could think about was finding a way to help you." She searched his face like she still couldn't comprehend the beauty of it, so he tried again. "Tell me about last night."

She sniffled and swiped her knuckle beneath one eye. "What about it?"

"After I left, how did you feel?"

She frowned, and her gaze slid down and to the side. "Restless." She refocused on him. "I had a hard time falling asleep."

"Because mates—once they've found each other… touched each other—want to be together. The more that happens, the more being apart doesn't feel right. That's the bond, Elise. It's there already. Waiting. Growing.

Getting stronger. But the female controls it. Always. Until you accept it, nothing's final."

"So, what? You're stuck with me? You don't get a choice?"

Another clue. A kink in how she viewed things created by her past. "Elise, you don't give yourself enough credit. Apparently, you don't see the woman me and everyone else sees when you look in the mirror." He paused just long enough to make sure she was listening. Really listening. "I made my choice. I took one look at you and knew the Keeper had gone so far beyond my expectations of a mate, I happily accepted what I'd been given."

"But you left." A mocking chuckle slipped up her throat. "Almost ran out the front door not even thirty seconds after you met me."

Oh, he remembered. Had replayed that critical stretch of time over and over in his head and cursed himself for the way he'd reacted. But, as Priest had reminded him repeatedly in the hours and days that followed, following his base instincts would have been a bigger hurdle to overcome. "I wasn't running, *mihara*. I was protecting you. From me. You were new to the clan. Afraid. Thrown into a whole new reality after learning you were being hunted by a madman and looking at me with those big eyes of yours. If I'd done what I wanted, you'd have been up against a wall and learning the feel and taste of me before you learned my name."

Her eyes widened and a comprehension to match the bright floor lamp overhead settled behind her gaze. "Really?"

"Really. It was natural. Perfect. Like walking out of a black-and-white world and finding color for the first time in my life. I wanted to gorge on the gift I'd been given and wasn't the least bit in control." He eased back and stroked her hair. "I'm yours, Elise, and proud of it." Straightening, he pulled the table and the tray on top of it closer. "Give me your mark."

She shook her head and wiped her palms on her jeans. "No. I don't care what I am to you. I'm not messing up Priest's work."

"Elise, look at it." He pushed his shoulders back, knowing full well the way he'd placed her name beneath the swirling knots and symbols Priest had inked after Tate's soul quest was perfect. "These are the exact same lines you did over and over again today."

"On fruit! Not your skin."

"Elise." One word said strongly enough she seemed to hold her breath. "I want this. I'm asking you to give it to me."

"To send a message to Vanessa."

"No. Because I want it. Rubbing Vanessa's nose in it after the way she's treated you is just a bonus."

"What if I screw up?"

"You're not going to screw up. It's no different than today."

Her gaze dropped to his chest and she swallowed huge.

"It looks right there," he said. "That voice or instinct you felt last night and today knows it. Don't be afraid. Give me what I want and make it real for me."

She studied the outline. The machine and ink ready and waiting beside her. Then searched his face and whispered, "This is crazy."

"Stop thinking. Just do it."

With a tiny shake of her head, she wiped her palms

on her jeans and scanned the tray. "Shouldn't I wear gloves or something?"

"Voláns with their magic don't contract infections like singura do. Plus, I'm warrior house, so surface wounds don't last long on my skin. Besides all that, you're my mate. I don't want gloves on you."

She nodded, picked up the machine and got it situated in her grip just as she had at the shop. She inked up like a pro, faced him and cocked her head, considered his position and then how she was perched on the chair's edge. "This doesn't feel right." Dropping to her knees between his splayed legs, she let out a slow breath through her mouth, leaned in and tentatively braced her hand on his shoulder. "Wow. This is…different."

Fuck different. It was potent. A supercharged profoundness mixed with a primal edge. "It's the bond. Trust it."

Narrowing her gaze, she fired up the machine.

The buzz jolted through him, but it was her breath against his skin that registered the strongest. The warmth of her hands and the nearness of her body. The needles made contact a second later and a wave of deep red rippled against his skin.

Elise jerked back. "What was that?"

He caught her with hands at her waist before she could get far. "Just my magic. A natural defense for warriors. A shield to block superficial injuries." He urged her back into position. "If it thought you were a threat, it wouldn't have let you in, but my magic knows you. It'll spread out and pull you in with it as you go." He smoothed his hands to her hips and prayed she'd be too occupied by what she was doing to notice the rigid length straining just inches away. "It's okay. Keep going."

He paced his breathing. Focused on every physical point of contact and willed his magic to settle. To surround and soothe her.

She settled into a rhythm. Inking the needles. Drawing a steady line. Dabbing the excess ink away and assessing her work. It was the same steady concentration she'd used at the shop, but there was more to it this time. A connection within her movements that built and strengthened with each line. A focus lasered on to something felt more than seen. Whether it was his magic pulling her in, their bond guiding her, or the act itself, he couldn't figure out, but she was fully in the moment. Invested at the most fundamental level and riding her instincts. Flowing with the wave they created.

He wanted her like that beneath him. Lost to only the sensations he gave her. Free of any thoughts but the ones they created together. Mindless and wild.

The buzz stopped, and the room's silence pressed heavy around them.

Elise swiped the last line, the lingering drag of her fingertip almost remorseful. As if she hated the fact there wasn't more left to give. "Done."

No, she wasn't. Not even close. One look at her face—at the curiosity and longing as she studied not just the mark she'd left behind, but his torso—and he knew with absolute certainty she was far from done. His mate was hungry. Intrigued and cautiously considering a whole new terrain.

Slipping one arm around her waist, he tugged the machine from her fingers, set it aside and then cupped the back of her neck. "It's okay, Elise. I'm yours. You don't need an excuse to touch me."

Gaze still locked to her name, she traced her fingers beneath the ink. As if the simple gesture might somehow underscore his words and help her come to grips with her new reality.

"More." Keeping one hand anchored at her nape, he covered her hand with his and flattened it against his sternum. "Take what you want."

Her gaze shot to his. "How do you know what I want?"

"Because I feel it, *mihara*. Need to give you what you want as much as you want to take it." He released his grip and leaned back on the ottoman, propping himself up on his elbows and giving her unimpeded access. "All you need to do is take what's yours."

Chapter Eleven

So tempting. A virile male—a prime one so far beyond Elise's imagination or fantasies she still couldn't believe it—stretched out in front of her. Offering her unimpeded touch. An exploration. And he was *hers*.

Her mate, if what he said was true. Chosen specifically for her. The revelation was both astounding and humbling, wrapped up in a healthy amount of disbelief.

She licked her lips, for all the good it did her. Her mouth and tongue were equally dry and showed no signs of catching up.

Her gaze slipped lower, lingering a bit too long on the obvious erection beneath his track pants before shifting her focus back to his face. "I'm not sure that's a good idea."

"Why not?"

Because she didn't know what she was doing. Because the last thing she wanted was to look like an idiot. "Because I'm not ready," she said instead.

He pushed himself upright and cupped both sides of her face. "I'm not offering this as a lead-in to sex. I'm offering you this as a starting point. A chance for us to learn each other. For you to explore." He paused a beat, his gaze roving her face, considering. "Do you want to touch me?"

"God, yes." It slipped out, fully uncensored and breathy with relief and need. If she had the courage to take what he offered, he'd be stretched out naked on the bed behind them so she could soak in every detail and feel every inch of him.

"Then do it." He shifted one hand to the back of her head and tugged her ponytail holder free. Digging his fingers deep along her occipital bone, he combed the thick strands from root to tip. "I want to touch you, too, Elise. Very much."

"That's kind of what I'm afraid of."

His mouth crooked in a wry smile. "Then you set the pace. For tonight, however you touch me—wherever you explore—sets the boundary."

Well, that was clear enough. And reasonable. Except for one thing. "Won't you…" Ugh, but she hated her inexperience. Hated not having the right words to use in this situation. She dipped her head toward the still straining length between them. "Won't that be uncomfortable for you?"

She'd expected laughter, or maybe an awkward moment. Instead, his golden eyes warmed and his smile softened. "Just because we're intimate doesn't mean either one of us has to get off."

It didn't? Because, from all the stories she'd heard, that was the end game everyone seemed most focused on. "But you'll still be…" She shrugged and glanced downward.

"Then you will be, too." He grinned huge, a wicked edge to it that made her sex clench. "Unless you decide to take matters into your own hands, of course. In which case, I'd enjoy like hell watching."

Another flutter. This one stealing a little of her breath and making her tighten her grip on Tate's thighs to remain steady.

He cocked his head, the sharpness in his gaze telling her he'd caught the subtle response. "You like cake?"

Huh? Cake? "Um…yes?"

"Ever lick the spoon while you were making the batter?"

"Of course."

"Did you like it?"

Okay, this was officially the weirdest erotic conversation she'd had in her life. Not to mention the *only* erotic conversation she'd ever had. "Yes."

"And the cake after it was baked…ever eaten it without frosting?"

"Sure."

"Would you turn it down without the frosting?"

"No."

He traced the line of her jaw with one knuckle, the heat and thoughtfulness behind his gaze electrifying the contact. "That's what intimacy is supposed to be like. The whole process is good. Something to enjoy. Just because you don't end up with icing doesn't negate how good the rest of it is."

Oh.

Okay.

No immediate need for icing.

Though, right about now, that felt like a damned shame.

His thumb skimmed along her lower lip, the contact making her realize they'd parted at some point in the process. "What do you want, *mihara*? Not what you think you should do, or what you think I want—but what *you* want?"

She wanted to touch. Wanted to take her sweet time and look her fill without worry. "I set the pace?"

"Only the boundaries you set."

Her heart's erratic rhythm thundered in her head and, despite the solid floor beneath her feet and the walls around her, she could have sworn her toes were poised at the edge of a ten-thousand-foot cliff. She coiled her hand around his wrist and held on tight. "Okay."

His rumbled exhale was rich with relief and pure masculine satisfaction, and the wildness burning behind his eyes made her breath catch. "My brave mate. All mine."

Twisting his wrist, he captured her hand and skimmed his lips along her knuckles. "Come on." Before she could process what he meant, he stood and pulled her to her feet.

"Wait. Where are we going?"

He pulled his hair free of its holder and backed toward the bed, breaking their joined hands only when necessary to stretch out on top of the comforter. "Where you've got plenty of room to work."

Whoa, boy.

This was *real*. Not a daydream. Not some detached wishful thinking void of witnesses, but the real freaking deal. She inched closer, utterly clueless on next steps.

"It's okay, Elise. Just kick your sandals off and crawl up here. There's no right or wrong. Just what feels good to you."

What felt good to her? *He* was the one being touched and, for some reason, wanting whatever she did to feel awesome for him seemed imperative. Still, he clearly knew more about how to navigate this scenario than her, so she went with it. Shoes off, she put one knee to the mattress and tried to kneel on one side of his hips, but he caught her other knee and guided her so she strad-dled him instead.

"Oh." She stood tall on her knees, glanced down at the still very prominent erection beneath his pants, then back behind her. "Won't it be uncomfortable for you if I sit here?"

He chuckled and urged her downward with hands at her hips. "Not like you think."

Right. And now she not only had a bird's-eye view of how hard he was, but the base of his cock was just an inch from her own sex.

He cocked his knees behind her, effectively shift-ing her balance forward so she had to catch herself with hands at either side of his head. It also obliterated what was left of the space between them and brought her core flush against his cock. It was just a hint of con-tact, but the impact it sent scurrying through her was on par with an electric jolt. "Wow."

His eyes crinkled at the sides with a hint of mischief. "Wow, good? Or, wow, too much?"

"Wow, good." Wow, *very very* good was more like it. So much so she wasn't entirely confident her body could process the rush all at once. She forced herself to take a deeper breath and let her gaze drift downward. Across the wide slabs of his pectorals, down his ster-num and the defined muscles in his abdomen. Touching him before had been one thing. A necessity to give him what he wanted with guilty pleasures thrown in as a side benefit. But this was intentional. A connection far more intimate. "I'm not sure where to start."

He tucked the hair that had fallen along one side of her face behind her ear. "Turn your mind off. Just go with what feels right and see where it takes you."

Her gaze snagged on her name now inked just above his heart. On the swirling black lines marred only by the red, irritated aftereffects of the needles piercing his flesh.

You're my mate.

The same flutter and flush she'd felt when he'd uttered those words stirred in her belly all over again, and that indefinable and overpowering force that had sprung to life this afternoon lifted its head, awake and eager for all he offered. She traced the tail of the stylized *E*, careful not to further aggravate the mark. "Do you have any idea how surreal this is?"

"Which part?"

"All of it." Emboldened, she splayed her hands against his warm skin. So much strength. Every muscle lean, deeply defined and covered by taut, tan skin. The dusting of gold hair along his pecs and sternum tickled her palms and she could have sworn her heartbeat settled into a rhythm to match the one beneath her touch. "The clan. What we can do." She shifted her hands up and outward, savoring the corded lines of his shoulders and down to his biceps. "Having a mate."

His hands settled on her hips. When he spoke, his voice was different. Deeper and a little strained. "Does that scare you?"

"Logic tells me it should. That the whole notion isn't possible."

"But?"

She smoothed her fingertips down his sternum and lower to his abs. A trail of hair slightly darker like his beard dipped low and disappeared beneath the waistband of his pants. Temptation nudged her to follow it. To tease the subtle line and see what response it garnered. "My mother told me for years about our clan. About our magic and the ability to shift." Slow and steady, she followed the path, her lungs straining harder for breath with every inch gained. "I listened to logic once and it was wrong. I'd rather follow my gut this time and see where it takes me."

"Elise?"

She didn't dare look up. Not with the dangerous undercurrent in his voice. She kept her focus rooted downward, instead, and smoothed her hands across his stomach, her thumbs dragging along the waistline of his pants. "Hmmm?"

"What's your gut want right now?"

To let go.

To see, touch and taste him everywhere and not give a fig about how little she knew. Except they'd made an agreement and taking things to the level she wanted with him would mean offering him the same in kind. She slid her hands toward his hips, the soft cotton of his pants an affront to her senses after the hot, tight press of his flesh. "I want to touch you."

He could have made fun of her shyness. Could have pointed out she already had her hands on him and forced her to be more specific. Instead, he cupped the side of her face and urged her gaze to his. "It's okay." He covered one of her hands with his and guided it closer to the straining length in front of her. "I want your hands on me."

Two heartbeats. Two ragged, unsteady kicks that went too fast and yet seemed to stretch over eternity.

And then she was there. Her palm pressed against his impossibly hard shaft and his hips flexing into her touch. Her breath rushed out in a shaky exhale. Fascinated by the feel of him, she stroked his length, outlining his shape through the soft cotton. "That's... different."

He chuckled, but there was a hint of strain behind it. An incongruent mix of humor at the situation and a struggle for control. "Not what you'd expected?"

"Not even close." What she actually had expected she couldn't have articulated if she'd tried, but her imagination had clearly come up woefully short. She dragged her finger down the center then back up again. Soft at first. Then stronger.

Through her explorations, he traced idle patterns along one shoulder. A subtle touch that both calmed and encouraged her.

As if she needed encouragement. With every stroke and every breath, her courage blossomed. Lifted its head and demanded answers. "Are you..." She cleared her throat and tried again, peeking from beneath her lashes and meeting his eyes. "Can I see you?"

In the lamplight, his amber eyes already ran a deeper, warmer color, but the second the reality of her question registered, they seemed to deepen further and his steady touch at her shoulder faltered. "You're sure?"

Was she? They'd made an agreement. She set the boundaries and taking this step would push her own limits a lot further out than where she'd thought they'd end up.

Yes.

The times in her life when she'd felt such clear direction were few and far between, but tonight it resonated with perfect clarity. Mind, body and spirit all aligned at once.

She nodded, too bound by whatever it was that moved between them to actually speak. The same energy and unique connections she'd felt between them from the start, only more palpable and crackling with awareness.

Holding her gaze, he lifted his hips and pushed his pants past his hips and down to his corded thighs. "Whatever you want, *mihara*. It's yours."

Wow.

Never in her life had she been so dumbfounded. So caught off guard and floundering for stable footing. But seeing Tate like this—laid out solely for her perusal and exploration—packed a wallop. An emotional looptyloop that left her thoughts racing to catch up.

She ducked her head and focused on pulling his pants the rest of the way off, praying the action covered some of her fuzzledness. Too soon, she tossed them to the floor and was left with him watching her. Waiting for her to take what she'd asked for.

He cocked one arm and braced it behind his head, propping his head up for a better view. The other hand he splayed above one pec, her name just below the heel of his palm. "I'm trying to be good, but if you keep looking at me like that, I'm going to run out of resolve real fast and claim my own turn."

Oh, no. He wasn't rushing her past this. Lack of experience or not, being with Tate made her a seriously greedy woman, and he'd just unveiled a whole new playground.

Rather than straddle his hips as she had before, she crawled between his knees.

He cocked them both and spread them a little wider, an appreciative rumble slipping past his lips. "I wish you could see what you look like right now. How wide your eyes are. How your lips are parted. How focused you are on every detail."

She grazed her fingertips from the inside of his knees upward, the light dusting of hair along his thighs tickling her palms. She was focused on details, all right. Namely, how his size seemed a whole lot more intimidating without clothing barring the view, and how the skin around his shaft looked almost painfully taut. She traced the sharp V at his hips. "I want to get it right."

That said, she didn't have a clue what to do next. Where to start, or how to make him feel good.

"Sweetheart, you're my mate. Short of coming at me with a machete, there's not a damned thing you could do to me right now that could ruin this moment, and even then, I'd probably let you have at me."

It was just the levity she needed. The easy laughter that bubbled up fueling a potent reminder that she was human. That they both were. This wasn't about acing an exam, or winning a competition. This was about getting to know each other. Exploring and laying whatever foundation worked for them.

"No sharp objects. I promise." She bit her lip, smirked up at him and gently scraped her nails along the tender skin on either side of his shaft. "Well, except for these, but I promise I'll keep those in check."

His cock jerked against his belly and he groaned. "On my cock, yeah, but when I'm fucking you, I wanna feel them in my back."

Flutters swirled and dipped in her belly and her breath hitched, the wild image he'd created with his words jolting her headlong into a whole different head-space. She held his gaze and repeated the stroke, softer this time, but letting the sides of her fingers brush the length of him.

His gazed heated, the predator locked inside staring back at her. "You like that don't you?"

"Like what?"

"The words." His lips curved in a dirty grin. "They shocked you, but they felt good, too."

For a second, she considered denying it. Even thought about drawing her hands away from him and ending their fun for the night simply to hide the vulnerability he'd uncovered.

But that same, animalistic response she'd felt this afternoon pushed forward instead, overcoming her in-securities and fears with an almost bulletproof confidence. Guided her to welcome the truth. To step into the possibilities he created and take what she wanted.

"I do." With trembling fingers, she stroked him root to tip. "I won't say I understand it, but I felt them."

Back down she went. Then up again. With each pass, she grew bolder. More engrossed in her learning and more intrigued with his response. Talk about a disconnect between theory and reality. Yes, she'd known what to expect in a textbook sense. Had even fed her curiosity with porn explorations over the years. But nothing came close to the real deal. To the discovery of how soft his skin would feel compared to the strength beneath. To the warmth of him against her palm. To the ragged breaths her touch generated and his hiss when she fisted him at the base.

She hesitated, gauging his body language and the fierceness in his stare. "Too much?"

"More."

A dare.

A demand.

Both lashing her back into motion and stoking her own response higher. Odd, how he was the one receiving pleasure, but she was right there with him. Caught in the moment and keenly aware of the growing ache in her own body.

She swirled her thumb in the precum pooled at the tip of him. Painted it along the flared head and along the prominent ridge beneath.

She wanted more of it.

Wanted to watch his release and witness the aftereffects. To claim that private moment with him and hoard it for herself.

A shocking realization, but deliciously primal. Freeing.

But she had no clue how to make it happen. To make the moment something beyond what her limited skills could provide.

Unless you decide to take matters into your own hands, of course. In which case, I'd enjoy like hell watching.

He'd suggested it for her, but the idea of seeing himself bring himself off was far more appealing. A chance to learn and enjoy at the same time.

With one last lingering caress, she pulled her hands free and sat back on her heels. "I want to see how you do it."

He studied her a moment, thoughtful. "How I do what?"

Dammit. She should have known he'd make her spell it out. But if he could speak so bluntly with her, surely she could manage the same. "I want you to make yourself come, and I want to watch it happen."

He slid the hand at his chest lower, hesitating above his belly and rubbing back and forth rather than grasping his shaft like she wanted. "That's a big jump from where we started."

A huge jump. One she was terrified she couldn't reciprocate in kind. But seeing him like this—this open and ready. This primal and hungry. Surely, it was worth the risk and the effort. "Is that too much? Because, I'll be honest. I don't know if I can do the same."

"Don't know if you can come, or aren't ready yet?"

Heat scored her cheeks and, if she hadn't been so soundly ensnared by the profound energy prickling between them, she'd have probably sprinted out the front door to hide her embarrassment. "On my own I can, I just...well... I don't know if I can get there with you watching."

"But you'll touch yourself for me? Let me watch you?"

Could she? Really?

The quiet swelled between them, tension, desire and lust drawing her deeper. Consumed her and pulled her under. She swallowed hard. "So long as you don't expect icing."

He smiled huge, the mischief sparking behind his eyes the only warning she got before he knifed upward and tumbled her to her back, the playfulness in his actions completely dispelling what was left of her anxiousness. "No expectations. None except that you do what feels good. You don't do things for me. You do them for you and because you want it. Understand?"

She nodded. Though, with the way he was looking at her right now and the foreign feelings swirling through her, she'd have probably marched through Times Square naked if he asked her to.

His smile slipped and he cupped the side of her face, a cautious expression stealing across his features. "You sure you want this?"

Was he kidding? Any level of certainty she'd had when they'd driven here tonight had fizzled the second he'd walked out of the bathroom shirtless. It'd been a nonstop tango through unfamiliar terrain ever since. "I learned I had a mate tonight, tattooed my name in his skin and have a naked man who's left me tongue-tied since the day I met him almost pinning me to the bed. My brain stopped working a long time ago."

He grinned. "Tongue-tied, huh?"

She tried to make a serious face and paired it with a healthy shove against his shoulder. "Shut up and show me what I want to see."

Of course, he didn't budge, but his grin deepened, and his eyes twinkled. "Keep stoking that attitude, mate. One of these days it'll get you a response that surprises you."

Before she could ask what he meant, he rolled to his back, reached for the top nightstand drawer and pulled out a clear bottle with a dark gray top.

Elise sidled closer. "What's that?"

He waggled it so she could see it better then stacked the pillows higher behind his head.

Lubricant.

She probably should have tried to act more grown-up about it, but she couldn't help but giggle and cocked an eyebrow. "Have that kind of thing handy, do you?"

He grinned and flipped the lid open with his thumb. "I met my mate over two weeks ago and haven't been able to touch her the way I wanted until tonight. I could have bought this stuff by the case." He sat the bottle next to his hip and raked her with a smoldering look. "Come closer. I want you next to me."

She stretched out beside him and he pulled her into the crook of his arm, guiding her head to his chest.

"Fucking love the feel of you next to me." He speared his fingers into her hair and inhaled deep. "Though, I gotta admit. I'm looking forward to feeling it without your clothes between us."

Good grief. She hadn't thought about that part. Though, now that he pointed it out, she was looking forward to it, too. Another exploration she had no doubt would prove as addictive as all the others he'd taken her on. She splayed her hand above his sternum, the beat of his heart against her palm far steadier than her own.

His hand in her hair slid lower, slowly trailing the length of her smile. "You realize it's probably going to take me all of five strokes to get off with you watching me."

She propped herself up on her elbow. "Then you better make them a stellar five strokes so I know how to handle the job myself next time."

One heartbeat. One jolt that moved like lightning between them.

He picked up the bottle and handed it to her. "If you're telling me you'll handle the job from here out, I might get things done in four."

Chuckling she took the bottle. "Why are you giving this to me? I'm not certified yet."

"Because if I'm gonna keep my shit in check, then I'm going to keep one hand on you to remind me my stamina card is on the line." He motioned for her to get on with things with a few quick crooks of his fingers. "That means you're on lube dispense duty."

It was a clever ploy, but she wasn't buying it. Tate never did anything without a sound reason, and his go-to approach where she was concerned was getting her as involved as possible—the fresh tattoo on his chest being her strongest case to date.

She tipped the bottle over and gave it a gentle squeeze.

"Jesus, you're the only woman I know who can make a simple thing like that look hot."

She snapped the lid shut and frowned at him. "I do not."

"You do, too. Concentrated on the task like you were reaching for the holy grail and bit your lip while you did it." He gripped himself way more aggressively than she had and dragged his hand upward. A long, leisurely stroke that left her slack-jawed and stupid. "I can't wait to see how focused you get in the next few minutes."

Focused? There wasn't a word in any language that summed up the level of concentration holding her spell-bound in that moment. *Riveted. Captivated. Dumbfounded* and *bewitched.* They all fell short. And while a tiny sliver of the innocent sensibilities she'd walked in here tonight with still whispered in the back of her mind, the new awareness he'd brought to life blossomed bigger and brighter with every glide of his hand. On the wet sounds of the lube against his taut skin and his earthy masculine scent filling her lungs.

His breaths shallowed and a low rumble rolled up the back of his throat. "You look like you want something, *mihara*." His hand at her back slipped lower, firmly cupping her ass. "Tell me what you want."

To help. To mimic each languid stroke and feel that velvety hardness against her palm. Rather than answer with words, she skimmed her fingertips down the faint trail of hair beneath his belly button.

"That's it." A murmured encouragement. A dark devil luring her deeper. "Take what's yours."

Hers.

That odd connection she'd felt this afternoon resonated its agreement. Urged her to release all her concerns and worries and just flow with the moment. To touch, taste and feel to her heart's content.

She pressed her lips to his belly then cautiously flicked her tongue against his skin.

"Fuck, yes." Tate palmed the back of her head, but his touch was tender. Careful. "Just like that."

She went with it. Savored his skin with her lips and fingers. Floated on the rasp of his heavy breaths. Watched his hand working his sex.

When she slid her hand down the top of his thigh, he widened his legs.

She circled upward, slowly inching her way toward his tight sac. Hesitating no more than an inch away, she risked a glance at his face.

A hunter stared back at her. A dangerous beast barely leashed. His eyes were solidly locked on her and burned with challenge. Over and over, he pumped his hand along his rigid length. "Do it, *mihara*. You want to watch me come, then touch me the way you want to. Make it happen."

Her call.

Her touch unleashing his release.

In that moment, she understood. It wasn't about performing. About executing anything just right or meeting anyone's expectations. It was about connection. Setting aside everything except the two of them and riding the moment. In fully engaging at the most fundamental level.

Her fingers whispered featherlight against the dusky skin and he moaned, bucking against his fist.

So erotic. An exceptionally primal male on display only for her.

She trailed her fingers lower, the weight of his balls pressing firmly against her palm.

My mate. All mine.

She tightened her grip, an instinct she couldn't quite understand driving her actions.

A feral growl filled the room, and he bucked against her hold, the muscles along his arms, torso and neck straining as he pumped faster. Harder. Milking his shaft as come jetted against his belly. Not once did he close his eyes. Just held her stare throughout his release, his gold gaze smoldering behind heavy-lidded eyes.

She lay back down beside him, tenderly whispering her touch parallel to one long, pearly white stream just above his belly button. Too fascinated to pass the opportunity up, she ran her fingertip through it. Sampled the silky glide and texture against her skin.

"I want to mark you with it."

Pleasure speared low in her belly and her sex clenched so hard it was a wonder she didn't come just from his words alone.

He cupped the back of her neck and teased his thumb

along her hairline. "I want to fill you with it. See it slip from your pussy and along your inner thighs after I've taken you."

Another tremor. This one more potent than the last and leaving her breathless. "Tate."

Whether she was asking him to stop or say more, she wasn't entirely sure, but his name on her lips was a lifeline. A much needed foothold on an otherwise perilous cliff.

"Elise, look at me." His low voice coiled around her, rich with a languorous rumble that danced along her skin. A temptation calling her to surrender.

Slowly, she lifted her head.

The calming stroke along the back of her neck never faltered. "I know what we agreed to, but you don't have to do anything you don't want. There's no hurry. Not between us."

Funny. He thought she was hesitant, but the truth was she'd die without his touch. Fears, modesty and insecurity or not, she craved him. Needed him to ease the ache he'd created. To guide her across the unfamiliar terrain. "I'm not changing my mind. Not after that."

A new and fascinating expression crossed his face. One of intrigue and wonder tempered by the indolence of his release. "My mate likes her dirty words *and* her visuals. I think I'm officially the luckiest man alive." He ran his knuckle along her jawline then traced her lower lip with his thumb. "I need to clean up. While I do, you're going to lay right here and relax. No thinking. No doing. Just being. Okay?"

"Okay." It slipped out soft and easy. Though, everything inside her railed at the idea of severing their closeness even for a moment.

He grinned as though he'd been privy to her thoughts, sat up and pressed his lips to hers. "You're pretty agreeable when you're worked up. I'll have to remember that."

Before she could wrangle up some witty or sassy retort, he gave her another quick kiss, rolled off the bed and padded to the bathroom.

She dropped to her back on the bed and let out a frustrated huff, the reality of where they were headed and the apprehensive feelings that went with it tangling with a clawing need for *more*. To dive in headfirst and fully immerse herself in all that was Tate and the exquisite sensations he created.

No thinking. No doing. Just being.

The soft *whoosh* of water from the bathroom blended with Tate's quiet movements. She'd overthought a lot of things in her life. Had taken subtle looks and idle comments made by other people and drawn ridiculous conclusions. Had filled in the blanks with all manner of self-judgment and fear and let those evaluations rule her life.

Maybe Tate was right. Maybe the key to growing with him was just to let go. To be honest about what she was feeling and what she wanted and simply be present. To say what felt good and own her desires.

The bathroom light flicked off and her heart lurched.

Tate strolled back into view and, just like that, her mind quieted. Stilled and steadied itself under his watchful gaze. Focused solely on him.

And oh, what a sight he was. His blond hair loose with those easy waves that made him look like a surfer god. His lean yet muscled body poised beside the bed and his tanned skin perfectly highlighted in the soft glow of the lamp.

He cocked his head and studied her. "Light on or off?"

She wanted to be brave. Wanted to leave it on and share with him what he'd given her, but she also wanted to relax. To give her tentative courage a solid footing.

Say what feels good.

Own it.

"Off."

He smiled like he'd expected as much and turned it off without a beat of hesitation.

Darkness consumed them, broken only by the soft moonlight shafting through huge windows and the shadowed outline of the lake and trees beyond. The bed dipped and the soft swoosh of Tate moving against the comforter filled the silence. His earthy scent blanketed her a second before his weight and his heat.

And then his lips were on hers. His mouth consuming hers in a long, slow, lazy kiss that disengaged her brain and left her floating. Coasting effortlessly into the moment. His fingers traced the outline of her face. Down her neck and along her collarbone. Over her shoulder and back again to cup the back of her neck.

He gently nipped her lower lip and inhaled deep. "Still good?"

Good?

She was great. Ravenous and yet oddly content to let him guide her through the feast he'd promised. She forced her heavy eyelids open. In the shadows, his sharp features seemed softer, but there was no missing the intensity behind his gaze. The acute concentration lasered only on her. "I'm not afraid. Nervous, maybe. Uncertain, but not afraid."

His hand at the back of her neck circled toward the

front, the width of his grip resting lightly just above the hollow of her throat. A possessive touch that would have terrified her had it been anyone else, but strangely centered her with Tate. His thumb skated along her carotid artery, a simple touch that wordlessly conveyed his awareness. As loud as her heart was beating he could probably hear her racing pulse as much as he felt it. "One word from you and I'll stop. No matter what."

His fingers slipped lower, skimmed the sensitized skin above her tank's neckline, then between her breasts and down to slip beneath her shirt's hem. He hesitated only a second, then lifted it up, guiding it up and over her head, then tossed it to the floor. She'd thought she'd have a moment to assimilate. To breathe and adjust. But he dealt with her jeans just as fast. Stripped them past her hips and discarded them with a welcome efficiency, leaving her only in her bra and panties.

Cool air danced against her exposed skin, but the sensation was nothing compared to the feel of his eyes on her. To the outline of him standing tall on his knees, one on either side of hers, and knowing he openly perused her in the moonlight. "You're beautiful."

Soft praise that came a heartbeat before his touch. A rasp of his roughened fingertips just below her belly button. So slow. One caress after another, agonizingly patient and drawn out as he learned her. Explored the curve of her hip. Teased the exposed upper swells of her breasts. The delicate stretch between her belly button and the line of her panties. When he spoke, his low voice was grated and thick with emotion. "It makes me a selfish son of a bitch to say this, but I'm glad you've never done this with anyone else. Glad no other man has ever seen you like this."

Oddly, she was, too. Her whole adult life, she'd felt short-changed by her lack of experience. But with Tate touching her as he was now—watching him watching her and hearing the proprietary edge in his voice—she was grateful for the wait. Thankful it was him who was guiding her into this new world and for every day that had led to it.

Sitting back on his heels, he dragged her bra straps over her shoulders then leaned in and pressed a kiss to the side of her neck. He slid one hand behind her back, his nimble fingers working the clasp even as his words rumbled in her ear. "No other man ever will."

Her bra loosened with a muted snap and her breath caught.

As he straightened, he pulled the fabric free, slowly exposing her breasts.

Goose bumps fanned in all directions and her already straining nipples hardened further, the tight points painfully distended and greedy for attention. While his covetous gaze soaked them in, his hands drifted lower, his touch more urgent. The contact more strained as he hooked his fingers in the waistband of her panties and tugged them past her hips. He tossed them to the floor along with everything else and sat back, his hands fisted on his thighs and his breath churning as heavy as her own. "Sit up and scoot down just a little."

The instruction was the last thing she'd expected. So much so, she followed his direction with zero hesitation. Her mind caught up eventually, though, and chimed in just as he shifted and sat behind her, one thigh framing each of her hips. "What are you doing?"

He dragged her back so her ass sat flush against him and guided her so she reclined against his torso.

Oh, dear God.

Of all the ways she'd expected to feel him against her for the first time, this hadn't even been on the list. But it was strangely comforting. Protective in the way his body cradled hers and yet decadent in the press of his bare flesh against hers. Especially with his cock pressed firmly against the upper swell of her ass.

Rather than answer her question, he wrapped his arms around her waist and tapped her outer thighs. "Open."

Not a request, but a command. One the dark side of herself she was coming to know thrilled to and eagerly wanted to obey. She inched them open, her legs shaking as though her muscles protested the vulnerable position. Air kissed her exposed and aching flesh, making her all too aware of how wet his touch and the night's experiences had left her.

"Very nice." He paired the praise with firm strokes up and down her quads and skimmed his lips from her shoulder to her neck. "I like seeing you spread like that. Ready for me."

Pleasure speared between her legs, the instinct to pull them back together and squeeze until the tremors subsided making her thighs quiver. She bit her lip instead, scrunched her eyes shut and willed her knees to stay where they were instead.

"Now's the time, sweetheart." His lips caressed her ear and his warm breath fanned her cheek. "Show me how you touch yourself. Teach me what you like."

It was weird at first. Tentative and a little awkward. But with each breath, her body settled into a rhythm. Matched each of his inhalations with one of her own and followed the steady thrum of his heart against her back. She cupped her breasts. Lifted and stroked them. Toyed with her nipples and plucked the tips until she didn't care that he watched. Only knew that her body had suffered enough and deserved release.

She slid one hand lower, slicking her fingers through her labia and up to circle her clit.

He palmed the breast she'd abandoned, matching the touch she'd given herself only more firmly, the heat of his palm and the strength of his touch wiping her mind blank. "How wet are you, Elise?"

"Soaked." No hesitation. No shame. Only need. Raw desperation.

He hummed and scraped his teeth along the stretch where her neck and shoulder met. His free hand dipped between her spread legs and teased the inner seam at the top of her thigh, so close to her labia she nearly wept. "Next time, I'll sit between your knees and watch."

Yes.

How she could want that—even crave it considering her lack of experience—she didn't have a clue. Only knew that it appealed at a surprising level and shoved her closer to climax. Not close enough to fall over, but right there, dancing just out of reach.

"What do you need, *mihara*? Tell me."

He knew.

Knew, but wanted her to claim it. To ask for it the same way he'd asked her. "I want you. Your touch to make me come. Not mine."

"You want me to play with your pussy? Stroke you until you come?"

Her sex tightened, release hovering so close. "Please."

Just a tease at first. A subtle graze of his broad fingertip against her swollen flesh. And then he was there.

Slicking through her wetness. Coating her lips and her clit with her arousal and building a demanding patter. Up and down. Skimming her entrance on each pass and driving her higher and higher.

She groaned and arched her back, desperate for air. For more of all he offered. "Tate."

"So wet," he said as though he understood. "Swollen and ready for me." He nipped her earlobe then licked the sting he left behind. "You want to know what I thought of while I brought myself off the last two weeks?"

She tried to answer. Wanted to know as much as she wanted release, but couldn't form any words save *please* and *more* in her mind.

Tate answered anyway, his rumbling voice a wicked temptation at her ear as he pressed one finger at her entrance. "My mouth right here." His finger drifted upward. "My tongue lapping up every drop you make for me." He circled her clit and pressed hard. "Sucking your clit in my mouth and fucking my fingers inside you until you come around them."

Gone.

Utterly and completely lost in the most astounding orgasm of her life. Bolder and more powerful than anything she'd thought possible. A whole-body experience that left her wrecked and utterly exposed even as she soared. Over and over, her sex clenched and released. Grasped for something it knew was missing, but reveled in all the same. Gloried in the promise of what was to come and the terrain left uncharted.

Through it all, he was there. His voice in her ear. His warmth at her back. His scent in her lungs and his touch guiding her through each sensation. Holding her through the explosion and then guiding her back to reality with each languorous caress. Yes, she'd come before, but never like this. With Tate it was different. Bigger. Bolder. Brighter and more powerful.

She rolled her hips against his slowing fingers and moaned, clenching her thighs together and rolling to one side. "Oh my God. I can't believe I just did that."

He chuckled at that, slipped his hand from between her legs and pulled her up so she lay cradled in his lap. His cock stretched hard once more between them, but he guided her head to his shoulder and smoothed his hand along the back of her head as though he wasn't bothered by it in the slightest. "Well, you did, and the image is burned into my brain, so if you need a detailed recounting of events, I can give it to you."

Her cheeks tingled and she buried her face in his chest.

"Oh, no you don't." He hooked her chin with one finger and guided her face toward his. "You don't come for me like that and think anything negative about it. It was beautiful. Perfect."

The burn in her cheeks got hotter, but this time it was the remembered intensity of the moment that cranked up the heat. "It was pretty awesome."

His smile softened and he ran his thumb along the apple of her cheek. "It was more than awesome, *mihara*. It was spectacular." He hesitated a beat and looked her straight in the eye. "It was also the beginning."

Chapter Twelve

Maybe she should have gone with the plain black leggings instead of her gray tie-dyed ones. Or shorts. Or just stayed home altogether and taken a little more time to build her courage before tackling her first training day with the clan.

Careful not to trip on any stray limbs or loose rocks scattered on the path to Priest's house, Elise reconsidered her black slip-on Chucks. "You're sure I'm dressed right?"

Walking beside her on the trail to Priest's house, her mom chuckled and rubbed one hand between Elise's shoulder blades. "You look fine. I've been there for the last two Saturdays and all the women wear comfortable clothes they can move around in."

Comfortable like her mom, maybe. In her loose cotton pants with their coral, pink and raspberry print and a solid coral top, she looked like a yogi flower child. Nowhere near the casual outfit Elise had picked. "Even leggings?"

"Even leggings. Though, you make them look more like a fashion statement. You always have. Those mesh inserts on the sides make your legs look miles long, and your top and Chucks make it spunky."

"Spunky, huh?" It wasn't exactly the look she'd been going for, but considering it would be her first solid foray into regular clan life, a little extra attitude and spunk wouldn't hurt. Tate had already clued her into what to expect—a few hours spent with each of the houses and training with specific magics, and then another hour or two with the warriors where they taught self-defense to everyone. She just hoped the loose black top would give her enough mobility to avoid paring down to the strappy black sports bra underneath when the latter half of the agenda kicked in.

"Relax, sweetheart. It's going to be fine. You'll see." Her mom pushed aside an evergreen branch blocking the path, then held it out of the way for Elise. "I have to say, I'm surprised Tate didn't come to walk you over this morning."

"He wanted to."

"But you didn't?"

"No."

Jenny stopped mid-stride and held Elise back with a hand at her arm. "Did something happen?"

Oh, something had happened all right. In a span of mere days, she'd gone from plodding through a mostly quiet, routine life, to surfing through experiences so rich and emotionally colorful she wondered if her feet would ever touch the ground. And it wasn't just Tate's regular displays of affection either. Wasn't just his drugging kisses or his soothing touch. It was his presence. His attention and care. The combination was overwhelming. Euphoric and frighteningly addictive.

Realizing the goofy smile she seemed to sport most of the time now had crept back onto her face, she ducked her head and motioned her mom forward. "Nothing's happened. I just realized how much time I'd spent with him the last few days and wanted a little alone time with you."

She'd also wanted to leave herself an out in the event her nerves got the better of her and she wanted to chicken out of showing up today. Though, even if she'd tried that approach, Tate likely would have shown up at her front door and carried her to Priest's house.

"You know, you don't have to worry about me, Elise. Being alone isn't a bad thing. I've known since the day you were born that someday you'd find your wings and make your own life."

This time it was Elise who paused in her tracks. "What makes you think I'm leaving?"

Jenny stared at her, a tiny, knowing smile tilting her lips.

"Did you know about Tate? About what he is to me?"

Her mother hesitated a beat, then nodded. "He told me the night of Beltane." Stepping closer, she cupped Elise's shoulders and smoothed her hands up and down her arms. "I'm happy for you, sweetheart. Thrilled to know the Keeper blessed you with such a wonderful man. To know that you'll never have to hide your heritage. That you'll be with someone who'll care for you and support you in everything you do."

Unlike the relationship her mom had had with her father.

She didn't come right out and say it, but the undercurrent was there in her tone. So many things her mom had given up. Her magic. Her companion. Her clan. All because she'd fallen in love with an outsider before she found her own mate. "I'm not leaving you, Mom."

"Not yet. But you will. And I want you to know…

it's okay. I want this for you." Jenny smiled huge and cupped the side of Elise's face. "Now come on. I've seen how some of these Volán men act with their mates. If we don't show soon, Tate will track us down and you'll end up making your first training day appearance slung over his shoulder."

It was a perfect May day. At nearly noon the chill from the night before was almost gone, replaced with a featherlight breeze and temperatures slowly creeping toward seventy. Not a single cloud dotted the brilliant blue sky and new, bold green leaves rustled in the trees around them. With every step toward Priest's house, the chatter of voices and laughter grew stronger, lifting Elise's heart rate right along with it.

Up one gentle slope and the gathering came into view. The number of people was similar to those who'd gathered for Beltane, but the energy this time was different. More focused and purposeful. An abundance of food was laid out on three long folding tables and the four red coolers at one end were no doubt stocked to the gills with drinks, but there was an orderliness to the groupings of people that hadn't been there the last time. Kind of like when she'd done a physical therapy internship rotation with a football team and they had broken up into special teams for training.

She zeroed in on the two groups gathered in loose circles and seated under two different trees. One of them had to be the clan's healers given Vanessa's prominent placement near the center. "Where do I go?"

She hadn't realized she'd paired her question with a death grip on her mother's hand until Jenny covered hers with her own and whispered, "I have no idea. The last few weeks, Naomi carted me around to the different groups, but I don't know if that was the norm, or her just introducing me to everyone." She squeezed Elise's hand and drew her attention to the group of men and women on their feet and physically going at each other head-to-head. "I've got a feeling he knows, though."

Tate.

Dressed in lightweight gray warm-up pants and absolutely nothing else, he was fully engaged in a bout with Alek and dodging punches and kicks thrown so fast she could barely track them all. Why just seeing him eased the tightly coiled tension in her gut she couldn't say, but her lungs rejoiced at the freedom to actually draw a decent breath, and her body perked up in a way no amount of coffee could ever replicate.

Footsteps sounded on the wooden steps from the raised deck behind her a second before Kateri's smooth voice jolted her out of her dumbstruck ogling. "They're fun to watch, aren't they?"

Elise cleared her throat and prayed the heat crawling up her neck wasn't as noticeable as it felt. "I'm not sure *fun* is the word I'd use." Fluid, maybe. Powerful and deadly, for sure. She dared another look, only to find Tate had noted her arrival and left Alek hanging to jog her direction. "It looks dangerous."

"Maybe," Katy said. "But the more you watch them, the more you realize that's what their magic's about. They're deeply physical and the movements come naturally." She chuckled and lowered her voice. "By the way, nice work on the tattoo. I'm *so* going to make Priest teach me how to do that."

"Oh my." This from her mother on an indrawn breath that spoke of shock and wonder. "Did you do that?"

Before she could answer, Tate was there and pulling

her flush against him. Not the least bit concerned with her mother's presence, he cupped the back of her head and pressed an intimate, yet firm and lingering kiss to her lips. "Hey," he murmured against her mouth too few heartbeats later.

"Hey." As clever responses went, it was terribly lame, but per usual when Tate was close or touching her, her brain refused to function at anything more than the most basic level.

Behind them, Katy cleared her throat, effectively rattling reality back into focus. "I guess the tattoo wasn't enough to make a statement."

"It was either that or beat his chest like a caveman," Priest said moving into sight just to one side of Tate. He clasped Tate on the shoulder and leaned in enough to murmur, "You might want to slow your roll a bit, killer. Maybe let her get her bearings."

His words brought the gorge's utter silence into laser sharp focus. No chatter. No laughter. No grunts or shouts from the warriors beyond.

Just utter, fixated silence.

The anxiousness that fired through her must have shown on her face, because her mom bit her lip in an effort to curb her smile.

Elise frowned up at Tate, thankful his body mostly blocked them from view. "Everyone's looking at us, aren't they?"

He grinned, utterly unrepentant. "God, I hope so."

"Yep. Total caveman." This time Priest used the hand at his shoulder to urge Tate away. "Hands off and let me get her settled. You can preen and prance around with her later."

Tate relented, but snagged her hand as he unwound his arm from her back. "She can stay with the warriors."

"She'll have time to work with each of the houses over time, but today she's starting with the healers."

"She doesn't have to start there," Tate said. "Her grandfather was warrior house. She gets equal time between the two until she knows her magic."

"She starts with the healers, Tate." A final command, given with zero give.

Tate glared up at him, his mouth a hard line and his eyes burning with arguments left unspoken.

Pure instinct and the need to get the silent spectators behind them focused on something else, Elise moved in close to Tate and pressed her palm to his stomach. "It's okay. I'll be fine."

Priest noted the action, volleyed one of those shrewd, assessing parental looks between the two of them, then zeroed in on Tate. "Something I need to know?"

"No," Elise said before Tate could answer. "I'm good learning whatever I need to learn. Tate's just being protective."

Priest's gaze narrowed further then shifted to the healer group before rounding back to Elise. "Did something else happen?"

"Nothing I can't handle." And she would. In the last few days, she'd thought long and hard about Vanessa and the parallels their encounters ran to Elise's past. She'd wished for years for a chance to do things over. To find the courage to stand up for herself and see how differently things played out. Fate had finally given her that chance. This time, she was going to make the opportunity count.

She smoothed her hand up Tate's chest and covered

her name over his heart. "Really, I'll be fine. It's the right thing to do."

His grip on her hand tightened and the sour look on his face said he wasn't buying it.

As matter-of-fact as could be, Katy stepped in beside her. "I'll be there. I haven't spent much time with the healers yet, and it's not like I have anyone but Priest to train with anyway."

"Me, too." Her mom moved in on her other side. "But after we're done I want to hear about the tattoo thing and how you got Elise to do it."

The double whammy diversion tactic seemed to work, Tate's glower morphing into something closer to a manly pout.

Priest eyeballed Jenny and Kateri and jerked his head toward the healers still mostly blocked from Elise's view by Tate's body. "You two head on over. Elise and I will be there in a minute." Not waiting for them to shift into motion, he slapped Tate on the back. "Kiss your mate and get back to business. We'll take care of her."

Tate sucked in a huge inhale, and his nostrils flared like he was seconds away from just picking her up, hauling her out of the gorge and telling the whole world to go to hell. Instead, he cupped the back of her head and sealed his mouth to hers. It was the same fit as when he'd greeted her. The same lingering contact. But this kiss was a claim. A promise and a challenge to anyone watching rolled up into one. He rested his forehead against hers. "Don't let her mess with your head."

"I won't." At least that was the goal. Though, she had to admit, the whole facing-her-fears pep talk she'd given herself the last few days was a whole lot easier to listen to when there weren't over a hundred people on hand

for game time. She stroked her hand down his sternum
and backed away. "Now go, so I can get this over with."

He jerked a terse nod, aimed a pointed look at Priest
she couldn't quite decipher as he backed away, then
jogged toward the waiting warriors.

Yep.

Definitely over a hundred people.

And while some of the chatter from those gathered had picked back up and a smattering of people
had grown bored with the show, the vast majority still
watched and waited.

They're just an audience.

No different than the meets she'd attended for gymnastics or the parents who'd endured long dance recit-
als or competitions.

She lifted her chin and faced Priest with what she
hoped looked like more confidence than she felt. "Okay,
so what do I do?"

His lips twitched and those mystic gray eyes of his
sparked with laughter barely held in check. "Well, I
was going to give you one of those chin-up-and-own-
your-destiny talks, but I think you've already got that
one under control."

Under control was debatable. More like the stubborn
nature that had made her so good in competitive sports
had finally woken up and found a new focus. "Yeah,
but I don't have a clue what I'm wading into. How does
all this work?"

He guided her toward the healer group with a hand at
her shoulder blades, his pace an easy gait that allowed
them time to talk. While the circle they were bound for
was the farthest away, he still lowered his voice. "You

see the woman next to Vanessa? Long gray hair with braids on one side?"

Funny. Until Priest had pointed her out, Elise had completely missed her. But now that she really looked at the woman, it wasn't that she was insignificant, but more that her peaceful countenance and graceful posture made her blend in with the world around her. And while it had looked like Vanessa was running the group at first glance, the fresh perspective proved the older woman was firmly in control. Vanessa was just rooted next to her and ready to jump in the first chance she got.

"That's Meara," Priest said. "She's 189 and the oldest person in our clan we know of still living. She and your grandmother were very good friends."

189.

Almost two centuries old.

No matter how many times Elise tried to imagine what it would be like to live so long, her brain refused to cooperate. It wasn't until movement registered in front of Meara that Elise realized there was someone stretched out on the ground. "What's she doing?"

"It's not what *she's* doing. Look closer."

A woman sat on Meara's other side, her head bowed over the person in front of them so her dark hair covered her features. "That's Sara."

"And the little girl in front of her is Janie. She twisted her ankle a few days ago and Sara's fixing it."

"So, training day for healers is kind of like open clinic for the clan?"

Priest grinned down at her. "Something like that. Where warriors use the self-defense portion of the day to bond with people from the other houses, healers do the same and strengthen their skills by seeing to everyone's ailments."

"What do they do when there's no one to heal?"

He chuckled and paused in the center of the gorge, motioning to the people around them. "We've got about a hundred and twenty here today. There are probably another fifty to sixty who live nearby and another hundred or so that live farther away. There's almost always someone to heal. Even if it's only a scratch or a pulled muscle." He dipped his head toward the warriors going at each other like their lives depended on it. "And those knuckleheads are guaranteed customers on training days. It's not *if* someone gets hurt, but *who*."

Her gaze locked on to Tate, thankfully not engaged with anyone at the moment, but standing with his arms crossed at the edge of his group and watching Elise like a hawk.

Priest tapped her shoulder. "Come on. He's not going to stand down until he knows you're okay."

The introductions went by in a blur, far too many names for her to have a prayer of remembering when the day was over. Unfortunately, Priest saved Meara for last and guided Elise to the top of the circle rather than letting her settle in at the far edge of the group like she'd planned. "Meara, this is Elise Ralston. Cara's granddaughter."

Not an outright statement that Priest was banking on Elise being the next prima, but a solid reference to her lineage nonetheless.

Meara beamed up at her, her smile brilliant even if her pale blue eyes seemed unfocused. "Finally." Still kneeling on the ground, she held up both hands toward Elise, their aim toward Elise just a fraction off. "Priest said you might venture out today, so I had my daughter drive me in for a visit. Come. Sit next to me."

Not unfocused eyes.

Sightless.

And yet something about the joy behind them stilled the bulk of Elise's worries and doubts the way her mother's presence and soothing touch could wipe away the worst nightmares.

"Meara lives about four hours south of here," Priest said. "Just south of the Ouachita Forest near Hot Springs."

Elise shifted enough to grasp her hands and squeezed. "I hope you didn't drive all the way up here just to meet me."

"Of course, I did. Your grandmother was one of my best friends and an exceptional prima." Keeping Elise's hands in hers, Meara twisted her head to Vanessa beside her. "Scoot over a little and make room for her, Nessa."

Vanessa might have covered her anger during Priest's subtle reference to Elise's prima grandmother, but there was no missing the indignation on her face at being displaced as Meara's right hand.

Unerring in her aim despite her blindness, Meara leaned toward the blonde-headed little girl stretched out in front of her and stroked her forehead. "How does it feel, Janie?"

Janie circled her foot. "It feels good to me. No pain anywhere."

Sara still didn't move, just kept her gaze rooted on Meara, her mouth pinched as though uncertain.

Still leaning over the girl, Meara stilled, only her thumb moving in a calming back-and-forth rhythm on Janie's forehead. Finally, she nodded and sat back on her heels. "You did a fine job, Sara. You're getting stronger."

Sara let out a heavy exhale and smiled huge. "That's a relief." She leaned forward enough to offer her hand to help Janie up. "Thanks for trusting me, kiddo."

Janie took the hand, but given how nimbly she made it to her feet, it was more of a polite gesture than a necessity. "Thanks for fixing me!" She hugged Sara with an easy exuberance that almost toppled Sara backward, then darted off toward a cluster of children playing well away from the training groups, shouting, "Hey, Joey! Look! I'm all fixed!"

Soft laughter rounded the circle.

As it slowly died off, Meara covered Elise's hand and addressed the group. "Okay, let's pair off and see to those who're left." She paused just enough to aim her cloudy eyes toward Vanessa at Elise's left. "Nessa, why don't you roam group to group and offer some guidance rather than heal today."

To Elise's ears, the direction seemed innocent. A request for assistance and an honor given all rolled up into one. But the aggravation on Vanessa's face and the almost palpable anger coming off her screamed of a woman stripped of an opportunity. "But I haven't had a chance to practice today. How can I get better if I don't practice?"

"Part of learning is in the giving. Your skills are strong. Sharing with your other healers will make you stronger."

For a second, Elise expected Vanessa to argue.

Instead, she pushed to her feet, studiously avoiding Elise's gaze as she brushed a stray leaf off her leggings and almost stomped out of earshot.

"She's gifted, but misguided." As low as Meara said it, Elise wondered if she'd even meant to say it out loud. Then she squeezed Elise's hand and confirmed the information had been shared with intent. "She'll be yours to wrestle soon enough. It's good you're facing the challenge now rather than later."

Okay, that was freaky. Tate had mentioned the clan tended to have a healthy grapevine, but she hadn't realized it ran all the way to Hot Springs. "You picked up on that, huh?"

"The second you and your mother arrived, I felt it. She knows she'll never be the prima, but she's been one of our strongest healers and having you here poses a threat to her position." A sly smile curved her lips. "The fact that you've found your mate even before you received your magic is just salt on the wounds."

"I guess that means she saw the tattoo?"

"Saw the tattoo. Heard the other warriors congratulating him on being gifted with such a fine mate. Heard everyone anticipating you being here today. She's wound up and ready for a fight, but you'll overcome it. You come from a strong line of exceptional women." Meara sucked in a slow breath, patted Elise's hand, then tucked her hands in her lap. "Now. Tell me all about life in Louisiana."

The next half hour flew by, Elise answering every question Meara threw at her. The nonstop queries had just started to slow and Elise was thinking she'd finally be able to ask a few of her own when a sharp cry and an eerie thud sounded from the warrior group.

Settled farthest away, Elise and Meara were the last to reach the crowd. They'd have never made it through the crush if it weren't for Meara's stern "Move. Now."

Her heart in her throat and body racing with adrenaline, Elise scanned every warrior gathered as she led Meara through the crowd. Just as she cleared the front line, her gaze locked on to Tate standing directly behind Vanessa who'd crouched next to the injured woman awkwardly splayed on one side.

Vanessa kneeled so the woman's head was directly in line with Vanessa's knees. "It's her neck. Let's roll her to her back."

"No!" Either the volume behind Elise's command or sheer shock froze everyone where they stood. "You can't move her."

For a healer, the glower Vanessa shot Elise was better suited for murder. "I'm a healer."

"So am I."

"Don't give me that. You don't even know what you are yet."

"Not a healer in Volán terms, but educated enough to know physiology. The way she's lying, if you move her she won't be alive for you to heal."

"You're not my prima. You don't tell me what to do."

Priest's low and unforgiving voice settled on the clearing like a gavel. "No, but your priest does." Like a judge and executioner who'd watched unnoticed from the edges of the crowd, Priest unfolded his arms and walked forward. "Elise, what would you do?"

Meara shifted her grip on Elise's arm and nudged her forward at the small of her back, the simple action an unmistakable encouragement.

So many people, and yet every person was quiet, only the injured woman's strained breaths mingling with rustling treetops overhead. Elise crept forward and kneeled on the opposite side of the woman. She felt more than saw Tate's presence solidify behind her all of a heartbeat later. Not so close as to crowd her, but there, lending his strength and support. "What's your name?"

The answer was so quiet, Elise had to lean in to hear it. "Kallie."

Elise smoothed the hair that had escaped her ponytail off her face. "Kallie, can you move your toes for me?"

Kallie's breathing hitched, and a tiny sob slipped past her lips. "Did they move?"

Murmurs sounded behind her, the tenor of them echoing the dread in Elise's gut. Rather than answer directly, Elise stretched out and firmly pinched Kallie's ankle. "Can you feel that?"

"No."

She tried again on Kallie's wrist. "Can you feel that?"

"No."

Bracing herself with a deep breath, Elise wiped away a fresh tear from Kallie's face. "It's okay. You're going to be okay." At least she hoped the woman would be. If Vanessa or Meara couldn't heal her, Elise would be an absolute liar.

She locked gazes with Priest first. "You can't move her. If you can heal her, do it where she is."

"I can do it," Vanessa bit off.

"Not with that energy you won't." Led by Sara, Meara shuffled forward and motioned Vanessa out of the way. "If it's as serious as Elise says it is, then you'd need to be more emotionally grounded to do the job needed."

"I'm grounded," Vanessa said.

"This isn't a game." Where the steel in Elise's voice came from, she didn't have a clue, but it was strong enough Vanessa's gaze whipped to her and widened with shock. "Whatever your beef with me is, we'll deal with it, but not when a woman is this seriously injured. Step back and let Meara do it."

Vanessa stared at her for all of a beat, then scanned the gathered crowd, her gaze landing on Priest next to Elise last.

He didn't speak. Just stood there with his arms crossed. Waiting.

Lowering her head, Vanessa nodded, pushed to her feet and stepped back.

Almost the second Meara settled next to the girl and placed one hand at the back of her neck, the air around them changed. Stilled with an indefinable reverence. Seconds that should have been riddled with concern and tension drifted into easy, yet heightened minutes and Elise could have sworn even the forest held its breath, waiting and lending its strength.

Finally, Meara leaned forward and whispered something in Kallie's ear.

Kallie's foot shifted a second later, followed by the slow stretch of her leg. "I can feel them."

Whatever she said after was lost in the chorus of shouts and praise for Meara's work, the weight of potential tragedy happily traded for triumph and relief.

Elise let out her own shaky breath, the onslaught of post-trauma adrenaline making her light-headed enough she'd have likely tipped over had she been standing.

Tate steadied her with a hand at her shoulder and moved in closer so his torso blanketed her back. "You did good."

"I didn't do anything. Meara did."

"Elise." He squeezed her shoulder as if to drive the rest of his words home. "If you hadn't stepped in, Kallie might not have gone home at all today. You did good. Not to mention, made a huge impression on the clan."

All around them, people waited for their turn to pay Meara their respect and hug a now bewildered looking Kallie where she stood beside her. Everyone but Vanessa. Even her usual crew seemed missing in the crush, leaving her isolated and on the far end of the fray.

But she was there. Her arms crossed and her gaze glacially cold. And every bit of her anger was directed squarely at Elise. "Maybe some of them. But there's at least one who likely wishes Draven had found me before Priest did."

Chapter Thirteen

His mate was quiet. Too quiet now that Tate thought about it. In the two weeks since Elise's first training day with the clan, he'd learned many things about her, but at the top of the heap was how she only got quiet and distant when she was gnawing on something in her head.

Walking steady by his side, her footsteps were nearly as silent against the forest's undergrowth as his own, each stride far more confident in the darkness than they'd been their first night walking home. Considering she didn't have the benefit of an animal's sight and only a crescent moon hung overhead, it was a hell of a feat.

But there was something else about her silence that bugged him. An uncomfortable current that made his coyote's hackles bristle. He slowed his steps and gently squeezed her hand in his. "What's on your mind?"

She startled a little as though he'd yanked her from a daydream. "What?"

"You haven't said a thing since we left Priest's house." And even then, she'd been a little distant. While they still hadn't moved further physically than their first night in the cabin, most nights had been a mix of easy flowing conversations and sexual exploration, each day reflecting her growing comfort. But tonight, lingering around the firepit behind Priest's house, she'd been distracted. Unplugged from the rest of the conversation around her.

She shrugged and eased close enough her shoulder brushed his arm. "You're going to think I'm nuts."

"I highly doubt that. Jade's nuts, so I know firsthand what it looks like."

Her soft smile scattered some of the tension moving through her, but not enough to completely dispel it.

"Spill," Tate said. "Brooding's bad for the soul."

"That sounds like a Priest-ism."

"That's because it is. I think I heard it on a daily basis from the time I turned fourteen until my early twenties."

She nodded, but kept her gaze rooted on the ground.

Rather than press, Tate kept his silence.

It took another handful of seconds, but she finally pulled in a long breath and said, "I'm worried about Vanessa."

Now, *that* was the last thing he'd expected. He halted dead in his tracks and pulled her to a stop beside him. "Why?"

"Because she wasn't there tonight."

"That's a good thing."

"She wasn't there last week either."

"Double bonus."

She tried to fight her smile with an exaggerated frown, but it couldn't quite hide the mirth in her eyes. "Okay, I'll admit it's been nice not to have the drama, but aren't you worried about her? I mean, she can be a bitch, but I don't want anyone from the clan feeling ostracized. She's a healer. A good one. The last thing we need is to lose someone with her skills."

That right there.

That single display of concern and her focus on the bigger picture was why he was certain to his bones Elise would be the healer prima. "You're thinking of her as one of your healers, not as an adversary."

"I'm thinking of her as a person." She shrugged again and started meandering toward the house again. "Probably makes me a glutton for punishment, but I just wondered if there wasn't something I should do. Maybe reach out to her somehow and see if she's okay."

He caught an outstretched limb directly in line with her head and pulled it out of her path right before she walked into it. "If it was anyone but Vanessa, I'd say you were probably right, but she created her situation. A sting that lasts awhile is one you tend to remember longer."

She chuckled, a little of the lightness he'd grown so accustomed to the last few weeks pushing past her pre-occupied demeanor. "That sounds like another quote from Priest."

"Yeah, I heard that one a few times, too."

Ahead, the back porch lights from Elise's house glinted between the thick tree trunks. Tate snatched her hand and spun her so the widest one was at her back, effectively blocking her from the wide windows at the back of the house. "You sure that's it?"

Elise wrinkled her nose. "Thinking about Vanessa all night's not enough?"

"You have a point." He cupped the side of her neck and backed her one last step so her shoulders were flush with the tree. Even with her thoughts out in the open, something still felt off, but he was loath to push it. Especially with the topic he'd been itching to bring up all day. "I don't like leaving you at night."

For the first time all afternoon, her face lit up, her smile pure joy in physical form. "We've been coming back so late at night, it hardly counts to say we're apart."

"I want to make it so we're not apart."

He'd meant to lay the concept out with a little more finesse and considering the instant heat that flashed across her face, he figured fast-and-to-the-point hadn't been a total fail.

Her lips parted, and he'd damned well bet in better lighting he'd have found a flush on her cheeks and neck. "I'm not sure I know how to interpret that."

"You and me under one roof. You falling asleep next to me and saying good morning instead of good night."

"But Priest's house is already packed with you, Alek, Naomi, Katy and Jade."

"Priest has already broken ground on the house he's building for Katy. That knocks the headcount down inside three to five months, and if it bugs you being around them all in the meantime, then we can stay at the cabin."

She splayed one hand above his heart, the simple touch so much more confident than those first hours they'd spent alone he could hardly contain a howl. "I like the cabin."

Fuck, he did, too. Loved all the memories they'd made there already. Loved seeing her curves high-lighted by moonlight and shadows—a regular occur-rence considering she'd yet to bare herself to him in any stronger light.

"But if I leave, my mom will be alone."

Her near whispered statement would have sucked the hope right out of his sails if he hadn't already spent an inordinate amount of time hashing possible options.

"She doesn't have to be. Naomi's patient as a saint, but she'd gotta be tired of sharing space with Jade. She loves your mom and might appreciate being around someone she can relate to."

Her gaze dropped to where her fingers played back and forth against his T-shirt above his sternum. "I don't know." She met his stare and frowned. "You don't think that might make Naomi feel weird? Like she's not wanted or something?"

"Are you kidding me? We're talking about a natural born matchmaker. I'm halfway surprised she wasn't the one to suggest it."

Actually, now that he thought about it, he'd gotten the idea three mornings ago when Naomi had offhandedly over breakfast shared how much she missed chatting with other women her age. For all he knew, it'd been a tactical comment custom tailored to send him in the right direction. Naomi was crafty as hell that way. "So, what do you think?"

That odd sensation he'd been sensing all night kicked in again. Not uncomfortable this time so much as different. Foreign and stirring his coyote's awareness.

Elise pressed her palms up and outward, stroking his shoulders and triceps in a surprisingly aggressive way. She urged him closer. "Can I think about it?"

The tone didn't match her words. If anything, the underlying message was a resounding yes. Especially with the way her gaze was rooted on his lips.

He gave her the contact she wanted and angled her face to his with a hand at the back of her head. "I'm not going to rush you." At least, he was trying not to, even if his dick had its own agenda. Like right about now, all it wanted was a chance to sink inside her pussy and glory in the wet heat his fingers had been privy to. He braced his free hand on the tree behind her and forced himself to go slow. Fit his lips to hers and prayed the hunter inside him would hang on just one more day. One more minute.

She sighed into his kiss and eagerly opened for him. Teased her tongue against his and playfully nipped his lower lip.

He groaned and deepened the kiss, an action she encouraged with nails sinking deep into his shoulders. Fisting his hand at the back of her head, he dragged her mouth away from his and arched his neck and shoulders into her wild grasp. His coyote's warning growl rumbled up his throat and his muscles strained.

"Tate." No fear in her voice. Not a drop. Just pure hunger. A ravenous hunger that rattled the cage on his control.

Not yet.

Not now.

Fuck, she couldn't even bare herself to him fully yet. If he took her with his beast in charge, he'd scare the living hell out of her. "Go inside."

"I don't want to go inside."

"Elise, go. Now."

"Why?"

Chest heaving, he forced his eyes open and faced her, knowing full well what she'd see.

A predator's eyes—part man, part beast, but the whole of him ready to possess what he wanted.

She gasped and would have knocked the back of her head against the tree had it not been for his hand holding her steady. Still, she stayed rooted in place.

"Elise, you either go inside, or the first time I take you will be right here, pinned against this tree."

Her eyes dilated and, for a second, he was certain she'd sink her nails in deeper and demand he follow through.

But she dipped her head and released her grip, instead. "Are you okay?"

"I'll run. I'll be fine." Hell, in the last two weeks, he'd covered every inch of Priest's sizable land burning off the edge leaving her left him with. Tonight, he might have to run the length of two states.

He uncoiled his fingers from her hair, too unstable to risk another kiss, and somehow managed a shaky step backward. "Go. I'll pick you up for work in the morning."

With one last lingering, uncertain look, she turned and started toward the house. Slow at first, then breaking into a jog as if it was the only way she could manage the separation.

The bond was definitely there. Not sealed by any means, but getting stronger every day. Tonight, it had practically pulsed between them, the changed energy inside her flooding the connection so completely letting her step inside the house bordered on impossible.

Soon.

The confident message from his companion was all knowing. Grounded in wisdom beyond Tate's human comprehension and calling him to surrender to his other half. He welcomed the change. Absorbed the sting against his skin as the magic burned through him and his coyote took over. The peace was instant, his companion's form a welcome cage for the roiling need she'd stoked too close to the surface with her kiss.

Elise paused at the back door, scanned the tree line and smiled when her gaze locked on his beast. "Good night, Tate." A simple statement offered in a soft voice no singura could have heard at his distance.

But Tate heard it. Felt it in every part of him. He answered with a lift of his muzzle and a sharp bark that sent her hurrying inside. The unmistakable slide of the thick dead bolt registered a second later and her shadow drifted behind the closed living room curtains.

Still, he waited. Watched her bedroom light come on. Listened through the muted rush of water and the faint strains of music. Only when her light went off and every sound inside the house settled did he move, stalking the house's perimeter as he had every other night before leaving her to run. A stronger wind than normal rustled the treetops and carried with it a hint of the smoldering fire the straggling clan members were no doubt still gathered around outside Priest's house. Otherwise, all was as it should be. Every chirp, hoot or croak of the forest's inhabitants a balm to further still his restlessness.

A twig snapped.

Tate froze and zeroed in on the sound, its source directly opposite where he stood near one corner of the front entrance.

Leaves whooshed and light, but steady footsteps trekked toward the main highway.

There.

Definitely a person. And whoever it was was dressed in dark clothing and no taller than Elise or Jade.

Tate followed, running parallel to the shadowed form until he'd gained enough ground to circle around and gain a solid visual. A light flowery scent hung on the air. Something manufactured rather than natural.

I'm worried about Vanessa.

She hadn't been there tonight and she was a fan of perfumes. So much so, his coyote had always bristled after too much time in her presence.

Close, but still not to the road, the footsteps slowed and stopped.

A car door chunked open, then slammed shut.

The service road.

He'd forgotten about the new road Priest had begun to build for his new home. A perfect place for someone to park if they wanted to get close and roam undetected. All pretense of stealth pushed aside, he shot forward, pouring all his magic into his speed.

An engine revved to life. Tires spun against soft soil and headlights flooded the darkness, burning and blinding his eyes. With one last burst of energy, he leapt, straining to focus through the overpowering brightness.

Pain exploded in his hip, a blast of searing agony that ricocheted up and down his spine. The forest spun, and his head and shoulders took the brunt as his body crashed to the main road's asphalt.

Broken.

Elise.

Danger.

His coyote's thoughts were his last before the shift blasted through him, leaving him huddled in human form on the ground. The kaleidoscope red of receding taillights narrowed and faded.

Then…nothing.

Chapter Fourteen

Elise bolted upright in bed, her gasp still hanging shroud-like in the dark room and her heart pounding an irregular beat.

No threat. At least none she could distinguish in the room's shadows. But something had woken her. Ripped her from an eerily deep sleep and thrust her headlong into what felt like a waking nightmare. A cold sweat fanned along her forehead and the fine hairs along the back of her neck and down her arms prickled as though unseen ghosts danced around her. "Mom?"

Silence.

With trembling hands, she pushed the covers aside and hurried to the window, her light cotton sleep pants and the fitted tank she'd worn to bed doing nothing to fight the sudden chill.

Moonlight.

Stillness.

Everything exactly as it should be.

But she couldn't shake the unease. The iron-weighted lethargy in her bones. The deeply seated certainty that something was terribly wrong.

Tate.

A shiver ran the length of her spine and urged her

into motion. She snatched an oversized sweatshirt she'd thrown over her desk chair, shrugged it on and nabbed her cell phone on the way out the door. Pausing at the bottom of the stairs, she scanned the open foyer. The living room. The kitchen beyond.

All quiet.

Her mother's voice sounded from the top of the staircase behind her. "Elise?"

Where was Tate? He was here. She felt it. How, she didn't have a clue, but he was there. Somewhere. And he was hurting. Badly.

"Elise, what's wrong?"

"Call Priest."

"Why?"

She had no clue. Only knew that whatever it was, she wouldn't be able to handle it on her own.

Moonlight shafted through the front door's square panes, leaving a geometric spotlight on the floor to her left. *Outside.* "Just call him. Tell him to hurry."

She was out the front door and racing across the wide wooden porch before her brain bothered to catch up, instinct a whip that dogged her every step. Gravel and scattered twigs along the long drive to the highway dug into her bare feet.

"Tate?" Her shout rounded through the forest, an eerie boomerang effect that left her cold and empty. "Tate, where are you?"

Nothing. Not even the normal sounds she'd grown so accustomed to in the weeks she'd spent roaming the woods with her mate. Lungs heaving, she reached the end of the drive. Darkness stretched in both directions, the only color to break the emptiness the white and yellow lines that marked the asphalt.

Except one of the yellow lines had a break in it. A long-ish chunk that stood out in the darkness.

No.

Not a chunk.

A huddled mass.

"Tate!" She ran across the road and dropped to her knees, the uncontrolled descent and the road's harsh surface scraping the flesh beneath her sleep pants. The pulse at his neck beat steady, but was far too weak. Blood trickled from a head wound near his temple and, curled on his side at an awkward angle, there was no way she was moving him. Not without someone far more skilled than she was to properly package him onto a backboard with a cervical collar.

The growl of a big engine moving fast rumbled in the distance and headlights glowed around the bend.

"Please be Priest." Elise thumbed the light on her phone, waited until the vehicle rounded the corner, then waved it overhead. Priest or not, she wasn't risking either of them adding hit-and-run to the list of damages.

"Get off the road." Tate's voice was the last thing she'd expected to hear, and as low as it was, she almost missed it over the increasing roar from the vehicle moving closer. Quiet or not, the command behind his words was pure alpha. "Not protected."

The wards. They only went as far as the road and with Tate out for the count she had zero protection.

She still wasn't moving. "Priest is on his way."

"Get off the road."

"I'm not leaving. Tell me where you're hurt."

He tried to move, pushing up on one forearm and bracing the other low on his hips. One leg seemed to cooperate, but the one closest to the ground didn't budge.

"Tate, no!"

"You need to get back on our property."

"I need you to stay still. Is it your leg? Your hip?"

The car rounded the curve and raced toward them.

Still stubbornly trying to get up, Tate dragged himself in front of her, his painful groan knifing through her.

"Tate, stop it. It's Priest."

Sure enough, Priest's black Tahoe screeched to a halt on the opposite side of the road.

Priest had barely gotten both feet out of the truck before Tate started in again. "Get her back behind the wards."

"I'm fine," Elise said, grateful to see Katy hurrying around the hood to join them.

"Someone was watching her house," Tate bit out to Priest. "A woman. A Honda, I think. Newer. Black or dark blue, maybe."

One look from Priest said he not only wanted her back behind the wards as bad as Tate did, but had a mind to make it happen no matter Tate's condition. "Go. I'll take care of him."

"No."

Katy crouched beside Elise, her voice calm and compassionate despite the wild energy spinning around them. "They need to focus, Elise. Until you're safe, that's not going to happen with either of them."

"He's hurt."

"Elise?" Her mother's voice drifted across the highway over the engine's steady idle. "What happened?" She hesitated mid-stride across the road, spied Tate sprawled on his side in front of her, then high-stepped it the rest of the way there. "My God, Tate. Are you okay?"

"Fine. Get Elise to the house." Tate looked from Jenny to Elise, his eyes obviously glazed with pain and his chest heaving. "Please."

"Go," Katy said. "Priest and I will get him in the truck and up to your house. We'll call a healer. He'll be fine, but loading him up without hurting him more than necessary is going to take some time and neither of them are going to focus as long as you're off protected land."

"Elise…" Tate clenched his jaw and squeezed his eyes shut.

"Okay. I'm going." She forced herself to stand and take a step back. The pulsating connection that had guided her to him in the first place vibrated with a silent fury, fighting the distance she created with every step. Even the weight of her mother's arm around her shoulders and her comforting scent didn't help. Only made her want to trade it for Tate's strength. To drown in his woods-and-earth scent and feel his skin against hers.

Tucked tight to her mother's side, she made the long trek back to the house on adrenaline-shaken legs, the gravel and sharp debris that had been so inconsequential to her bare feet only minutes before now a brutal punishment.

"Just breathe, Elise." Her mother hugged her closer and smoothed her hand up and down her arm. "He'll be just fine. You've seen for yourself what the clan's healers can do, and Tate's in nowhere near the condition Kallie was a few weeks ago." She tried to guide Elise to the porch swing.

Elise shrugged it off and paced the length of the railing, her gaze rooted to the soft glow from Priest's Tahoe at the end of the drive. "We had Meara here for

Kallie. Vanessa's the next strongest healer we have, and I pissed her off. Even if she's good enough to fix whatever's wrong with him, she might refuse to help."

"Then we'll deal with it. Tate's strong. He was wide-awake and ready to do battle if it meant getting you back inside Priest's wards. Fear is just skewing your perspective."

Fear? Fear was chump change compared to the emotion roiling around in her gut. To the razor-sharp sting cutting beneath her skin. The way he'd been able to move, any debilitating spinal injury was unlikely, but there was no telling what internal damage he might have suffered.

"Have you bonded with him, Elise?"

It was a reasonable question. Especially the way she'd been ripped out of a dream and guided to him. "I don't know." She'd felt something. That much was certain. But there was a part missing, too. Invisible puzzle pieces she was too terrified to look at. She squeezed the porch rail and stared down the driveway, willing the steady headlights to move. Strained her ears for the elevated sound of an engine in motion. "He wants me to move in with him."

Her mother moved in beside her. "It's where you're supposed to be, sweetheart."

An hour ago, she might have argued. Might have pushed for slowness and more time, but after tonight— after clawing through the dread she'd awoken with and clawing through the terror now—now she knew better. "I don't understand it. Not any of it." She swallowed hard and met her mother's compassionate gaze. "But I don't want to fight it either. It feels *right*."

"But you're worried about me."

Her vision blurred through a surge of tears and her lips trembled. "You're the only one who's ever been here for me. The only one who understood the stuff at school. The things I struggled with. You were always there for me." Her breath hitched and a tear slipped free. "But when you needed me, I didn't believe you."

Jenny pulled her into a hug and tucked her face in the crook of her neck, the slow, calming stroke of her hand against the back of her head comforting as only a mother's touch could be. "It's okay, Elise. You did the best you could. You thought what most sane people would think with what I was able to show you. It's over. And just because you're living with Tate doesn't mean we're not together." She paused a beat. "I don't want you missing even a second of what I lost. When you worry about me, think about that instead."

Headlights swept across the front porch and the throaty rumble of Priest's Tahoe coming down the drive punched Elise's heartbeat back into top gear. He hadn't even put the truck in park before she jerked the back door open.

Nothing.

And no one in the passenger's seat where Katy should have been.

"Where is he?"

Priest slid out of the driver's seat with far too much calm for her liking and rounded to the back hatch. "I checked him before I moved him. No internal injuries that I could sense, but his hip's mangled." He popped the hatch and her breath caught.

Tate lay flat on his back, out cold, with Katy beside him.

She started to scramble inside, but Priest cut her off,

leaning in and carefully hauling Tate into his arms. "What happened to him?"

"I knocked him out."

"You what?" She hurried after him, following him through the front door her mother held open and up the stairs.

"I knocked him out."

"It's not what you think," Katy added from tight behind Elise. "Priest's magic gives him control of his clan. The pain would've been too much for him otherwise."

Priest paused at the top of the stairs long enough for Elise to slide ahead of them and through the door to her room. Only when Tate was laid out on her bed and she was next to him did her heart find a heavy yet regular rhythm. "Have you called Vanessa?"

Rather than answer, Priest toed off his boots.

Kateri studiously avoided Elise's gaze.

"Priest, what are you doing? You need to call Vanessa."

Her mother must have sensed the odd mood in the room, because she took a few steps backward toward the door.

Down to his bare feet, Priest peeled off his shirt, displaying the mass of rugged tribal tattoos along his shoulders and back. He faced her, but his focus was solely on Tate, and the look he aimed at him was angry frustration. "I'm not calling Vanessa."

"What? Why?"

Kateri lifted her head and locked stares with Priest. A feminine warning shared without a word spoken.

Priest sighed and shifted his gaze to Elise. "Because I promised him I wouldn't. He doesn't trust her and doesn't want her hands on him."

"That's insane. She's the best healer we've got nearby."

"And he's a mated Volán male. He'd take his own life before he betrayed you."

"That's not betraying me. That's keeping me from going insane." She redirected to Kateri. "Give me your phone. I'll call her."

"No." Priest padded to the bed and rolled his shoulders, the action combined with his appearance making it look like he was prepping for a fight rather than healing anyone. "His timing is shitty, but I made him a promise and I'll keep it."

"What do you mean his timing is shitty? It's not like he planned this."

"Someone's nearing their soul quest," Katy said. "Priest knows when they're close. He started sensing one a few hours ago."

To hell with soul quests. Right now, all she cared about was Tate and somehow containing the explosive anger burgeoning behind her sternum. "Then call Vanessa! You already said your skills weren't as good as a healer's. Are you even sure you can fix this bad of an injury?"

"Oh, I can fix it." He kneeled on the bed beside Tate's hip and assessed him for a second. "It just won't be as good as what you'll be capable of."

"Not exactly helpful since I don't *have* my magic! And you don't even know if I'll be a healer."

"Tate thinks you will."

"But you'll have already healed the bones."

He gripped each of Tate's hips and met her gaze. "Then I'll break them again and you'll do it right."

"You're nuts."

Priest refocused on Tate, then closed his eyes.

"Priest—"

Katy cut her off with a grip on her shoulder, a caring yet tight hold, as though she wasn't entirely sure Elise wouldn't launch across the bed and keep Priest from his work. Her voice was quiet and close to Elise's ear. "It's what Tate wants. Trust him. Trust Priest."

She felt more than saw her mother move in behind her. Her touch mirrored Katy's on Elise's other shoulder, but the intensity was softer. Encouraging. "It'll be okay, Elise. We'll deal with the rest later."

An odd stillness settled on the room, the same she'd felt when Meara had worked on Kallie, but with a different edge. A commanding, otherworldly presence.

Elise squeezed her mother's hand. Forced herself to breathe.

And waited.

Strung one anxious minute after another for what felt like eternity. Bit by bit, the anger that had set aside the deep fatigue she'd woken with ebbed and the lethargy wove its way back into her muscles. Lulled and coaxed her to give in. To stretch out next to her mate and surrender to sleep.

Her body trembled, and her eyes burned, so much so she couldn't tell if the silvery glow drifting along Tate's body was a figment of her imagination, or Priest's magic at work. She blinked over and over, but the odd aura only grew. Thickened into a mist that called to her.

"Elise?"

Her mother's voice.

Then others. A mix of masculine and feminine tones carried on words that made no sense.

But there was one voice among them she wanted to hear. *Needed* to hear.

The mist surrounded her. Blinded her with its brilliance.

"Give in, Elise."

There it was. Tate's warm baritone voice. So far away, but awake and safe.

"Yes, I'm safe. You can let go now."

Let go? And how had he known her thoughts?

Her body shifted, unseen hands lifting and cradling her inside the silver nothingness that surrounded her.

Tate's scent surrounded her. His warmth a comforting blanket despite the vast unknown. "Sleep, *mihara*. Just give in. I'll be here when you wake up."

Sleep.

Sleep was good.

Necessary.

The first step.

Toward what she had no clue, but Tate was here. Safe and holding her close.

She closed her eyes, sighed at the instant relief and surrendered to the dark.

Chapter Fifteen

The clock was missing. Why that was the first thing she noticed in Dr. Nilson's office was truly weird. Even more bizarre than what she was doing here. She hadn't visited the Lafayette psychologist who'd helped her after high school in well over a year. Maybe more.

The maroon carpet beneath the fluffy tan couches looked newer than when she'd been here before, but the doc's desk was just as scattered with folders and books she often loaned out to clients as it always was. Outside the small window above the doctor's desk, the world was pitch dark. Not even a hint of moonlight to show the other professional buildings that made up the complex where her office was housed.

Odd. Elise couldn't remember ever visiting Dr. Nilson at night. And where was the doc anyway?

Priest's voice startled her out of her wonderings. "Who's Dr. Nilson?" Sprawled casually in the couch perpendicular to her own, he didn't seem the least bit fazed at being in a strange doctor's office with her.

But he hadn't been there a few seconds ago. "Why are you here?"

"To help you."

"At my shrink?"

His mouth quirked in a wry smile that did little to ease the fatigue lining the outer edges of his eyes. "I don't think they like to be called shrinks."

No. They didn't. At least Dr. Nilson didn't. Especially since every time Elise had used it in the past had been as a negative reflection of her need for counseling. "How do you even know Dr. Nilson? Did she call you or something?"

"In a manner of speaking. But I don't think this is going to be a regular session."

Great. More weirdness to pack onto all the other weirdness. "Why not?"

Soft footfalls sounded on the stairs outside the door.

Priest picked up on the sound as well, his gaze shifting to the door briefly before he met her eyes once more. "Because the soul quest I sensed tonight was yours, Elise. You're not in reality. You're in the Otherworld."

The light.

The need for sleep.

Tate.

Elise shot to her feet, her heart jolting hard enough it could have propelled her into motion if panic hadn't already handled the job on its own. "Where's Tate? You're supposed to be taking care of him."

The door opened behind her, filling the room with an energy that stole her breath. The sweet, soft voice that had talked her through countless experiences and feelings drifted in along with it. "Your mate is fine. Perfectly healed, holding your physical form close, and beside himself he can't be here for you."

The same voice, yes, but *definitely* not Dr. Nilson. There was too much power beneath the message. A larger than life compulsion to obey even though no command had been spoken.

Elise turned, both terrified and intrigued as to who or what she'd find behind her.

Dressed in simple black slacks, a fitted white blouse with a cowl neck and sensible black shoes, the resemblance to her doctor was perfect. Right down to her chestnut hair styled in a chin-length bob and her impish smile.

"You're the Keeper?" Elise said.

"I am." With the same professional grace she'd come to expect from her counselor over the many sessions they'd spent together, the Keeper motioned toward the couch behind Elise. "Have a seat and let's get started."

Surprising even herself, Elise refused the command. "What did you mean by Tate being perfectly healed? Priest said he couldn't handle the full extent of his injuries on his own."

"She intervened," Priest answered instead. "Used my energy as a conduit and healed him for you."

"For me?" She looked to the Keeper. "Why?"

The Keeper angled the wingback behind her desk so it faced the couches, sat and crossed one leg over the other. She clasped her hands patiently in her lap. "Your will is exceptionally strong. It was either intervene or wait longer than I wanted to meet Cara's granddaughter face-to-face." She cocked an imperial eyebrow and eyed Priest across the room. "Not to mention, the idea of one of my warriors suffering through a second round of pain didn't sit well with me."

"You made the bonds and our males the way they are," he fired back, clearly not the least bit intimidated.

"Don't be surprised when we dig in our heels and honor what you give us."

The Keeper smirked, an appreciative gleam in her eye, when she turned her gaze to Elise. "And *that* is why I picked him." She dipped her head toward the couch behind Elise. "Now, sit. Your mate might be good physically, but his agitation is painful to watch."

The mere idea of Tate anything but confident and grounded dropped her like a stone to the couch behind her. Though, this time, she stayed perched on the edge, ready to bolt if the situation warranted. She gripped her knees, just now realizing the two sizes too large tan cargo pants she had on were the same ones she'd relied on years ago to help hide her figure. The simple olive tunic she wore with it did the same and added to the unimpressive colors designed to fade into the background. It'd been years since she'd worn something so unflattering and, with it, came a host of old emotions.

"You never blended in," the Keeper said. "No matter how hard you tried."

The Keeper's unexpected foray into Elise's thoughts ripped the few remaining emotional shields she had left free and shoved her square into uncomfortable territory. "You can hear what I think?"

"You're Volán. Mine as much as you are the Creator's. All your thoughts, all your wants, needs and pain move through me the same as they do you. I know your hopes. I know your dreams. And I know the fear that holds you back. Keeps you rooted on the edge of all you want." She stood and prowled toward Elise with a preternatural gait, stopping only an arm's length away. "You wanted a second chance, Elise. Tonight, you'll have it—assuming you're ready to face your fate."

"My fate?" She looked to Priest. "I don't understand. How am I supposed to answer what I'm willing to do if I don't know what's being asked?"

Priest leaned forward and braced his elbows on his knees, his hands clasped loosely between his wide knees. In such a position, his already massive shoulders seemed twice as impressive. Intimidating. And yet, his voice was pure velvet. "She's asking if you're willing, *nahina*. And you answer with no knowledge of the task you'll be given. Only with the courage and desire to see it through and earn the gifts meant for you."

Her choice.

Her chance to claim the magic her mother had given up. To step into her heritage and earn her own companion.

If she could just face the task chosen for her—whatever that looked like.

Body humming, she stood on shaking legs and met the Keeper's steady stare. "I'm ready."

"I'm glad, Elise. You've carried your regrets too long." With a tender touch that belied obvious strength, the Keeper cupped the side of her face. "Face that which frightens you most and claim your freedom."

One breath and the room was gone, replaced with one of Butte La Rose's smaller clothing stores, the pale blue walls and silver racks nowhere near as stylish as those at the mall in Lafayette. For a junior's area, the styles weren't bad. Just not as plentiful to choose from.

God, she hadn't been in this store in *years*. Not since…

Pieces clicked together. A long-forgotten memory thrust straight to the front of her thoughts and dug icy claws deep in her chest.

Her first bra.

She hadn't wanted to come. Had dreaded everything about it. Had cried for two days after her coach had pulled her mother aside in front of the other girls and explained that maybe it was time for Elise to have some supportive coverage considering the form fitting nature of her leotard.

The girls behind her had snickered and Elise's cheeks had burned from the shame so badly they hurt.

She hated that day.

Remembered it as the beginning of all her problems.

"It starts when you do, Elise."

She spun and found Priest behind her. With the tattoos peeking out from under the sleeves of his black T-shirt, his long dark hair loose and faded jeans, he looked woefully out of place in the environment. "What am I supposed to do?"

"You'll find the rhythm. The path to walk. That's how it works."

"You won't be with me?"

His stern features softened. "I'll be there when you need me. But that time isn't now." He dipped his head toward the wall of garments hung on the far end of the building. The top of her mother's head barely peeking over one rack. The color was darker, the rich dark chocolate it had been before time had begun its transition to gray.

"Go," Priest said. "It's time."

Elise stood there, that old clawing urge to escape blossoming through her chest and up her throat. To take whatever measures were necessary to stay safe and disconnected.

Face that which frightens you most and claim your freedom.

Her second chance. The real deal. Or as real as the Otherworld could make it. How many people had such a chance? To truly experience how a changed response would ripple through their life.

The clothes and people around her went by in a haze, her heart doing double time. Everything was exactly as it had been that day, but this time there was more. The knowledge of exactly how reality would play out after this day adding a barbed layer of terror to each step.

"Oh, there you are." Her mother waved her over the second Elise rounded the rack that had stood between them. "Come see what you think of these." She held up two different bras, both a neutral beige with thinner straps and different styles of lace lining the tops.

Laughter sounded behind her and the same shame that had pierced her heart all those years ago stabbed deep.

Yvette and her friend Tina.

Somehow, she'd forgotten that detail of the memory. As if her brain had determined the two of them hearing the coach's gentle guidance to her mother that day had been enough and chosen, out of sheer necessity, to bury the recollection they'd unfortunately visited the store the same day.

As if on some automatic track from the past, Elise found herself pointing to a white one hanging among all the others. No frills. Nothing girly. Just a simple tank style she'd hoped would do a decent job of making her budding breasts go away. "I want one like that."

Her mom tucked the one she'd picked under one arm and picked the white one off the rack, her gaze narrowed in consideration. "I guess it would be okay for gymnastics, but it won't do much shape wise."

Her current self wanted to chime in. Wanted to stop and consider her mom's words, but her old self pushed ahead, drawing her deeper and deeper into her history. "I don't want shape. I want flat."

Giving up all pretense of studying the bra, Jenny faced her. "Why on Earth would you want flat? Most girls like it when they start developing."

The snickering sounded behind her again and Elise gave serious thought to crawling behind the clothes on the rack beside her. "I'm ten, Mom," she whisper-scolded and tried to subtly motion to Yvette and Tina behind her with her head. "No one else has boobs."

Her mom noted the girls behind Elise, cleared her throat and firmly raised her chin as she faced the bras once more. When she spoke, her voice was much softer, but loaded with emphasis. "You're not supposed to be like everyone else, Elise. You're supposed to be like you."

The same words her mom had spoken that day, but this time their message hit a different part of her. Ricocheted off the experience she'd brought to the past with her and resonated with a truth she'd missed the first time around.

Dr. Nilson had essentially said the same thing in countless sessions in the time she'd visited, and Elise had worked hard to learn and grow in that area in the years since, but the information she'd needed had been there from the get-go. A lesson missed.

She *wasn't* like anyone else.

No one was. Not really. No matter how hard they all tried to conform for the sake of acceptance. Now was her chance to show she understood with the simplest of choices.

Her younger self started to balk, but somehow her older half pushed through. "Okay." The answer came out a little loud, making more than one head turn their direction, but Elise didn't care. Just grabbed the bras her mom had selected and forced her feet toward the dressing room. No way was she repeating the mistakes of her past again, including going one or two sizes too small for the sake of hiding her body.

Her mom tight on her heels, Elise wound through the racks, knocked on one door to make sure the room was empty and opened it wide.

The change in scenery was so drastic, she nearly face planted. Not onto the dressing room floor she'd expected to find, but into the high school library behind a floor-to-ceiling bookshelf. The industrial-grade gold carpet was a little frayed and faded, and the size of the space was nowhere near as impressive as what other, bigger school systems boasted, but was redolent with the scent of old books. Hushed voices hung on the air around her, most coming from the long study tables she remembered all too well on the other side. Held tight against her chest were two books and a spiral notebook.

"You know, I saw her last weekend with a few guys who graduated last year. Not one, but *two*."

One sentence, but the content and the haughty tenor of Yvette's voice at the table directly opposite the bookshelf rooted Elise on the exact spot she'd been sent to. She'd stood in this same spot before. Overheard and wept silently as she listened to two other girls she'd thought were her friends pile on their own fictional sightings.

"Elise?" Tracey said. "You're out of your mind. She's too focused on gymnastics right now to bother with going out with one guy. Let alone two."

June chimed in right behind it. "But you've got to admit, she's gorgeous enough for an older guy like that to ask her out."

"You mean *built*," Yvette said. "Too bad she has to rely on her body to get their attention. She probably puts out, too."

"No," June said. "I mean she's gorgeous. And if you think for a second Elise would put out for any guy, you're nuts. I don't even think I've seen her pay attention to the guys at school. Let alone kiss one."

More words were spoken. An active back-and-forth debate where the two friends who'd so quickly knifed her heart with rumors in real life now stood as staunch defenders between Yvette and her tales. But Elise couldn't really process the context. Couldn't shake herself out of the sheer shock and amazement at how things were changing.

Was it possible? Could the one simple decision she'd made to not hide her developing body bring such a drastic change?

She blinked her eyes over and over, as if her brain needed the extra action to clear the muddled thoughts running through her head. She'd bought those bras when she was ten. She'd overheard the rumors her sophomore year.

Six years.

If that much changed, what else had?

She hustled on quiet feet to the window along the far edge of the aisle. The old oaks that lined one side of the high school parking lot outside were thick and green and the sky was a glorious blue, but what stole her breath the most was the woman reflected in the glass.

Cute jeans that hugged her curves in place of loose cargo pants. A simple, but fitted white V-neck T-shirt in lieu of her standard oversized shirts. But the most surprising thing was her hair and her face. Gone was the ponytail she'd worn every single day, replaced with stylish bangs and loose curls that hung easy around her face. She even had on makeup. And jewelry.

One act of faith—of courage—and look what she'd become. And if she'd wrought this much change, what else could she do?

Facing the long empty aisle behind her, Elise started forward. Slow at first, then picking up steam as her confidence built. Years ago, she'd waited, listened to every malicious word spoken, then crept out the far library door to the parking lot, the early spring air cold against her tear-streaked face.

But not today.

Not this time.

She paused at the end of the bookshelf, one hand braced on the solid wood as she sucked in a deep breath, then stepped out into the main area. A boy seated at the table closest to her looked up from the book in front of him, met her gaze and smiled. Behind and to one side of him two girls she remembered from the track-and-field team glanced up, waved and went back to their work.

Perfectly normal. No judgment. No sideways looks. No whispered asides.

Emboldened by the response, she aimed straight for Yvette, making absolutely sure her shoulders were back and her chin held high. She stopped less than an arm's length away. "I *am* built. It's who I am and there's nothing wrong with it. What's wrong is when someone spreads lies about someone else simply because they're different." She paused long enough to meet June's and Tracey's eyes. "For what it's worth, thank you for what you said. It meant a lot."

With that, she turned and strode toward the main library entrance. The weight of several stares pressed at her back and sides, and her palms were so damp it was a wonder she didn't drop her books on the long trek to leave, but she kept going. Clung to the fresh surge of empowerment with everything she had and acknowledged every person she passed along the way who met her gaze with either a smile or a simple nod.

She wasn't a victim. Not now. Not ever again. So high was her confidence and certainty she'd learned her lesson, she pressed open the library door expecting to find herself back in the visage of Dr. Nilson's office and the Keeper and Priest waiting for her.

Instead, she found herself in the girls' locker room. Dressed the way she always had been at the end of a practice in light workout pants and a school T-shirt. Her hair was wet and loose around her shoulders and her duffel sat packed and waiting on the wooden bench in front of her. Per usual, everyone else had already cleared out, only a few random echoed shouts from masculine voices from the basketball court beyond.

That day.

Yes, her clothes were different. *She* was different. But there was no question the Keeper had sent her back to the time when those damned pictures were taken. The day when her life had unknowingly taken a drastic turn.

Dread closed around her as thick and humid as the lingering warmth from the showers, the remembered pain and humiliation that had cut so deep the following day surfacing so fast she nearly choked on its power.

Face that which frightens you most and claim your freedom.

Twice now she'd done it, the emotional muscle memory still shaky beneath the uncomfortable memories, but less hesitant to respond. She hefted her duffel bag onto her shoulder and forced her feet into motion. Whatever changes she found this time, she'd deal with it. Would hold the positive manifestations of her courage close and battle to win one more.

Outside the gym, the student parking lot was nearly empty. Habit insisted she turn left and circle the back of the gym to the faculty parking lot where her mother always picked her up. But a stirring inside her urged her to do something different. To upset the apple cart once more and walk straight through the after-school crowd that always lingered in the halls and in front of the main entrance. To face those who might judge her tomorrow before the photos even surfaced.

Opening the door at the far end of the main hall, she entered the place that had been hell on Earth for nearly two years. The scent was just as she remembered it, cleaning materials, books and good old-fashioned time. The crowd at the opposite end wasn't nearly as full as she'd expected, but a decent number of people were visible on the landing outside the glass double doors and in the front drive beyond.

Her tennis shoes barely made a sound against the green, white and black marble floors, but her heart hammered so hard behind her sternum she half expected it to echo against the white painted walls.

"Oh, come on. It's just a little prank."

Elise slowed at the sound of Yvette's voice, the direction of it coming from the hallway ahead she hadn't yet reached.

A masculine voice that seemed vaguely familiar answered. "Man, I don't know what your problem is with her, but you need to let it go. Elise is a nice girl."

"Are you kidding me?" Yvette said. "You said yourself you're pissed at her."

"I said I was *disappointed*. I asked her out and she turned me down. That's not a reason to fake a bunch of pictures that'll hurt her. What'd she ever do to you, anyway?" Footsteps sounded a second before the boy she'd always believed was responsible for the doctored images stalked around the corner, headed for the double doors. So focused from his conversation with Yvette, he didn't even see Elise. Just punched the bar latch on the door with an impact that sent a shotgun echo down the hallway and jogged down the school's front steps.

Elise stood rooted in place, the simple realization that it had been Yvette who'd taken the pictures to begin with unraveling what was left of her bitterness.

One woman with a long-standing grudge. One she'd enabled over and over again by refusing to accept who she was. By running and taking the easier, softer approach. By letting her past linger and taint her future.

At the end of the day, respect for herself had earned respect from those around her. Maybe not from Yvette, but standing in her newfound perspective, Elise wondered if Yvette's need to tear someone else down wasn't grounded in the same need for self-love.

Such complex thoughts. And yet, in the wake of them came a lightness that was staggering. That left her feeling a foot taller and flooded with a newfound inner strength. Sunlight slanted through the double doors, calling her to step forward. To finally surrender the tether to her past and step into the warmth of today.

One step.

Then another.

She sensed Yvette's appearance at her right, just walking out of the hallway, but Elise didn't look. Didn't care. The things that had kept her life in such an excruciating grip before weren't there anymore. Replaced by acceptance. Understanding. Peace.

Outside the sun's rays grew so bold and bright, the teens gathered grew hazy. Blurred shapes in a reality that didn't matter anymore. The door's bar latch was cold against her palm, but the weight as she pushed the door open was nonexistent. Pure white light consumed her. Wrapped her in its sweet embrace, then unwound its arms and delivered her somewhere utterly unexpected.

To her left a river meandered with water so still the sky's azure blue reflected back a mystic turquoise color. Aspens and pines lined either side of it and majestic mountains striated with every color from the palest sand to rich plum reached to the heavens. But what surprised her most was Priest. He stood beside what once had been a sizable bonfire, the barest wisps of smoke lifting upward in lazy spirals. His torso and feet were bare, and his dark hair was loose down his back, but the pants he wore were unlike anything she'd ever seen on him before. A style that looked a lot like blue jeans would, only looser and a light tan in color. He stared at the charred wood and ashes, seemingly unaware of her presence or the chilled air despite his exposed skin.

In deference to his somber appearance and the quiet

beauty around her, Elise stole as quietly as she could toward him. "Where are we?"

He stood stock-still, not acknowledging her presence in any way. In fact, his focus on the fire's remnants was so absolute, she wasn't entirely sure he'd heard her. For all she knew, he couldn't.

"Our last full presect was here," he finally said.

A cold breeze slipped through the valley, cleansing in its touch even as it seemed to mourn with whatever held Priest so still.

He met her gaze, his mystic gray eyes brighter than she'd ever seen them. "This is where your grandmother died. Where all the primos died when my brother stole their magic."

Death. In such a beautiful place. It didn't seem possible. The narrow, winding basin seemed too pure to have ever been touched by the slaughter Priest had told her about the day they'd first met. But here they were— nestled in the heart of where the clan's current struggles had all begun.

"New life comes from death."

Elise spun to find the Keeper behind her, still dressed in the same professional outfit as before. Only rather than aiming her potent gaze on Elise, her attention was locked on Priest behind her as she meandered their way. "You could learn a thing or two from Elise, Eerikki."

Eerikki.

No matter how many times Elise heard Priest's true given name, it still rang incongruent with the larger than life man she'd come to know.

"You did the best you could with what you had to work with," the Keeper said. "Only wisdom learned through time allows us to change our responses. The pain of the past is what makes us who we are." She stopped just out of reach and shifted her focus to Elise. "I'm proud of you, Elise. Proud of all you've learned. Delighted with your courage."

She was, too. Maybe it was wrong to feel that way, but of all the competitions and physical challenges she'd tackled growing up, none felt so liberating as those she'd faced today.

The Keeper smiled, one of those knowing ones that said she'd not only heard Elise's thoughts, but approved. "Will you accept the gifts I'm willing to give you?"

Her magic.

She'd made it.

And while a part of her hoped—even prayed—that Priest and Tate were right and healing would be her place inside the clan, in this moment, she was happy just to be a part of the whole. No matter what magic she was given.

Elise bobbed her head, her heart skipping with an elation that left her body singing. "Yes."

The Keeper smiled and stepped closer. "I'm glad."

Priest moved in tight behind her and braced his hands on her shoulders.

"Remember what you've learned today," the Keeper said. "The freedom that comes in facing your fears. The compassion shown. The inherent strength that comes from loving and appreciating who you are."

She leaned in, her lips aimed straight for Elise's.

Priest's fingers tightened and held her steady.

And then she was floating. Present only in spirit and free from the physical weight of the world. Surrounded in an evergreen light and buoyed by pure love and strength. A second later, her breath caught, and her eyes opened.

Still in the valley. Surrounded by beauty.

Beside her, Priest stood patiently, the odd attire he'd worn before replaced with his standard black tee, faded jeans and boots. The Keeper was nowhere in sight, but a thick black leather cord circled Elise's neck, the medallion that hung from it resting warm and heavy just below the hollow of her throat. "What's this?"

"What do you think it is?"

She tried to dip her head for a better look at the design, but where it lay on her chest, seeing the full image was impossible. Loads of Voláns wore charms around their necks or on bracelets. Others, like Jade, wore them woven into braids in their hair. Every symbol was different, each representing some aspect of protection or strength.

But none looked like this one. None except the ones Alek and Priest wore.

She held Priest's gaze and her fingers trembled against the metal. "She made me healer prima?"

Priest barked out a laugh that seemed to echo off the mountains. "You're the only person who ever doubted that would be the case."

A healer.

A leader.

And while the latter half of that equation struck a healthy spark of trepidation, both distinctions humbled her clear to her soul. "I didn't think… I mean, I thought because I hadn't grown up with everyone else, she'd pick someone else."

"Sometimes fresh perspectives are what we need. I certainly wasn't what everyone expected when the

Keeper picked me as high priest." He cupped the back of her head and pulled her in for a hug. "You're going to be a fine healer, Elise. I promise."

An eagle's cry rang out against the bright, clear day, as if to punctuate Priest's statement.

Priest chuckled and released her, pointing to the sky behind her as he stepped away. "You've got a visitor."

Elise turned in time to watch the magnificent bird bank a sharp corner and fly toward them, its wings stretched wide to each side and at least eight feet long. It landed on a big boulder not ten feet away, lifted its wings wide and ruffled them before settling them close to its body. "He's beautiful."

"He's a she," Priest corrected.

Well, she'd have to take him on faith on that score. Wildlife hadn't ever been her strong suit, but something about the creature in front of her held her spellbound.

"They're fascinating birds," Priest said, still standing behind her. "Their vision reaches up to three miles away and, once they lock on to their prey, they never take their eyes off it until they capture it."

"Wow, really?" She cocked her head and studied the bird who seemed to be doing the same thing to Elise.

"Really." Priest moved in beside her. "They also fly *into* storms instead of away from them like other birds. They use the storm's winds to lift them higher up."

Despite the information and the hidden message it seemed Priest was trying to share with her, she couldn't look away from the eagle. "Why is she watching me?"

"Because, she's waiting on you."

Waiting. On her. "For what?"

Priest lowered his voice, the sheer reverence in his words moving across her like a solemn prayer. "She's

yours, Elise. And she's waiting for you to accept her."
He splayed his hand at her back and nudged her forward. "Go. Meet your new companion."

Chapter Sixteen

Tate was going to kill his primo. It might take a surprise attack when Alek was otherwise engaged in a head-to-head session with Priest, or when he was unconscious to do it, but one of these days Tate was going to kill him. Or at least land a punch to his jaw hard enough to knock him out for a few days. Granted, he was just trying to help Elise level out with some light sparring so she could try her hand at magic and shift for the first time, but the fucker deserved something nasty for putting his hands on Tate's mate.

Waiting with Priest and Katy in the gorge behind Priest's house, Tate leaned one shoulder against a huge oak, crossed his arms and fought the push from his coyote to shift.

"Relax," Priest drawled from beside him. "He's not doing anything inappropriate."

Pushed too far, Tate snapped back in a tone he'd never dared used with Priest, "I don't see Katy sparring with another man."

Priest shrugged, so disaffected by Tate's reaction he didn't even bother to look away from Elise struggling to break free of a chokehold. "My mate's not a prima. Yours is. She needs a bond with Alek."

"She needs to bond with her mate."

This time Priest met Tate's glare head-on and his voice was pure steel. "Your mate's going to have her hands on a lot of people if she's going to do her job. Men included. Time for you to get used to it."

Fuck.

He hadn't thought about that aspect of their life. But now that he stopped long enough to consider it, he clearly remembered the frequent bouts of fury his dad had had to fight for the same reason. And his mom hadn't been a prima.

"I see that sunk in." Priest smirked and went back to watching Alek and Elise. "Don't worry, though. In another ten minutes or so, Elise's buzz is gonna level out and you'll have your work cut out for you."

The vague undercurrent behind Priest's words yanked Tate upright, his arms uncurling and body bracing for a fight. "What's that supposed to mean?"

Priest eyeballed Tate as though gauging whether he could handle the answer. "It means my gut tells me we'll need Elise's skills sooner rather than later, so I'm going to push her. You're my best leverage to get her there fast and I'm going to use it."

Katy stopped her silent spectating long enough to volley a considering look between Priest and Tate. "Why do I get the feeling we should have called a few more healers in for backup?"

"We won't need them," Priest answered without breaking Tate's stare. "Tate will take whatever it takes to get her there. Won't you, Tate?"

The realization of where Priest was headed materialized in Tate's head with all the subtlety of a wrecking ball. Watching her spar with Alek was one thing, but participating in something that would cause her full-scale panic was something else. "You can't."

"Give me one good reason why not."

"Because it'll hurt her."

"Whoa. Hold up." Katy braced herself between them, clearly prepared to intervene. "Can't do what?"

"Reflex training," Priest answered.

Just hearing the approach voiced out loud iced Tate's bones to the marrow. He'd seen the technique work a million times, particularly with warriors. Had even had Priest use the tactic on him a time or two. He'd just never considered Priest would try it with a healer. "You throw the person into a situation where they don't have any choice but to respond and the magic answers on instinct." He focused on Priest. "You didn't feel her panic when she found me on the road. I did. I'd have still been out cold when you got there if it hadn't been for her pain waking me up."

"You're wrong," Priest said. "We may not have a bond with her, but every one of us who came into contact with her last night felt what she felt. And you're not giving her enough credit. There's a reason you're fully healed instead of partially so."

Tate looked to Katy. When all she did was shrug in lieu of an answer, he shifted his attention back to Priest. "What's that supposed to mean?"

"It means your mate's will was so damned strong in refusing to meet the Keeper in the Otherworld— fighting slipping into her own soul quest—that the Keeper intervened and did the bulk of the work for me so Elise would let go."

The silver light.

He'd thought it'd been a dream or a by-product of

Priest knocking him out. God knew he'd never seen Priest generate that kind of light when he'd healed Tate before, and Tate had come home for Priest to patch up with some doozies.

Priest's voice dropped to a low murmur. "Look at her, Tate. Not who she's working with, but her and how fast she's learning."

She was beautiful to watch. A mix of grace and feminine power. It emanated in every movement, her focus as she trained absolute.

"She was meant for this," Priest said, "and my gut tells me we're going to need her skills." He paused a beat and let the weight behind his words sink in. "What I need to know is if you're willing to help her get where she's going as fast as we need her to be there."

Tate's throat clenched so tight his answer was more guttural growl than words. "I'd do anything for her. Anything but hurt her."

"Oh, trust me," Priest said. "She's not going to be the one that hurts. You will." Not waiting for Tate's reaction, he ambled forward and let out a sharp whistle. "Alek, take a break."

The break in action was almost instantaneous, Alek unwinding the hold Elise had likely only been seconds from breaking free of and stepping back, even as he kept a steadying hand on her shoulder.

Priest stopped just five feet from the two of them and waved Tate forward. "Tate, you're up."

Flushed from her bouts with Alek and the newfound magic streaming through her body, Elise smiled huge. Had it not been for the cold reality of what was about to happen slicing through him, Tate would've strutted the distance between them. As it was, he took the smile for everything it was and prayed it wouldn't be the last one she gave him.

"Shirt off," Priest said to Tate as he prowled closer.

Something in Priest's ominous tone must have tipped Elise off because her smile slipped, and her gaze darted back and forth between them. "What's going on?"

Tate tossed his shirt to the ground and squared himself to Priest. Whatever injury Priest intended Tate couldn't fathom, but there was no doubt it was going to hurt like hell.

"How's your energy?" Priest said, avoiding her question entirely.

"Good." She looked to Tate and raised an eyebrow.

Tate didn't dare speak. Hell, just standing there knowing what was about to happen and not sharing took everything in him.

Priest stopped right in front of her. "Can you feel your magic?"

Elise lowered her head, her attention loosely aimed at the ground in front of her and her gaze distant. "I think so." She lifted her head. "It's like a buzz, right? A hum beneath your skin?"

"That's the one." He craned his head from side to side as though warming up for a fight. "Focus on it. Center yourself in it."

Elise closed her eyes and the clearing around them stilled in an instant. Midmorning sunshine filtered through the full treetops overhead and the steady drone of a boat on the lake hummed in the distance, but within their immediate reach a preternatural softness permeated everything.

The healer's concord.

Tate had experienced it hundreds of times growing

up with his mother. A natural connectedness that sprung from every healer when their magic melded between the Otherworld and Earth. The ground practically sang with it, and the breeze took on an almost singsong quality.

Pure power.

That of a prima finding her way.

Priest felt it, too, the hard edge he'd approached them with now coated in pure certainty. "Open your eyes, Elise."

She did as he asked, her normally light green eyes darkened by the depth of her magic.

"What you feel right now—the energy flowing through you—is what you need."

She cocked her head just a fraction. "What I need for what?"

Too focused inwardly on honing her gifts, she seemed to miss Priest fisting one hand at his side. Silver shimmered down his right arm. "To heal your mate."

One second.

One blindingly fast swipe of Priest's arm and a flash of his panther's claws and Tate was on his knees, the searing burn across his chest too great for his body to process and stay standing at the same time.

"Oh my God!" Elise was there in an instant, kneeling before him. His blood seeped over her fingers as she tried to stem the flow with her palms.

She didn't stand a prayer of stopping it. The cuts were too deep. Too jagged for anything but magic or a well-trained trauma team to repair. She glared at Priest over her shoulder, undiluted fury and terror whipping the once peaceful forest into a maelstrom of dangerous energy. "Are you out of your mind? Fix him!"

Priest held his ground, his voice utterly dispassionate. "No."

Her rage shot higher, lashing through their still growing bond with all the mercy of a barbed whip and ripping a low guttural moan he had no hope of containing up the back of his throat. He gripped her wrists. Tried to focus through the pain and steady his breathing. To slow his ragged pulse. "Elise."

Her focus on him was instant and the energy around him softened, though nowhere near as still as what she'd need to heal him.

"You." His arms shook and, despite what his mind insisted he say, his mouth struggled to cooperate. "Not Priest. You."

"Are you out of your mind?" She twisted back to Priest. "I don't know what I'm doing! Help me!"

"He won't." The muscles in Tate's thighs and torso trembled to the point he swayed and nearly pulled her off balance with him. "You have to."

The horror and helplessness etched on her face cut him deeper than the jagged claw marks across his torso. "I don't know how!"

"You don't. Your magic does." Blackness crowded the edges of his vision and the forest spun. The next thing he knew, the brilliant blue sky was above him. Priest towered to one side of him, his arms crossed resolutely across his chest.

Elise knelt at the other, the press of her palms against his bleeding chest and tears streaming down her cheeks.

Tate tried to wipe them. Needed to ease the pain crashing through their bond. "Hurts."

"Tell me what to do," she said between choked sobs. "Please."

It doesn't matter if it's a simple scratch or a terrible wound. His mother's voice, paired with a memory that crowded out the present and dragged him back to one of the first times he'd watched her heal a little girl who'd stepped on a piece of broken glass. With a featherlight touch, she stroked the three-inch wound. *Healing is a connection. Two souls brought together by pain. The magic knows where to go. How to heal what's been torn apart. So long as my heart is open, it flows as easy as a river.*

"Your heart." Cold weighted his legs and feet, and his hands were already so numb the warmth of her own hand beneath his barely registered. His eyes slipped closed, too heavy to stay open any longer. He tried to pull more air into his lungs. To add more strength to his voice, but the words still came out grated. "Heal from your heart."

An instant shift.

Warmth and light surging through him.

Movement sounded beside him. The soft whoosh of decomposing leaves beneath solid footsteps.

"Just like that." Priest's voice. Much closer than before. "Open to him. Guide the magic."

The warmth grew. Blossomed into a commanding heat that threaded through every cell and sinew. His back bowed, drawn upward by a relentless force knotted squarely behind his sternum.

The bond.

Not fully formed, but stronger than he'd ever felt it. Pulsing and alive. Flooding him with strength.

The slow, aching throb beneath his wounds ebbed. Shifted to a stinging tightness. Air flooded his lungs and his eyes snapped open.

Katy stood near his feet, her pale face marked with wonder and a healthy amount of shock, but Priest crouched beside him, a pleased smile that bordered on smugness aimed at Elise. He splayed a hand on her back. "Breathe, Elise. He's fine."

Elise ignored him. Kept every shred of her attention focused on Tate's torso as her trembling hands skimmed across the healed flesh, seemingly clueless to the fact that he was awake, aware and fully whole. "But what if I missed something? What if there's something inside still bleeding?"

"Elise."

At the sound of Tate's voice, her head snapped up, her honey-gold hair loose around her tear-streaked face and her eyes wild with raw distress. She blinked over and over, as though her mind couldn't quite grasp the reality of what she'd done. Her breaths came short and ragged, but otherwise she stayed locked in place, kneeling beside him with her torso protectively curved over his. "Tate?"

Odd. Seeing the blood smeared over his torso, he could understand the disbelief on her face, but despite the gruesome remnants of what had happened, he felt amazing. Fully recharged as though he'd rested for days. He pushed himself upright, braced himself on his knees in front of her and smoothed her hair away from her face. "You did it. I'm fine." He guided one of her hands across his healed chest to just above his heart. "See? They're gone."

Lips parted, she scanned his face. Then his chest. The wildness in her gaze eased, but a distance replaced it. An almost dazed appearance as though the world around her had dimmed and she couldn't find her bearings.

The bond between them vibrated with a frantic energy. A manic buzz with the discordant itch of a live wire. His coyote snarled and snapped, pacing and pushing for release. Tate gripped each side of her face and tried to get her to focus. "Elise?"

Her lips quivered, and a shiver snaked through her arms and torso. "Can't..." She lifted her chin as though trying to stay above rising water. "Breathe."

"Too much adrenaline." In one fluid move, Priest stood and hauled her upright. "Tate, brace her from behind. She needs to shift."

Tate shot to his feet and banded one arm around her waist and another around her shoulders, his own panic filling his head with a ragged drumbeat. "She can't shift like this." No one did their first time. Or their first ten tries.

"She'll shift. You didn't see her in the Otherworld. She's a natural." Priest got up close enough Elise couldn't avoid his gaze. "Elise, look at me. Think about your companion. Remember when you merged. Call her."

Elise opened her mouth, then closed it, the choking sound that eked up her throat enough to make Tate's constrict in equal fashion.

"Dammit, Prima, look at me." Priest punctuated the command with a firm grip on her chin and got nose to nose. "Reach for her. You want to breathe? Want the calm you can't quite find? Let her through. Fly."

Fly?

His mate had a bird for a companion?

The thoughts had no sooner zinged through his head than a brilliant emerald light blinded him, and the brush of soft feathers swept against his arms. From the center of the deep color a bird with a wingspan at least eight feet wide burst forth, its deep sable—almost black—body contrasted by its pristine white head.

An eagle.

A symbol of power and strength for their clan. A keenly insightful and courageous predator.

His mate.

As if it had heard his thoughts, the majestic creature's cry rang out over the forest. Its powerful wings beat in bold, leisurely strokes that sent it careening nearly straight up into the cloudless skies.

"She's beautiful." Katy shielded her eyes from the sun and craned her head to watch the show taking place overhead, every dip and turn fluid and graceful.

"She earned every feather," Priest said with a reverence and respect Tate had never heard spoken outside of reference to his mate.

But reverence and respect or not, Tate was done with spectators. Done with forcing undeserved hardships on his mate. She'd earned her magic. Donned her wings. And when she landed it would be with Tate and *only* Tate waiting. "Go."

The harsh directive was the only one he'd ever dared utter to Priest his entire life, but in that second neither man nor beast cared. Elise was the only thing that mattered. Elise and making up for all the shit she'd endured since he'd left her last night at her back door.

Priest hung his head and rubbed the back of his hand across his mouth, trying unsuccessfully to hide the knowing smile on his face. "Right. I'd say you've earned that play." He motioned Kateri closer and held up his arm to welcome her close. "Come on, *mihara.* Let Tate take care of his mate."

"But what about her shift back?" She volleyed a clueless look between them. "Won't she need help?"

Priest wrapped her up, squeezed her affectionately and kissed her temple. "I think you've forgotten the aftereffects of a first shift."

Her eyes got big and cheeks flushed, memories of her own transition back to human form no doubt crashing in. "Oh."

"*Oh*, indeed." Priest chuckled and kissed her temple. "Besides that, her eagle's not an alpha like your lion. By the time she lands, she'll happily trade places if it means being with Tate." He met Tate's gaze, not bothering this time to hide his humor. "I take it you'll want me to tell Jenny her daughter won't be home tonight?"

Not tonight. Not ever if he had any say about it. And once he got Elise back in human form and pressed against him it was the second topic up for discussion. The first was groveling until she forgave him for participating in all that had happened today.

Rather than answer directly, he turned his gaze on the sky and marked Elise soaring in the distance. "We'll be at the cabin." With that he surrendered to the push from his companion, welcomed the stinging burn of the transition and loped into the forest after his mate.

Chapter Seventeen

Rich green treetops below her. A blanket of blue all around her, broken only by thin white wisps of clouds in the distance. The meandering, shallow beaches of Beaver Lake and the soft ripple of wind against its surface. Bits and pieces of one exceptional view. Intricate details Elise had only been able to take in one at a time on land, but could absorb as a whole from the air through her companion's eyes. Could see and appreciate the beauty of the bigger picture from a fresh perspective.

Rather like her life.

She'd thought she'd understood where she was headed. Believed her time seeking help for the harsh experiences she'd endured in high school had shone an understanding to help her cope and grow. But until today, she really hadn't had a clue. Hadn't been able to truly grasp how she needed those lessons—every hardship and every tear—to make her who she was today. To prepare her for the broader landscape of her life she'd yet to explore.

Below, a flash of gold, white and gray darted between the trees. A big coyote keeping pace with her travels and racing through the forest.

Tate.

The space behind her chest surged with a mix of exhilaration and worry. A silent communication within the strengthening bond she couldn't deny anymore. The exhilaration pulsing through it she understood. Felt the answering rush from her own companion with each beat of her wings.

Freedom.

Not just from gravity, but from all the complexities of the human mind and the overanalysis it brought to every equation. In animal form she simply was. Existed and enjoyed every second one by one. Honored and abided by the instincts given to her by the Creator.

The worry, though...that part agitated her bird. Logically, her muted human thoughts could rationalize the reason for it. Knew beyond the shadow of a doubt that her mate was struggling with his part in how the last twenty-four hours had impacted her, but her eagle didn't like it one bit. To her, what was done, was done. The raging fire was over. And while it had been excruciating at times and had left an indelible mark on her soul, she'd flown out stronger. Wiser. More confident as to what she was capable of and better prepared to face the next phase of her life.

Including her place as his mate.

As if he'd heard her thoughts, a sharp bark shot skyward.

Her heightened gaze sharpened in an instant, lasering in on Tate's coyote in a mostly circular clearing with a manmade structure near the center. Compared to the other homes dotting the lake's perimeter, this one was smaller. More cottage-size like so many of the bed-and-breakfasts Eureka Springs was known for, its simple black asphalt tile roof barely standing out among all the green that surrounded it.

The cabin.

Their cabin.

When it had earned that distinction she couldn't say, but any doubts she'd had about spending her nights as well as her days with him were gone. Replaced with a resoluteness that resonated to the tip of each feather.

She banked left and circled toward the structure, letting out a cry of understanding as she did.

Funny. While soaring above Priest's vast property, she'd had no concept of time. No need for it. Only knew that the sun had shifted well past its zenith and that her companion had been content to fly as long as she needed to find her center. But now, knowing Tate was waiting—knowing what she was about to fully step into—a new, uncompromising urgency pushed her faster.

The ground raced closer. The air sluiced between her feathers and her heart raced with the promise of what lay ahead. So many days and nights they'd played, each one with Tate slowly introducing her to touch and her sensuality. But not once had she felt this open. This safe and ready.

Her wings lifted on instinct, slowing her descent to the earth.

And then she was there. No more than fifteen feet from the front porch where Tate waited, his coyote already traded for flesh and blood male. Not one scratch marred his bare torso and the blood that had catapulted her so quickly to learn her magic was gone. His hair hung loose to his shoulders and his training pants hung low on his hips.

Her eagle fidgeted and ruffled its feathers.

"She doesn't like being so low and exposed." Tate ambled down the two steps from the raised entrance. Something black was gripped in one hand. A soft fabric. But between his tight grip and so much of his skin on display she couldn't quite manage the curiosity to puzzle out what it was. "She guided you here though because she knows you need a good foundation to shift."

Right. Before she could have what she wanted—what her past and consequent fears had kept from her until now—she'd have to cross one more bridge.

Tate stopped just over five feet away and crouched so his body no longer towered over her, the tight black bundle clasped loosely between his hands. "She knows the way back, but you're the one who guides it. Feel for the path. The same one you felt in the Otherworld when she merged with you. The same as when you brought her to you today."

No, not a path. At least that's not how it had felt this morning. More like a tunnel minus the same gravitational pull as real life. Or a water slide at a near ninety-degree angle engulfed in a blinding light. Her companion had all but pushed through. Lifted up and burst forth without a beat of hesitation. But how was she supposed to do the same?

Her eagle let out a series of quick, high-pitched squawks and lifted her wings. *Two halves. One whole.*

Not a direct message, so much as a thought. Paired with a pressure that shouldn't be possible without a corporeal form.

Follow.

A tingle blossomed behind the pressure. A borderline burn like when she'd spent too much time in the sun.

Two halves.

One whole.

Was it really that simple? A case of giving in to the push and trading places? Of moving with the subtle tug her companion had created?

She leaned into the sensation, leading with her heart. Welcomed it the same as she had her magic when healing Tate.

The burn escalated, singeing through her bodiless being with vicious snaps and crackles. Instinct urged her to step back. To play it safe.

Trust. Leap.

No more safe. Those days were over. She knew it. Her companion knew it. Envisioning the swoop and swirl of her first transition and the sweet flight as she'd ascended toward the sky, Elise surrendered to the pain. To the sting and the overpowering brightness beyond.

An emerald light embraced her. Swept her through the stinging pain with no heed for gravity.

Birdsong and the rustle of leaves in the trees above her.

Leaves and soil warmed by sun beneath her bare feet.

Sunlight and the sweet caress of a spring breeze against her still stinging skin.

Eyes closed, she tilted her head back and smiled to the skies, a silent thank-you to her companion for her guidance as she soaked up each heightened sensation.

"You did good."

At the sound of Tate's voice, she opened her eyes, eager to share her own delight.

Her words dried up at the sight of him. Still crouched as he'd been before, now his head was down, his gaze firmly rooted on the ground in front of his feet. He held up one hand, offering the folded black fabric. "I thought you might want this."

Not fabric.

A T-shirt.

Because she was naked.

So thrilled with her transition and the sensations that had welcomed her back from her spirit form, she'd missed it entirely.

But Tate had known what to expect. Known and anticipated her anxiety the way he always seemed to and had been prepared to ease it.

She crept forward, stopping only when her shins were inches from his bowed head and her feet were in his direct line of sight. She covered his outstretched hand with one of her own and combed her fingers through the hair at the top of his head with the other. "You're always looking out for me."

The muscles along the back of his neck and shoulders tensed and he waggled the bundle for her attention. "Take it, Elise."

Such strain in his voice. Fighting his desires and natural instincts—for her. Releasing his hand, she dragged the T-shirt from his grip. "Thank you for taking care of me." She dropped the shirt at his feet. "But I don't need it."

His hands fisted near his feet and the rest of his body went so still he seemed more like a sculpture locked on a supplicant pose than the alpha she knew him to be. "You don't have to rush anything with me, Elise. I can wait."

"Tate." Just his name on her lips felt different. More potent. A key to the first step in the rest of her life. "I've waited long enough. For everything."

His hands shifted to her ankles, the touch a mix of deep respect and stark need barely contained. "I hurt you."

The healing.

Of course, that would be the first thing on his mind. Especially with how hard the experience had hit her emotionally. Mates were wired to protect each other. Not actively participate in anything that caused them pain. But he'd done it to help her.

"You did. But you helped me, too. Got me across a bridge that could have taken forever to cross. Now I'm asking you to walk me across another one."

He growled and tightened his grip, the barely leashed strength behind the touch a stunning promise of what was to come. "Elise…"

A warning.

A plea.

"Look at me, Tate. I'm ready." For him. For what they could be to each other. Whatever that looked like.

He sucked in a slow, deep breath, the raspy sound of it as sensual as the glide of his rough fingertips across her sensitized skin. Up, up, up his palms went. Along the outside of her calves, over her knees and up her thighs. His gaze followed. Achingly slow. Consuming every inch at a delectably languid pace. Her sex. Her belly. Her breasts. Then finally her eyes.

No censure.

No judgment.

No leering or calculated gleams.

Just wonder and deep appreciation. A man looking on a gift and heartily accepting what he'd been given.

And damned if it wasn't intoxicating. Liberating and compelling all in one visual stroke.

He palmed her hips and rolled to his knees. "My mate." His fingers dug into her flesh, but the kiss he pressed just below her sternum was pure reverence. A vow and a claim all in one. His warm breath danced against her skin and the soft tickle of his beard sent delicate tremors fanning down her belly. "So beautiful." Sliding his hands around her, he pulled her flush against him, one hand anchored high on her ass and the other smoothing up her spine. He pressed his forehead against her. "Elise..." He lifted his head and met her gaze, frustration and worry warring behind his eyes. "Sweetheart, if you're not ready for more, you need to tell me. Now."

God, he felt good pressed against her. Pure warmth and solid muscle. And was it just her? Or was his scent stronger than normal? The earthy hints that clung to his skin richer like after a fresh rain. She sighed and smoothed her hands from his shoulders to his neck, spearing her fingers in his hair at the back of his head. Her hips flexed on instinct, the press of her pelvis against his flesh making her crave an entirely different layer of contact. The weight of him. The length of him blanketing her body.

"Tate." She fisted her hands in his hair and rolled her hips once more, demands she had no skill or knowledge on how to voice stomping through her with the all the stealth and grace of an elephant. Letting her head drop back, she savored the onslaught of sensations even as her mind grappled for some coherent way to communicate her needs. "Please."

Arms tightening around her, Tate groaned. "Christ, you're there already."

Already where? Lost? Found? Insane? Any seemed

appropriate answers considering the escalating need inside her, but all she cared about was touch. Tate's touch. Preferably everywhere at once with no hope for reality to interrupt either one of them. She needed more of his hands against her skin. His mouth, or any other part of him she could wrangle actively participating in building the sensation pulsing in her core. "Why are you talking?"

"Fuck, Elise. You don't get it." Slowly, he sunk down so he rested on his heels, his lips licking and sucking a decadent path down her belly. "It's your first shift. The sexual urge after is intense." His tongue dipped just below her navel and pleasure stabbed straight to her sex. "I can smell you. Your pussy's ready for me and I haven't even touched you yet."

A shiver rocked her head to toe, the coarseness of his words ratcheting her need higher.

But he was right. She *was* ready. Eager. Ravenous and insatiably determined to fill the void inside her. The low and husky words that came out of her mouth were a shock even to her own ears. "Then do something about it. Give your mate what she needs."

A growl. Low and eerily ominous. "Elise, don't push me. You don't know how rough this could get. If you're not ready, you need to tell me. You need to be sure."

Oh, she was sure. Her body practically sang its agreement. Preened under the primal energy coming off him. She forced her eyes to open and met his heated stare, certainty and hunger thickening her voice. "I know what I want. And right now, I want my mate to take what's his."

His nostrils flared and the emotion behind his amber eyes shifted. Heated and deepened until only a predator stared back at her. He stood, each brush of his body against hers as he did and the intensity behind his gaze shifting the dynamic between them. A transition her everyday mind couldn't quite comprehend, but that her instinctive self welcomed and accepted as *right*. Towering over her—holding her stare and pinning her in place with it—she was utterly bound. Captured without a single restraint. His voice was pure velvet. A command and an enticement all in one breath. "Say it again."

"I want this." More a ragged breath than a declaration, but her spirit soared with it. "I'm not afraid. Not anymore."

"You might be before I'm done." He skimmed his fingers along her jawline, the languid journey from the tip of her chin toward the back of her head deceptively soft in contrast to the edge in his voice. "Who do you belong to, Elise?"

Her stomach pitched and swirled to match the aerial acrobatics of her bird and her breath caught in her throat. Of all the sides to Tate she'd seen, this one was new. Dangerous. Demanding. Unflinchingly dominant. And the fledgling side to herself she'd only just begun to uncover easily stepped forward to answer. Flung every feminist and independent ideal right out the window and offered, "You."

His fingers tangled in her hair, his big palm cradling the back of her head as he squeezed her hip with the other. His lips ghosted against hers and his chest teased her already tight nipples to the point she whimpered. "That's right." He tightened his grip, drawing the roots of her hair taut and dragging a startled gasp past her lips. "All mine."

His mouth crashed against hers, the kiss he sealed

his words with unlike any of the others that had gone
before it. It was a declaration. A demarcation of life
before and after this moment. And good Lord, did he
feel sensational against her. Her breasts flush against
his torso. His arms implacable bonds around her shoulders and waist. His hard length an insistent press against
her belly.

In one impatient move, he lifted her up, guided her
legs around his waist and stalked to the house, his ravenous, all-consuming kiss never flagging in the process. Her lungs burned with the need for more air, but
the part of her brain normally focused on the basics of
survival and rote functions was too caught up in his
kiss to prioritize oxygen over his taste.

Why the hell had she ever fought this? Ever balked
at surrendering to something so naturally primal and
decadent. Granted, she'd never even been tempted with
anyone but Tate, but to think of how much she'd missed
in the time she'd known him left her halfway crazed
and desperate to catch up.

Only when Tate kicked the cabin door shut and the
cool shadows embraced them, did he slow his pace.
He eased her to her feet just steps from the bed, each
agonizing inch as he lowered her downward a tantalizing, erotic caress. Despite the care with which he
handled her, his touch still reverberated with barely
leashed control. A live wire cinched tight and primed
to unleash its energy.

He nipped her lower lip and backed her toward the
bed, his gaze stark with hunger and his voice pure pos-
session. "What are you?"

Oh, hell.

The backs of her knees met the mattress and her sex clenched. "I'm yours."

The low rumble that vibrated through his chest danced along her skin like sparks off a Fourth of July sparkler. A unique sensation her brain insisted could cause her harm, but that her body was too enamored of and curious to explore to heed its warnings.

He manacled one wrist with his fingers and lifted her hand, stroking his thumb up and down her pulse point. "Freely given."

The contact rippled through her. Jolted her heart and sent goose bumps fanning out in all directions. "Freely given."

He pressed her hand to his heart, the steady rhythm beneath her palm as unrelenting as his predatory stare. "Get on the bed."

Run.

She zeroed in on the door.

"Don't even think it." Tate crowded closer, his chest rising and falling at an accelerated pace and a wildness painting his features. "If you run, I'll chase you. You think you're scared now, you've got no idea what you'd unleash with a hunt."

A hunt.

Why the idea thrilled her, she couldn't comprehend, but it went hand in hand with the compulsion she'd felt to high-tail it out the door. As if in doing so, she'd force him to prove himself. To test how far he was willing to go in staking his claim. In providing for her and their family.

It was primal.

Sheer animal logic.

"I'm not scared." Not exactly, anyway. Anxious, yes.

Uncertain, absolutely. But there was no way on Earth Tate would hurt her. That much she knew clear to her soul. Legs trembling, she sat on the edge of the bed and scooted backward. "And I'm not running either."

"No. You're not. Not yet, anyway." One slow yet unceremonious shove of his training pants and he stood naked before her. The early afternoon sun cut through the wide wall of windows behind them and cast his prime body in a golden halo. In the two weeks since they'd begun their physical explorations, she'd had ample opportunity to see him. To touch and explore him all she dared. But in this second—seeing him this raw and exposed—was like seeing him for the first time. All of him. The core essence of him unveiled for her alone.

Keeping his unflinching gaze on her, he planted one knee on the edge of the bed, smoothed his hands along the tops of her feet to her ankles and eased them apart enough to kneel between them. "I won't hurt you, Elise. Won't ever give you more than you need." His hands slid higher, the rough pads of his thumbs dragging a wicked path along the insides of her shins. "But you're going to feel me."

A shiver wriggled down her spine and a tiny whimper eked past her lips.

The hum he answered with was pure contented alpha. The satisfied purr of a man confident he'd not only found but exploited a highly sensitive spot. He circled his thumbs along the inside of her knees. "You want that, don't you? Want to feel my claim as much as I want to stake it." His fingers tightened, and he firmly splayed her knees wide, fully exposing her sex. "What are you?"

Her sex spasmed and her back bowed, her taut,

heavy breasts pressed upward and eager for his attention. The answer came easy. Stronger and more determined. "Yours."

"All of you. Every inch." He cupped her ass, lifted his gaze from her aching core to meet her stare and blatantly licked through her folds. "Mine."

The word vibrated against her heightened skin a second before the wet silken heat of his lips surrounded her clit.

And dear God, it was sensational. Bliss in physical manifestation. The pull of his mouth. Each decadent sweep of his tongue. The implacable grip of his hands on her ass as he held her to his mouth and feasted, and the erotic image of his head working between her thighs.

She widened her knees and speared her fingers in his hair, shamelessly holding him to her and rolling her hips to meet each sensation. It didn't matter that there were no shadows to hide her. No darkness to mask her insecurities and worries. This was Tate. Her mate. He wanted *her*. Flesh and blood. Heart and soul.

As easy as breathing, the sweet, aching tension of a nearing release rolled in. Drew the tender muscles of her sex tighter and tighter as the last of her inhibitions floated away. He slicked his fingers through her folds and circled her entrance.

Her hips lifted in silent invitation. Eager to feel them press deeper. To ride the wet friction he'd taught her to crave as they'd played and learned each other.

Instead, he lifted his head, palmed the insides of her thighs and dragged in a long, sensual breath, openly enjoying the sight of her bared to him.

She dug her nails into the back of his neck. "Tate."

His exhalation was equally wicked. A sigh that said he welcomed the pain. A hunter in no hurry to finish its prey. "Easy, *mihara*. I'll give you what you want." He leaned forward, bracing one hand beside her head and caressing the curve of her hip with the other. At her rib cage, his hand shifted inward, then firmly cupped one breast. "Except tonight when you come, it'll be on my cock, not my fingers."

He punctuated the comment with a roll of his hips, nudging her clit with the broad head of his beautiful cock.

"Oh my God." She held on for dear life, the grip she kept on his shoulders no doubt painful even with her limited strength, but she needed something to ground her. An anchor to hold her steady as the foreign sensation rolled through her. Back and forth, he guided his shaft against her. Forced her back toward the ledge he'd so casually pulled her away from.

His lips skimmed the tip of one nipple and his warm breath fanned light against her skin. "You'll feel me just like this, Elise." Plumping her breast, he flicked the tip with his tongue. "Inside you. Stretching you. Filling you." He nipped the tip then surrounded the peak with his devious lips, drawing so deep that a tightly woven mix of pain and pleasure speared straight between her legs. For all the things he'd taught her—all the leisurely physical explorations he'd taken her on in the last few weeks—none were on par with this. This raw and unabashedly primal.

He shifted his attention to her other breast. Licked, nibbled and sucked her nipple and stroked her flesh until reality ceased to exist. There was only Tate. His scent. His touch. His taste.

With a frustrated growl, he sat back on his heels and palmed her hips. His cock jutted between them, its hard length a tantalizing weight against the top of her sex. "Last chance, Elise." His fingertips dug into her flesh and he ground his hips against her. "I might be able to stop now, but once I'm inside you, I don't think I can."

Stop? Was he insane? "If you stop, I'll hit you with my own car and not let anyone heal you."

She'd meant it as playful. Even tried to inject some levity into her breathless voice.

But Tate's response was unexpected, a hard, exhilarating edge she'd sensed countless times, but had never witnessed in full force. "I don't think you're thinking that one through, *mihara*." His hands coasted inward, his thumbs teasing the seam where her inner thighs and sex met. "If you don't heal me, then I can't fuck you like you need to be fucked."

It should have shocked her. Should have doused the moment or made her reconsider where they were headed. Instead, she bucked against him, the sheer rawness of his words and the primitive energy pouring off him waking a side to herself she hadn't known existed.

And she *loved* it. Loved the freedom. The uncivilized and ravenous urgency that blasted wildfire hot beneath her skin. She squeezed his wrists and writhed against him, his hard shaft a delicious friction against her clit, but nowhere near what she wanted. Foreign or not, her body knew what it needed. What it craved to ease the insatiable ache. "Tate. Stop talking. Let me feel you."

The snarl he answered with would have terrified her weeks ago, but tonight it settled something inside her. Incited a natural transference of power that might have felt wrong in the face of reality, but drifted through her now as soft and confident as a summer wind.

"Stop talking?" One blink and her hands were over her head, pinned beneath one of his own. He cupped the side of her face, a barely leashed power resonating through the touch despite its tenderness. "If I do that you won't know what I'm thinking." He traced her mouth with his thumb, the pressure behind the contact such she couldn't help but part her lips. "Especially the dirty parts."

Her eyes fluttered closed and a whimper slipped free.

"Oh, no you don't. Eyes open." He waited until she complied, the steel behind his amber gaze more effectively pinning her in place than his hands or his weight. Slowly, never breaking her stare, his hand slid lower. Down her neck. Between her breasts. Across her belly. "I want you to remember this. Everything you see. Everything you feel. Everything you hear." He shifted his hips, grasped his cock at the root and slicked his cockhead through her drenched folds.

"Tate." A whisper. A plea. A demand. Heck, she wasn't sure what she was trying to convey with the simple release of his name from her lips, but it was the only word that felt right. That made sense in the moment. A bulwark in the middle of a raging storm.

He centered himself. Notched the barest tip of him at her entrance, then stretched himself above her, lacing his fingers with hers and pinning them on either side of her head. "What are you?"

Dear God. Every time he asked the question, the response stabbed deeper. Left her bared at the deepest part of her soul and trembling with need. But with him poised as he was at the mouth of her, it was pivotal. An indelible moment thick with meaning. She squeezed his hands and lifted her hips as much as she could with his thighs pinning her legs wide. "I'm yours."

He pressed forward. An inch. Maybe less. But a revelation. "All mine." The muscles at his abdomen bunched as he flexed deeper. A delicious and overwhelming stretch so far beyond anything she'd imagined her lungs seized. "Only mine."

She fought to move. To pull her hands from his and tug him to her. To wrap her legs around his hips and glory in the feel of his hot, hard body. To claim his mouth even as his shaft sunk inside her. But breaking his hold was impossible. A cage her body reveled in even as it battled for more. "Tate, please."

With a ragged groan, his eyes slid closed and he drove the rest of the way home, burying his thick length so his pelvis pressed flush to hers.

So good.

Pain and perfection.

Too much and not nearly enough.

She squirmed beneath him, greedy for more of the delicious dichotomy he'd created. To embrace the unknown stretched out in front of her and freefall into maelstrom of all that was him. "Please." She arched her back and squeezed his hands in hers until her nails dug into his skin. "Let me touch you."

"Not yet." A ruthless denial on the surface, but a stark vulnerability rode beneath it. A tiny quaver that spoke of fractures webbing through his control. He slowly dragged his hips backward, the thick head of his cock rousing the tender, stretched walls around it and stealing her breath along with it. "Too soon." As if to prove his point, he thrust forward and seated himself to the hilt once more.

Heaven.

A dark, velvet heaven rich with heat and succulent sensation.

Over and over, he lured her deeper. Pumped his shaft inside her until it seemed her blood pulsed in time to the rhythm he created. Until her thoughts had no room beyond assimilating the most immediate inputs bombarding her. His earthy scent. His labored breaths drifting across her sweat dampened skin. Each flex and release of his muscles and the demanding push and pull of his sex inside her. Time and reason had no place. No bearing on the course he set.

And her body was content to follow. To cede control and happily yield whatever he asked.

"Perfect." His lips coasted against hers, his tongue licking inside her mouth to dance and duel with hers. He fisted his hand at the back of her head, drawing her head back for more of his demanding kiss. "So fucking perfect."

Free.

How long she'd simply ridden the pulsing tide without realizing he'd released his hold, she couldn't say. Didn't care to evaluate in the wake of his drugging kisses. Only knew that a whole new realm of possibilities lay before her. A bold landscape to explore.

She banded her arms and legs around his shoulders and hips and surrendered to the feel of him. To the wildness he stoked higher and higher with each second.

Mine.

A feral claim that rang wanton and unfamiliar in her head, but so profound it resonated beyond mere physical interpretation. The space behind her sternum swelled. Pulsed and reached for something unseen but desperately needed.

Mine.

The reflex and training she'd earned over the last few weeks clicked into place and pushed her into motion.

One shift.

One unexpected use of leverage and she was out from under him, her knees braced on either side of his hips and his cock a thick enticement slick with her arousal against his belly. She gripped it, positioned herself above it and braced for the sweet feel of him sliding home. Filling her completely.

But the world spun before she could claim him. Her shoulders hit the mattress and her breath whooshed out of her as Tate's face flashed primitive and primal above her. And then he was inside her. Buried until there was no separation between them, his teeth biting mercilessly into the tender juncture where her neck and shoulders met.

His snarl fired through her. Rained a flammable tempest on the broiling wildness inside her until there was no place left to go but upward. Shooting into the limitless sky and forcing her release. "Tate!"

A whimper, maybe. Or a shout. In her head it was the latter, her body zinging as her sex clutched his shaft. Fisted it eagerly without even a twinge of remorse.

The tightness around her heart expanded. Burgeoned until she thought her skin and the bones surrounding her chest would have no choice but to rend and split apart. She dug her heels into his flanks and sunk her nails into his shoulders.

His hips bucked against hers and his cock jerked inside her, his teeth bearing down until pain and pleasure were all she knew. All she needed. "Tate."

Maybe it was the sound of her tremulous voice. Or the shudder that wracked her body. But the indescribable pinch of Tate's teeth at her neck lessened in an instant. Replaced with the tender stroke of his tongue and the soothing glide of his lips. He rolled his hips against hers, a languid motion sated with pleasure.

The tug inside her chest strengthened. Drew taut and full. Ready and waiting.

Tate lifted his head, his eyelids heavy over his rich amber eyes. His gaze that of deeply pleased and satiated male—until he focused on the spot at her neck. "Fuck. Elise…"

In a blink, the tight sensation behind her heart ebbed and retreated, still strong, but no longer stretched and reaching forward as it had been before.

Tate tensed inside her arms and steered her head with a firm grip of her chin to one side for a better look.

Her eagle ruffled its feathers and crooned a soft chuffing sound in her head.

Your pain is his pain.

Or more that he perceived he'd caused her pain. Which was so damned far from the truth, she almost laughed out loud at the absurdity of the idea. Especially with her sex still quivering from the aftershocks of the release he'd given her.

She jerked her chin free. "Tate, look at me." When he wouldn't comply and peel his focus from her neck right away, she shifted so he had no other choice but to meet her eyes. "I'm fine."

Doubt.

Fear.

Gut-wrenching pain.

It was all right there. Laid bare in his expression. "I didn't mean to hurt you." His gaze slid back to the throbbing spot on her neck. "I was fine. Had him under control…"

And then she'd pushed him. Challenged her alpha until he'd had no choice but to respond. But what he didn't get was what he'd given her tonight. What he'd unleashed with every touch and word spoken. "Tate, I need you to look at me. Really look at me and listen to what I'm going to tell you."

For a second, he looked like he'd balk. Like an internal war raged inside him with a riotous jury raining judgment in his head, commanding he gut himself with his bare hands. But then he swallowed and met her stare.

She teased her fingers along his jawline. Savored the soft brush of his beard then traced his lips. "I loved it."

He swallowed hard, but held his tongue.

"I like the words," she said. "All the things you say. How you say them. I love your hands on me and the feel of you against me. Inside me." She wrapped her arms around him and skimmed her fingertips soft as a whisper along his spine. "And I love the side you just showed me. Including your bite."

"You haven't seen it," he ground out. "You're bruised already. There's no telling how bad it'll be come morning."

She smiled at that, part of her tempted to scurry from underneath him and see what it looked like for herself. Instead, she tilted her head just enough to give him a good look and caressed one finger above it. "Then I'll be able to remember how I earned it."

His expression darkened, a hint of the predator who'd

mastered her just moments before warring with the male convinced he'd harmed his mate. "You should heal it."

"Like hell I will." Where the bold retort came from she couldn't say, but it mingled with the low, throaty chuckle of a woman growing bolder not just with her sexuality but her place in her new life. "You remember that first night? How fascinated I was by your come and how you said you wanted to mark me with it one day?" She tightened her legs around his hips and smoothed her feet along the backs of his thighs, rolling her hips against his. Luxuriating in the slickness of their combined release. "You got your wish. It just so happens you marked me in more ways than one."

Whether it was the memory she'd dragged to the forefront of his mind, or the feel of her moving against him, his tension eased enough to let the beast in him retreat and the tight press of his lips softened. "It's not the same."

"Isn't it?" She traced the outline of her name above his heart. "A tattoo. Your release on or inside me. Your bite. They're all a claim. A statement. A declaration. A vow." Though, now that she said as much out loud, a part of her wondered at the powerful tug behind her chest. At the sudden loss she'd felt as it nestled back behind her heart. Was that the bond? And if she'd been ready to offer it—to fully seal the fated connection between them—then why didn't she feel the tether to him now?

"I don't want to hurt you."

His words rattled her awareness, a sub context she couldn't quite grasp in the moment buzzing through the hazy edges of her mind. For a moment, she was tempted to analyze it. To let her thoughts churn, twist and spin around the topic until she found the mysterious thread tugging her instincts.

But if she did that, she'd lose the moment. Plus, the one thing she'd learned in working a physical therapy internship, some things were simply meant to be understood in their own time. Whatever it was she was missing would come to her. Until then, she could soothe her mate, linger in his arms and bask in the memories of what he'd given her. "You didn't hurt me, Tate. You made me feel wonderful. Beautiful and free."

He frowned at her like he wanted to argue. Even dragged in a breath as though winding up for another self-scathing retort.

So, she opted for a diversion. One guaranteed to get his mind refocused and let her indulge in the cabin's cozy yet well-equipped bathroom. "You know, that claw-foot tub looks amazing, but I haven't had a chance to put it to good use. I'm thinking a long soak with my mate planning the next few days might be in order."

The ploy worked, confusion and the promise of dallying with her skin to skin knocking him visibly off-kilter. "What's happening the next few days?"

She smiled and threaded her fingers in his hair at the back of his head, urging him close enough to whisper her words against his lips. "I'm moving in with my mate."

Chapter Eighteen

One major bonus when it came to belonging to a clan was that help was never more than a phone call away. Or in this case, movers were never more than a phone call away. In the space of twenty-four hours after Elise's soul quest, Jenny, Naomi, Katy and Jade had not only huddled to pack Elise's things, but gathered a crew of men to deliver them to the cabin shortly after that. And while Tate would've been happy to do all the packing and hauling himself, the private, quiet time someone else doing the work had earned him with Elise was hands down the best gift his clan could have given him. A Volán version of a honeymoon, as it was.

Already done with putting away the larger items Elise had directed him to handle, Tate stretched out on the queen-size bed, one arm anchored between his head and the pillow and the other resting easy on his bare chest, not a thing on but his track pants. In the last three days, they were the most clothing he'd worn, and he'd done his damndest to make sure Elise stuck to nothing. Right now, though, she was cross-legged on the floor in only his T-shirt, unpacking all manner of clothes from a cardboard box, refolding them, and then precisely stacking them in an order he wouldn't even try to pretend he understood. "Wouldn't it be faster just to hang them in the closet when you pull them out?"

The smile she answered with was one he'd grown addicted to. A mix of playful and pure happiness. "I didn't have a chance to go through things when Priest moved us to Eureka Springs, so I thought I'd go through them now. Maybe see if there's anything I don't wear anymore that's more useful being donated."

Well, that kind of made sense. Though, even if she gave half of it away, he still couldn't figure out how she'd ever wear it all.

Box empty, she pushed it aside, stood and braced her hands on her hips, the action lifting the hem of his T-shirt just enough to grace him with a glimpse of her delectable hips. He was so distracted by the view, it took him an extra beat or two to figure out she was frowning at the stack she'd created.

"Don't tell me your stacks got mixed up."

For a second, she looked at him like he'd lost his mind, then comprehension settled in her gaze and she aimed a cute little scowl his way. "You're making fun of me."

"Not even close." Using more speed than was fair given his warrior gifts, he shot forward, snatched her around the waist and tumbled her to the bed. "But I don't like seeing you frown, so what gives?"

Before she could answer, her stomach growled.

Right behind it, she threw her head back and set free a laugh so rich and full his coyote settled in with a contented sigh. Eyes still smiling, she cocked her head at a playful angle and circled her arms around his neck. "Clearly, I'm hungry."

So was he. But he had a feeling he'd already pushed

her about as far and fast as her body could go sexually for today and it was only late afternoon. "How about we take a break and dig into one of the casseroles Naomi brought?"

Another bonus of clan life. One thing Voláns did with great abandon was celebrate good times and enjoy great food, and Naomi, in particular, was one hell of a cook.

Apparently, his mate had already charted the same plan, just with an alternate route. "I was hoping I could talk you into warming a casserole up while I hung the last of my stuff in the closet."

Oh, no. She'd worked enough for today. Had, in fact, plowed through box after box with a single-minded focus he couldn't help but appreciate. But now it was time for her to play. And for him to share something he'd had Jade sneak in with the rest of the boxes they'd delivered. He lowered his head enough to slide his nose alongside hers and breathed in her sweet, exotic scent. "If you put me in charge of food prep you're risking turning Naomi's food into something inedible."

"Right. Like you can't preheat and pop a frozen casserole in the oven."

"True. But if you're hanging clothes you won't be able to open the present I had Jade bring for you."

Her whole expression shifted, sheer delight and openness beaming up at him like a rising sun on a spring day. "I like presents." With that she unceremoniously shoved him to one side, scrambled out from underneath him and hustled to the kitchen. "Which casserole? Chicken tortilla, or beef and bean taco?"

"Is both an option?"

A sound between a snort and a giggle drifted back to him. "Honest to God, I don't know where you put it all.

The way you eat, you ought to be as big as this cabin. We're gonna have to ask Naomi for more provisions."

God, he loved seeing her happy. She'd been addictive even when she was shy and uncertain, but the last three days, her newfound confidence and joy had shifted to something more fundamental to his makeup. A necessity as vital as the blood pulsing through his veins.

And that mark on her neck…his coyote all but howled every time he saw it, even if the man in him still wrestled with the guilt that came with how brutally he'd put it there.

True to what she'd said that night, Elise didn't seem the least bit fazed by its presence. Hell, if anything, he caught her running her finger over it and adding just enough pressure she couldn't help but feel the bruise. And nearly every time she did it, there was a tiny smile on her face. A wistful look that made him wonder if maybe, just maybe, he might eventually be able to let his hunter side out.

"I thought you were getting me a present."

Yep. No shortage of confidence for Elise these days. Not where sass was concerned, or her rapidly rising sexuality. He rolled to the edge of the bed, folded over and slid free the unmarked cardboard box he'd stowed underneath the mattress. "How long will it take to preheat?"

"I don't know. Fifteen—maybe twenty minutes." She padded around the corner and planted her hands on her hips. "You've got more experience using this oven than I do."

He chuckled at that. "I've never so much as touched a knob on that thing. If I can't cook it in a microwave or a grill, it doesn't get eaten. Not if I'm the one making dinner, anyway." He laid the smaller wood box out where she could see it, scooted back so his shoulders were propped against the padded headboard and patted the space in between his legs. "Come here."

Eagerly, she crawled toward him and settled between his wide knees like she'd done it a thousand times before. "What is it?"

He sat the box in her lap and guided her backward so she rested against his torso, giving him an optimal view for the reveal. "So, you know how I said my mom was a healer?"

"Yeah."

He fingered the latch that held the dark pecan wood top panel closed. "Well, she was pretty respected. Nowhere near as powerful as you or your grandmother was, but no slouch either. Most of all, everyone in the clan trusted her. It was a tradition back then for the healer primo or prima to pick one person to maintain the clan records and healing knowledge." He opened the wide cover. "My mom was that person."

Inside, a book over a foot wide and nearly as tall lay nestled in black velvet. The plain black leather cover was soft from years of use and obviously tanned by hand at a time well before today's modern standards.

Leaving it in the protective case, Elise smoothed her fingers over the top of the book. "I don't understand. I thought healers just used their magic to fix people like I did for you."

"That's part of it. But the older generations blended herbs and handcrafted remedies, too. Plus, the records in that book include a whole lot more than just healer knowledge. All the customs and rituals surrounding presect are in there, along with some of the stuff that taught Draven how to tap into the darker side of his magic. That's why not just anyone was trusted with it. That kind of knowledge in the wrong hands is dangerous stuff."

Carefully, Elise lifted the cover.

The spine crackled, and the thick parchment paper whispered as though relieved to feel the touch of a healer once more.

"Tate, you can't give me this. It was your mom's."

"Technically, it's yours. I'd planned to give it to the healer prima whenever we found them. I just never imagined that would end up being my mate."

She turned the page and traced the intricate markings along one side, the black and red ink that made the tribal knots faded by time. "These look like Priest's tattoos."

"That's because they're protection marks. You know Draven's dark magic got trapped in Priest when he recaptured the magic his brother stole from the primos. What you might not have known was that mine and Jade's moms used those marks to help him find his balance. To fight the darkness."

She shut the book with a decisive snap, closed the wooden cover and sat the box to the side like she'd just discovered a snake inside. "I don't want to know anything about that stuff."

"Sweetheart, it's your job to know about that stuff. More than that, you'll need to find another person worthy of keeping the records like my mom did."

She frowned and opened her mouth to answer, but a knock at the door cut her short.

Before she could scramble off the bed to see who it was, Tate caught her at the waist and hauled her back. "Woman, if you think I'm letting you answer the door in only my T-shirt, you're out of your mind." He chin-lifted toward the stack of clothes still waiting on the floor. "You grab some pants and I'll run interference."

Funny. Outside of Elise's things being delivered along with some much needed provisions, Priest and everyone else had left the two of them alone—texts to check in and extra razzing from Jade aside. And while he'd expected reality to come calling eventually, he'd at least expected a heads-up by phone rather than a house call.

He opened the door and just barely managed to contain a startled step backward.

Not just one guest.

A whole damned crew, including Priest, Kateri, Alek and Jade.

Tate sized them up in one swoop. "You guys realize this cabin barely has enough space for two. Let alone a whole damned council."

Priest smirked at the smart-ass remark, but it was Alek who sauntered across the threshold without waiting for an invite. "We figured it might take a village to pry your asses out of your love nest, so we came in full force."

Katy rolled her eyes, but her grin said there was some truth to her brother's statement. "I held them off as long as I could. I swear."

"It's okay," Elise said coming up behind Tate. She wrapped an arm around his waist like she'd welcomed people into their home a hundred times before. "We were just about to put a few of the casseroles in. I don't know if it's enough to feed everyone, but we can give it a go."

Priest shook his head, waited for Jade to file through

the door, then waved Kateri ahead of him. "No need. We won't be long."

The words were polite and delivered with a casualness on the surface, but Priest wasn't the type to pay a social call for no reason, and he sure didn't do it with a small army in tow. "No notice and no plans to hang around. Either you were worried I was holding Elise hostage, or something's wrong. I'm going with the latter."

Jade pulled out one of the two chairs at the tiny kitchen table and cocked an eyebrow at Priest as if to say *I told you so.*

Priest ignored it with the same stoic demeanor he'd used to keep them in line for years and steered Kateri to the chair opposite Jade. As soon as she was settled, he leaned a hip to the kitchen counter behind him and crossed his arms. "Tell me again about the car you saw Saturday night."

A ghostlike touch drifted down the back of his neck. His coyote felt it, too, lifting its head from the easy slumber he'd enjoyed since his run with Elise's eagle this morning. "Either black or a midnight blue. Two-door. I could have sworn it was a Honda, but I could have bungled that detail when the front end demolished my left hip."

"Which part of the car hit you?" This from Alek who'd taken up eyeballing the picturesque view out the cabin's wide back window.

The sun spearing through the back window dimmed and the tiny stretch of seconds when he'd leapt across the road overlaid the present.

Blinding headlights. A shadowed form behind the wheel. His companion stretched nearly perpendicular to the car's front end. Then the excruciating impact. "Driver's side. Right at the corner of the bumper."

"And you said it was a woman behind the wheel?" Alek asked.

"No doubt about it. The height and build were right, and the perfume was hard to miss." Tate focused on Priest. "Where was Vanessa?"

"It wasn't her," Jade said. "No one outside our immediate family knows what happened to you and I talked with a few of her friends. They all say she was with them the same time you got hit."

"Jade's right. It wasn't Vanessa, but we've zeroed in on whoever it was," Priest said. "We've had teams out since Sunday combing the town and lake properties. One of the women on Garrett's team found a dark blue Honda Civic with Wyoming plates at an old motel about eight miles from here."

"There's an impressive dent on the driver's side right where you said you got hit, too." Alek grinned and dipped his head toward Tate's hip. "Healer for a mate or not, I'm not sure how the hell you're up and walking."

"Who is she?" Tate said to Alek, then shifted his attention back to Priest. "And what the hell was she doing at Elise's house?"

"Don't know yet," Priest said. "Garrett called all of an hour ago and has three people with eyes on the place in case whoever it is decides to move, but we figured it was time to clue you in. We're using clan connections to see if we can find someone with an inside track to the guest list."

"Or we could just go knock on the door and talk to whoever's inside."

At Elise's suggestion, the room got crazy quiet. Everyone, that was, except for Jade who snickered and pilfered a chocolate chip cookie from a bakery run they'd made yesterday afternoon. "Now there's a novel idea. Cut right to the chase and avoid all the cloak-and-dagger." Jade bit into her cookie and smirked at Katy. "I so love having more women in the house. Lots less nonsense to wade through."

Katy fought a smile by rolling her lips together and ducking her head.

"What?" Elise said peering up at him. "You're all making an assumption whoever this person is was there for some nefarious reason."

Alek turned from the peaceful view of the lake, his tone as lethal as Tate had ever heard it. "Draven slaughtered my parents."

At Alek's dark tone, Tate braced himself between Alek and Elise, his low growl overloud in the small cabin.

Alek didn't care. Just kept pacing toward them. "He's possessed the man who's probably our sorcerer primo and killed God only knows how many others. You really want to walk up to an unknown person without a clue as to who we're dealing with?"

"Alek."

One word from Priest and Alek stopped in his tracks, but his eyes stayed locked on Elise.

Moving in behind him, Elise smoothed her hand down Tate's arm. A soft and delicate touch, but behind it lay a strength to match her words. "We breed whatever we bring to the table. Suspicion equates more suspicion. Distrust builds more distrust. Maybe what we need more of is tackling our foes and our unknowns head-on rather than circling around and waiting for the right moment to pounce."

Alek's nostrils flared and his lips flatlined.

Tate braced, ready to intercept.

"She has a point." As low and off-handedly delivered as Priest's words were, they ripped the rug out from under Alek's anger, open shock replacing his menacing scowl in a heartbeat.

"Are you serious?" Alek said.

For a beat, Priest didn't move. Didn't say a word. Just stared at Alek with that unrelenting look that had let Tate and Jade know with utter certainty they'd not just pushed a limit, but seriously cross it. "I've got two primos. If we're lucky when this is all over, I'll have two more and we'll get back to the business of tending to our magic the way the Keeper intended. Every opinion and viewpoint they bring me has merit. I won't discredit their place as primo without weighing every one of them." He shifted his attention to Elise. "Now, tell me why you think the direct approach makes more sense."

"Well, for starters, Tate found them on your property. If whoever it was had something to do with Draven, could they have done that? I mean, I know the wards are supposed to keep us off your brother's radar, but if your magic made the wards, wouldn't you sense if someone functioning under his control crossed inside their influence? It's the same magic you use on your tattoos and you use them to locate people all the time."

Kateri smiled.

Jade nodded and dug out another cookie.

Priest uncrossed his arms, braced his hands on the counter's edge and cocked his head, considering. "The wards are an extension of me, yes, but we don't know the extent of what my brother can do either. It could be his spirit inside another body hides him from my magic." He paused, checked Alek as if to get a read on how he was holding up, then refocused on Elise. "What else?"

Elise shrugged. "Whoever it is isn't exactly hiding. If Draven was smart enough to hide his plans to steal every primo's magic as long as he did, he's smart enough not to leave a hit-and-run vehicle out in the open. Plus, this is a woman we're talking about. Have any of you considered it's someone who needs our help as opposed to someone out to hurt us?"

Priest's eyes narrowed in a second. "What makes you think that?"

Elise straightened and blinked her eyes over and over again. Almost as if the question had startled her out of a daydream. "I have no idea. It was just there." She glanced up at Tate then refocused on Priest. "I get being cautious, but taking a defensive stance doesn't feel right."

"It's instinct." Tate moved in tight behind her and cupped her shoulders. "A healer's intuition might be different from a warrior's, but it's no less valid." He looked to Alek. "Healers focus on people. Not threats. If her gut tells her to tackle it this way there's a reason for it. One we'd be smart to pay attention to."

For the first time since the topic had come up, Alek seemed to reconsider his original approach. "You really think this isn't someone under Draven's control?"

Elise let out an ironic chuckle and shook her head. "I have no idea. I don't even think I understand what's driving my thoughts. I just know when you said you'd found a car and started talking about covert ways to get information, everything in me balked." She looked to Priest and covered one of Tate's hands at her shoulder, the tiny squeeze behind the contact as if she sought his strength to lend to her words. "If we need to take precautions, then fine—take them. But if Draven's using his magic to possess people and looking for our seer primo, then aren't we better served to meet whoever's in that motel room face-to-face?"

The room grew silent.

Priest studied Elise. Then Alek. Then shifted his thoughtful gaze to the forest and lake outside the window. Only after a solid thirty seconds, did he push away from the counter and guide Kateri to her feet. "Alek, keep eyes on the motel for now and work out whatever plan you think's appropriate for contingencies. Tate, get your mate fed and things wrapped up here." He motioned Jade to the door ahead of them, then paused a beat to give Tate and Elise his undivided attention. "You've got an hour to meet us at the main house and then we're knocking on our stranger's door."

Chapter Nineteen

Having an alpha male for a mate was tricky business. Alone and left to their own devices at the cabin, Elise hadn't just appreciated his protectiveness and attentive nature, she'd wallowed in it. Embraced every subtle action that showed his desire to look out for her. Moving boxes for her wherever she wanted them. Keeping himself between her and the street when they'd made a bakery run one morning. Sleeping curled around her after he'd worked her body through each amazing release and waking her up with long leisurely kisses and coffee in bed. It had been perfect. An ideal time away from the world.

But sitting beside her in the back seat of Priest's black Tahoe and faced with the prospect of putting her anywhere near danger, he was as riled up as a sleep deprived grizzly.

Or an irritated coyote.

Apparently, they could be just as testy.

The drone of tires against the asphalt filled the SUV's interior and the thick trees that lined the winding country roads swept past the thickly tinted windows. Seated in the front passenger's seat, Katy maintained a peaceful, yet focused demeanor, while Priest looked like he was ready for battle. Probably more of the same alpha overload Tate was battling. Though, to his credit, he hadn't balked about Katy's insistence on coming with them. At least not publicly.

Beside her, Tate scowled out the front windshield. Unlike the last few days, his long blond hair was pulled back in a low ponytail and tension rode his shoulders hard. If it weren't for the way his arm was protectively draped along the seat back behind her or the hand on her thigh, she'd have sworn he was mad at something she'd said or done.

She covered his hand, gave it a reassuring squeeze and lowered her voice only for him. Though, knowing how powerful Priest was, he could probably hear her blood flowing in her veins if he wanted. "You know this is the right thing to do."

His expression softened in a blink and he turned his intense amber eyes on her. "I don't doubt it for a second. I trust your judgment."

"Then you have to know it's the right thing for me to be here when we knock on that door. What kind of person would I be if I gave a recommendation like that and wasn't here when people acted on it?"

He didn't growl, but the look on his face said he wanted to. Badly. His jaw worked just a fraction side to side as though wrangling his words into something that wouldn't backfire on him. "You're not just my mate. You're a prima. I get that. I respect it. But I need you to understand that *any* kind of threat to you—whether your position calls for it or not—isn't something I'll ever take to easily. It doesn't have anything to do with trusting your judgment. Or your skills. It's who I am.

What any decent male would be when it came to keeping his mate safe."

A Volán male, maybe. And even then, she had a feeling Tate was far beyond *decent* expectations. She skimmed her fingers along his jawline, the soft brush of his beard reminding her all too clearly how it felt with each kiss. Against her belly and her thighs when he tended to her with his mouth. "I understand. And I'll try not to put you in this position if I can avoid it."

He cupped the back of her head and pulled her to him, guiding her deeper into the crook of his arm so his arms and his scent surrounded her.

The SUV slowed and turned only moments later.

To his credit, Tate only hesitated in letting her push herself away from his torso for two or three seconds. "You think Alek's going to keep to the plan?" he said to Priest.

The plan being the four of them approaching as two couples in what they hoped would come across as non-threatening so they could start out with a decent dialogue as to what the stranger had been doing on Priest's property.

Almost at an idle in the parking lot, Priest scanned the old motel outside his driver's-side window. The once crimson painted siding was muted with age, and the gray asphalt shingles had to be the lowest and most unappealing commercial grade available, but overall the upkeep to the place was decent. There were even flower boxes hung outside the motel office windows planted with yellow and purple pansies.

Done with his examination, his eyes shifted to the rearview mirror and the trees on the opposite side of the road behind them where Alek and his men sat watching.

"Unless you or I give him a reason to come in fighting, he'll hold his ground." He inched the truck farther into the parking lot toward the Honda Civic parked in front of the third door from the end. "I think between Elise's logic and the fact that they haven't seen anyone come in or out of the room since they found the car, he's realizing Elise might have a point."

"What name was the room registered under again?" Elise asked.

"Terri Smith," Kateri answered with a dry chuckle. "What do you bet it's a bogus name?"

"The plates on the car tie back to a rental under the same name, so we've got nothing to track there either." Priest pulled into the spot beside the Civic, killed the engine and twisted for an eye-to-eye view of Tate. "I know this goes without saying, but if you tweak to anything, your only responsibility is Elise. Not strategy. Not hunting. Not other people getting hurt. Nothing. Alek and Garrett can handle whatever else happens."

"Yeah, that's not gonna be a problem."

Priest huffed out a short chuckle and nodded to Elise. "Okay. Time to see if your gut's right."

At nearly seven o'clock at night, the sun was well into its descent, casting all of the parking lot and the walkway along the long building in shadows. She'd caught all kinds of flak from Tate for picking a hunter green fitted V-neck tee since it left his mark so prominently displayed, but with the cooling evening air whipping around her, she was a little chagrined she'd won the battle and made it out of the house without something a little warmer. Her skinny jeans had been a point of contention, too. Though, once she'd proven the fabric was stretchy enough to let her handle whatever self-defense maneuvers were called for, he'd conceded, cupped her behind and heartily approved her wearing them whenever she wanted.

Priest took the lead while Katy and Elise walked side by side behind him and Tate followed at the rear. Rather than knock as soon as they reached the door, Priest crowded close enough anyone watching from a distance couldn't see his action and splayed his big hand about sternum height against the black door.

"What's he doing?" Elise whispered to Katy.

Her eyes stayed locked on Priest when she answered, as if she were at the ready to take action at a moment's notice. "The darkness in Priest recognizes Draven. It's what he felt the day we first met you. What told him there was someone watching us from the bayou. If Draven or anyone possessed by him is in that room, he ought to be able to sense it."

Stepping back from the door, Priest met Kateri's eyes and shook his head. "Nothing."

Tate's hand cupped Elise's shoulder and squeezed, though whether it was a subtle encouragement or him positioning to shove her out of the line of fire, she couldn't be sure.

Priest knocked.

Behind them, a big truck rumbled down the street, the equipment trailer it pulled behind it loaded down with lawn mowers and other yard tools rattling loud against the evening's peaceful quiet.

Then nothing.

Not a single movement behind the door.

He knocked again, this time cocking his head as though listening at a whole different level.

"She's in there." Tate's voice was low enough only

to reach Priest, but the certainty in his statement was unmistakable. "It's the same scent as Saturday night. Not as strong, but it's there."

An idea sparked. Or an instinct. "Can I try?"

Tate's hand on her shoulder tightened.

Priest shared a look with him that she could have sworn conveyed an entire man-to-man conversation in all of two seconds. He refocused on Elise, dipped his head and stepped back. "Do what you need to do, but Tate goes in first. Understand?"

Oh, she understood. She'd had a crash course in Tate's safety demands in the time since he'd finally accepted she wasn't going to stay cloistered at Priest's house and wait for an update. Still, she nodded and moved in closer to the door. She lifted her hand to knock, but stopped mid-motion and flattened her hand against the door's surface as Priest had done.

Panic.

Terror.

Exhaustion.

She jerked her hand away so fast, she lost her balance and would've fallen if Tate hadn't been practically plastered to her back. "Get us in. Now."

Tate hesitated, glancing to Priest for affirmation.

"Tate, get that door open." The command came out of her mouth not as a mate, but as a prima. One laser focused on helping the suffering soul inside and running on pure intuition.

"Do it," Priest said from behind her.

Whether it was Priest's go-ahead, or the urgency beating off Elise, Tate moved in, gave the knob a twist that wouldn't have been possible from an ordinary human and pushed the door wide.

Darkness consumed the bleak room, broken only by the waning sunlight through the doorway and the faint glow of the television on the plain black dresser. Two double beds took up the bulk of the room, their simple bedspreads an unremarkable pattern of red and blue. But it was the woman huddled with her knees tight to her chest and her back plastered against the headboard that held Elise's attention. Her chin rested on the back of her knees and her dark hair hung wild around her face so much of her features were obscured, but there was no missing the franticness behind her eyes. A glazed disconnectedness locked on to the television screen that said she was so far removed from reality she was dangerously close to shattering.

Tate started forward, but Elise blocked him, plastering her hand against the doorframe and holding firm with a strength that startled her. "No." Only when she was certain he'd heard and acknowledged her direction did she lower her arm and meet his stare, fighting against the incessant tug that insisted she tend to the woman straight away. "No men. Not until I say so." Her hand still tingling from the sensation she'd picked up against the door, she splayed it over Tate's heart. "I need you to trust me. She needs me."

Fear and frustration crackled and sparked against her already heightened healer instincts and for a second, Elise halfway expected Tate to refuse. Instead, he pressed his lips together with a visibly painful resoluteness and jerked his head in a sharp nod.

It was all she needed. A green light to give in to the compulsion driving her forward.

Two cautious steps past the threshold, the near muted chatter from the television superseded the natural sounds from outside and the stagnant discomfort of stale air pressed her on all sides. A high-end laptop sat open on the desk next to the dresser, its screen black. Beside it lay a semi-organized smattering of snack food—none of it healthy and most of it the type most easily picked up at a convenience store.

Another two steps in and the shadows grew thicker, the need and desperation she'd picked up before now whispering like ghosts against Elise's skin. Carefully, she stepped directly in front of the television and into the woman's line of sight.

The woman jumped as though she'd been startled out of a deep sleep and her eyes sharpened on Elise. A second later, she scrambled to the far side of the bed, her gaze darting between Elise and the doorway. "Who are you?"

Elise froze and held up her hands. "It's okay. You're safe, I promise. My friends and I just wanted to see if you were okay."

The woman squinted as though trying to focus through the shadows. "You're Elise Ralston."

Well, that confirmed they were dealing with the right person. The question was how she knew Elise in the first place, because she sure hadn't ever seen this woman before. "I am, but I don't think we've met. What's your name?"

Hesitating, the woman's focus shifted to the doorway.

"Listen, I don't know what's wrong with you, but I know you're hurting," Elise said, inching a little closer. "I also know that you were at my house on Saturday. If there's something you want—something you need—we

can help you, but it would sure be a lot easier to start
with if I knew your name."

"You're safe," the woman whispered.

"Yes, I'm very safe. Protected. But I'd like to make
sure you are, too, and I have a feeling you haven't felt
that way in a very long time."

Deep, aching sorrow pierced deep in Elise's chest,
the magnitude of it so powerful her knees buckled, and
she stumbled forward a step.

Before she could catch herself, Tate was there, his
arm a steadying band around her waist.

"You," the woman said, almost accusingly. She
backed off the bed completely as though prepared to
bolt. Though, where she thought she could run considering the room's layout and four of them between her
and the door, Elise couldn't imagine.

"It's okay. Tate won't hurt you. He's my mate. He'll
help you. We all will if you'll let us."

She frowned at that, her gaze still rooted on Tate. "I
saw you. Heard you. You were looking for her."

Plates from Wyoming.

Tate had gone there with Garrett following a lead
at the same time Alek, Priest and Kateri had come to
find Elise and her mother. They'd said all they'd found
were dead ends.

"Tate wasn't looking for me," Elise said. "He was
looking for someone else we thought might be in danger. The same way I was in danger. But Priest and
Kateri found me and moved me someplace safe." She
paused long enough to let the information sink in. To
let the truth of it resonate. "Please. Will you tell me
your name?"

She braced one hand on the old paneling behind her,

her body trembling with what Elise sensed was the last of her strength and far too much adrenaline. "Sabina." She stole a glance at Tate and swallowed hard. "Sabina Sterling."

Tate's arm around her waist tightened, but otherwise kept his response in check. "The lead we followed," he said low near Elise's ear. "The name our seer saw was Sterling."

They'd found her.

Finally.

Or rather she'd found them.

But if Elise couldn't find a way to build some immediate trust and deflate whatever anxiety gripped her, the woman they hoped would be their seer prima might not be sane long enough to help them. She straightened and urged Tate's arm from around her waist. "Sabina, tell me why you're afraid. Tell me why you thought I wouldn't be safe."

Sabina's voice quavered when she answered, so thready and shallow it barely registered over the television behind them. "I thought they were helping him."

"Helping who?"

Abject terror and desolation painted her features and her face blanched a ghostly white. "The man in my dreams."

Chapter Twenty

The forest was perfectly still. The waters in the cove just down from Elise's mother's house lay smooth as glass. If the midday sun weren't hidden behind a thick sheet of clouds it would have been a picturesque moment, but the deep gray sky and the energy in the air promised a torrent of rain at any moment.

If Tate's instincts were right, that wouldn't be the only storm on the horizon. Not after the things they'd learned from Sabina last night.

Priest sat silent in the Adirondack chair beside him, nursing what had to be his fifth cup of coffee in the last two hours. If he was anywhere near as keyed up as Tate was, he didn't show it.

"How do you do it?" Tate asked.

It took a solid two heartbeats before Priest pulled his thoughts back from wherever they'd drifted. "Do what?"

"Not keep Kateri locked up in the house where it's safe."

Priest's slow grin was that of a man not just aware of the kind of turmoil Tate was wrestling, but able to commiserate. "Don't think I don't consider it at least five times a day. Even if I tried, she's got enough magic in her to decimate the house and go on about her business anyway." He cocked his head and studied Tate. That shrewd once-over he'd honed since that fateful day Tate had followed his dad into the forest for training. "Our mates are strong for a reason. If we lock them up, we rob the clan of what they bring to the table. They'll face their own challenges in their own way. Our job is to be there and give them the backing they need to make it out safe."

Safe.

Tate scoffed and refocused on the cove. "Easy for you to say. You can *see* Katy's opponents. The ones Elise has to face, I can't do anything but stand back and watch." A task he'd done for hours last night watching Elise try to heal the fragile inner workings of Sabina's mind—a by-product of Sabina's self-imposed sleep deprivation over the past two months to avoid Draven reaching her in dreams.

"Elise is our healer prima for a reason," Priest said. "Trust her to know her limits."

"She's had her magic for four days. Her instincts are spot on, but no one's told her how dangerous it is for her to deal with the mental aspects of healing. If Draven's been in Sabina's head, there's no telling what kind of traps he's managed to leave in her mind. Elise wouldn't have a clue what to look for yet. And who knows if she's going to have to do more healing on Sabina once she wakes up or if some decent sleep will do the rest of the work for her?"

"You gave her your mother's records. She'll learn."

Not the answer he wanted to hear. Not even close. Especially when Elise had done nothing but pore through the journal since Priest had helped Elise ease Sabina into restorative sleep in the wee hours of the morning. Lack of knowledge or not, he'd have much rather seen her get some rest herself than cram on all things Volán.

The sliding glass door to the porch whooshed open.

For a guy who'd been primed and ready to do battle this time less than twenty-four hours ago, Alek seemed to be back to his usual laid-back self now. "Hey, how's Sabina?"

"Still sleeping," Priest said. "My guess, she's gonna stay that way most of the day before she's in any condition to surface and see if Elise's healing was enough." He finished off the dregs of his coffee and set the mug aside on the table between his and Tate's chair. "You get any confirmations nailed down on Sabina?"

"Everything checks out." Alek leaned one hip on the rail surrounding the wood deck and crossed his arms. "Born and raised in Jackson, Wyoming. The Sterling name first shows in Jackson just shortly after your thing with Draven went down. Six months later, Sabina's dad was born. The mother's name was Melanie. No father listed. No other siblings."

The calm Priest had carried about him all morning turned weighted and as dark as the clouds overhead in a second. "I remember her. Quiet. Complete opposite to her husband." He paused and sucked in a slow breath, as though wading through the memories of that night all over again. "It sucks she couldn't acknowledge her husband on the birth certificate, but after watching him be murdered with all the other primos, I can't say I wouldn't have done the same thing if it meant keeping myself and my kid safe."

"So, the Volán heritage runs through Sabina's dad's side of the family?" Tate asked.

"Looks like it." Alek smirked in a way that said he had some bonus information to share and was mighty pleased with himself because of it. "That's not the interesting part of the story, though. You know how Sabina said she'd overheard Tate give Elise's name when he took a call outside her house, and she decided to track her for fear someone was after Elise, too?"

Rather than answer, Priest just shot him an impatient look that said to get on with it.

Alek chuckled and rolled with it. "Well, turns out saying *she tracked her* is a bit of an understatement. Sabina's a private investigator. A really damned good one. If you think about it, the way things played out makes sense. A woman doesn't want to go to sleep because her dreams are chock-full of some guy who wants to do her harm. Sleep deprivation feeds paranoia, so she's on guard all the damned time, wondering if the guy who's making it so she doesn't feel safe to sleep is going to show up in real life. Then Tate and Garret show up, obviously snooping around, and mention another woman's name. PI instincts kick in and she moves out of defensive mode and into protector mode looking out for Elise. Her being here Saturday night was probably all about trying to see for herself if Elise was okay."

"And with Elise and her mom showing as relocated only a little over a month ago, it probably looked like they were on the run on paper," Tate said.

"Exactly," Alek said. "And you chasing her that night—combined with the lack of sleep and paranoia—probably put her over the deep end. It would sure explain her tearing out of here the way you said she did."

No shit. Tate had never met Draven and couldn't pick him out of a lineup if he had to, but warrior magic or not, he'd at least consider hightailing it for safe ground if he thought the asshole was bearing down on him.

Priest stood, moved around his chair as if headed back inside and snatched his empty coffee cup off the table. "Well, the good news is she's here now and safe. If we can get her healed up from what she's been through the last few months, the only major hurdle we'll have left is finding Jerrik."

"Ah, but you're missing the best part," Alek said.

Stopping midway to the sliding glass door, Priest twisted to meet Alek's stare and cocked one eyebrow in silent question.

"She's a PI."

Priest waited.

"A really good one."

The fact that it took as many seconds as it did for the pieces to click together for either of them only highlighted how little rest any of them had had in the last twenty-four hours. But it finally sunk in.

Tate looked to Priest. "We finally got the person we needed to find the last primo."

Chapter Twenty-One

She had a tattoo. An honest to God work of art that spanned her collarbone, delicately touched the crest of Elise's shoulders and then dipped downward in a tempting V toward her spine. While the shape of the protective marking was the same as what Priest had given Alek—a traditional formation reserved for those chosen as primos—the patterns were entirely different. Intricate swirls that hinted of flowering vines intertwined with tribal knots that denoted an undeniable balance of femininity, grace and strength. And while the bulk of the work had been done in simple black ink, he'd incorporated the rich green of her house's magic in the shading. A subtle touch that gave the overall appearance a surreal depth.

All too aware of Priest behind her and watching her response in the mirror, Elise traced the healer's symbol just below the hollow at her neck—a beautiful flowing design that looked like a bass clef on sheet music with an inverted impression below it and joined by an infinity loop between them.

But her eyes went to her neck. To the space where Tate's mark was missing.

"He'll give you another one," Priest said.

"Another what?"

He chuckled and gave her a look that said she wasn't fooling anyone. "I never know where my designs will take me when I do one with magic. Especially protection ink. I had to heal it to have a good surface to work with, but he'll give you another one. Trust me."

In that, she wasn't so sure. Yes, he seemed to finally be convinced that she'd liked it—both the look of it and the way she'd earned it. Had even watched her running her finger along the tender area and studied her response with a guarded curiosity. But other times, when he thought she wasn't watching, he'd scrutinized the mark with an expression she couldn't quite put her finger on. As though he both hated and coveted the action that had put it there and craved more despite his internal struggles.

Around the room where he'd lived with Priest until only days ago were little reminders of the mate she'd only just begun to know. Ticket stubs from sporting events tacked onto a corkboard. Artwork in various stages of completion stacked on the desk and framed on the walls. A closet that stood open, now void of clothes post-move to the cabin. "Do you think that's odd?"

"Which part? That you miss the reminder? Or that getting another one is almost guaranteed?"

She turned and met Priest's gaze. "Maybe both."

He cocked his head, his eyes just a little more narrowed. Considering. "Does it matter what I think? What anyone beyond Tate thinks?"

He had a point. A really freaking good one actually. And in the last few days, she'd had plenty of time to consider the impact his actions had had on her that night, as well as his careful, almost too tender attentions since then. "Yeah, well, Tate's not exactly talkative on that point. Which is weird considering how open he's been with everything else."

In all of a heartbeat, Priest's expression shuttered. A careful neutrality that said she'd tiptoed into either uncomfortable or sacred territory. He turned to his tattoo supplies lined up on Tate's dresser and started cleaning up.

She gripped the towel wrapped tight around her breasts and ducked her head, the jeans she wore underneath and the soft terrycloth fabric not nearly enough armor for the conversation she'd started. "Sorry. I shouldn't have gone there."

Priest hesitated, stared down at the floor for a beat, then started back with packing his ink. "There's nothing you can't ask or tell me, Elise. Part of my job is to be here for my primos."

"Not about relationship stuff, though. Especially not with how close you and Tate are." She grabbed her top and bra folded on top of the desk, fully prepared to execute a retreat. Not that she really knew Priest's house well enough to know where to go once she got past the bedroom door. "I'm sorry I made it awkward."

"You didn't make it awkward." This time a smile was in his voice. And while the most she could make of his expression was in profile, there was no missing the thoughtfulness as he packed the rest of his things in his duffel. He zipped it up, slung the strap over one shoulder and met her stare head-on. For a handful of seconds, he just looked at her, then seemed to come to a decision. "Mated Volán males have one drive that overrides everything else—see to their mate and their children. Every other concern or consideration is secondary. But our companion is part of us, too, and brings its own instincts and drive into the equation. When the two are in conflict, sometimes it takes a decisive action, or reaction, to force the two halves to find an order they can work with."

"An action?"

"Or reaction."

Considering he was actually trying to help her, frowning at him the way she was probably wasn't the best move, but with the amount of time and energy she'd put into healing Sabina and working her way through the journal Tate had given her, patience wasn't exactly in short order. "What are you trying to say?"

Priest huffed out a sharp laugh, shook his head and turned for the door. "Coyotes are hunters."

"And?"

"And I'm telling you sometimes action is more effective than talking." He opened the door and jerked his chin toward the backyard. "Hurry up and get downstairs. We've got over a hundred people ready to see you and celebrate. Not to mention, Katy's due here anytime with Sabina. It's her first glimpse into clan life. If you take too long up here, Tate will come up to get you, you'll both end up distracted, and then Katy and I won't have any help introducing her to everyone."

Boy, that was the truth. Tate might have been more cautious with her in the last few days than he had been that first night, but his sex drive hadn't abated in the least. Frankly, she was surprised Priest had managed to get him to leave her alone in the same room with another man, father figure or not. "Fine, but you have to promise to spend a little time talking to me about the journal before tonight's over. There's a mark next to some of the rituals that I don't know how to interpret. There's no legend to go with them."

Priest's brows dipped into a sharp V. "What mark?"

"It's weird looking. Nothing like the other marks I've seen. Two circles. One big one and a little one on top of it. Kind of looks like BB8 but with a cross perched on its head."

One second and Priest's whole demeanor changed, a darkness she'd never seen in him surfacing like a long dead demon. Just as fast, he seemed to shove whatever had gripped him back into place and shook his head. "Nothing with that symbol next to it can help you do anything except know what *never* to do. They're recorded as a warning only."

Black magic.

The kind Draven had used to steal each primo's gifts and killed them in the process—her great-grandmother included.

"If they're so dangerous, why record them?"

"There are two choices. Leave our future generations ignorant, or take a chance and at least provide a warning. Which option is worse?" Not waiting for a response, he nodded toward her shirt still clutched in her hand. "Get dressed. Forget about the journal for tonight and come meet your healers. Something tells me we'll have more than our share of darkness to contend with soon enough."

He left without so much as a backward glance, quietly closing the bedroom door behind him and leaving her to ruminate on the things he'd said. Located upstairs and furthest away from the gorge where most of the gatherings at Priest's house happened, Tate's room gave no clue as to the number of people who'd come to help celebrate the arrival of a new prima. Certainly nothing to warrant the number Priest said to expect. But the silence was a comfort. A tiny buffer in the seconds before she faced the full scope of her new reality.

She was a leader.

A powerful one.

Maybe not in the way Kateri was with her sorcerer magic, or fast and strong like Alek, Priest and Tate with their warrior magic, but an important piece in the clan's makeup.

She wriggled into her bra and pulled on her shirt. While she hadn't selected the trendy cotton tank with its low scooped neck and narrow straps with the end result of her tattoo in mind, it did a remarkable job of leaving much of the work on display. The contrast of its bold coral color with the understated green Priest had worked into the shading made it even more compelling. A bold, yet beautiful statement.

Funny, how much she'd changed in such a short span of time. Yes, she'd grown through therapy since high school, but nothing like she had in the last four weeks. For the first time in her life, she *wanted* to be seen. Wanted to share the joy of what she'd been given with the people who shared her heritage.

Maybe Priest was right. Maybe tonight she should just enjoy the moment. Tuck all the responsibilities of the future aside and simply focus on celebrating right now. Be with the people who'd so readily accepted her and see if she couldn't share the same with Sabina.

Resolve in place, she gave her loose hair a quick fluff and hurried to the door—only to have it open before she could get there.

Tate stood in the opening. In a matter of seconds,

he scanned the room, her and the ink now lying beautifully against her skin. His amber eyes warmed with mischief. "Aren't I supposed to get a private showing before everyone else does?"

Oh, no. If Tate got anywhere near her sans clothes she'd never get out of this room. Let alone have the social skills to face so many people for the first time as prima. "I think the point of having the celebration is for me to actually be there." She braced her hand at his sternum and pushed him backward, giggling as he gripped her wrist and used the momentum to pull her flush against him. She wrapped her arms around his neck and her laughter melted into an easy sigh, just the press of his body against her and his warmth settling what was left of her apprehension. "How about if we save the private viewing for when we get home so we can take our time?"

"Home." He cupped the back of her head and skimmed his nose alongside hers, the low rumble of his coyote's approval mixing with his own pleased hum. "That word has a whole different feel to it when you're a part of it." He pressed a lingering kiss to her lips then murmured against them, "And I can definitely see the benefits to not being in a rush when I get an unobstructed view of Priest's work."

God, the man was addictive. Not just the feel of him against her, but the rich baritone of his voice, too. The subtle hint of earth that clung to him. She closed her eyes and breathed in deep. "I do believe this is the first time I've considered ducking a party for a reason other than avoiding being social."

His low chuckle coiled around her. "Under normal circumstances I'd not only approve, but aid and abet your absence, but this time, Priest would flay both me and my coyote." He reached behind his neck, grasped one of her hands and guided it to his mouth for a kiss. "Come on. Katy, Jade, Sabina and your mom got here just a few minutes before I came up to get you. The way Sabina eyeballed the crowd, I think she needs a stiff drink and a hand to hold on to."

Getting to the isolated cluster of lawn chairs where Katy, Jade, Sabina and her mom had set up camp proved to be more of a challenge than either of them had thought. Where everyone in the clan she'd met to date had been pleasant and polite before, they'd also been a bit reserved. As though they hadn't been entirely sure what to make of the outsider Priest had brought among them, but were cautiously optimistic on what her future with the clan might be.

Today was a whole different experience. A throng of well-wishers intent on sharing their happiness in the form of hugs and blessings for the days ahead. If those she met were healers, the conversations were even more intense. A mix of reverence and gratitude she didn't even remotely feel she'd done anything yet to earn woven into each word.

By the time she and Tate finally reached everyone at the edge of the crowd, she felt almost as exhausted as Sabina looked. "Hey, Sabina. How are you holding up?"

Sabina scanned the people meandering from group to group behind them with the same wide-eyed wonder Elise had probably had the night of Beltane. "I'm still not convinced I'm not dreaming."

"Boy do I remember that feeling," Katy said. Dressed in a flowing chambray skirt and a white blouse that made Elise think of poets and flower children, she sat in a sling patio chair with one leg crossed over the other. As relaxed as she looked, there was no way to tell she'd only learned of their clan a few months ago. "Even after I saw Nanna change into her hawk the first time, I thought for sure I'd either lost my mind, or woken up in an alternate reality." She focused on Sabina and smiled. "It'll settle in eventually, though. You'll see."

Sabina didn't look convinced. It wasn't every day a person found out their heritage included shapeshifting and magic. And while the dreams Sabina had had of Draven over the last month had made her more receptive to the idea than most, it was obvious the reality had yet to fully settle in. Her physical appearance, on the other hand, was remarkably improved. The paleness that had almost obliterated the rich olive coloring of her skin was long gone, and the gaunt, desolate weight that had burdened her every movement was now replaced with a curious, yet cautious wonder.

Priest insisted it had been Elise's persistent healing over the last few days, but Elise suspected the bulk of it was from healthy, uninterrupted sleep. "Have you eaten?"

She should have known the answer without asking. Getting Sabina to tackle any more than a bite or two at a time had been a struggle since the first time she'd woken up. Though, she had perked up this morning when Naomi and Jenny had double-teamed the kitchen for an old-school breakfast fitting for a day's worth of manual labor. Then again, it was hard to say no to bacon. "I got distracted talking to Jade."

Jade rolled her head on the back of the lounge chair she'd stretched out on toward Sabina. "Oh, no. You don't get to use me for that one." She focused on Elise.

"Naomi and I both tried to ply her with homemade snickerdoodles and sugar cookies right after lunch and she defied us both."

Standing slightly behind her with his hand resting on her hip, Tate gave her a gentle squeeze. "I'll go grab you both a plate." He kissed the side of her neck, the subtle rasp of his exhalation as he did so sending a welcome shiver down her spine. "I know damned well you didn't eat the whole time Priest was working on you."

She *was* hungry. Enough so her stomach let out a muted rumble of agreement. But Sabina needed more than food. She needed grounding and a chance to realize this new reality was...well...real.

She stopped Tate with a hand over his at her hip, craned her head up and back so she could return the kiss to the strong line of his jaw. "How about if you take a load off and Sabina and I go explore what everyone brought?"

Whether it was the firm undercurrent in her voice, or just his experience in watching his mother work with people growing up, understanding moved behind his eyes and he dipped his head in agreement. "Makes sense to me." He turned her and pulled her in for a chaste, but lingering kiss. "Just be sure you skirt the edges of the crowd instead of cutting straight through it. Otherwise, it'll take you too long to get back to me."

"Yuck," Jade said with more than a little sibling disgust in her voice. "Tate being all macho is bad enough. The lovey-dovey stuff is painful."

Katy and Elise's mom both laughed, but the warmth and happiness in her mom's eyes as she watched them said she didn't care how mushy Tate got. Only that she was thrilled to see Elise so well taken care of.

More hesitant to pull away than she cared to admit, Elise forced herself to step out of his arms and waved Sabina out of her chair. "Come on. Let's go see what everyone brought to eat, and you can tell me what you and Jade talked about today."

Sabina glanced at Katy on her right, then Jade on her left, at least one or two excuses obviously poised on the tip of her tongue.

"You should go," Jenny said before Sabina could speak. "You've had enough time being alone and afraid. The sooner you meet everyone, the sooner you'll realize how safe you are now."

The comment hit its mark. A fact evidenced by a stubborn resoluteness that flashed across Sabina's face. "Right." She stood and smoothed her hands over her hips. Her sleek near black hair gleamed in the softening sunlight, the single length, yet angular cut landing just at her jawline and accenting her sharp features. Whether she'd intended to or not, the stonewash jean shorts she'd paired with a white Rolling Stones tee fit perfectly with the casual attire of everyone else in attendance. "Lost time is never found."

"Who said that?" Jade asked. "Thomas Jefferson?"

"Ben Franklin," Priest answered, stalking into their tiny group. *"'You may delay, but time will not, and lost time is never found again.'"* Stopping in front of Kateri's chair, he braced his hands on the arms, leaned in and kissed her forehead.

"It scares me a little how far away you can hear," Katy murmured as he straightened to his full six-foot-five height.

He flashed her a wicked grin and settled into the empty lounger beside her. "It's not me who's listen-

ing. It's my panther. Your lion could too if you'd learn
to half-shift."

"That's a thing?" Elise said.

"Sure it is," Tate said. "Once you're further along,
it's almost natural. Like shared resources between you
and your companion. The bodily form isn't there, but
all the senses are available for you to use."

Sabina inched a little closer to Elise, her gaze locked
on to Priest. "You're a panther?"

The smile he shot her was full of amusement. "Don't
worry, I'm not inclined to hunt the woman who's probably my seer prima."

"Priest, stop it." Katy grabbed his hand and gave it
a squeeze. "He's harmless." She frowned. "Mostly."

"This is crazy," Sabina muttered. "I've barely adjusted to seeing Jade shift into a lynx. I might be better off with a beer than food at this point."

Elise laughed, wrapped her arm around Sabina's
shoulders and steered her toward the food laid out on
three long tables closer to the house. "How about if we
wait to mix alcohol into the equation until *after* your
eyes aren't as big around as dinner plates."

Fortunately, the people they ran into on their food
run pulled Sabina out of her startled bewilderment, the
need for good manners and general decency forcing
her fears to the background. As they'd been the night
of Beltane, those they talked to went out of their way
to be respectful and polite, asking general questions
about where Sabina was from and what she did for a
living. If any of them knew the circumstances that had
brought her to Eureka Springs or the fact that she hailed
from the seer primo's family, they sure didn't show it.

Left alone as they filled their plates, Sabina sidled

closer to Elise and lowered her voice. A confession shared in a stolen moment. "I can't believe it. I felt you in my mind. I watched Jade shift with my own eyes, and I still don't believe it."

God, she understood that feeling. Totally comprehended the clawing panic and disbelief that followed everything she'd thought to be true being turned on its head. "I get it." She spooned far too generous of a helping of ambrosia onto her plate then forced herself to throw in some raw veggies to balance it out. "The first shift I saw was Alek. His companion is a gray wolf. A huge one. Right after that, Kateri showed me her sorcerer magic. Built this huge ball of...oh, I don't know what it was. Energy I guess. Then she hurled it forward and took out a tree that had to be a hundred years old almost half a mile away." She faced Sabina. "Even after I'd seen it, my mind insisted it was a trick. Honestly, I think the only reason I adjusted as fast as I did was the fact that my mom had been trying to tell me about my heritage for years. I just never believed her."

"Your mom knew about all this?"

Elise nodded. "Jade told you about soul quests? How sometime in your early twenties you're called by the Keeper to the Otherworld and are given a choice to accept your gifts and your companion, or live an ordinary human life?"

"She told me." Sabina sighed and scanned the food spread out in front of them as though she was just as overwhelmed by the selections as she was with all she was learning. "Honestly, I can't say it makes much more sense to me than anything else."

"Well, my mom chose not to accept her gifts. She regretted it later, but she spent most of my teenage years trying to convince me she wasn't making things up. I still haven't really forgiven myself for not at least trying to listen."

Sabina pulled in a big breath and surveyed the people gathered in the wide gorge. "It's a bit fantastical."

"Fantastical, yes. But also very real." The memory of her first shift blossomed with the same rush as when her eagle had soared out and upward into the sky. "I've lived it, Sabina. This isn't an illusion. And the best news is, you're with people now who can keep you safe from Draven. At least until we can find him and deal with him."

"Yeah, Alek talked to me about that today."

Figured. Though, Elise supposed she should be glad he'd waited a full forty-eight hours before hitting Sabina up for help. "You're going to help us?"

Sabina hadn't really had a lot of opportunities to smile in the time since they'd found her at the old motel, but the lopsided one she shared with Elise in that moment was sweet. "I've had more solid sleep in the last few days than I've had in the last month combined. I might not understand everything I'm learning yet, but I'd help just on the basis of feeling sane again."

Naomi bustled up to the table with casseroles in each hand. "You two need to spend less time talking and more eating." She slid each dish into place, one of them some kind of an Italian dish and the other covered in an abundance of cheese, then frowned at Sabina's near empty plate. "Oh, sweet girl. Couldn't you find something you liked?"

Sabina smoothed her hand along her stomach. "It all looks great. I'm just not convinced any of it would go down well."

"You know what you need?" Naomi said. "Ginger ale." She shifted some dishes around and consolidated two plates of cookies into one. "Just let me get these tidied up so we have more room and I'll get you some."

"I'll get it," Elise said. "In the fridge upstairs?"

"No, there's another fridge in the storage area under the patio." She dipped her head toward the door just to the side of the wood staircase that led up to the raised patio. "Priest keeps it stocked with all kinds of drinks for training days and get-togethers like these. I'm pretty sure I saw some ginger ale earlier today."

"I'm on it." Elise hesitated mid-departure and locked stares with Naomi. "You'll stay with Sabina, right?"

Naomi smiled that sweet yet ornery smile of hers. "Oh, I'll stay with her. Though, as pretty as she is and without you to keep the curious types away, she might have a few of our men with her when you get back."

Typical Naomi. If she wasn't cooking and plying people with food, she was matchmaking and getting into mischief. She spared a quick glance for Sabina. "She only halfway means that. My guess is she'll at least wait a week or two to try and fix you up with anyone." With that, she wound through the crowd, sharing smiles and accepting congratulations along the way. Odd, how she could be among so many people—a good chunk of whom she couldn't yet call by name—and yet still feel so accepted. Even before the Keeper had chosen her as prima, she'd been welcomed. The only difference between that first night Tate had introduced her to everyone and today was her willingness to accept their inclusion. To really lower the shields she'd used to keep herself safe and believe she truly belonged.

The storage room proved to be more of an improvised enclosure. Tight latticework stained to match the wood patio above surrounded what had once been an open space and tiny beams of soft evening sunlight streamed through the narrow diamonds to give the open area a secret hideaway feel. Inside was everything a person would need to throw the kind of gatherings Priest held. Lawn chairs, Tiki torches, tables, coolers, blankets… Basically an outdoor party mecca.

Elise wound through the neatly arranged contents to the fridge standing in the farthest corner. All around her, the soft chatter of voices and music from outside mingled with the shadows. She popped open the door, more than a little surprised to find every single space on the shelves and all the drawers chock full of everything from beer to juice boxes.

"I don't care if they're mates. She won't hold his attention. She can't."

Elise froze at the unmistakable bite of Vanessa's voice, the direction of it coming just behind the bookshelf to one side of the refrigerator.

"Mates don't cheat, Vanessa." Whether the near whispered response was Bren or Taya was hard to say, but there was no way it was Dacie or Renda. Neither one of them seemed capable of saying anything without a giggle.

"Then he'll be miserable for the rest of his life," Vanessa said. "Have you seen them together? He treats her like she'll break if he looks at her wrong. I know Tate. He needs the hunt. Craves it. The few times he fucked me, he was unmerciful, but the way he acts around her, he'd never go there. I'm telling you, if he can't hunt, they won't last."

"They're mates." This from Taya for sure, the strength

in her voice rising just a little above the rest of the crowd. "The Keeper doesn't screw up. If she thought Elise was right for Tate, then there's a reason for it."

"The Keeper doesn't screw up for people who know what it means to be Volán. She's clueless. More singura than she is one of us."

It was bullshit.

Unadulterated and absolute *bullshit*.

Elise knew it as sure as she knew the sun would set tonight. But there was a part of her—that tender, vulnerable center she'd spent so many years trying to shield and protect—that quavered at Vanessa's claims. That wanted to curl inward and safeguard itself from the risk of loss.

Nothing to lose.

Only more to be gained.

The thought from her eagle flowed through her as easily as the wind rippling against her feathers. An encouragement and a command, her fearless nature urging her forward. To fly into the challenge presented rather than seek shelter, exactly as Priest had promised she would.

The chilled air from the refrigerator washed over her and the vast selections laid out inside sat like an odd metaphor of all the paths she could take in light of what she'd heard.

You know what you want, her companion whispered. *Take it.*

She *did* know. Maybe she hadn't known the details of it or been in a place where she could articulate it, but she'd felt it. Had sensed the something missing— the loss—when Tate had seemed to rein himself in that first night. Had craved an intangible wildness every time she'd stroked her finger against his mark and felt the tender bruise he'd left on her skin.

He needs the hunt.

She forced herself into motion, found the ginger ale tucked into one of the shelves on the door and hurried back to Sabina and Naomi. She still didn't understand exactly what Vanessa meant by *the hunt*, but she had a good idea it was tied to the tight control Tate kept on himself. Maybe even why the bond hadn't formed when she'd felt it so close that first night.

Coyotes are hunters, Priest had said. *I'm telling you sometimes action is more effective than talking.*

Oh, yeah. She had resources now. Lots of them. And she'd figure out what Vanessa meant in short order.

Then she was going to fly headlong into the storm.

Chapter Twenty-Two

Something was wrong with Elise. Or maybe not wrong, so much as different. Dangerously so. For the life of him, Tate couldn't figure out what the change was, but his coyote felt it, too, and was restless and irritable. Pacing inside him and refusing to settle. Which made it hella hard to focus on the work in front of him. Especially when the client was in her early twenties and putting off vibes that said she wasn't just comfortable in her sexuality, but open to exploring it with him.

He finished the last of the shading, wiped away the excess ink and rolled his stool back enough to consider the overall outcome. Placed high on one outer thigh, Merry's new turtle looked as if he were out for a stroll toward her feet, but had paused for a moment to glance up at her face. Whatever doubts he'd had about her sexual interests before they'd started working this afternoon had been cleared up quick when she'd asked him to add Shibari rope around the turtle's body in an intricate diamond pattern. He had to admit—fucked up worries about Elise or not—the result was not only stellar, but beautifully original.

"I'm naming him Jürgee," Merry said.

"Yeah?" He snatched the healing ointment and bandages he needed to get her finished up. Normally, he'd appreciate some decent post-art conversation, but without Elise here to balance him out, it felt awkward. Wrong. And why the hell she'd pushed back on coming to work with him like she had the last few weeks, he still didn't understand. "Any particular reason?"

"I'm a football nut. I love Jürgen Klopp."

Interesting. He could count on one hand the number of females he'd met who loved soccer. Even less who so subtly, yet openly expressed their interest in kink. If he'd met her a few months ago, this conversation would have unequivocally gone an entirely different direction. Now? His heart just wasn't in it. "Why a turtle?"

"They know how to endure. How to keep going." She hesitated long enough for him to meet her eyes and cocked her head. The way her short dark hair was cut added a certain impishness to her faery features. "They never give up."

Insightful, too. Too bad Alek was holed up with Sabina at Jenny's house following any and all rabbit trails to Draven. He had a feeling Merry could give him a run for his money. "No, they don't." He finished up the bandage, tugged off his black latex gloves and tossed them in the trash. He was just about to bypass any further banter by digging into aftercare instructions when Katy strolled through the open doorway and braced one hand lightly on the doorjamb.

"Hey, Tate. Elise just called. She asked if you could sneak away and help her with something at the cabin."

He tugged his phone from his back pocket. No missed calls showed on the screen and the signal strength showed maximum reach. "Why'd she call you?"

Katy shrugged, but there was a mischief behind her

gaze. "Beats me. Maybe she knew you had an appointment and didn't want to mess you up?"

Maybe.

But the late-afternoon appointment had just been
scheduled this morning, so how would she have known?

His coyote paced and grumbled, its predator instincts
prickling right alongside his own. "Did she say what's
wrong?"

She shook her head. "Nope. Just said she needed
something. I checked with Priest. He can cover for the
rest of the night, so you don't have to come back."

Lie.

Not the part about Priest. That much she'd really
done, but not knowing what was up with Elise was utter
crap. His companion scented the deception behind her
words and actions as clearly as the stench of a decay-
ing carcass on the wind.

For a split second, he considered pushing for more
info. Or at least nosing around until he got a better feel
for what was going on. But Katy was an alpha in her
own right and Priest's right hand for a reason. He'd have
about as much luck getting intel out of her as he'd have
of Jade minding her own business the rest of his life.

He stood, pulled one printout of the standard aftercare instructions from the stack on his shelf and handed
the paper to Merry. "Do we need to go over these?"

She took the paper and smiled, a secret one that
spoke of a whole new level of interest. "Who's Elise?"

He tucked his phone back into his pocket and went
about breaking down his equipment. "My mate," he
answered too quickly. But then, given Merry's appar-
ent orientation, she probably wouldn't make as much of
the label as an ordinary singura. He glanced back at her

and tried for a calm, unhurried tone. "If you have any problems, call the number on the bottom of that sheet."

Not the least bit bothered by the fact that all she had on her lower half was a lacy thong or Kateri now leaning one shoulder on the doorjamb with her arms crossed at her chest, Merry stood and unfolded her jeans from the sofa along the far wall. "I know the drill. I'll be fine." Her low chuckle mingled with the rasp of the denim against her skin. "Not sure about you, though. Your mate sounds like she's got some kind of surprise waiting for you. I'm almost sorry I'll miss it."

The next thirty minutes went by way too slow, Tate cursing the time it took to semi-politely get Merry on her way and the subsequent drive from Main Street to the lake. Every mile was a torture. An extended opportunity for his mind to ponder and twist possible scenarios that might be in store for him. By the time he finally pulled off the main road and onto the bumpy road that wound to the cabin, his patience was too frayed to baby his Camaro with a slow pace and he nearly screeched to a halt only five feet from the porch.

Elise strolled out the front door just as he slammed his car door shut. Whether it was the look on her face, or her appearance that kept him locked in place he wasn't sure, but both man and beast paused, assessing the energy that gripped her. Visually, she was the epitome of comfort and ease. Bare feet. A simple green cotton dress that barely reached three or four inches below her ass and tiny straps he could snap with a minimal tug. Hair loose and wild around her face.

But it was a ploy.

His coyote sensed it. Bristled at the external ruse and subtle challenge burning behind her deep green eyes.

Mine.

The claim rose up in an overwhelming surge, nearly knocking him back a step. The need to chase, to possess and mark her in every way he could consuming him completely. Driving him. Lashing him with a primal demand.

He braced one hand on the top of his car and tried to still his ragged breaths.

Elise noted his hand on the car then gauged the distance between them. You couldn't quite call the answering response on her lips a grin, but there was no missing the pleasure in her expression. "Everything okay?"

"I thought I'd ask you the same thing. Katy said you needed help with something."

This time her mouth quirked and a coy smile slid into place. "I might have misrepresented things just a little."

So playful. And yet there was steel behind her response. A dare uttered indirectly. "What's going on, Elise?"

She ducked her head and slowly descended the two steps. With her curves, even a simple stroll was a sensual delight, but today her hips swayed with invitation. "What makes you think there's something going on? Maybe I just missed my mate and wanted to see you." She stopped just out of reach and peeked at him from beneath her lashes. "There's nothing wrong with that, is there?"

Too far away.

Too tempting.

"You're playing with me, *mihara*. That's a dangerous thing."

"Is it?" She lifted her head and met his stare head-on. "I wouldn't know." Her gaze slid down his body and her expression softened. Warmed with that liquid sensuality that drove him insane. "I'd like to, though."

Ah, hell.

He couldn't do this. Not yet. It was too soon. Too early in their relationship.

She tilted her head to one side and skimmed her fingers along the curve where her neck and shoulders met, tracing the spot where his mark once was. "I miss it."

So did he. Had fought the last two nights replacing it and giving her even more. But he didn't trust himself. The drive that followed was too savage. A risk he wasn't willing to take.

She ventured another step forward. "I'm tired of wondering what my mate is holding back. Tired of imagining what it would be like to feel you lose control. To be the one who pushed you too far."

Fuck.

"Elise…"

"Of course, you're not the only Volán who likes to hunt, are you?"

One second. One barely veiled threat and his beast demanded release. Snipped and snarled and clawed against Tate's wavering restraint. He prowled forward, the growl in his voice a lethal warning. The harshest he'd ever given her. "Careful, mate."

She stood her ground, her smile pure wickedness. A woman fully immersed in her feminine power and refusing to balk. "Why? You're being careful enough for both of us."

He reached for her, intent on calming both him and his companion with physical contact.

She dodged his grip and braced on the balls of her feet, a triumphant grin tilting her lips. She dipped her chin. Not in surrender, but in blatant provocation, her eyes locked on his and her body braced for attack. "Oh, no you don't. If you want to touch me, you'll have to earn it."

Mine.

He shot forward, the primitive compulsion he'd held in check for over a month eradicated on the simple thought.

But Elise was already gone, her quick footsteps crashing through forest's undergrowth headed toward the lake.

His coyote's instincts pushed forward, latching on to her scent and the trajectory of her escape even before the shift completed. The landscape changed. Sharpened. Every hunter compulsion in him fully engaged and compelling him forward.

Trees blurred past on either side of him. The wide expanse of the lake stretched out ahead and the late evening sun spilled deepening shadows throughout the forest.

But the only thing that mattered was the floral-and-sugar scent that drifted on the air. The crash of her feet against leaves not yet decomposed from the winter and the random snap of twigs.

Still on foot.

She could have easily taken to the air and escaped him for however long she wanted, but she'd stayed in human form and mostly stayed to the path they'd run the last few days.

She wants the hunt.

Not an observation from his companion, but a demand. An inevitable truth he couldn't fight anymore. Didn't want to.

He surrendered to it. Let his coyote have the lead and welcomed the wildness. No censure. No restraints. Just him, his beast—and their prey.

His heart settled into an accelerated, but steady rhythm. His muscles stretched and warmed from the thrill and the chase. His mind sharpened and his blood hummed with anticipation. Over boulders and fallen stumps. Between trees and prickly shrubs. Every step she'd taken he followed. Recreated her path even as his hunter instincts projected her trajectory.

There.

A flash of green too artificial to blend with that created by nature and a glint of sun off her blond hair. Less than two hundred feet from the tiny cove they'd discovered yesterday morning.

He poured on the speed, not bothering to hide his pursuit. She needed to hear him coming. To know and accept what she'd earned with her challenge.

He veered off track. Cut beneath the underbrush and aimed toward the cove.

Another twig snapped, and a tiny whimper cut through the air.

Barefoot.

And she'd run like a madwoman through the forest that way.

He'd fucking paddle her ass for that move. Would tend to whatever wounds she'd created in her reckless maneuvers, then bend her over, spank every inch of her delectable skin until she'd never do something so stupid again.

Right after her fucked her.

Hard.

He burst through the tree line at the far side of the cove just as she came into sight on the opposite side.

Startled, she stumbled as she broke through a scraggly hedge and fell to her knees, catching herself with her hands on the loamy bank. She froze and watched him, her eyes wide and her breaths coming in ragged, uneven pants. Her hair was tousled and a sprig of evergreen sat tangled in one strand along the side. Along her arms and legs were tiny cuts borne from crashing through the briars he'd gone out of his way to make sure she'd avoided on days prior, the sight of her blood lashing his fury even higher.

He growled and prowled closer, his head lowered and muscles coiled to spring forward.

"Tate." A plea and a question all rolled up into one. A need to see where this new side of him would take her and a request for assurance at the same time.

When all she got was a snap of his coyote's teeth, she crawled backward, then pushed upright on her knees as though ready to flee again.

He shifted mid-stride, the sting of the transition against his flesh more fuel to the fire. "Stay down."

She gasped and sunk back so she sat on her heels, her knees just slightly parted. Whether it was the fact that he'd forgone his clothes in the shift, or how hard and tall his cock stretched against his belly, her eyes got bigger and her jaw slackened. "Tate."

"You wanted my beast, *mihara*." One beat and he flashed forward, gripping her hair at the back of her head and craning her head back as he leaned in close. "Now you've got him."

A groan.

Not a whimper like he'd expected, but an honest to

God groan so thick with lust his cock jerked in approval. "You like it, don't you?" It was more of an observation spoken aloud than a question, but even as he said it, the man in him had a hard time grasping the reality.

"Maybe," she managed through a raspy breath. "The jury's still out. You might be a total bust."

Another challenge.

And he fucking loved it.

He tightened his fist and tugged her forward, forcing her back on her hands and knees.

She moaned, and her eyes slipped shut for a second, then snapped right back open. A silent demand for more. From where he stood in front of her, her mouth was poised almost directly in line with his dick, her lips slightly parted and her eyes locked on to his.

"You think you can make me lose control? Think because you forced a hunt you can make me falter?" Twisting his wrist, he released the grip on her hair, coiled it around his hand like a leash and pulled. "Give it your best shot, mate."

Comprehension settled behind her green eyes in an instant. Bold and unmitigated feminine power ripe for release. It wasn't the first time she'd been given the chance to use her mouth on him, but it was damned sure the first time she'd brought this energy to the equation. A primal submission rather than an innocent exploration.

She inched closer, tentatively testing his hold on her hair and releasing a shaky exhale just inches from the base of his shaft.

Her hot breath washed over him. Drew his nuts up tight and made his dick stretch even farther. "That's it." Tempted as he was to spear his fingers through her hair and pull her to him, he kept the tension and held her firm. "Push me as much as you can. See what it gets you."

She smiled, a devilish curve of her lips paired with a gleam in her eyes that gave him serious pause. Holding his gaze, she licked the base of him, her tongue dipping downward for just a beat between the top of his balls then traveling up the length of him. She paused at the ridge, flicking the tip of her tongue along the sensitive spot then pressing her full lips around it and suckling gently.

He growled his approval, rolling his hips just enough to glide his length against her plump lips.

It didn't daunt her. Nothing did. Not the sounds rumbling from his chest. Not the hold he kept on her hair, or the way he moved against her. She licked. Sucked. Explored and savored every inch of him. Experimented and studied every response he gave her, keeping her keen eyes on him as much as possible.

She circled the head of his cock, teasing the slit at the end as though eager for a taste, then consumed him. Sunk her plump lips down until he grazed the back of her throat and firmly cupped his balls in the palm of one hand.

A snarl slipped free and he palmed the back of her head, the need to control—to dominate and claim what was his—clawing at the last of his restraint. The tug he'd felt the first night he'd taken her swelled behind his sternum. The same connection that had stretched taut and demanding one minute, then retreated.

The bond.

It was there.

Waiting.

Not on her. On you.

He'd been the one who'd missed it. Who'd shunned her offering by holding back who he was and robbing them both in the process.

As if she sensed it, too, she hollowed her cheeks, drew harder on the next upward glide and fisted the base of his shaft. The head of him slipped free of her lips and she aimed a wicked smile up at him. "You know, I don't think this is the best way to push you." She teased the sensitive ridge with the tip of her tongue and hummed. "But I have a feeling this is."

One blink and she was in motion, shoving him away with hands at his hips and scrambling to her feet.

The predator in him answered. Surged beyond the last of his control, wrestled her to the ground, and pinned her face down with an unforgiving grip at the back of her neck. He ripped her dress free in one yank, exposing her perfectly bare body beneath.

The bond between them surged. Pulsed and burgeoned to the point he could barely breathe, let alone voice his command. "Ass up."

Her gasp and the consequent shiver that wriggled through her worked him with the same decadent stroke as her mouth had done and made his cock jerk in approval. She braced her hands beneath her shoulders and lifted her hips as much as his body above her would allow. Raw need and lust coated her husky voice. "Tate. Hurry."

The ripe musk of her arousal hit him like an uppercut and his companion growled in appreciation. He nudged her knees with his. "Wider."

She eagerly obeyed, the greedy tilt of her hips and her exposed sex the most erotic vision he'd ever seen in his life. "Oh, Elise." The low rumble that rolled from his chest felt like thunder rippling through the earth. He slicked his cockhead through her drenched and swollen folds. "If you think I'm hurrying this, you're sadly mistaken." He notched himself inside her.

She tried to push back and take him deeper, but he used the hand at her neck to stay her and, through some goddamn miracle, forced his hips to keep their distance. When she finally settled and accepted she had no control, he blanketed her back and pressed a deceptively tender kiss to the space where her neck and shoulders met. "You feel it don't you?"

She whimpered in answer and her eyes slipped closed, the hands pinned beneath her shoulders fisting in frustration.

"You felt it the first time we had sex, too, didn't you? You figured it out and decided to push me."

"Yes." Not an ounce of regret registered in her voice. Only exasperation that he hadn't yet given her what she wanted. "I want *you*. All of you."

All of him.

The man and the beast. The light and the dark.

He licked the tender space beneath his lips and reached his hand beneath her, toying with her distended clit. Pushing his hips just enough to get her attention, he grazed his teeth along the same spot. "Who do you belong to?"

"You. Only you." She wriggled beneath him. "Please."

The bond strengthened. Stretched tight and pounded with a primal beat, demanding its due. "Mine."

He surged forward and sunk his teeth deep. Filled her with all of him even as he yielded to the bond's claim.

To her heat. To the wet, grasping clutch of her sex and the sweet brush of her relieved sigh in his ears.

It was wild. Utterly savage and untamed, and yet blindingly perfect. Beautiful in its hedonistic simplicity and fundamental nature.

One man. One woman. Perfectly joined in the most vital connection.

He yanked her upright, collared her throat with his hand and thrust upward, burying himself to the hilt. Sunlight bathed her torso, painting her skin in a golden glow and highlighting her plump tits as they bounced and jiggled.

She dropped her head back against his shoulder and cupped her breasts. Lifted them and teased the hard tips as though offering them for his pleasure. Her eyes opened, the lids weighted with lust and need and the green of her eyes nearly consumed by her pupils. "Please."

Anything.

He'd give her anything.

Annihilate any threat. Conquer any foe. Give until his body couldn't give any more.

Fingers drenched with her arousal, he circled her clit. Teased the tight bundle of nerves until her cunt fluttered around his cock—then gave her the pressure she needed.

The bond pulsed and a deep piercing sensation stabbed around his heart.

Her back bowed and she cried out as her pussy convulsed around him. Fisted to the point he had no choice but to respond. To drive deep and fill her. To mark her with his come and bind her to him in the most ancient way possible. His cock jerked inside her. Flooded her even as the slick muscles of her sex milked his release.

Whole.

His.

Finally.

Loosening his grip at her throat, he skimmed his lips above the blossoming mark at her neck and sucked in much needed air, the combined scent of the lake, forest and their release leaving an indelible imprint on his memory. How fitting that they'd sealed their bond here. Surrounded by nature in a place uncannily similar to the place where he'd first tasted her kiss. Where they'd begun their slow and careful dance.

But the days of careful were over.

She knew him now. Had not only accepted him and opened herself to the bond between them, but had welcomed him eagerly. Matched his ferocity with her own relentless spirit and forced what he'd been too hesitant to face.

She nuzzled his neck and sighed. "You're thinking too much."

He chuckled at that, his muscles protesting the simple action even as the lighthearted reaction forced his thoughts back to the present. To her sweat-dampened skin against his and the subtle undulation of her hips against his as she found her way back to reality. "That's usually my line."

"I think today proves you're guilty of overthinking just as much as I am."

He met her sated gaze, the sun setting in the distance bringing out tiny flecks of gold in her otherwise deep green eyes. "I should have trusted you with who I was."

"You had your reasons." She traced his jawline, dragging her fingertips through his beard in that thoughtful, affectionate way he'd grown to crave. "But I love this part of you, Tate. Love knowing you can draw a part of me to the surface no one else can. That no one else but you will ever see." She paused as though searching for the right words. "Today I was free in the most fundamental sense of the word. You gave me that."

Free.

Of all the ways he'd imagined her characterizing what they'd shared, that hadn't been on the list.

But it fit.

He cupped the side of her face and claimed her lips. Offered his thanks and reverence for all she was the best way he knew how. By the time he lifted his head, she lay boneless against him, the sun kissing the horizon and his bite deepening to a stark purple. He dipped his head toward it. "You got your mark back."

"I did." Straightening away from him, she went to all fours, then gracefully rolled to her back, cocked her knees to one side and her arms stretched overhead like some forest nymph sent by the Keeper to tempt him. Her sexy smile made his coyote huff with pleasure. "I am a little disappointed, though."

So playful. Reveling in the last rays of sunlight. Sensually aware and toying with him like she'd been born for this. He sat back on his heels and studied her, his cock stirring with the promise in her voice. "Disappointed? And here I'd thought you'd gotten what you wanted."

Her raspy laughter moved easily through the air around them, sultry and rich. "Well, I was rather hoping for more than one. At least two. Maybe more." She cocked an eyebrow and slowly parted her legs, guiding her hand so it teased the top of her mound. "Assuming my hunter is up for it?"

He straightened and braced himself over her, his body humming and ready to go despite how hard he'd just come. "Oh, *mihara*. Where you're concerned you have no idea what I'm up for."

Chapter Twenty-Three

Perspective really was everything. Perspective and experience. It had barely been five years ago—only a few months after Elise had graduated from high school—when she'd spied a girl in a store with her arm around her boyfriend, laughing and cuddling close to him in a way some would have called an overdose of PDA. It hadn't been the affection that had captured Elise's eyes, but the bold mark on her neck. A hickey, her mom had called it with a giggle when Elise had asked about it.

Elise had judged it unsophisticated. Crass and crude. But she hadn't understood. Not even a little bit.

She twisted in front of the cheval mirror in the corner of the bedroom and traced the blossoming bruise high on one ass cheek. It was one of four. And seeing every one of them in her naked reflection brought a sense a pride. Of ownership and the dark, delicious memories that came with earning them.

"You look mighty pleased with yourself." Tate shifted in the bed behind her, the brush of his skin against the crisp sheets filling the otherwise quiet room with a sensual hiss. With the angle of the mirror, his muscled torso and tanned skin was displayed perfectly against stark white sheets. The masculine knots Priest had tattooed into his flesh added an animalistic edge. Reminded her of the hunter she'd finally begun to know.

She pressed the tender skin just enough an echo of the pain she'd felt as he sunk his teeth deep rippled out and unsteadied her breath. "I have every right to be pleased. I earned these marks." She faced him and padded to the bed, the sway in her hips fueled by the idea wriggling through her head. She held his languid stare as she crawled onto the bed. "And I thoroughly enjoyed every second of it."

"I've created a monster." He cupped the side of her face and pulled her to him for a lazy kiss. "Not that I'm complaining, you understand."

She smiled against his mouth. "I'm not a monster. I'm just a very devoted student." She backed away just enough to meet his eyes. "I mean, I might not be an expert on mates, but it stands to reason we'd be smart to learn what makes each other tick."

His eyes narrowed, either the playful tone in her voice, or the grin on her face tipping him off to her devious mood. "Putting together a playbook, are you?"

"More like a quick reference guide. You know…so I know how to distract you when I need to." She cocked her head and bit her lip. "Or if I decide I need more pretty decorations on my skin."

He slid his grip to the back of her head, his fingertips tightening against her skull. "Yeah? And which buttons have you figured out get what you want?"

"Well…" She smoothed her fingertips over her name just above his heart. "Running is a good go-to. Of course, that can be problematic if I don't have enough room to run. Say like when we're here in the cabin."

"Mmmm." Said like a man who was far more focused on what she was doing than what she was saying. Which was exactly what she needed.

She leaned in and pressed a kiss to the same spot. "I've also figured out you're a fan of wrestling and you'll never let me stay on top for long."

Keeping his hand in her hair, he chuckled and stroked the length of her spine with the other. "You're on top right now."

"Yeah, but you won't let me stay here." She kissed and licked a path toward his neck. "Then there's the rise I got out of you mentioning other males."

His hand fisted in her hair in a heartbeat and his companion's growl filled the cabin.

"Easy." She teased her fingertips along his jawline and brushed her lips across his. "That was just a one-time deal to get you off dead center."

"Smart. Otherwise, I'll mark your ass with something other than my teeth."

Her sex clenched at the image his words created and the wanton hussy who'd all but taken up full-time residence in her head scribbled a new to-do:

Note to self—play the jealous card at least one more time.

"Anything else?" he prompted.

Tempting as it was to lose herself in a long, mindless kiss that would no doubt lead to an explorative, languorous interlude, this morning she wanted her hunter. Wanted one last taste of wildness before reality forced its way into their world. She forced a speculative hum to hide her devious intent and skimmed the curve of his shoulder with her mouth. "Well, there's one idea I'm toying with." She licked and sucked a lazy path toward the curve of his neck. "I'm not sure if it'll get the response I want, but I figure it'll turn out a winner for me either way."

"Yeah?" Again, with the distracted tone that said she could tell him she'd spent all of his money in a single shopping spree and he wouldn't care. "What's that?"

She was out of her mind doing this. For all she knew, she was crossing some badass alpha line that would turn him off completely, or earn her a spanking faster than she was ready for.

But what the hell.

She'd come this far.

And she could always heal it if things didn't work out like she hoped.

She pressed a lingering kiss to the base of his neck. The same sweet spot where he'd first marked her. "I'm curious what happens when I do this."

She bit him.

Hard.

Put everything she had—everything she'd felt in all the other times when he'd done the same to her—into the contact.

Tate's back bowed off the bed and he fisted her hair at either side of her head, his lethal snarl filling the room.

And that was it. The last second she had of control before she was on her hands and knees, her face pinned to the mattress and her sex full of Tate's cock.

It was exactly the wild she needed. The untamed wonder she'd come to not only crave but welcome.

By the time he was done with her, the bed covers were on the floor, both of them were sweaty and out of breath and she had not one, but two new bites—one at each curve of her hips.

She rolled to her side and splayed her hand against his thrashing heart. "I take it that's a button you're not opposed to me pushing?"

"Sweetheart, you can bite me any damned time you want." She could have sworn it was his coyote that smiled back at her. "So long as you're ready to get double from me."

"Houston, we have a problem."

The sound of Tom Hanks's voice from *Apollo 13* blaring from their kitchen was the last thing she'd expected to hear.

Even more surprising was how fast Tate rolled out of bed and headed that direction.

The same phrase repeated and she propped herself upright. "What's that?"

"Priest's ringtone."

"Your ringtone for Priest is a movie quote?"

"It's appropriate." He snatched his jeans off the back of one kitchen chair and dug his phone out of the back pocket. "I can count on one hand the number of times he's called me and they usually mean I'm in trouble." He slid his thumb across the screen. "What's up?"

From deep inside, her eagle squawked and ruffled its feathers, an uncomfortable warning itch tickling beneath her skin.

"You're sure?" Tate asked. His gaze narrowed on Elise and for the first time since she'd learned it was possible, she realized how handy being able to use her eagle's hearing could be going forward. "Yeah, give us thirty minutes and we'll be there."

He ended the call, slid the phone to the dinette and started pulling on his jeans. "We gotta get dressed and get to Priest's house. Sabina got an in with a cop who's been working the crime scene where Jerrik's parents were killed. Alek's pulling in Garrett and a few key warriors, and Naomi's pulling together the strongest seers we've got." He strode to the bed, leaned over and gave her a sound kiss. "Get dressed, beautiful. Priest wants all hands on deck to see if we can figure out what Draven's up to."

In the end, they made the trip in twenty minutes. Katy met them both at the door, wrapped Elise up in a quick hug and then waved them the rest of the way in. "Sorry for the wakeup call, but Priest wanted his primos here before he talked to everyone." Her gaze dipped to Tate's bite mark on her neck and she grinned. "Though, I'm pleased to see the plan worked."

Tate chuckled, draped his arm around Elise's shoulder and pulled her in tight to his side. "If that's the outcome from you meddling, you're officially allowed to plot and scheme with my mate anytime you want."

"That good, huh?" Walking through the entry at Elise's other side, Katy leaned in and muttered, "By the way, you owe me. You have no idea how hard I had to work to make sure you and Tate were the last two Priest called."

The last two called was right. The room was already full and a heightened, almost anxious energy filled the open space. While the far edge of the room usually boasted an exceptional view of the lake, this morning the landscape was blocked by two tri-fold display boards set up on long folding tables. Nearly everyone was gathered in front of them, each taking their time to study the pictures on one side and a map with pins in it on the other. "Where did those come from?" Elise asked.

"Sabina's been busy." Katy directed them both to

the board on the right. "Between her and Alek, they've turned up a lot of information. These pictures are from the crime scene where Jerrik's parents were murdered. It's a mostly empty warehouse that's been up for sale or rent for over a year."

Elise stopped dead center in front of the board and soaked in the images. Dark, like something from a horror flick with only a few stray columns of light slanting from slender rectangular windows high on one wall. The flashes from the cameras, though, did a more than capable job of highlighting the gruesome symbols painted on the old concrete floors and a few cheap candles burned to the nub. "Is that blood?"

Katy nodded and pointed to another picture directly next to the one Elise had studied the longest. "This one is identical but it's actually a different set. Crime scene reports show one set ties to the blood of Jerrik's dad and the other matches his mother. There's a third blood type, but the cops don't know who it belongs to."

"Jerrik," Elise said.

"That's what we're thinking."

Behind her a few of the warriors traded hushed comments she couldn't quite make out and on the far side of Tate a seer whose name she couldn't remember gently pressed her fingertips to the corner of a picture and closed her eyes. "Has anyone come up with any ideas? Seen anything?" she asked quietly so as not to disturb the woman.

"Not yet," Katy said. "Alek and Sabina are up in Tate's old room working through other details they can bring down. Priest thought he'd give them time to finish combing through details before we huddle up and start brainstorming ideas."

The sliding glass door that led to the raised wooden patio opened and Priest stalked in dressed only in loose black cotton pants and his usual charms on leather cords around his neck. Despite the number of people in the room, his gaze cut right to Kateri and the intensity that had gripped him eased just a fraction.

"Ah, fuck," Tate murmured with the same dread a teenage boy busted after curfew would use. "How bad is it?"

Kateri responded almost as quietly, but the pain in her voice was palpable. "Bad enough the only time he hasn't been in panther form since meeting with Sabina this morning was when we were making calls."

"What triggered it?"

"The pictures."

"Wait." Elise focused on Kateri. "What's wrong with him?"

"Draven's dark magic." Katy frowned and nodded toward the pictures. "The second Priest saw them, it reared its head and won't shut up."

"But I thought the two of you kicked that."

"We didn't kick it. It just decided to play nice. Or, more to the point, it decided it liked me. But when it saw and recognized Draven's handiwork, it decided it was time to wake up."

"It works against him," Tate said. "Like a really bad case of negative, evil thoughts all the time."

"That's how it used to be," Kateri corrected. "This time it's pissed. It knows Draven nearly killed me. Seeing the pictures woke it up and it wants vengeance."

"So, Draven's magic is working against him?"

"Something like that."

Priest prowled up behind Kateri and banded his arms around her waist. "You told them what Sabina found?"

She covered his arms with hers, an affectionate contact intended to ease and comfort. "Most of it." She twisted to look at the maps and the tacks anchored at various locations across the US. "I haven't explained those yet."

Not waiting for a segue into details, Elise slid past a man she hadn't met yet, but recognized as a warrior by his vibrant red aura, and stood in front of the map. The number of red pushpins marking different locations weren't exactly vast, but they were considerably spread apart and all of them were close to natural habitats. She scanned from a little state park just outside of Austin, Texas, to Roosevelt National Park in North Dakota. "What do the marks mean?"

"The team working the case in Blacksburg found mention of similar symbols, also drawn in blood, in other cases." Priest motioned toward the pushpins. "One thing led to another and these are the other cases that match."

"He's been at this for a while, then," Tate said. "No way he's hit all these locations in just the last few months."

"And who else has he possessed or killed in the process?" Katy added.

Elise cocked her head, a thought that wouldn't quite crystalize coming in and out of focus in her head. The coverage was massive, but it didn't look random either. More like there was an art to it. A shape partially formed.

She took a step back. Then another.

"Elise?" Tate's voice was right beside her, his presence an anchor in the middle of a swiftly rising storm.

Behind her sternum it seemed her eagle fought for release. Either that or was trying to warn her of something.

Not warn.

See.

Her eagle's sight. It was tenfold better than her own. A gift of nature from the Keeper.

As soon as the thought floated through her mind, the pattern solidified—two circles. A big one on the bottom, and a little one on the top. The cross was there, too. "He's performing a rite."

The room's chatter went silent in a heartbeat.

Tate's heat pressed tight against her back and his hands rested firmly on her hips. "How do you know?"

"The symbol." She tore her gaze away from the pushpins and met Priest's tense stare. "The one I told you about. It's right there. It's missing a few spots, but it's the same one. He's performing a rite."

Priest faced the map, studied it for all of ten seconds, then frowned and faced her. "You only saw it listed next to the rituals, though. Never in the ritual itself, right?"

Maybe. Maybe not. She'd crammed more studying of that journal into the last ten days than she'd studied through all her time in college.

Reanimation.

For a creature lacking a human vocabulary, her bird had a striking memory and ability to communicate. But she was right. There'd been one rite—one of the last ones listed—that focused on restoring a physical form. "Has anyone actually seen Draven? Like the way he used to be?"

Kateri shook her head and cast a wide-eyed look at Priest. "I only saw him as Jerrik and as Jerrik's owl." She scowled. "But there was a dark cloud for a second. I threw my magic at it and it scattered like ashes."

"He doesn't have a body." Naomi's hushed voice cut through the silence from behind them. Her gaze was distant. Unfocused. But there was no question of the clarity flashing inside her head. A second later, her gaze sharpened and she scanned the room, her sole focus landing on Elise. "He wants his own body and he's using his Volán victims to bring it back."

Chapter Twenty-Four

Dark, dank and depressing. As a setting for what everyone hoped was the final showdown with Draven, the isolated warehouse just outside of Rapid City, South Dakota, that Naomi had seen in her vision was something Elise would have cast for a B-rated horror flick. From the exposed and weathered wood beams overhead and the slender murky windows high on each metal wall, to the dirty concrete floor strewn with random, discarded packing material, the place was as dismal as they came. Especially in comparison to the beauty and majesty of South Dakota's Black Hills National Forest just miles away.

It'd taken them five days to plan, prep and travel— two of them spent driving in a motley caravan because logistics for a group of fifteen by air had been too much of a hassle. Plus, there had been Priest's darker half to contend with. As agitated as the darkness inside him had become, flying would have been a risk of nightmare proportions.

Katy and Sabina stood silent in the deepening shadows on either side of her, two sizable stacks of crates hiding them and the four guards around them while Priest, Alek and Tate prowled the rest of the building for signs of activity. Only the barest hint of sunlight still colored the skies outside.

"Do you think Jade's okay?" Sabina whispered.

Doubtful. She'd been furious when Priest had done an about-face just before they left for the long drive and insisted she stay home, and no amount of begging or outright demanding from her or anyone else had caused him to change his mind. "I think she's going to be a major thorn in Priest's side for a long time after this is over." The resolute determination on Priest's face as he'd shared the news reflected in Elise's memory once more, tickling some hazy realization that wouldn't quite come into focus. "I still don't get why he changed his mind."

A stillness came over Katy. A subtle hitch in her breath, before she glanced at Naomi sitting cross-legged on the top of a wide crate with her eyes closed roughly twenty feet away. Ready. Open. Waiting for more direction from the Keeper.

Katy sucked in a quiet breath. "Priest didn't say as much, but I'm pretty sure Naomi saw something. If that something involved Jade, I'm not surprised we couldn't talk him out of it. Frankly, if it means keeping her or anyone else safe, I'm fine dealing with her pouting."

The switch from Jade coming to Naomi taking her place.

How Garrett rarely left Naomi's side and the two extra guards that trailed them everywhere.

Braced for attack.

Yes, the logic absolutely made sense. It also explained why Katy and Alek had been so uptight leaving the hotel tonight. Knowing your grandmother was willingly putting herself in danger couldn't be an easy pill to swallow. "But if she's seen something, she knows what to look for, right? How to counter?"

"I don't think it works that way," Sabina said. "From what Naomi and Jade have taught me so far, visions are more like clues. Snippets to be used as guideposts or omens. To give anything too concrete violates free will and the cycle of destiny. The only differences between what seers are offered and those given to everyone else day to day are the visual aspect and the strength they're delivered with."

A slight rasp sounded well behind them. The subtle grate of loose dirt against the concrete floor.

Both Katy and Sabina twisted to see what it was, but Elise knew what had made it. Or, rather, who. Had been all too aware of Vanessa's presence the entire trip and the stubborn distance she'd kept from everyone except a few unmated warriors. A distance Elise had tried more than once to broach with polite conversation, but had been met with nothing but stony silence. As if Vanessa couldn't decide whether to wring her neck for daring to speak to her, or simply couldn't find anything decent to respond with and opted to keep her mouth shut.

"I'm surprised you brought her," Katy murmured, turning her attention back to the open space beyond. Considering she knew not only the way Vanessa had treated Elise in front of the clan, but what Elise had overheard the night of her celebration, Elise had done an exceptional job of displaying an impartial demeanor publicly. Privately, was an entirely different matter.

The same held true for Sabina, though her way of showing Elise support was usually more silent and backed with a glare that said she wasn't above guerrilla tactics to even the score if any more underhanded crap happened. "It's a good maneuver as the healer prima. It shows the clan Elise won't let her personal feelings get in the way when she's making decisions."

That was some of it. Another factor was that Meara had no business being in the middle of what could turn into a full-scale battle and Vanessa was the next best option. The bulk of her reasoning, though, was far more self-serving. Namely, that she had complete confidence Vanessa would heal Tate to the best of her abilities just to spite Elise if anything should happen to him.

I'm expendable. You're not.

Tate had all but drilled the mantra into her head from the time Naomi shared her full vision until just before they'd left the hotel tonight. Logically, Elise understood it. Absolutely grasped the magnitude of her position within the clan and what it could mean to the Earth's magic if she, Priest and the other primos didn't survive the next few hours. But that didn't mean she had to like it, or that she wouldn't do everything within her power to make sure he stayed safe.

Including rely on Vanessa.

Two shadows moved on either side of the building, sharpening her awareness.

No, not shadows. A coyote and a wolf, their lighter coloring nearly muted in the room's darkness.

The third beast registered only seconds before it was upon them, Priest's massive panther blending completely into the blackness. He shifted only four feet in front of them, the usual silver wash of light that came with the transition eerily absent and making it seem as though Priest appeared out of thin air.

Tate's hands settled on her hips a second later, his

earthy scent and delicious warmth soothing the uncomfortable chill that had blanketed her skin.

Alek materialized just behind Sabina. "We're clear. No one in the building, but this is definitely the place he's planning to use." He nodded toward the farthest edge of the building. "He's got a good supply of ropes, candles and the knife Naomi described ready to go behind that crate."

The last ritual.

Where the Keeper had been limited with her visions before, this time she'd given far more. They'd still had to work at it. Had to piece together the moon phases to figure the correct timing and sort through a slew of warehouses inside the immediate region to find the one with the right sign out front, but they'd pulled it off.

Now it was down to Elise. Down to trusting that she'd interpreted the information from the ancient journal she'd been given the right way.

Tate must have sensed her apprehension because he wrapped both arms around her waist and pulled her flush against him. "It'll work."

Directly in front of her, Priest met her stare. Confident. Unflinching. "What you're feeling right now—let it go. The Keeper gave you your instincts for a reason. They were right for Sabina and they'll be right this time, too. Trust them. The rest of us do."

Easy for him to say. He wasn't the one who'd gone against feedback from the rest of those who'd studied the rituals outlined in the journal and insisted on one with far less details.

Judgment by Blood.

Even thinking about the ritual now, her body hummed with a certainty that left her a little dizzy.

Her logical mind had other ideas, though. At least a half a dozen arguments as to why she should have picked other, more obvious options. "I still don't understand why I think this one's the right one to go with."

"Instincts aren't meant to be understood," Priest said. "They're meant to be followed." He faced Kateri and the tight lines in his posture eased a fraction. "You know what to do?"

"Distract, distract and then distract some more. Preferably with lots of blasty, fiery magic that makes him lose his cool."

Priest cupped the side of her face. "You've met my brother, *mihara*. Don't underestimate what he's capable of."

"Oh, I'm not underestimating him. I'm just ready to give him some of his own medicine and enjoy myself doing it."

"I'll second that," Alek said.

Shaking his head, Priest's mouth quirked in a wry smile...until his gaze settled on Naomi, still silent and motionless. His expression sobered. "Give me a minute." With that, he squeezed Kateri's shoulder and stalked to Naomi.

"Whatever she knows, I have a feeling we're not going to like it," Sabina said.

"I already don't like it," Alek said.

Katy lowered her voice back to a whisper. "Did she tell you something?"

"Not a thing, but you know Nanna. When she sets her mind to something, she doesn't budge, and she's more tight-lipped on this than she was about our heritage, so you know it's gotta be bad."

If Alek's words weren't enough to confirm it, the

solemn way Priest spoke to Naomi and the way he reverently cupped each side of her face and touched his forehead to hers would have cinched it.

"Garrett won't let anything happen to her," Tate said. "He'll keep her safe."

Alek stared at his grandmother, his wolf's sharp eyes acutely focused. "Maybe from Draven, but I'm not sure how he'll keep her safe from herself."

"What do you think she's up to?"

"No clue." Alek met his gaze. "But with her there's no telling. She's the bravest woman I know."

Stepping away from Naomi, Priest motioned Vanessa and her guards forward. As soon as he could speak without projecting his voice too far, he dipped his head toward the open center of the warehouse. "Naomi says it's almost time. Elise, show everyone what to do. Vanessa, you're behind this line at all times unless someone goes down." He looked to the three men around her. "You keep her safe."

They each nodded.

The rest of them moved out from behind the towering crates.

It was all the same space, but somehow moving out from behind the makeshift wall and the wards Priest had built made the moment seem more poignant. As if, in stepping into view, they were making their declaration and facing a turning point in their destiny. The air felt more stagnant, too. Thick and charged with energy like the eerie calm before a violent storm.

Elise stopped at the southern point. "Sabina, this is you." She faced Sabina, opened the messenger bag slung crosswise over her torso and tugged the slender box covered in scarred black leather free with trembling fingers. Crouching, she motioned for Sabina to do the same. "Give me your hand."

Sabina glanced at everyone gathered around her then back at the door they'd come in through over an hour ago. Finally, she kneeled in front of Elise and held out her hand, palm up. "Have I mentioned I'm not fond of this part?"

Surprisingly, it was Alek who moved in for moral support, dropping to one knee beside her and steadying her hand with a firm grip at her wrist. "The dagger's sharp. Sharp enough you won't feel the cut. Only the sting after and it'll pass."

She cocked an eyebrow at him like she either thought he was nuts or wanted to argue.

Elise took advantage of the distraction and sliced quick and deep along the tender stretch at the back of her forearm.

Sabina's hiss ricocheted through the building, but to her credit held mostly still, cringing as her crimson blood dropped to the dirty floor.

"The blood of one lost, given to hold the one accused." How loud she was supposed to project her words, Elise didn't have a clue, but the moment seemed to call for solemnity more than pomp and circumstance, so she opted for going with what felt like a prayer on her lips. Using Sabina's blood and her fingers, she drew the seer's symbol on the concrete. A pear-shaped top with a long stem and a crisscrossing pattern running through it all.

Elise stood and stepped back.

Alek helped Sabina to her feet and motioned her and her three guards back behind the crates. "Keep her protected until Priest and Katy get Draven contained, then bring her out."

From there they repeated the pattern, once for Alek at the west, and once to mark her own symbol in blood opposite him in the east. Once done, she stood and eyeballed the still open spot for Jerrik on the north point. "I'm still not sure this will work with us marking the corners out of order."

Tate pulled her around and urged her back behind the crates. "We all talked about it. You told everyone what you were concerned about and we decided together to go with your gut. Now, let it go."

Elise might have argued, but the intense attention Vanessa had aimed on the two of them scattered every retort. With her head cocked just a fraction to one side, Vanessa's brows formed a sharp V and her eyes were narrowed in a way that seemed to imply a whole new set of information had just come online at once. To ignore her and keep her distance probably was the smarter move given the circumstances. The last thing any of them needed right now was a distraction, but her gut told her to try one more time. To see if she could at least start to mend the bridge between them, even if their connection proved to be nothing more than something used to the benefit of their clan.

She veered off the course Tate had set for them and stopped in front of her. "Are you okay?"

Vanessa's eyes widened, and she glanced between Elise and Tate like she hadn't even been aware of their approach. "Me?" She blinked a few times and shook her head as though to clear it. "I'm fine."

No bitterness.

Just confusion.

Not exactly the response Elise had hoped for, but it was better than what she'd gotten to date. Elise nodded to the guards around her. "They'll keep you safe. Just listen to what they tell you to do and do your best. Though, I'm hoping there's nothing for any of us to do."

Vanessa dipped her head, the acknowledgment so minute Elise suspected she didn't even realize she'd given it.

Rather than create the safe distance between them as she had before, Elise turned and peered out at the open space on the other side of the crates. Tate moved in slightly to one side and behind her, his heat and his possessive hand at the curve of her hip a silent show of support.

"You brought me for him, didn't you?" Vanessa said. There was no way she could couch her voice low enough for Tate not to hear, but she murmured it anyway, keeping her gaze locked straight ahead. "Not because you wanted to, but because you wanted to have someone to look out for him."

She could lie. If nothing else, pointing to Vanessa's strength as a healer would undoubtedly go further in her goal of peaceful coexistence. But lying never helped anything. Only delayed the inevitable. "I have to be prepared to help the primos and Priest. I knew you'd put everything you had into it, if for no other reason than to prove you could. Not just for him, but for everyone."

Silence stretched out between them, broken only by the steady inhalations and exhalations of those close to her.

"You love him," Vanessa said, her voice thick with the weighted realization Elise had glimpsed on her face. "And he loves you."

Love.

Things had moved so quickly. So naturally she hadn't really stopped to try and put a label on it. From the day she'd seen him, everything between them simply was. A light turned on in a room that had stood empty for years and a whole new range of emotions untapped. "He's my mate. I'm not sure *love* is an adequate word to describe what's between us, but someday you'll know. You'll feel it and you'll understand."

A low rumble sounded beyond the warehouse's metal walls, an engine closing in.

"I'm sorry," Vanessa whispered. Nothing more. Nothing less. But the delivery was genuine.

Tate tensed beside her. No doubt wanting to rub her apology back in her face and remind her what a bitch she'd been.

But bitterness only brought more bitterness and they'd had plenty of that already. "What you feel right now…if you heal from that place, harness it and let it change you…your life will be so much different." She turned enough to meet Vanessa's gaze. "I hope you can because I need someone to help me. Someone to guard our secrets and keep them safe."

Her gaze shot to Tate then back to Elise, clearly realizing the position she referred to. "Why would you pick me?"

"I haven't yet. I'm only saying I think you have the potential. How you choose to let that lead your decisions is up to you."

The rumbling grew louder, idled just beyond the walls, then stopped.

The soft warning chuff of Priest's panther filled the warehouse and the room went eerily silent.

A car door slammed.

Then another.

Heavy footsteps crunched against thick gravel and the heavy metal door at the farthest end of the building opened with a squeaky groan. Jerrik marched through a second later, a body slung over his shoulders and his gait measured and weighted as though his purpose wasn't his own.

But then, that made sense. Outside of Draven's attempt to overtake Priest the day he'd come with Katy and Alek to introduce Elise to her heritage, Jerrik had likely had little freedom from Draven's presence, if any.

And therein lay the biggest risk of all. It'd been nearly three months since Jerrik's parents had been found murdered in Blacksburg and no one had any clue what kind of impact such prolonged exposure to Draven's dark magic would have on Jerrik's psyche.

At nearly the center of the room, Jerrik paused, scanned the perimeter and seemed to scent the air.

Tate tensed beside her and the prickling energy she'd first experienced the day she'd tattooed her name above his heart washed over her in a warm, rippling wave.

His magic.

Protecting her. Engulfing her in warmth and comfort even as he braced for the worst.

More slowly than before, Jerrik finished his trek to the center of the room and slung the body off his shoulder. He caught the person's head just before it hit the concrete, each movement as he finished arranging the body stiff. Fatigued and forced. As if a battle for control raged beneath the surface.

Jerrik snapped upright and spun to the back of the room. In an instant, the air around them sparked with energy. An uncomfortable electric charge that warned of danger.

Priest prowled out of the darkness. Dressed only in loose black pants, everything about him promised an all-out war. His mystic gray eyes glowing with resolve. His muscles taut and the ancient markings along his collarbone, shoulders and arms pulsing with a luminous power she'd never seen before. "Another life to add to your growing tally? How many have you taken now? Do you even know anymore?"

The evil laughter that came out of Jerrik's body was all wrong. Deep and warped with a malevolence that raised goose bumps along Elise's arms. "I'm not plagued by conscience like you are, brother. That's your downfall, not mine."

Tate squeezed her hip, a silent nudge to prod her toward her first and most important task.

She wanted to close her eyes. To feed the words with all of her healer gifts, but with Draven's hostile spirit growing in intensity she didn't dare. "The body is sacred. A gift of the Creator given to one spirit."

Jerrik twisted side to side, scanning the crates for the source of her voice.

He wouldn't find it. Not without significant work. Kateri and Priest had spent too much time on the wards that hid them and, in a few more seconds, he'd have his hands too full to focus.

Elise focused on Jerrik's face and poured everything she had into her words. "Your spirit does not belong. It has no rights. No place inside the physical haven it's seized."

With a roar that echoed against the metal walls, Jerrik struck, unleashing a deep amethyst bundle of energy the size of a bowling ball into the crates along one wall.

Tate moved in front of her and murmured, "Keep going."

Her heart pounded, and her lungs hitched at the stench of smoke and Draven's ugly magic. "By the power given by the Keeper, you are banished. Forced to surrender the body you've taken and present yourself. Relinquish your hold. Form your true self."

Jerrik spun. "Where is the little bitch? I'll kill her, too."

"You'd have to get through me first," Priest said.

"And me." Katy strolled from behind the crates opposite those Draven had destroyed with his attack, for all appearances the epitome of casual confidence. "And I've learned so many new things since we last met."

Jerrik struck, unleashing another bolt directly at Katy's head.

She dodged and volleyed with her own, Priest adding another that collided from the other direction in nearly perfect timing.

And then it was on. Magical warfare on an astounding scale. Lights flashing. Bodies moving at preternatural speed. Grunts and moans as some impacts landed and the splinter and crash of wood as others didn't.

Tate backed up a step, bringing his back flush against her front. "Elise, finish it."

This time she did close her eyes. Opened her hands and surrendered to the power flowing through her. Pulled on the frenetic energy swirling around them and repeated the command. "The body is sacred. A gift of the Creator given to one spirit. Your spirit does not belong. It has no rights. No place inside the physical haven it's seized."

Own your magic.

Own and direct it.

Feel it.

Guidance from her companion, or perhaps the Keeper, but shared with the strength of an ocean's wave against the shore at high tide.

She used it. Channeled it. Let the magic pour through her. "By the power given by the Keeper, you are banished. Forced to surrender the body you've taken and present yourself. Relinquish your hold. Form your true self."

A long, grated shout rang out. The agonized wail of a man being torn apart. The tortured sound hung in the air for all of a second, and then she was in motion, Tate tugging her forward with one hand in hers as the others rushed into place.

At either side of the building, Priest and Kateri stood with hands outstretched. Streams of deep plum magic poured from Kateri's palms while the silver of the Otherworld beamed from Priest. The combined power swirled around a dark cloud hovering high overhead. A cage containing Draven's dark spirit.

"Elise!"

Tate's sharp command yanked her out of her stunned stupor. She grabbed the dagger and dropped to her knees beside Jerrik's unconscious body. Whether it was the warriors standing guard who'd dragged him to his position on the northern side of the rite, or Tate as he'd all but hauled her across the open space, she couldn't say. "Someone hold his arm."

Tate was there in a heartbeat, his focus and calm burning through the shield he kept around her.

"The blood of one lost," she said, drawing the sorcerer's symbol in the blood that streamed to the concrete floor, "given to hold the one accused."

As soon as the words died off, the thrashing cloud contained inside Priest and Kateri's combined power stilled and a brilliant white light superseded the combined silver and purple of Katy and Priest.

"It's working." Tate heaved her upright and urged her to her own place.

Sabina stood shell-shocked in the southern position, her wide eyes locked on Draven's dark spirit.

Alek waited opposite her in the west. Unlike Priest and Katy who had their attention trained on Draven and stood ready to intercede at a moment's notice, his focus was solely on Elise. He jerked his head in a sharp nod, a silent command to get a move on.

Her voice rang out, surprisingly clear and steady despite the ragged, thrumming pulse in her ears. "Draven Rahandras, you're called to the Keeper by Judgment of Blood. Bound by all four corners of the Earth and by the ancestral blood of those whose lives you stole. Four souls taken. One executioner. Stand now and face the consequences of your actions. The sentence for the forbidden path you've chosen."

The dark cloud shuddered and wavered, but otherwise nothing happened.

Elise looked to Tate.

He shook his head and squeezed her shoulders. "Don't doubt it. Focus."

She studied the cloud. Opened her gifts and let her

intuition guide her. Recited the words she'd studied almost nonstop for the last five days again in her head.

The darkness lightened, then slowly took shape.

A man, the form more that of a ghost than one of flesh and blood. His arms were outstretched to the side as though bound by unseen rope and his body completely naked. Vulnerable.

Draven.

The likeness to Priest was there. The same powerful body, skin tone and nearly black hair. But anger and resentment permeated his being. Twisted what could have been a wholesome, peaceful countenance.

Draven shook his head. His body. Every movement as though desperate to dispel a swarm of insects crawling on his flesh. "No!"

"Oh, yes." The Keeper. There was no body to go with it. Only the mildly spoken feminine voice from the Otherworld delivered with a fierceness that promised fathomless strength. "Harm done and damage inflicted will not go unanswered. You willingly trespassed against the law of ultimate good. Defaced the gifts you were given and stole from me and my clan those who are precious to me. You *will* stand judgment."

A low hum vibrated through the building. A living presence that imbued everything around them. The concrete. The walls. The very air in her lungs.

Draven's back bowed, his head dropping back and the veins along his neck and shoulders popping out in stark relief. "I will not be held. My power will match yours. Surpass yours."

"You made a sacrifice," the Keeper said, still calm in her response. "An innocent given to bridge your journey into the darkness. One willing to offer their own sacrifice negates your powers. Will sever you from the dark. And then, Draven, you're mine."

The hum intensified. Supercharged the room with an energy that licked and snapped against Elise's skin.

"You have my offering." Naomi stepped from the shadows, Garrett a stoic shadow behind her as she calmly walked forward. The bright light containing Draven's ghostlike form radiated off her simple white skirt and matching tank. "My gifts. My life. To bring things into balance, both are yours."

"No!" Alek tried to bolt from his place at the west, but Priest was there before him, holding him back in an unrelenting grip. He said something to Alek, the context impossible to hear over the growing sound around them, but whatever it was sucked the wind out of Alek's struggles. Deflated him in a second.

Kateri stayed locked in place, her eyes huge and trained on Naomi. "Nanna."

Naomi smiled, a beautifully serene look shared by a woman who'd not only come to grips with this moment, but welcomed it. "He took my mate. He took my son. He will not take my grandchildren."

The tradeoff with Jade.

Naomi hadn't been worried about someone getting hurt. She'd been worried about not having an equal sacrifice. Someone to sever Draven's powers once and for all.

"The sacrifice is offered," the Keeper said. "One laid before me with willingness. Your sacrifice was forced. Stolen from the life of one too young to know better." A tiny pause. A heartbeat that pulsed like thunder. "Your powers are void. Stripped and buried back within the darkness where they belong and your spirit banished alongside them. Your freedom is unobtainable. Your suffering endless and bound by the leniency and compassion you've shown your victims."

The bright glow around Draven's form grew bolder. Blinding.

A deafening explosion filled the cavernous space and an inexplicable force blasted them on all sides, the impact crashing into her and Tate with the force of a tidal wave.

Tate rolled with it, wrapped her up and broke her fall, the sharp thud as his head hit the concrete and the Keeper's voice the last thing she heard before an endless blackness swallowed her whole. "Draven Rahandras, your judgment is final."

Chapter Twenty-Five

Living in the moment was a hell of a lot easier to practice when the moment in question didn't suck. For Tate, sitting in a hotel room, watching his mate try yet again to rouse Jerrik from unconsciousness while so many others in his clan waited in their own rooms and mourned the loss of one of their own, this moment and the last three days in general definitely sucked. Worse, Elise had nearly run herself into the ground trying to pull off a small miracle and was practically dead on her feet.

A shadow moved behind the drape-covered window, the harsh late-afternoon sun outlining an unmistakable silhouette.

Tate pushed off the wall where he'd waited the last hour and quietly twisted the doorknob before Priest could knock. "Hey. How's Alek?"

Priest's gaze cut to Elise bent over Jerrik's body and Vanessa a near mirror image on the other side. The two weren't best buddies yet by any stretch, and frankly, he'd just as soon Vanessa not get within twenty feet of his mate, but they'd reached a peaceful agreement. A treaty, of sorts, brought about by tragedy and triumph and sealed in growing respect.

Motioning to the second-floor walkway outside the door with a jerk of his head, Priest stepped away from the door. "Let them focus. They've got enough to deal with without us adding distractions."

For Priest, it was a pretty polite summons. Under normal circumstances, he'd have simply commanded Tate's presence, but all of them had been a little less ballsy lately. A little more humbled and mindful of what they had.

And what they'd lost.

Tate followed him out, leaving the door propped open just enough he could hear Elise if she called or could get back in without the key. Isolated from most of the tourist venues around Rapid City and the Black Hills Forest, the hotel was empty save the people they'd brought with them. A good thing considering the odd hours they'd come and gone within the last several days. "So, has he talked to you yet?"

He being one highly pissed off Alek. Where everyone else had faced their grief with a certain amount of solemnity and respect, Alek had woken from the Keeper's explosive pronouncement with a palpable anger that had morphed to raging fury when they realized Naomi's body was missing.

Priest had faced it down like he did everything else—head-on with absolute resolve. But the guilt and weariness were written all over his face. "He finally let Kateri into his room. She's trying to talk him into a trip to Black Hills for a shift and a run."

"He can't avoid you forever."

"He won't. But he's got a right to be pissed at me. He needs time to work through it and his wolf will help."

"It was Naomi's decision."

"I know that. You know it. But logic's cold comfort for a man like Alek. For anyone who's lost someone they love."

Considering how things had turned out, *lost* seemed an especially apropos word choice. In addition to Naomi's body being MIA by the time they'd all woken from the Keeper's body blast, the rest of the building had looked untouched. Still as drab and dreary as when they'd first walked in, but minus the crushed and torched crates and litter cluttering the floor. No blood marks and no sign of the body Jerrik had carried in when he'd first arrived. It was like nothing at all had happened. A reset like the movie *Groundhog Day*, but with a much eerier vibe that none of them cared to repeat.

But Draven was gone, his dark magic and the threat he brought to their clan eradicated along with him.

Priest lifted his chin toward the room behind them. "Still no change?"

"Nothing. Physically, they both say he's fine, but they can't get him to wake up."

Face hardened to a cold mask Tate hadn't seen in years, Priest twisted to stare past the parking lot to the forest in the distance. They'd hoped with Draven's banishment, the darkness inside Priest and whatever lingered in Jerrik would be banished with him, but Priest had assured them the parasite he'd fought for the last fifty years was still there. Quieter than before, even somewhat content that its maker had suffered a gruesome fate, but still just as dangerous and deadly. Like a dormant infection just waiting to raise its ugly head.

Assuming Jerrik woke from his unconsciousness, that meant he was likely in for the same arduous journey back to sanity Priest had fought years ago. Then he'd still have to find the will to fight. After all they suspected he'd been put through—all the atrocities he'd undoubtedly committed under Draven's hand—finding the will might be a long shot.

"You don't think he wants to wake up," Tate said.

"I think if his journey's anywhere near what mine was, he's got a long road in front of him." He faced Tate. "We'll get him there, though. We'll take him home and work him through whatever he needs the way your mothers helped me."

The door behind them opened and Elise padded out, her tired eyes narrowed on the skies above the Black Hills beyond rather than on either of them.

Vanessa trailed close behind her, but all of her attention was on Elise, a concerned expression pinching her features. She looked to Priest and Tate. "Something's up. She was sitting there…totally focused…and then straightened like someone had woken her up from a dream. The next thing I knew she was headed out here."

Elise paused at the white railing, her hands lightly resting on the top and her head cocked as though straining to hear something far away. "I'm fine."

Not exactly a response that gave Tate a whole lot of warm and fuzzy on the surface, but the wonder and curiosity in her voice and the steady thrum of the bond between them kept both man and beast in check. Whatever it was that held her attention, it was something good. Something good enough to lift her lips in a soft smile and make her green eyes spark in the bright sunshine.

"Go get Kateri and Alek," she said on a near whisper. "Hurry." With that, the deep forest green of her healer's aura burst around them, and her eagle swept forward, its welcome cry filling the wide-open space around them.

"I'll get them," Vanessa said, then took off at a near run to Alek's room at the far end of the walkway.

Tate looked to Priest. "What the fuck?"

"I have no idea." Priest shook his head, obviously as confused and dumfounded as Tate was. "What I do know is your mate's got a keen instinct. One that's got us past a lot of shit the last few weeks. If she's on to something that gets her that keyed up and hopeful, I'll frog-march Alek out here myself."

Voices sounded down the walkway. First Vanessa. Then Katy. Then a much terser response from Alek.

Elise's eagle kept going, soaring outward and upward until all that remained in sight was a quaver of black against the bold blue sky.

"Goddammit, Alek!" Katy bellowed from Alek's room. "I don't care how pissed you are. Elise said she needs you, so suck your shit up and get out there!"

Tate chuckled. "I think you're rubbing off on her."

Priest hung his head, but the first smile Tate had seen in days split his face. "No, I just helped her open the door." He lifted his head and met Tate's stare. "Kind of like what you and Elise did for each other."

A sharp screech cut across the sky, not Elise's eagle but another bird of flight.

Elise's eagle answered and the bond inside Tate pulsed with a white-hot joy that struck deep. "She's not alone."

Priest straightened, all levity erased and his keen gaze fixed on the horizon. "And that's not another eagle. *That's a hawk.*"

As if to confirm his statement, the screech came again. Bolder this time and filling the air around them.

"Alek!" Priest roared and strode to the concrete steps

that led to the parking lot below. "Kateri, get him out here."

But he'd already heard it. Everyone had. Sabina, Kateri, Alek, Garrett and the rest of the warriors all filing out of their rooms and following Tate and Priest down to the asphalt.

The two birds came into view, the massive span of Elise's eagle and dark coloring against the bright sky easily dwarfing the smaller hawk behind her.

But she was there.

A hawk.

Naomi.

"Is it her?" Kateri murmured as she moved in between Priest and Tate.

Priest pulled her close to his side, an uncustomary anxiousness etched on his face. "I don't know, *mihara*. Until we see her—"

"It's her." Alek strode forward.

The hawk and eagle swooped downward. A sparkling gold light blended with Elise's more potent green.

And then they were there. Elise obviously tired and a little shaky, but beaming a smile to rival the sun and Naomi beside her, for all intents and purposes seemingly untouched by any harm. Not even a stray gray hair out of her perfectly wound braid.

Alek caught her up in a bear hug and held her tight, his grumbled words unintelligible to the rest of them.

But they made Naomi laugh.

Made her throw her head back and clasp the back of her grandson's head and hold him a little tighter.

Kateri was next.

Then Priest.

But Tate went to Elise. Pulled her tight against him

and guided her cheek so it rested on his chest. "How did you know?"

"I didn't." She lifted her head and smiled up at him, her eyes wet with tears that hadn't quite spilled over yet. "My eagle knew. She heard Naomi's hawk from the Otherworld and told me to follow. Naomi's been there the whole time. Protected by the Keeper."

Priest stepped back from Naomi, the realization on his face proving he'd heard every word. "The willingness was the key."

Naomi nodded.

Alek stood close beside her, his stance such that he was still firmly in the grasp of disbelief and fearful she'd disappear again.

"When the vision came to me," Naomi said, "it also came with the night of Draven's sacrifice. A young girl slain to claim enough power to overtake the primos. Completely unwilling." She grabbed Alek's hand and squeezed. "A willing sacrifice made is always more valuable. More powerful. But the Keeper didn't want my magic or my death. The intent and faith was enough."

"You've been gone three days," Alek said, clearly agitated by the delay in returning Naomi to them. "If she didn't intend to keep you, why keep you away this long? We thought you were dead."

"We grieved." Where the guidance came from, Elise couldn't say. And frankly, after all she'd learned and experienced in the last month, she didn't care anymore. Only knew that her intuition and her magic were incredible gifts meant to be used. To be headed above logic. "The emotion made the sacrifice more formidable. A sacrifice of many versus a sacrifice of one."

"A sacrifice made for three days," Garrett said. "A

triad—one to bind Draven's body, one to bind his spirit and one to bind his soul."

"But it's over, right?" Kateri said. "It's not just a temporary deal. You're back for good and Draven's dead?"

"Souls never die," Naomi said, her smile a little softer than before. "But his is bound to the darkness. And yes, until my time comes, I'm here for good."

"Do me a favor," Alek said to Priest. "Don't let her talk you into that shit again."

"Personally, I'm hoping we don't have reason for any more grand gestures," Katy said before Priest could answer.

Priest glanced back at the hotel room where Jerrik lay unconscious, the barest hint of a frown marring the relief of having Naomi back.

Elise picked up on it, too, the single-minded determination she'd shown the last three days to give Jerrik whatever he needed to find his way back clicking back into full gear. She pushed against Tate's chest and tried to free herself from his hold. "I'll go try again."

"No." Priest said it the same time Tate tightened his arms. "You've done enough. So has Vanessa." He scanned the people gathered around who'd gone silent at his quiet command. "What he needs now is time. We'll take him home and see to him there." His gaze sharpened on Elise. "What you need is rest."

Elise frowned up at Tate. Then at Priest. "But someone needs to stay with Jerrik."

With the warriors who'd gathered behind Alek, Vanessa had all but disappeared in the crowd, but her tentative voice rose above them. "I'll stay with him." She stepped more fully into view. "I slept last night, and you could use a break."

Funny. They'd had some pretty serious jaw-dropping moments in the last week, but Tate had never seen the crew who'd traveled with them grow as silent as they were in that second.

Elise, though, didn't miss a beat. "Thank you." While her body was mostly lax against him, she grinned up at Tate with a sly smile that belied her fatigue. "To be honest, though, I'd rather fly than rest. Maybe explore the Black Hills a little more?"

Explore his ass. He knew that look. His mate might need some serious sleep, but she had more than a little adrenaline to burn off after the burst that had likely hit hearing Naomi's hawk. While she might not be up for a full hunt, he had zero problems giving her a good chase. He smoothed his palm down Elise's spine and met Priest's gaze over her head. "When do you want to head back home?"

Priest smirked, tucked Katy tight to his side and muttered to the other people around him, "That's code for, *We shouldn't plan to see them until sometime late tomorrow.*" He chuckled along with everyone else and jerked his head toward the forest stretching out behind them. "Go. Have fun."

Elise's laughter as she pushed free of his arms was the lightest he'd heard in days. "Well, he'll have to catch me first." She wiggled her fingers in a playful good-bye a second before the green that marked her as healer house consumed her and her eagle burst free.

Alek snickered along with a handful of the other warriors. "Yeah, good hunting, Tate. You'll have a hell of a time finding her before nightfall."

"Oh, I'll find her." His coyote paced and pushed for release, the sting and burn that came before the shift rippling beneath his skin and the bond between them pulsing bright. He paused to meet Alek's stare a second before he gave his companion free rein and welcomed the shift. "She was made for me. I'll always find her."

* * * * *

To read more books from Rhenna Morgan,
visit her website at www.rhennamorgan.com.

Acknowledgments

In this story, Elise earned a new clan and had the joy of learning what it meant to be supported and protected by them. I find it ironic that Elise found her clan at the same time I found a new one of my own—or maybe it was simply life reflecting itself in fiction. Who knows! But I can say without question, that I'm so very grateful to those of you who've supported me in my new journey. To each and every one of you—thank you!

To my core writer team—Cori Deyoe, Juliette Cross, Dena Garson, Lucy Beshara, Jennifer Mathews, and my *amazing* daughters, Abby and Addie. There is nothing I can't accomplish with your support to hold me steady.

I also want to thank the crew from Rhenna's Romantics. It's so much fun sharing my writing journey with each of you. I deeply appreciate all you do to get the word out when new stories release.

Finally, a heartfelt thanks and huge hugs to Angela James, Kerri Buckley, Stephanie Doig and the entire Carina Press and Harlequin teams. I'm a long-winded writer, but there just aren't enough words to properly express how honored and thankful I am for your time, care and talents.

*Priest Rahandras has lived with the darkness
trapped inside himself for years. Betrayed by his
own brother and forced to watch his clan's brutal
annihilation, the only thing Priest wants more
than to escape the curse that haunts him—as both
man and beast—is to rebuild.*

*Until the mate he's longed for walks into his life
with an elder from his past. She's everything he's
wished for, and the key to the clan's very survival.*

Chapter One

Safe with the Keeper. Guarded from the dark.

Over and over, Priest repeated the protective words in his head, merging his magic with the ancient symbols he inked at the base of Jade's nape and down her spine. Black and red swirling links with shades of gray joined each sacred talisman. No one would hurt her. Not her or Tate so long as he drew breath.

His forearm ached from his constant grip on the tattoo iron, but the steady drone and vibrations from the coils as he worked deepened his trance. Beneath his free hand, Jade's body trembled from the rush of pain-induced endorphins she'd endured for nearly four hours.

Safe with the Keeper. Guarded from the dark.

He swiped the excess ink away from the intricate design. The same intertwining scroll and symbolism that marked his shoulders, back and collarbone—and likely the only thing that had saved his life and sanity in the early days. Had Jade's and Tate's parents not guarded him after his brother's betrayal and marked him with the sacred symbols, the darkness would have consumed him entirely.

"Priest?" Jade pushed to her elbows on the padded table and peered over one shoulder. "Are you done?"

The art was perfect. A sufficient start in hiding her from the threat he sensed closing in. A malevolence he'd first felt with an unexplained summons to the Otherworld. Never since he'd been named high priest had he ever been called there so abruptly. Without warning or purpose.

Priest set his equipment aside and peeled off his latex gloves. As eerie as the memory had been, even if he covered Jade in ink, it wouldn't feel like enough protection. "For now."

Jade grinned, swiveled on the padded table, and snagged her blue tank top off the counter next to them. "How does it look?"

The tiny chimes above the front door jingied before he could answer, and Tate stalked through, his hands laden with yet another haul of the fast-food breakfasts Priest detested. The coffee, though—that he could use in abundance.

Through the open door, morning sunshine glinted off the storefronts on Eureka Springs's Main Street, only a few cars and Harleys motoring down the main drag. Not surprising for a Thursday, but by late tonight or early tomorrow they'd be flooded with tourists and bikers soaking up the spring weather.

Tate kicked the door shut and threw the bolt. The fifties throwback neon clock showed straight up eleven o'clock, only one more hour until the shop opened.

"Tate, check it out." Jade shifted in front of the full-length mirror behind her and held the blue hand mirror higher for a better angle on Priest's work. "Mine's as badass as yours and Priest's."

Ignoring Jade, Tate set the orange and white paper bags and cardboard drink holder aside and stalked to the window overlooking the street. "Hey, Priest. Have you got an early gig today?"

A prickling awareness danced across his skin. Not danger or evil. Either of those would have stirred the darkness trapped inside him. Instead, it lay still and dormant like midnight fog. He turned from cleaning up his tools. "First client's at noon. Finishing up that biker from Fayetteville I started last weekend. Why?"

Tate twisted enough to meet his gaze. "'Cause there's a little old lady and two people about my age outside in the parking lot. They keep staring up here."

Jade sidled up beside Priest. "You sure you didn't schedule an early one?"

Hell yes, he was sure. Appointments before or after hours were only for customers needing more than art. Those needing protection, peace or comfort woven into his coveted designs. "Get away from the window."

Tate stayed put and studied the parking lot. "Looks like the old lady's coming in."

"Get away from the window. Now." Two weeks he'd waited, petitioning the Keeper as much as he dared for guidance. For some insight into the danger he sensed or Jade's subsequent terrifying vision. The Keeper's only answer was a promise that messengers would be sent to guide him, but his instincts screamed to brace and prepare. "Stay behind me. Say nothing until I know who they are."

"But I locked the door. We're fine."

The bolt flipped before Tate finished his argument, the remnants of air Priest used to unlock the mechanism fluttering the paper want ads on the corkboard beside the door.

"I want to know who they are, but I want you out of the line of fire," Priest said.

Footsteps sounded on the wooden stairs to the shop's raised patio, a light tread that would have gone unnoticed to someone without the benefit of a predator's keen hearing.

The door latch clicked and the chimes overhead tinkled as an older woman eased through the door. Her attire seemed more on par with something from Jade's closet—comfortable cotton pants the color of a robin's egg and a fitted, white T-shirt. Around her neck hung three charms, each dangling from simple black leather cords.

Charms fashioned in the symbols he'd honored since birth.

His gaze snapped to hers. Deep blue-gray eyes he remembered from his youth stared back at him, the woman's shoulder-length gray hair framing her delicate face. "Naomi."

"Eerikki," she whispered, the emotion behind the sound so deep and fraught with bittersweet memories his knees nearly buckled. Countless nights he'd wondered if she was safe. If she and her children had survived the night his brother murdered so many—Naomi's mate included.

Before he could shake the surprise that held him rooted in place, she closed the distance between them and wrapped her arms around him. "I'd hoped you were alive. I tried to track you through my visions for years, but couldn't find you until a few weeks ago."

The messenger he'd been promised.

Finally.

His arms tightened around her, and the solitary

weight he'd shouldered since Tate's and Jade's parents had died eased a fraction. As if the presence of someone from his own youth altered the gravitational pull around him and soothed his beleaguered soul.

Jade's and Tate's quiet footsteps sounded on the tiles behind him, their curious stares a tangible press against his back.

Begrudgingly, Priest released his old friend and stepped aside, bringing his two companions into view.

Naomi studied them. "These are your children?"

By now, he should be used to it. Everyone asked the same question, and yet it still knifed through him. He loved his wards. Would do anything to protect and guide them and never regretted their place in his life, but he craved his own mate. His own children.

A dangerous proposition with the tainted magic trapped inside him.

"No," he said. "These are Lisana and Rani's children. Lisana and Rani healed me after my brother's attack."

Naomi blanched, but tried to mask her response with a weak smile. He couldn't blame her for her fear. The mere thought of his brother, Draven, still flayed his insides.

He motioned to his wards. "Naomi Falsen, meet Jade Mitchell and Tate Allen. They've lived with me since their mothers passed."

Hand outstretched, Tate stepped forward first. "Not too many people know Priest's real name."

This time her smile was genuine, and her eyes lit with joy the likes of which Priest had long forgotten. She cupped Tate's hand with both of hers. "I've known Eerikki since before the Keeper named him high priest.

My mate, Farron, mentored him before his soul quest and afterward served him as warrior primo."

Tate released her hand and puffed his chest up a little broader than before. "I'm warrior house."

As soon as the words were out, Tate's excitement deflated, the reality of Naomi's information belatedly connecting with Priest's history lessons. How Priest's failure to ferret out Draven's plans before it was too late had cost every house primo their life and countless clan members as well.

Naomi patted Tate's shoulder, her petite stature compared to Tate's towering height making the gesture almost comical. "It's okay, Tate. Let it go. My mate faced his destiny the same way Eerikki and all the rest of us will."

"You mean Priest," Tate said.

Naomi swiveled toward Priest and frowned.

"The world's different now," Priest said. "Eerikki's not exactly a name that blends in. Rani started calling me Priest in the seventies." He shrugged. "It stuck."

"Ah." She scanned him head to toe, obviously connecting how the name tied with his image. He might have been an innocent when he'd stepped into his position fifty years ago, but now he reflected the hardened years in between. "It stuck because it fits. In more ways than one. Though, for your mother's sake, I'll use the name she gave you unless we're outside our clan."

Decision made, she turned her gaze on Jade and studied her aura. "You're a seer. Who's the primo for your house?"

Jade hung her head, and it was all Priest could do to stifle his flinch. "We have no primos," Priest answered for her. "Our numbers are down. Most from the last generation refused their quests."

Naomi frowned and opened her mouth as if to share something, then closed it just as fast and dug in her purse. "Give me a minute. There's someone I want you to meet." She pulled out her phone and typed out a message fast enough to rival Jade and Tate on a texting frenzy.

The same warning buzz he'd wrestled for weeks surged between his shoulders, both beast and man sensing a shift on the horizon. As though the answers he sought crouched nearby in thick shadow, poised to launch into the light. Whether the change he sensed was good or bad remained to be seen, but the sensation was too big to ignore. An emotional stirring that warned whatever lay ahead would pack a serious punch.

My mate faced his destiny the same way Eerikki and all the rest of us will.

If he remembered right, Naomi and Farron's son had been eight or nine at the time of Draven's betrayal. And yet Priest had never been summoned to join his soul quest. "Your family has always led the warrior house. Where's your son?"

She averted her face and dropped her phone back in her purse. Her aura dimmed, the vibrant gold of the seer house paling as though a cloud had moved across it. "My son and his wife couldn't come."

His wife. Not his mate. More evidence her son had shunned his gifts like so many others.

Before he could question her further, the shop door opened and sent the chimes overhead jingling. A tall and oddly familiar looking man with short dirty-blond hair and a beard in the making stepped just inside the entrance, one hand braced on the knob. He scanned the room, his muscled torso locked tight until his gaze snagged on Naomi. "Everything's safe?"

"It will be now." Naomi shot the man a relieved smile and waved him in. "Get your sister and come inside."

Priest tweaked at her choice of words. "Why wouldn't it be safe?"

The man ducked outside, leaving the door open, and soft voices murmured from the raised porch beyond.

Naomi subtly inclined her head toward Jade and Tate. "I'll explain later. After you meet my grandchildren."

Well, that explained the familiarity.

Her grandson strode back through the door and stepped to one side, holding it open for the woman behind him. The second she came into full view, Priest froze.

"Eerikki, this is my grandson, Aleksander, and my beautiful granddaughter, Kateri. Kateri, Alek, this is our clan's high priest, Eerikki Rahandras. Though, now, he just goes by Priest."

Granddaughter.

Beautiful.

Kateri.

Some dim corner of his mind registered Naomi had shared more with her lighthearted words, but those were the only three that mattered. Except the woman in front of him wasn't just beautiful. She was perfect. Dressed in a flowing tan skirt and fine white linen shirt tied at the waist, her willowy body gave the illusion of fragility, but strength beamed from her intelligent blue-gray eyes. Her hair fell well beyond her shoulders, a soft blond the color of endless wheat fields.

But it was her aura that gripped him most. No colors

to represent a house, but powerful nonetheless. Shimmering as though the moon shone directly behind her.

My mate.

His beast stirred and scented the air.

"Eerikki?" Naomi's touch pressed just above his elbow, her fingers light against his skin, but trembling. "Is something wrong?"

Nothing was wrong. Not anymore.

Seventy-seven years he'd been alone, but now she was here. His to win. To protect. To provide for and pleasure.

The darkness rose, and crude, devastatingly vivid images blasted across his mind. Him above her. His cock powering deep and her breasts bouncing with each thrust. Her soft cries filling his ears.

Kateri crept forward and held out her hand. A lifeline and a temptation. "My nanna's told me a lot about you."

He should step away. The evil was too close, waking with a devastating hunger and licking the edges of his control. To hurt this woman would be the end of him. The annihilation of his soul. He clasped her hand in his anyway, the contact zinging through him as profound as his connection with the Otherworld. He needed more. Wanted her hands pressed against his chest. Her nails scoring his back and her palm working his shaft.

Tugging gently, he pulled her to him.

She stumbled slightly, but didn't resist, splaying her free hand above his thrashing heart. She lifted her face to his, her beautiful eyes wide and mouth slightly parted, her soft pink lips ready for his kiss.

His panther chuffed and purred, the uncontainable response rumbling up the back of his throat and filling the room.

Two seconds. No more than that and his mate was ripped from his arms and thrust behind the unknown male, her startled gasp still lingering in the air around him.

"What the hell?" The stranger's terse voice slashed through the otherwise quiet room.

Priest's cat screamed and clawed for release. The tingle and burn that came scant seconds before each shift raced beneath his skin, and his breath crept up the back of his throat in a hot hiss. He stalked forward, his prey mirroring each advance with a step backward.

Logic tried to surface, a flicker of knowledge as to the man's name and who he was clawing at the back of Priest's mind.

It doesn't matter who he is, the darkness whispered. *He took her from us. Kill him.*

Through his beast's lethal focus a movement registered. A woman blocking him from his target. "Don't move, Alek. Not so much as a step."

Priest stopped. He knew that voice. Trusted it. He fought the thickening black haze around the edges of his vision and focused on the woman in front of him.

Naomi.

An innocent.

An elder and a friend.

Her words pierced through the murderous fog, a pinprick at most, and echoing as though she whispered from the depths of a cave. "He's her sister, Eerikki. Their parents were killed two weeks ago. He wants only to protect her."

Her brother.

One of his clan.

Safe.

He touched her, the darkness countered.

His cat growled in agreement.

Eliminate him. Take what's rightfully ours.

Naomi inched closer. "Alek, take your sister to the car. Wait for me there."

The two shifted for the door, but froze at the warning growl that rumbled up Priest's throat. "No."

"He'll bring her back." Lowering her voice, Naomi crept within killing distance. "Your companion is angry. Insulted and raw. He doesn't care that he's her brother. Only that he's a stranger he doesn't know. But *you* know, Eerikki. Take the time to find your balance. Tate and Jade can go with them. Tate's a warrior. You can trust him to keep her safe."

As though she'd summoned him with her words, Tate stole closer to Priest, the wary nature of his coyote obviously sensing Priest barely held his panther in check. He kept his silence, but his watchful amber eyes burned with curiosity and confusion.

Never in all the years they'd been with them had Priest ever lost control. Hadn't sunk this deep into the darkness in years.

Still braced protectively in front of Kateri, Alek stared Priest down. Such innocent bravery. Clueless of the torture Priest could wield with little more than a thought.

End him. The dark encouragement danced all too enticingly inside his head and sent fire licking down his spine.

Behind Alek, Kateri watched him with wide eyes. Not afraid. Surprised, yes, and curious given the tilt to her head, but not afraid. She swallowed and flexed the hand clutching her brother's shoulder.

His panther bristled at the sight, jaws aching to sink its teeth into the usurper who enjoyed her touch.

"Go," he ordered Tate, not daring to break eye contact with his mate for fear he'd lose what little control he had left. His muscles flexed and strained, blood pulsing with a ferocity that left an aching throb in its wake. Naomi was right. If he didn't find his balance, he'd slaughter Alek where he stood. "Stay close, but don't let her out of your sight. No one touches her." The darkness and his beast coalesced with his own voice and unleashed a feral claim. "She's mine."

Chapter Two

It couldn't be real. None of it. Katy padded down the wooden steps from the tattoo shop, her footsteps nearly silent in comparison to those resonating from the three people behind her. The crisp spring morning temperature kissed her sweat-misted skin and the sun beamed just shy of its zenith. Normal. Safe. The same world she'd grown up in.

Except that the world wasn't what she'd thought it was. For the last two weeks, her scientist's mind had insisted that the things Nanna had told her—even shown her—weren't possible. But that man. Eerikki. Priest. Whatever his name was. Her logic couldn't ignore that. Had heard the animalistic sounds roll past his lips and felt the power emanating off him. Electric like the snap and tingle that came before a lightning storm. That was no trick of the mind. No figment of her imagination or wishful thinking as she'd tried to explain her grandmother's foresight and shifting abilities.

And his body...

She shuddered at the memory of the hard muscles she'd felt all too briefly. The heat of him. Between his edgy biker appearance, loose black hair well past his shoulders and deep olive skin, he was every deep, dark fantasy rolled into one. Had her brother not yanked her behind him, she had no doubt she'd have happily pressed herself flush against him and purred like a desperate cat in heat.

Talk about illogical responses.

She released her shaky grip on the handrail and stepped onto the aged asphalt parking lot, praying her adrenaline-overloaded body could navigate without the extra support.

Behind her, the woman she'd yet to formally meet asked, "Are you guys hungry? We've got some great cafes and coffee shops on Main Street."

Katy paused on the sidewalk that ran along the west side of the street and rubbed her arms to ward off the chill. The traffic had picked up since they'd pulled into the parking lot, but the quaint storefronts nestled along the softly sloping street and massive budding trees that framed it on either side seemed to ground the bustling area in a quiet peace.

And, boy, did she need peace right now. Even with the rumble of motorcycles and chattering tourists milling up and down the street, the fresh air and birds chirping soothed her as nothing else could. Nature was what grounded her when nothing else could. The simpleness of it. The soul-calming beauty. Two weeks ago, she'd been a few formalities away from making it the foundation for her future, her Bachelor of Science in Environmental Science and the coveted environmental protection internship she'd fought for almost guaranteed.

But then her parents had been murdered and her neat, tidy life had been turned on its head. "Is there somewhere we can sit outside?"

Alek's deep, clipped voice sounded a second before his hand clamped onto her shoulder and redirected her to the parking lot where his red Jeep Wrangler waited. "We're leaving."

Before Katy could even dig in her heels, Tate was between them and the cars lined in orderly rows. When she'd first seen him in the shop, she'd thought him a cross between a male model and a hipster—his long hair pulled back in a low ponytail and a honey-blond color a lot of women paid hundreds to achieve. Now, seeing his slightly darker beard framing bared teeth as he growled at Alek, he was pure predator. Shoulders back, arms tense at his sides and braced on the balls of his feet, he appeared only seconds from taking Alek to the ground.

Jade shoved Alek's hand off Katy's shoulder and positioned herself between Katy and Alek. She was shorter than Katy, five-two at best, but the soft blue tank top and tight-fitting jeans accented firm muscle and curves the likes of which always left Katy envious. "Keep your hands off her." She studied each of the men and shook her head like they'd both lost their minds, the same silver clan charms her grandmother wore woven into small braids in her long dark hair and glinting in the sun. "Jesus, don't you know *anything* about our race?" she said to Alek. "Priest said no one could touch her. Tate's coyote takes that literally."

Maybe Katy *should* have followed her brother. Or at least put a little extra distance between her and Tate. Instead she stepped forward, her indomitable curiosity overpowering the need for caution. "Your animal's a coyote?"

Tate scanned the distance between her and Alek

and relaxed enough to jerk a terse nod. Only after he'd drawn a few more breaths and straightened from his fighting stance did he shift his attention to Alek. "Your family has always anchored the warrior house. Why don't you know about us?"

Alek frowned and gritted his teeth so hard the muscles at the back of his jaw looked as if they'd snap. "I don't know. Nanna said our dad made her promise not to tell us. Said he didn't do his soul quest, or whatever you call it. Something about not wanting his gifts. After what I've seen the last few weeks, I'm starting to see why." He glared at Katy. "We should go. Nanna can finish her big reunion with Mr. High-and-Mighty and call us to come get her." He huffed out an ironic chuckle and shook his head. "Oh, wait. She's a hawk, right? She can fly to us when she's done."

No way was she leaving. Not when she had a chance to pry information out of two people who clearly knew what they were talking about. Even if she didn't have a solid motive for wanting to learn more, the scientist in her insisted on digging deeper. On finding some reasonable explanation for the things her nanna had summarized as simply *magic*. "Don't you want answers?"

"What I want is for my sister to not end up like our parents. Have you seen the way these people act?"

Memories of the blood-splattered walls and coppery stench that had filled her parents' living room fired as bold as real-life, pricking her carefully buried rage. To lose control was unacceptable. The worst offense she could show her parents after what they'd suffered. "What I want is justice. The only way we're going to get it is if we talk to the people who can help us find him. I don't care if they have spots or shift into unicorns. I'm staying."

"Justice for what?" Jade shifted her gaze to Alek, confusion clouding the green depths that matched her namesake. "What happened to your parents?"

Mouth pressed in a hard line, Alek stared at Jade for all of two seconds, then spun to face the street, a muttered curse Katy couldn't quite make out drifting on the wind.

"Our parents were killed two weeks ago." Two weeks that felt a lifetime away and yet her words still shook with barely contained fury. "It was bloody. Gruesome."

Jade glanced at Tate as if to gauge if he was following the topic any better than she was. "What?"

"Murdered," Alek said, shifting enough to scowl at Tate. "By a Volán. You really think I'm inclined to trust anyone from your race after what happened to them? After the whacked-out shit I just saw from Eerikki or whatever his name is?"

Tate smirked and cocked an eyebrow. "He goes by Priest. And I hate to point this out, but if you're Naomi's grandson, you're Volán, too. One from the warrior primo family."

"A warrior what?" Katy said.

Jade's gaze cut behind Katy to a couple meandering down the sidewalk. She cleared her throat and motioned for Katy to step out of the way. Only when the couple was out of earshot did she speak, but her voice was still hushed. "Warrior primo. Every house has a leader that serves the high priest and mentors their people. Your family has led the warrior house for as long as anyone remembers."

Alek scoffed, stuffed his hands in the pocket of his jeans and glared into the distance. "This is bullshit."

Katy understood the sentiment. Had echoed the thought more times than she could count since Naomi first shared her family's mysterious heritage and shifted into a hawk for the first time. But this was the first time she'd seen Alek struggle with the concept of their race. Yes, he'd grieved and wrestled with anger the same as her since they'd found their parents slaughtered in their family home, but he'd seemed more open to the idea of magic. Even eager to learn more about it. Or he had been—until he'd come face-to-face with Priest.

"Call it whatever you want," Tate said. "But it's reality. If you don't accept what's yours, the Keeper will hand the honor to someone else."

"Who's the Keeper?" Katy asked.

"Wow." Jade's eyebrows hopped high, and she scrunched a handful of her soft black hair on top of her head. After considering Katy and Alek for a second, she planted both hands on her hips, scanned Main Street from left to right, then made pointed eye contact with Alek and Tate the same as a scolding mother would her errant sons. "Okay, can you two hold your shit in check long enough for us to find a place to talk?"

"I'm fine," Katy said. "It's the men doing all the flipping out, not the women." Although, if she was honest with herself, Alek's attitude had been getting worse even before their parents were killed. Like the quiet patience he'd always shown growing up had sprung a slow leak that showed no signs of stopping.

Jade crooked a grin that spoke of a saucy attitude Katy could absolutely appreciate under normal circumstances. "Not exactly a trait unique to our clan, but still true." She glanced back at Tate, a genuine concern and question in her soft gaze. "You good?"

Tate paused long enough to scrutinize Alek who still refused to look at the rest of them. He nodded. "Yeah. Just keep him at arm's length."

That got Alek's attention. He squared his shoulders toward Tate and started forward, but Katy held up her hand before he could get two steps in. "Stop it." She lowered her voice. "Whatever it is that's going on with you, let it go. They're not going to hurt me. No one's going to hurt me. But I want answers and they've got them. If you can't deal with that, go wait in the car, and I'll find you after we're done."

It took a good fifteen seconds and more pride than Alek was likely comfortable swallowing, but he finally dipped his head, the tiny acquiescence leaving his features hard and pinched.

Jade sighed and motioned toward the top of the main strip where a pub sat on the opposite side of the street with motorcycles lining the front of it. "Let's hit the Cat House. Breakfast sounded good thirty minutes ago, but right now a drink sounds better than coffee, and we can sit on the patio."

Less than fifteen minutes later, they were seated at a balcony table overlooking Main Street. There'd been another tense moment when Tate had claimed the seat beside Katy—effectively caging her between the balcony rail and him—but between the give-it-a-rest glower she aimed at her brother and Jade's placating demeanor, Alek took a seat beside Jade on the opposite side of the table. If the waitress found it odd they all ordered hard liquor at straight up noon, she didn't show it.

Eureka Springs truly was a beautiful town. The

soft rolling hills, quirky shops and buildings from a more peaceful era was a place she'd enjoy exploring. But while she loved the thick foliage and the winding streets, what she wanted most right now were answers. Checking the proximity to make sure no one could overhear them, Katy started with Jade. "Can you shift, too?"

One blink and the watchful tension that had gripped Jade nearly nonstop since Alek had yanked Katy out of Priest's arms flashed to bright happiness. "I can. My soul quest was just a little over a month ago."

"What's your animal?"

Her smile grew bigger. Prouder. "My companion's a lynx."

Alek snickered. "You mean you're a cat."

Katy shot him a warning glare. "A full-grown Eurasian lynx would come up to your thigh and could spot you coming as much as 250 feet away. They're also superb hunters. I'd hardly call her a cat."

Tate's reply wasn't nearly so subtle, the low growl of his coyote winding around them all.

"Let it go, Tate," Jade said then turned her attention on Katy. "How do you know so much about them anyway?"

"I took an advanced zoology class before I declared my major in Environmental Science." She glared at her brother, still more embarrassed than she cared to admit. "I don't know what's up your ass lately, but I've just about had it with your attitude."

"I don't have an attitude, I'm just tired."

"Trust me. You have an attitude. All the time. And when you're not biting everyone's head off you're passed out in bed."

Jade and Tate shared a look, one borne of many years together and unspoken understanding.

"What?" Katy asked them both. "Does that mean something?"

Ducking her head, Jade tapped her thumb against the scarred wood tabletop.

"How old are you?" Tate asked Alek.

Alek hesitated as if he sensed a trap or a prank coming on. "Twenty-five, why?"

"Bad temper? Sleeping a lot?"

Alek glanced at Katy and shrugged. "I guess. Yeah."

Tate nodded. "Most Voláns are called on their soul quest between twenty-one and twenty-six. Most never make it past twenty-five and men almost always share the warning signs of fatigue and anger. If you're not generally a giant dick, I'd say you're close."

For the first time since he'd gone all protective-big-brother with Priest, a little of Alek's bravado faded. An especially surprising response considering Tate's blatant verbal taunt.

"You really don't know much about our race at all, do you?" Jade asked quietly.

Alek shook his head, barely meeting her eyes. "Nanna told us about the magic and the basic houses. She said she was a seer and showed us she could shift, but other than that... I think she was afraid to share more."

"You said you went on a soul quest," Katy said to Jade. "That's when you learn to shift?"

"Sort of." Jade stared at the table for a second, her eyes distant while she seemed to struggle for the right words. "In the Otherworld, you face the parts of yourself the Keeper feels are necessary for you to navigate this realm with magic. Once you do, you're assigned a house and the magic that goes with it. It's only after your quest that you meet your companion."

Odd. She'd heard that expression several times since her grandmother had divulged their race's shapeshifting gift and it still didn't make sense. "I don't get the companion part."

"If you think it's weird now, wait until you have one." Tate chuckled and crossed his muscled forearms on the table. "Think of it this way. Today there's just you. When you think to yourself, all you hear is your voice. After you're given your companion, you'll hear two. Yours and your animal's. It's the Keeper's way of ensuring our race stays in tune with nature and magic."

Fascinating. Far-fetched and completely insane, but fascinating in theory nonetheless. "And there are four houses, right? Seer, warrior, healer and sorcerer?"

Jade nodded. "The sorcerers are rare, though. Very powerful and highly respected. Or they were. We don't know of any that are still alive."

Alek shifted in his seat, obviously uncomfortable. "The primo thing. You said our family led the warriors. What's that about?"

While he'd directed his question to Jade, it was Tate who answered. "Your grandmother's mate was the last primo for the warriors. Unless the Keeper deems otherwise, each primo stays within a family line. No clue what she'll do since your father refused his gifts."

"And what do primos do, exactly?" Katy asked.

"They're the strongest in their house and serve as mentor for the people they lead. But they also serve as Priest's advisors and share their magic with him at presect."

"At what?"

"Huh?"

Both Tate and Jade smiled at Alek's and Katy's dumbfounded responses, but it was Tate who answered. "When the seasons change, our clan comes together for a sacred rite called presect. It's simple really. An exchange designed to honor, balance and keep the Earth's magic thriving. Only, we don't have any primos right now. Without them to help Priest, the rites aren't as effective. We need them. Bad."

"So, what happens without the primos?" Alek asked. "Our race's magic dies out?"

"Not just ours," Jade said. "The Earth's magic."

Katy groaned, planted her elbows on the table and planted her forehead in her palms. "Earth magic. That's insane."

Tate chuckled. "Seriously? You've seen your grandmother shift into a hawk, and been up close and personal to Priest fighting back his panther and you don't believe in magic?"

He was right. She'd seen Nanna shift. Watched her as a trance pulled her under and followed what she'd learned in her visions guiding them right to Priest.

And Priest…no one could ignore the power inside him. She'd felt it the second she'd stepped across the shop's threshold. Had been drawn to him in a way her mind still couldn't find a decent way to categorize.

She rested her forearms on the table and sighed. "I don't know what I believe anymore. Maybe the Volán have magic, but you can't tell me it's out there for everyone. Normal life is just that. Normal."

Cocking her head, Jade studied Katy with a quiet intensity. "Maybe your definition of magic is too limited."

"Too limited how?"

Jade scanned the parking lot below, her gaze lingering on the clusters of patrons milling beside their bikes and laughing like they had all the time in the world to enjoy the day. "The magic is everywhere if you're open to it. The comfort you feel when you're with your friends. In the quiet of a spring day or the rumbling thunder of a violent storm. That's not just for the Volán but for the singura, too."

"The singura?" Alek asked.

"Companionless humans." Tate grinned. "Basically, what you thought you were."

Warming up to her explanation, Jade motioned to a couple on the lower patio. The woman was perched atop the wide protective rail that separated the patio from the parking lot, and the man stood between her spread knees, his arms possessively coiled around her. It was an intimate moment. Powerful in its simplicity. "Look at them. You can't see something like that and not believe in magic."

Warmth blossomed beneath Katy's skin, the all-too-vivid memory of how Priest's muscles had felt beneath her palms and how his presence had enveloped her in a protective cocoon lifting to the height of her awareness.

And his scent. She pressed her knees together under the table and fought back a groan. She could still smell him on her. A mix of summer storm, leather and the deepest woods. Her voice came out softer, when she answered. Deep and husky. "That's just attraction. A chemical response in the body."

Jade grinned. "Is it?"

She's mine.

The remembered words sluiced through her in the

most exotic caress. Possessive at a level she both craved and railed against. She cleared her throat and laced her fingers together on the table, forcing a detached expression. "Priest said I was his before we left. What did he mean by that?"

Jade looked to Tate, a request for guidance without a word spoken.

Tate shook his head. "I can't know for sure."

"But you *think* you know."

He hesitated, glanced at Alek as if gauging how well his temper was holding, then shifted his compassionate amber gaze back to Katy. "It's not up to me to share. Priest will tell you."

"But the way he acted...how he lost control," Katy pressed. "Surely, you can see why I want answers."

For the longest time, Tate merely studied her, consideration and concern marking his handsome features. "I do. It's still something he should talk to you about, but I will tell you this." He paused as though carefully considering his words, not just for her but for her brother who'd drawn scarily motionless beside her. "Of all the people who walk this Earth, there is no one safer than you."

Read Guardian's Bond *by Rhenna Morgan today!*

About the Author

Rhenna Morgan is a happily-ever-after addict—hot men, smart women, and scorching chemistry required. A triple-A personality with a thing for lists, Rhenna's a mom to two beautiful daughters who constantly keep her dancing, laughing and simply happy to be alive.

When she's not neck deep in writing, she's probably driving with the windows down and the music up loud, plotting her next hero and heroine's adventure. (Though trolling online for man-candy inspiration on Pinterest comes in a close second.)

She'd love to share her antics and bizarre sense of humor with you and get to know you a little better in the process. You can sign up for her newsletter and gain access to exclusive snippets, upcoming releases, fun giveaways, and social media outlets at www.rhennamorgan.com.

If you enjoyed *Healer's Need*, she hopes you'll share the love with a review on your favorite online bookstore.